MW00454469

WHITE LINES

A FRANK HARPER MYSTERY

GREG ENSLEN

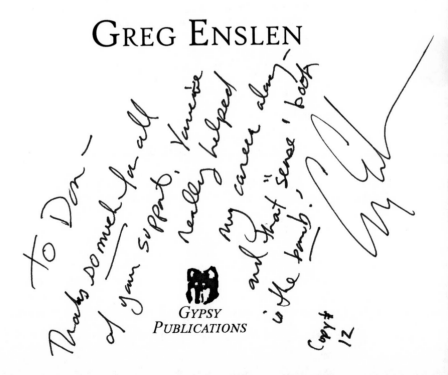

GYPSY
PUBLICATIONS

Published in 2017, by Gypsy Publications
Troy, OH 45373, U.S.A.
www.GypsyPublications.com

First Edition

Enslen, Greg
Frank Harper Mysteries Series
White Lines/ by Greg Enslen
ISBN 978-1-938768-76-7 (paperback)

Edited by Diana Ceres
Cover by Nikky Hopkins
Cover Design by Pamela Schwartz

For more information, please visit the author's
website at www.GregEnslen.com

ACKNOWLEDGMENTS

Writing this book was a challenge. With this third Frank Harper mystery, I decided to expand the scope of Frank's life and tackle something larger than just him and his cases. I wanted to explore his interaction with an ongoing crisis, and I chose the opioid crisis taking place here in the Dayton region. Although this book is set in 2012 and is obviously fictitious, I tried to say something about this crisis and the epidemic of dealers and users that seems to have many Midwestern cities and counties by the throat. As I was finishing up this book in May 2017, Dayton was given a dubious distinction — according to ArrestRecords.com, Dayton was the number one city in the country for drug overdoses.

Somehow, I don't think that will make it into the local marketing campaign.

Many people have opinions about the best way to tackle illicit drug use. Even after writing this book, the largest of the Frank Harper mysteries, I'm still not sure how I feel about it. I think that in some ways, the "war on drugs" has been a horrible failure, wasting countless billions of dollars and countless years of prison terms. Has it made things better? Would things be better or worse now if there hadn't been a crackdown?

I hope someone comes up with a solution. In the meantime, lives are being destroyed, drugs are pouring into our country over our porous border, and criminals, gangs, and terrorists are profiting. And unfortunately, I think things are worse in real life than they are in my fiction. At least I can wrap things up with a nice bow on top. But hearing about all the young children orphaned by the ongoing crisis reminds me that real life—and real problems—are rarely so tidy.

In the two years I spent researching this book, I learned a lot more than I wanted to about the opioid crisis and how it's affecting southwestern Ohio. And while the task force I write about is completely fictional, there are groups out there combating the drug epidemic. Keep them in your thoughts. If you or anyone you know is dealing with addiction problems, call the Partnership for Drug-Free Kids at 1-855-378-4373.

This book was a group effort in many ways. I'd like to thank:

- My parents, Dee and Albert Enslen, for reading and rereading this book and making it so much better with their tireless efforts.
- My editor, Diana Ceres, for vastly improving the book with her rigorous edits. She adds so much to these books (and my other titles) and keeps Frank sounding like Frank.
- My Beta Readers, consisting of Amanda, Cherie, Dave, Dee, Jim, Rose and Tony. You guys rock. Without these folks' early reviews and recommendations, the book wouldn't be as good as it is today.
- My publishers, Gypsy Publications, for taking a chance on me and getting me into print.
- and my wife Samantha, who supports me every day...even though I'm pretty sure she's sick of hearing about Frank Harper.

Lastly, I would like to thank the wonderful folks of Tipp City, Ohio. The locals have embraced Frank Harper and made him one of their own. People stop me at the coffee shop to ask about him as if he was a real person. I think Frank would love Tipp City, though he might not like the way the train mucks up traffic occasionally. My advice to him? Head to Sam and Ethel's and relax over some pie and coffee.

— Greg

WHITE LINES

CHAPTER 1
The Raid

A thick silence hung over the dilapidated neighborhood.

Snow blanketed every surface this early Sunday morning, heavy on the dead lawns and rows of run-down homes. A light flurry fell through one home's collapsed roof, drifting between burnt rafters and settling on abandoned furniture. In the street, more flakes of snow swirled along the black gutter. In one empty lot, a rusted shopping cart stood overturned, rusty wheels pointing at the sky.

From up the street, three large black vans rolled quietly, crunching on the icy street. Their headlights were off—they'd been off for the last half mile of the drive, navigating only by the meager early-morning sunlight and the cones of light from the occasional unbroken streetlights.

The black vans rolled quietly past the empty lot and the upturned shopping cart and slowed, stopping along the curb. The vans idled, snow falling silently around them.

The passenger door of the lead van swung open and a man, dressed head to toe in black, jumped down onto the street. He regarded one home in particular, half a block down. The man took out a black spotter's scope and held it up to his eye. He studied the home for a long, silent moment. Cold clouds of breath puffed through his mask. Finally, he nodded and walked to the back of his van, pulling the doors open.

"Keep it quiet," he whispered loudly, then walked away.

Behind him, six more dark figures jumped down to the street from the back of the van. Their boots hit the snowy pavement with only the slightest crunch. All wore helmets and tactical gear and black knit masks like the man with the scope.

They formed up at the rear of the van and waited, each checking their automatic weapons. One helped another adjust his thick bullet-proof vest.

The man with the scope crossed to the other two vans and tapped lightly on each rear door. At the signal, each opened and more task force members emerged. From the last van, a figure climbed down—a woman, still fiddling with her gear. Patricia Hawkins leaned against the van and checked her sidearms. She was a thin woman with dark reddish-brown hair and the glint in her eye of someone who didn't like to be fooled with. She had a hardness to her that translated into her brief, precise moves. While most of the others carried semi-automatics M4 carbine rifles, she seemed to only be equipped with two angry-looking pistols. For each Glock 10mm, she popped the gun magazine out, checked the bullets inside, and then reloaded and slid the top to push one bullet into the chamber.

Satisfied, Patricia holstered her guns and turned to the man with the scope.

"We good, Sarge?"

He nodded. "Yup, no movement. I'd be surprised if they're up yet." He stepped behind the van and pulled his mask and helmet off, tucking them under his arm. Sergeant Roget had a full head of dark hair and a thick beard. He looked like he could be a lumberjack—or a Viking—in another life.

"You bringing anything besides your little pistols?"

She smiled. "You know I don't like those big automatics," she said, patting her holsters. "I've got these and the ankle gun, plus my Taser. Someone's gotta be a little stealthy."

He lowered his voice. "I like it when you're stealthy, Hawkins." He gave her a wink and pulled his mask back on.

She smiled. "Shut up," she said under her breath. "We're gonna get caught one day."

Roget nodded, taking out his guns and checking them one more time—he was carrying an M4 carbine, like the others, and a heavy black 9mm SIG Sauer loaded with hollow points. Lately, the local gangs had started wearing vests of their own, and the standard ammunition just wasn't enough.

"Good. I'm tired of all this sneaking around," he said, winking. "Maybe then we can get married."

"Oh, really? Which one of us is gonna stay home? They'll make one of us quit."

He shrugged. "I'll transfer. You stay with the task force, and I'll work at one of the PDs up north."

She nodded. "Keep dreaming."

Another figure appeared around the back of the van. "Teams are ready, sir."

Roget handed the scope to Hawkins, then put his helmet on and waved the others to follow him. Hawkins followed, putting on her own mask and helmet. The assembled group of nearly twenty men and women in full tactical gear gathered behind the lead van. They were split into three teams, with Roget heading Team A.

"We're guessing five to seven inside," Sergeant Roget reminded them. "They're with the Fifth Street Runners. Could be their main production location."

"That's from a report four days ago," Hawkins added, speaking quietly to the group. "It's the best intel we've had on this gang in a while. We're here to round up and prosecute, not blow anyone away," she said, looking around at them. "Anyone who discharges their weapon better have a damn good reason."

If their information was correct, this was the prime lab for the gang, one of the largest in west Dayton. Along with Keystone and the Northsiders, Fifth Street pretty much ran this half of the city, supplying pot and coke and heroin to whoever wanted it, including users in the city and from all points north: Vandalia, Cooper's Mill, Troy, even up to Sidney.

Roget put in his ear piece, which was connected wirelessly to a computer in the lead van. "Radio checks," he said. They each spoke in turn, saying their names and team. Masked, he couldn't tell any of them apart, but that was just as well. At this point, they were all part of the same weapon: a spear, designed to stick into the heart of this drug operation.

"Okay, team leaders," Roget said. "Check your people one more time and then form up and move out. A follow me—we'll take the front. B take the back, C secure any vehicles and back Team B."

The groups moved silently off. Hawkins and the rest of Team A followed Roget as he approached the house—it was like any other in the neighborhood, built in the 1950s and looking like it hadn't been painted since. Shutters leaned away from the rest of the home like they were trying to escape. A rusty car sat in the driveway, the snowy concrete beneath it painted a dark, oily smear.

They crossed the street and approached the front of the dark house, crouching down near the gate of the chain-link fence. It led to a short path up to the house.

Roget looked over at Hawkins' masked face. "You ready?"

Hawkins nodded.

Roget did a final radio check with the other two teams, then stood and walked up to the front of the house. Close behind him were Hawkins and Officer Bellows, who carried a sledgehammer. They walked quietly up the front steps and then stepped to the side. The cop movies always got it wrong—standing square up with the door was just asking to get shot. Roget stood to the left of the door with Hawkins and put his hand up, making a fist. He waited, listening to his earpiece. Teams B and C reported back that they were ready.

"Okay, let's go," Roget whispered into his radio. He reached over and tried the doorknob, but it was locked. He nodded at Bellows, who stepped up and swung the heavy metal sledgehammer back. He then brought it forward, crashing into the door just below the doorknob. The door burst open and Bellows stepped through. Roget and the others rushed in from all sides, catching the men inside still asleep.

It was all over in a matter of minutes.

Team A cleared the front half of the house, searching for suspects and arresting those they found. Team B took the kitchen and back half of the house, and Team C followed them in, racing upstairs and securing the second floor.

Ten minutes later, Roget and Hawkins stood in the living room, looking over the five young black men sitting on the floor in front of them, all their hands zip-tied behind their backs. No shots had been fired, and none of the task force members had been injured. Two of the gang members were bleeding from superficial injuries.

All in all, a very good effort, Roget thought.

"Okay, you guys know the drill," he said, looking at each of them and holding up a small package on coke. "We know this is a Fifth Street house. The little '5' you stamp on everything kinda gives it away."

None of the men looked up.

Roget looked at Hawkins. "I guess none of them has a sense of humor."

"It is pretty early," she answered, pointing at her watch.

He looked back at the men in zip-ties. "I'll give you the standard offer, which I know you'll pass on. You could talk, but you want to serve your time, I know. Really looking forward to it. Be a good little soldier for Fifth Street; maybe get stabbed in prison. Sounds like fun, right?"

None of them made a sound. Out front, Roget could see several Dayton Police Department (DPD) cars had arrived to help secure the scene. "You are each looking at significant time," Roget continued, sounding bored. "Eight years, minimum," he lied. They hadn't finished the inventory and still had no idea how much was in the home. "But I'm happy to make all that go away if you give me some names. Your boss, their bosses, etc." Roget did his best to sound bored. Sometimes it worked. Maybe one was new, or hadn't been around long enough to be brainwashed by the whole "snitches get stitches" mindset.

"Don't waste your time, Sergeant," Hawkins added, playing her part in a conversation they'd had a dozen times. She looked at the men, all of whom were staring at the dingy carpet. "None of these guys will rat—they're hardened criminals," she said, glancing at Roget and smirking. "They're all excited about doing some hard time. Maybe they'll bunk with some huge dude named 'Tiny' who wants to be friends, right?" At that, one of them glanced up. The black kid was the youngest in the house, thin and scared. Roget knew he had a winner.

"Okay, wrap them up," he barked at the two DPD officers who had just walked in. The officers started pulling the men to their feet and walking them to the door. "We'll talk to them at HQ," Roget said loudly. He nodded at one of the officers and pointed at the scared kid.

"Your car," he whispered, and the cop nodded.

CHAPTER 2
Brooding in B-ham

Frank Harper sighed at the television and sipped more of his beer. There was nothing on TV this afternoon but some stupid European car race.

Lately, Frank had been feeling old. He was only in his mid-fifties and in good shape for his age. He'd always been wiry and lean, even back in his days in the military and with the New Orleans PD. And Frank had been through some tough times. But lately, he hadn't felt very spry. It had been weeks since he'd worked out, something he used to do religiously, ingrained in him since basic training.

It had started with him getting shot in the back last October as part of a kidnapping investigation. Six months later, his back was now healed, but the months of prescription—and recreational—drugs he'd taken since had dulled him. Before, he felt more like the edge of a knife, sharp and ready. Now, his focus came and went, depending on his latest dosage.

Frank knew people around him were starting to notice. But Frank didn't care. He had his beer and his little bottles of Oxycontin to help with the pain and nothing else really intruded upon his daily worries.

The race went to commercial—he was watching the car race as there were no "real" sports on. March was a shitty month for sports—too late for football, too early for baseball. He watched whatever was on, but it was just something to watch. Just something to fill the time. And any sport was better than CNN—all they wanted to talk about was the upcoming 2012 election, now only six months away.

Maybe Frank should take up "binge watching," whatever that was. He'd seen an article about it in the Birmingham paper—folks who got Netflix or some other on-demand service would spend days or weeks watching one entire show, all the way through. It sounded like a cure for insomnia to Frank. Who wanted to sit down and watch every episode of "The West Wing" back to back? He might consider it, but only after the apocalypse. When he was stuck in some underground bunker somewhere. Knowing his luck, he'd be stuck with nothing but the collected DVDs of "The Wiggles" or "Gilligan's Island."

He glanced around his small apartment. Frank Harper lived in a not-great building in a lame part of Birmingham, Alabama, and right now the place was a mess.

He stood and made his way across the floor of the living room, steadying himself on the wall at one point. There was a stack of pizza boxes in one corner and another on the dining room table. He headed in the general direction of the bathroom, ignoring the growing number of flies in his apartment.

Oxycontin did that to you. Oxy made everything feel normal. It made you stop caring about silly things like showering or food rotting in the corners of your apartment.

He leaned against the wall and started coughing. After a while, he staggered on toward the bathroom, kicking over an empty bottle of bourbon. It rolled across the floor and hit the wall, breaking into several large pieces.

"No way I'm bringing a woman back here!" He shouted at the top of his lungs, eliciting a banging on the floor from his downstairs neighbor.

Frank wasn't wining and dining women and bringing them back to his apartment anyway. Money was tight again—Oxy was expensive. He was down to watching television with cans of cheap beer to keep him company. The bourbon was nearly gone—he only had a little of the Ten High Blended bourbon left and was saving it in a flask to take to work. After that, he'd moved on to a cheap vodka that tasted like engine cleaner, but it was all gone too.

At some point later, he woke up in his chair in front of the TV. Something different was on—some old movie. He'd blacked out. How long had it been? He'd been stumbling to the bathroom. He couldn't remember anything after getting up to go take a piss. Now he was watching TV again. Had he imagined getting up? Or was he imagining this now? Was he stuck in a loop of TV and beer and piss?

Frank slapped himself hard across the face—hard enough to make his eyes water. It hurt like hell and kept hurting.

The Washington family. They were real. According to his friend Jake Delancey's most recent phone messages, they were getting tormented every night. Frank had tried to help up in Ohio last month by confronting one of the gang members that had been menacing Jake's tenants. Frank had threatened the gang, telling them to back off and leave the Washingtons alone.

But after that, what had he done to help them? Nothing.

Frank shook his head and stood up, the blood rushing to his head. He went to find his iPhone. It was old and didn't like to hold a charge, so he kept it plugged in most of the time on the kitchen counter. He found it and played back the last message from Jake again. For some reason, Frank just couldn't make himself delete it.

Jake sounded worried—the Washingtons were in danger. Things were getting worse and now the cops were involved.

The message ended. Frank looked at the phone and replayed it. Once it was done, he realized there was a message from his daughter, Laura. He hit "play" and held the phone up to his ear.

"Frank, it's Laura. Just wanted to let you know we miss you. Jackson said everyone is talking about you at the preschool and how you found Mrs. Mercato's husband. You're quite famous in these parts. Anyway, just wanted to see how you were doing. Haven't heard from you in a week or two and I'm starting to worry. Please call me. Soon."

He listened to it again, then looked at the phone. The message was from Friday, two days ago. Why hadn't he noticed it before? It had been a month since he'd seen her, a month since he'd been in Cooper's Mill.

In a rare moment of clarity, Frank suddenly realized why he'd been putting off calling Laura back—he wanted to sound coherent when he talked to her. Frank was waiting for a sober time to call, but they seemed to be happening less and less.

He wanted the bourbon, but he was saving it for work. It was the only way he could stand going to work anymore. His job had seemed pointless before, but after going up to Ohio and working a few cases, it had gotten worse.

Frank set the phone down, careful to not delete the message, and went to find the flask. It was in his jacket. He screwed the lid off and hesitated. If he drank it now, he'd having nothing for tomorrow. Mondays were the worst. Mondays were the most hopeless.

And Frank needed the job. He had no retirement or pension coming in—his only salary came from working at the Alabama Bureau of Investigation (ABI). Going in drunk would only lead to another fight with Collier, his annoying boss. The job sucked, but it paid for everything. As much as he hated it, it was all he had.

Frank decided he'd drink beer instead. He screwed the lid back on the flask and went back to the TV and sat down, grabbing open beer cans from the coffee table in front of him until he found one with something in it. Popping another Oxy from the bottle, Frank drank until the can was empty, gagging on tepid beer. Then he grabbed the remote, desperate to find anything to distract his foggy mind.

CHAPTER 3
Jake, Driving

Jake Delancy was having a tough time keeping the truck on the road. The flurries were starting to intensify, and the wind was gusting heartily as yet another winter storm moved into the area. The other challenge was his left arm, held close to his body by the fabric sling. He'd broken it in a fall a month ago. The cast had come off last week, and it was still tender. It seemed like he banged it on everything.

But this was a very important errand he'd been putting off.

Jake had many jobs and many interests—too many, he'd been told on numerous occasions. First and foremost, he thought of himself as a tinkerer and handyman. Few things gave him more pleasure then crafting a new set of cabinets or installing a stained-glass window.

Jake's smile faded as his thoughts returned to the task at hand. He drove south on I-75 and exited at Needmore Avenue, heading west into the rougher parts of north Dayton.

His main business—and the one that paid the bills—was owning and maintaining several apartments and home rentals in the Dayton area. Most were in the northern towns of Vandalia, Troy and Cooper's Mill. But he also had several smaller properties in the poorer parts of north Dayton that inevitably needed more maintenance and repairs. Tenant turnover was higher, but he made good money on the rent. It was paid directly to him from Ohio's Section 8 housing program, so he rarely had to deal with the tenant's money. Once he'd gotten on the list with Section 8, he'd started buying up cheap properties and fixing them up.

Things had gone great up until the gangs started moving in. Jake had seen it coming and adjusted his property mix, selling some places and buying new ones north of Dayton. He kept several in Dayton and maintained them well—his tenants were always happy, and reported as much to the folks at Section 8. But the gangs were making it harder.

One property in particular was giving him heartburn. He'd bought the small home on Eckhart Street at auction and fixed it up. Section 8 had put a great family, the Washingtons, into the home.

And things went well until the Northsiders showed up. The gang, one of the largest in the area, or so he'd read, threatened the Washingtons, telling them to move out because the "house belonged to them." Jake had reassured the family that they were living there legally—he had the deed. But the gang kept coming back, trying to scare the family off.

Jake had spoken to the Dayton Police, but they didn't seem interested unless a crime had been committed. Then Jake had another idea—he'd ask an acquaintance, Frank Harper, for help.

It seemed like a good idea at the time. Harper was an ex-cop, in town visiting his daughter and grandson. Harper had helped solve a high-profile kidnapping case back in the fall, and Jake asked if he did any work on the side. Frank listened to the particulars—Jake had done some cabinet work for a Russian family, but the Russians had refused to pay. Frank agreed to help, especially after hearing the Russians had pushed Jake down a hill and broken his arm. The "negotiation" came to blows, with Frank injured and the three Russians ending up in the hospital. But Frank got Jake his money.

Rolling the dice, Jake asked for more help with another situation—the Eckhart Street property. Frank drove down and spoke with the Washingtons, calming them. But then he took it upon himself to visit a strip club controlled by the gang and warned them off.

Unfortunately, it hadn't worked. Over the past month, things had escalated. The tenants felt in constant danger as the Northsiders tried to push them out of "their" house.

Unsure of how to proceed, Jake called Frank on multiple occasions. The last call hadn't gone well. "Can you come back up to Ohio soon?" Jake asked. "The family is really scared. Last week, they got another rock through their window.

Harper had dismissed Jake, telling him to call the cops. And Harper sounded drunk or high. Or both. Jake was starting to regret putting any faith in the man.

After that last call, Jake spent days pondering his options. The only solution he came up with was to move the family and get them set up in a new place.

Jake turned onto Eckhart Street. Half the lots were vacant—homes either burned to the ground or torn down by the city of Dayton.

The city did little to encourage people to move in—about the only thing they did was actively "manage" the occupancy rate. When a home was abandoned or people moved out, the occupancy rate went down. One way to improve the occupancy rates was to get people to move in by providing more security or better local services.

But there was another, far cheaper way to "improve" the occupancy rate: tear the empty houses down. It was happening all over, especially in shrinking Midwestern cities like Dayton. Instead of fixing the problems that made people move away, some cities just waited until people left and then tore down the dilapidated houses, thereby "increasing" the occupancy rates.

Jake thought Detroit had it right—instead of tearing homes down in a piecemeal fashion, the government was tearing down entire neighborhoods. In some places, they were even "unpaving" the roads and letting sections completely return to nature. When a city retreated from the edges, shrinking back onto itself, did that mean nature was winning?

He pulled up in front of the house on Eckhart Street and stopped. Climbing out, he noticed the sky was heavy with snow. Careful with his arm, Jake bent his head away from the wind as he walked up to the front door and rang the bell.

Markeys Washington answered the door. He was a skinny black man with very short hair and a nervous demeanor. But who could blame him? He and his family had been on guard for weeks.

"Hey, Mr. Washington," Jake smiled. "Can we talk?"

The man nodded and held open the door. "Sure, Mr. Delancy. And you can call me Markeys. It startin' to come down out there?"

Jake walked into their modest living room. Everything was neat and tidy. Jake loved seeing people take care of his property. "Yeah, it is. And thanks, Markeys. I wanted to talk to you about what's been going on. I think we should move you and your family."

Markeys' wife came in from the kitchen, carrying their young boy. "We're moving?" Markeys asked.

Jake nodded. "It's not safe here."

Markeys' wife put the boy down and looked at her husband. "That's what I've been saying. These fools around here…"

Jake nodded and pointed at the door. "I have a truck, but I can't carry all your stuff, so I rented a moving van."

Markeys started to argue, but his wife put her hand on his arm. "That's fine," she said quietly, looking at Jake. Her name was Denise, Jake remembered. How could he have forgotten? This family had been on his mind so much lately.

Markeys shook his head. "I ain't leaving. I ain't letting these fools think they won."

Jake started to say something but Denise interrupted him. "I don't care what you want. Noah and I are gettin' out of here. Last night they shot out the window," she said, pointing to a board where the glass used to be.

Jake shook his head. "I don't think the cops are gonna help," he said. "I've called a bunch of times."

Denise looked at her husband. "We gotta go, Markeys. It's been crazy."

Jake nodded and Denise looked at him.

"Where we goin'?"

"A hotel over on Miller Lane, for now," he said, mentioning an area of north Dayton with a concentration of hotels and restaurants. "I have several apartments, and two are going to be empty on the first of April. That's just five days from now," he said, doing the calculation. "It will take me a few days to get one of them ready."

"What about your friend, that ex-cop?" Markeys asked.

Jake shook his head. "He's not around anymore."

"Good," the young wife said. "He's the one that caused this trouble, going down to that stripper club and yelling at the Northsiders. Right after that was when we got the brick through the window. Remember that?"

Jake nodded. There wasn't anything to say, really, about Frank. These people didn't know the whole story. Hell, Jake didn't know the whole story, but it didn't change the fact that Frank had waded in and made things worse. Much worse.

"Do you want to stay somewhere else tonight? I can drive you," Jake said, looking at the door.

Markeys shook his head and glanced at his wife. "We need to pack. Tomorrow?"

Jake had thought there would be more arguing. It was one of the reasons he hadn't just showed up with a moving van. "Okay, I'll be back in the morning." Jake stood and turned to leave.

Denise spoke up. "What about our rent? Gotta be more than this place."

"I'll take care of it." Jake walked to the door. "I'll be back in the morning. 10:00 a.m."

They said their goodbyes and Jake walked back to his truck. Fresh snow scudded across the sky and fell from the darkening clouds. He climbed into his truck, trying to avoid banging the arm on the door jamb. It seemed like half the time he got into this truck, he banged his bad arm on something.

Once settled, he started up the truck and turned on the heat. It seemed like this winter was going to go on forever. He glanced once more at the house and drove away.

CHAPTER 4
Ride to HQ

While the rest of the task force members were heading back to headquarters, Sergeant Roget rode along with the Dayton PD officer and his young suspect. Roget started in on the "horrible" conditions in holding. The DPD officer picked up on the conversation right away. Holding actually wasn't that bad. It was far better than the Montgomery County Jail, where the kid would end up if he was ever sentenced, but the kid didn't know that.

"Yeah, it's pretty bad," the officer added. "Last week we had a guy get killed."

"Really?" Roget asked with mock concern. "How?"

"Stabbed."

"Geez." Roget wasn't sure, but he thought he heard a whimper from the back seat. He turned around. "What's your name, kid?"

"Um, Fango," he said quietly.

"Yeah, it was gross," the officer continued, talking louder than he really needed to. "The kid got stabbed in his room and bled for like five hours before anyone found him. Blood ran out into the hallway."

Roget covered his smile. That kind of stuff never happened. Holding was where suspects went before being charged, and everyone was kept far apart—but this Fango kid didn't know that.

"Did they find the killer?" Roget asked.

The officer glanced over, his eyes twinkling. "Nah. They really should do something about that—I mean, the guys in holding are just there for questioning."

"Well, the smart ones speak up and get sprung."

Roget just let that one hang in the air. The only sounds were the engine and the heater blowing and an occasional beep from the patrol car's radio. Other than that, there was nothing to distract the kid.

Roget knew what Fango was thinking. The kid was just like anyone else. He'd probably been caught up in a situation he couldn't control and now was paying the price. But if his loyalty didn't run too deep, maybe he'd flip.

Even though the task force worked for the mayor, they didn't have the manpower to secure crime scenes or process them. And most arrests, like this kid today, were still handled by the Dayton PD, headquartered on North Fourth Street.

"Drop you at the task force?"

Roget nodded. "Yeah, thanks."

The officer slowed in front of City Hall and dropped the sergeant off. It was a strange setup, but there nothing Sergeant Roget could do about it. The 50-member Dayton Area Heroin Task Force (DAHTF) operated separately from the Dayton PD, but they shared many resources. The task force just wasn't large enough. But the mayor had been clear: they were not part of the Dayton PD, which had struggled for years to contain the heroin and cocaine epidemic in Dayton.

Logistically, that meant the DAHTF, as part of the Mayor's Office, was located in the same building and on the same floor as the mayor and his offices in the Dayton City Hall. The Dayton PD had their own headquarters about two blocks down the road, next to the huge Montgomery County jail. The buildings were connected by a bridge over a shared parking lot.

Roget turned and watched the police car drive away. The kid in the back looked scared. Good.

Chapter 5
Trio

"Shut up, bitch."

Slug, a massive young black man, had the guy on the floor, a foot on the back of the old man's neck. The guy on the floor was the owner of a liquor store and a "customer" of the Northsiders, which meant the Northsiders provided "protection" for the store and the property inside. Bad things could happen to a store if it wasn't protected by the Northsiders.

Tavon watched the customers and kept an eye out for cops. He was uncomfortable with this part of his job. Skinny and 22, Tavon didn't much like the "enforcement" part of working for a gang. Actually, there wasn't much he liked about the Northsiders. Unfortunately, they were the best option around.

"Look, son, I already paid," the man said, his voice gurgling under Slug's shoe. "I paid in—"

Rubio leaned over the man. He was a little older than Slug and Tavon and ran their three-man crew. "You paid for March—I was here, man. And I ain't your son. We're here for April. Collecting early."

"It's not ready yet—" the man started to say, and Slug leaned forward. Tavon thought Slug was built like a linebacker—or a tank. The man on the ground waved his arms, and Rubio nodded at Slug, who backed off slightly. The man on the ground gasped for air and nodded weakly. "No problem, no problem."

Rubio helped the old black man to his feet. "Five hundred," Rubio said, walking him over to the cash register. "Plus another hundred. For making Slug put you down like that."

The man started to say something but then thought better of it. He was bleeding from the mouth and nose and shook his head, hitting a button on the cash register to pop it open. Rubio and the old man counted out the money and Rubio put it in his pocket. "We good."

Tavon turned to leave, but Slug wasn't having it. He reached back into this waistband and pulled out his gun, a short-nosed Beretta, pointing it at the bloodied shopkeeper. "We'll be coming every month now, not every other month. Same amount. Have it ready so we don't have to do something stupid," he said, walking over to a standing rack of newspapers and tipping it over. Papers scattered on the floor. "And don't make us regret letting you off the hook."

The shopkeeper nodded and said nothing.

Rubio and the others stepped back out into the cold—the snow falling harder than when they went in. Tavon pulled his jacket around him.

"Getting cold," Rubio said.

Tavon agreed but didn't say anything. He'd learned a long time ago to keep his opinions to himself. Slug and Rubio were short tempered, even in the best of times.

They walked toward the three matching Honda Civics parked in the lot. When they weren't enforcing for the gang, the trio was usually making deliveries. The Northsiders had invested considerable money into tricking out the three matching cars. Gig, their boss, had insisted the cars be able to out-muscle any other vehicles on the road, including the cops. Tavon and other mechanically-inclined gang members had spent countless hours tweaking the vehicles. In another life, Tavon would have been an automobile mechanic, working at a shop and changing oil for rich white folks.

Gig had them collect on the rare days when there wasn't any product to move. Tavon preferred those days—he was happiest behind the wheel of his Civic. Any day Tavon could get his Civic onto the local highways and up to 100 miles per hour was a good day. Chases were rare—the gang members routinely monitored the police scanner and different iPhone apps to track cop locations—but when pressed, these three vehicles were faster than most cop cars.

In addition, Gig had encouraged them to be creative. Tavon had come up with an interesting idea for escaping the cops during a pursuit. He had put his plan into motion and was looking forward to the next time the cops chased them to see if their setup would work.

"Where to next?" Tavon asked.

"Lemme check." Rubio looked at a piece of paper. He wrote everything down on these little pads of paper he carried around. Tavon never asked, but he hoped Rubio was smart enough to destroy them when he was done.

"Couple more places along here," Rubio said, starting off for their cars. "Gonna run through Burger King first," he said.

Tavon and Slug nodded and followed him to the cars. The Civics sat untouched, shining in the weak sunlight. No one ever bothered their cars. They were Northsiders, and not to be messed with. Not like that old white guy last month. That guy had stones. Stupid, but he had stones. Walked right into Riley's, a strip club up on North Dixie that the

Northsiders used as an office. Old white guy came over and talked to Tavon like they were best buds.

Crazy.

The guy was an ex-cop, that much had been obvious. Cops and ex-cops carried themselves with a confidence that came from carrying a gun around all the time.

The old man had warned them to stop threatening the new tenants of a stash house on Eckhart Street. Tavon and the others had been by the house a few times to scare them off, but Gig had left it at that—just intimidation, for now. Slug and Rubio were pushing to burn them out. Tavon knew better than to express an opinion.

Tavon got to his Civic and lifted the car door. It moved smoothly upwards for him to climb in. Reconfiguring the three cars, making sure the frame could handle the extra weight, had been fun. He'd ended up having to weld in new supports for each door.

Tavon skipped Burger King, idling in the parking lot while he waited for Slug and Rubio to go through the drive-through, wondering how he'd ended up here.

He lived with his mom and three sisters, even though he made enough to live on his own, which he'd done up until a few months ago. His mom worked her fingers to the bone, even with the money Tavon provided her. His father—well, he'd never met the man. Tavon tried not to complain. He'd had a good life so far. There was always food on the table, even back before he'd been old enough to work for the Northsiders and start bringing in money of his own.

Rubio's and Slug's cars exited the drive-through and Tavon fell in behind them, heading north. They drove along Salem Avenue, passing Riley's, where Tavon had talked to the old man and then the old man had bought some stuff from Stimpy, the local dealer. The Northsiders allowed Stimpy to sell at the club as long as they got a cut. He also acted as a lookout, in case a rival gang made a move on the location. Stimpy was always outside, winter or summer, and would notice a drive-by long before anyone inside would know what was happening.

After the old guy had left, Tavon had gone out and talked to Stimpy. He'd said that the old man had bought a couple hundred worth of Oxy. Tavon wondered if the Oxy was for the old man or if he was running and selling his own product on the side. Why buy it from Stimpy and pay full street?

CHAPTER 6
Backstabbed

"Nah, I don't think that's right," Fango said.

He looked around the small cell he'd occupied since arriving in holding. The Dayton PD officer had booked him, then walked him to holding. And then the dude from the task force had come in and interviewed him.

The guard looked at his clipboard again. "No, that's what it says. 'Transfer to GP.' That's general population."

"Look, you need to talk to Sergeant Roget, okay," Fango said again. "He said I'd be kept out of the general pop. For my own safety."

The guard shook his head. "Look, man, I'm just doing what the forms tell me, okay? It came over like two hours ago, and I'm just getting around to it. Turn around and back up to the gate."

Fango complied, and his wrists were zip-tied together. The guard opened the door and led Fango outside. He walked from the one side of the building, through a series of locked doors, and out into the general population, a large area that resembled a lunch room. Twenty or thirty men, mostly young and mostly black, were sitting around at long tables.

"What are these guys doing?"

"Waiting for arraignments or interviews." The guard looked at his watch.

"I'm not supposed to be in with these folks," Fango whispered urgently. "I'm not kidding here, man. I...the gang I'm with. I gave up names. The cop I was talking to was clear—if they find out, I'm dead."

The guard checked his clipboard yet again, looking through the paperwork. "That might be right, but look, kid. The form's right here. I can't disobey or I'll get busted. If you want, I'll call him when I get back to my office. Roget, right? Task force?"

Fango nodded. "Yes, please call him."

The guard nodded and removed the zip-ties from the man's wrists. "Just keep your head down."

CHAPTER 7
Burning Down the House

Later that evening, the three matching Honda Civics motored through the dirty, snowy streets of west Dayton, passing under the occasional flickering street light. Crime stalked this area, just as it did in scores of other depressed cities in the Midwest where neighborhoods collectively rolled up their sidewalks at dusk. Some citizens scrounged every penny they could find to move away, but most lived lives of quiet desperation, huddled inside their homes every night, praying that the sun would rise in a few hours and find the occupants still alive.

Tonight, it was Eckhart Street's turn for violence.

The three cars parked several houses down and shut off their engines. The car doors slid straight up, moving eerily in unison. Three young black men emerged and walked to the trunk of their vehicles, opening them.

Tavon looked down into the trunk of his Civic and wondered at the death it held. Guns, more than a dozen. He'd carried weapons, of course, and owned quite a few over the years. They were useful at scaring people or projecting power. Tavon had no problem scaring people if that's what it took to get them in line or get them off your back. But he'd never killed anyone. Something had always stayed his hand.

Slug walked up to Tavon. "Come on man. We gotta roll." Tavon saw he had a shotgun, along with a handgun tucked into his belt. Tavon always wondered at the wisdom of sticking a gun in your waistband, pointed at your junk.

Tavon nodded and picked out a handgun of his own. He always chose weapons based on how they looked. If he could, he'd carry a chainsaw or a Japanese sword. People were more scared of weapons when they could imagine the amount of damage they would do. And scared people were less likely to fight back.

He followed Slug over to the trunk of Rubio's car, where the man was removing several lengths of chain. Rubio handed two to Slug and one to Tavon, keeping one for himself.

"What are these for?" Tavon asked.

"Chaining the doors."

Tavon glanced at Slug, then shook his head. "No, we're just here to scare them. No need to trap them inside."

Rubio stood up from his trunk. He was now holding two red plastic jugs. Tavon saw the look on Rubio's face and knew the man wasn't kidding.

"Things have changed," Rubio said. "Gig called. Said we're burning the f-ers out."

Rubio flashed his toothy grin. "Shit yeah."

Tavon nodded, backing off. Rubio lifted the jugs. A liquid inside sloshed loudly. "Okay, let's do it."

Tavon didn't move.

"Nah, I'll stay in my car," Tavon said, shaking his head.

The others looked at him.

"You can burn the place to scare 'em out. I got no problem with that. But they got a little kid in there."

Slug cursed quietly as Rubio stepped up and leaned over Tavon. The man was at least a foot taller than the younger boy. "I don't give two shits what they got. We got orders," Rubio said slowly. "Too many folks around here don't listen no more. Gig said make an example. That's what we gonna do."

"No," Tavon said, handing his chain to Rubio. "I ain't killing them."

Rubio took the chain. "You serious?"

"I'll scare 'em," Tavon said to them both. "But I ain't killing a family. That's some shit. I mean, the point of this is to get 'em to move, right?"

Rubio shook his head. "Nah, man, you're missing the point. Orders come down, you carry 'em out. Like the Army. That's the way it works. Gig says so, and so does the Dragon. They got a plan, bigger than you and me. This is part of it."

Tavon didn't say anything.

"And this ain't about them," Rubio continued, leaning closer to Tavon. "It's about the Northsiders. You still part of that, boy? Or are you asking to get out?"

Tavon knew what that meant. No one left the gang. You stayed in or they put you "out." Dead in some dark alley. Ten toes up, they called it. The Northsiders never let anyone just walk away. There was no retirement, no 401-k.

Tavon shook his head.

"Naw, I ain't trying to get out. But killing a kid—that's just gonna make people hate us more."

"Don't matter if they hate us. We need people scared of us," Slug added. "Other gangs ain't giving us respect. You know how it is."

It grew quiet between them. Rubio had said what he was going to say and Slug had backed him up and now it was up to Tavon. He was either in or out. Either way, the house would burn and the family would die.

"Shit," Tavon said, putting out his hand. "Give me that chain."

Rubio smiled and handed it over.

"Damn, boy, you had me going," Slug said, punching Tavon in the shoulder. Tavon smiled at them both and wrapped the chain around his hand.

Rubio handed one jug to Slug. "Okay, I got the front of the house. I'll chain the door, then pour the gas. Slug, pour your gas along the side and back. Tavon, you chain the back door. Attach it to a grate or bar or something, then lock it," Rubio said, handing Tavon a heavy padlock.

Rubio and Slug started off, carrying the red jugs. Tavon skirted the snowy lawn and walked around the side of the house. Just as he moved out of sight, Tavon could see Rubio at the front door, using the length of metal chain to secure the metal screen door to the nearby metal grate that covered the closest window. He pulled it tight and latched it with a padlock.

Tavon's mind raced. He'd never killed anyone and wanted to keep that streak going. He walked around the back of the house and found a door off what looked like the kitchen. It opened onto a small backyard and an alley behind.

Tavon unwrapped the chain and fed it around the bars that covered the kitchen window, then through the handle of the metal screen of the back door. Slug appeared from Tavon's left, splashing his gas can on the ground under the windows. "You ready?"

Tavon nodded, pulling out the padlock.

Slug ran past him, pouring more gas along the base of the house and moving out of sight.

Tavon looked at the weighty padlock in his hand. Maybe he could just lock it on the chain, not actually attaching—

"What are you doing?"

Rubio was standing there, the red can in his hand.

"Putting on the lock."

"Naw, you're not. You're thinking, I can see it. That's what gets people killed, man." Rubio reached down and took out his piece. "Seriously, you gonna die over some stupid family you never met?" Rubio pointed his gun at Tavon.

"I'll do it. I'll do it," Tavon said. He leaned over and padlocked the two ends of the chain together.

"Back up," Rubio said, waving Tavon away. He walked over and checked the padlock. He looked back at Tavon. "Move it, man."

They walked around the front of the house. Tavon felt empty inside, knowing what was coming next. The family would die, that much was for certain. But now Rubio would be looking at Tavon differently, watching, waiting for any sign of Tavon's wavering loyalty to the Northsiders.

As soon as Tavon slipped up, he was a dead man.

They met Slug at the front of the house. The man was so excited he was shaking. Rubio dribbled the last of his gasoline in a line down the snowy driveway, then bent down and put a lighter to it. A thick ribbon of blue fire skittered across the snow, splitting in half and racing along the walls on each side of the house. In moments, a ring of yellow flames encircled the house.

"Nice," Slug said. "That'll burn the bitch down."

"Let's go," Rubio said. "Bring the cans."

Slug and Tavon followed him to their cars, and Tavon earned another long glance from Rubio before they all climbed in and drove away. The flames grew behind them, lighting up the night. Rubio and Slug raced away, but Tavon lingered, driving slowly. He watched, looking in his rearview mirror. Flames licked the sides of the small house. He watched, hoping to see some movement or signs of people escaping.

But Tavon saw nothing.

CHAPTER 8
Crossed Off

Sergeant Roget was sitting at his desk in the task force offices. It was past seven, but he had to brief the Mayor and others in the morning. The phone on his desk rang.

"Yeah," he said.

"Sergeant, this is Central. Your 'guest' got moved."

Roget sat up. They had to be talking about his witness, the one from the raid. "Yeah, he's in holding. Or he's supposed to be. His street name is Fango. I left him in isolation."

Roget could hear paperwork rustling. "That's what I thought, but he's not here. There's a transfer request in the file, moving him to GP a couple hours ago. Didn't know if you knew about it."

"No, that can't be right."

"Got it here. Signed by—well, who knows. I can never read these signatures. But came down earlier, all official. I took him over myself, then told him I'd call you when I got back. Then we had another incident, so I'm just getting a chance to call."

"Okay, thanks. Go find him, right now. No delays. And get him out of GP before something happens."

Roget hung up and grabbed his coat.

Two minutes later, the sergeant was pulling into the parking lot behind the police department. The jail was just north of the station and shared a parking lot. Roget could hear alarms going off as he approached the doors to the jail. A white exterior strobe light was flashing.

Inside, people seemed to be making their way to the exits. A guard at the metal detectors was pushing people toward the exit.

"What's going on?"

"Not sure," the guard said. "Better step back outside."

"Looked like some kind of fight," a man in a suit said, rushing past Roget. "I think an inmate got stabbed."

Roget felt his heart sink.

CHAPTER 9
Gone

The tinny ring from his cell phone woke him.

Jake Delancy sat up in bed, groggy and confused. He stood and walked over to the dresser. The wooden floor of his bedroom was cold on his bare feet. Someday he'd need to get a rug or something.

The clock read "1:10 a.m."

"Hello?"

There was a crackle of static and a voice came back. It was hard to hear over the sirens and shouting in the background. "Mr. Delancy?"

"Yes?"

"This is Captain James with the Dayton Fire Department. We understand you own a property on Eckhart Street in Dayton?"

"Yes, that's right."

"There's been a fire," the man said. In the background, Jake could hear hissing.

"What?"

"The house is fully involved."

Some part of Jake's mind offered up a translation—that was fireman-speak for "completely on fire."

"What?"

"The house is on fire right now, sir," the man said. "Our records show there were three occupants?"

"Yes, a family," Jake said, leaning on the dresser. He was suddenly cold. The man had distinctly used the word "were." Past tense.

"Are they okay? Did they get out?"

"It doesn't look like it, sir," the man on the other end said. "We found metal chains on the ground. We think both doors were chained shut—from the outside."

Jake's heart skipped a beat.

"Sir, are you there? We need you to come down."

"Okay, I'm on my way."

Jake started looking around and flipped on a light to look for his clothes and shoes.

"There is no hurry, Mr. Delancy," the man said. "We'll be here at least another hour. It's a huge mess. And Dayton PD needs to talk to you."

Jake thanked him and hung up.

Dead? Were the Washingtons dead? He'd just been down there a few hours ago. When the phone rang, he'd expected it to be the moving company canceling on him.

He shook his head and headed downstairs, pulling on his heavy coat and finding his keys.

Twenty minutes later, Jake drove through the dark and snowy streets of north Dayton. He stuck with the main roads where he could. It had snowed all evening and the plows were having trouble keeping up with it.

He saw the flashing lights, red and blue, before he even made the turn onto Eckhart Street. This was no little kitchen fire. The whole house was burning—orange and angry and flickering up into the night sky. If they had been inside, the Washingtons were dead.

Jake slowed and stopped his truck, parking near a huge firetruck and getting out. He could feel the heat from a hundred feet away.

"You can't park here," a woman firefighter said. She was decked out in firefighting gear with reflective yellow stripes on the arms and legs. Her yellow jacket had a patch on it that read "MCGINTY." Her hair was slicked with sweat and she looked exhausted.

Jake nodded at the house. "Captain James called me down here. This is my property."

"Oh, okay," she said, pointing at another firetruck. "He's over there."

Jake walked over, stepping carefully over the web of thick fire hoses that littered the ground like fat gray snakes. In places, snow and ice and water from the firefighting efforts had refrozen, creating a slippery path. He found a knot of men talking next to a firetruck and pointing at the burning house.

"Captain James?"

They all turned and looked at him. One of them spoke up. "The Captain'll be right back," he said to Jake. They turned and resumed their conversation, ignoring him.

"Did they find the family yet?" Jake asked of the group. "I heard they were trapped inside. Is that right?"

"You'll have to talk to the chief. Sorry."

Not sure of what else to do, Jake waited, leaning on the fence around a neighbor's yard. The scene was loud and chaotic: hoses hissing and throwing water on the house, firefighters and policemen yelling at each other, the loud crackle of the fire. Yet there were no spectators from the surrounding houses. Jake saw an ambulance nearby, and the EMTs looked bored. That was a bad sign.

He turned and looked up at the house. The massive flames licked the sky. He waited and watched them fight the fire until a large man in a yellow firefighter suit walked over and talked to the assembled group of men, who scattered, shouting directions. The man turned to Jake and lifted his helmet—he was an older white man, with white hair and a thin white beard and wrinkled, craggy skin.

"Delancy?"

Jake nodded.

"I'm Captain James, DFD. It's pretty much a done deal at this point," he shouted to be heard over the radio on his shoulder, which kept squawking.

"Any sign of the family?"

He shook his head. "Nothing yet. We see these arsons a lot down here. But this time we found chains on the ground—it looks like both doors were chained shut. I don't think they got out."

Jake looked at the wet ground.

"There had been threats—"

"Yeah, that's what the PD said," pointing at a police car over his shoulder. "You need to talk to them. The structure itself is going to be a total loss. Once we have it knocked down, we'll let you know. You'll need to get your insurance people out here—they get tricky when it's arson."

Jake shook his head. This was all too much.

The chief pointed one yellow glove at the yard. "Scorch marks on the grass. Usually they burn them from the inside. Pour some gasoline on the kitchen floor, light it up, run. Here, they did it from the outside. Gas around the perimeter walls, then a line of gasoline across the driveway. It burns in a particular way. Ignition area was near there," he said, pointing.

"Sick," Jake said, and realized he said it out loud.

He looked up at the captain, not sure what the man would say.

"Most criminals are, in my experience. Look, I gotta get back," he said, pointing at the fire. "But we'll call you, or the Dayton PD will, once they know what happened to the family."

"Okay," Jake said. "Thank you."

The man nodded. "No problem," he said and pulled the radio from his shoulder, shouting instructions into it as he walked away.

Jake stood and watched the fire for a few more minutes. Now they were watering down the houses on either side, probably to keep the fire from spreading. Jake saw at least one broken window on the house to the left, and the siding on the house to the right was singed and curling away from being exposed to the heat. Would his insurance cover the neighbor's damage?

After a few minutes, Jake turned and went to find the cops. He talked to several before finding the one he needed to speak to. The cop was nice—they all were, really. Cops got a bad rap, Jake thought. If he had to deal with this kind of stuff all the time, he'd probably lose it. He doubted he could keep up a cheery disposition with people killing each other around him, or setting each other on fire.

Jake and the cop quickly went through the particulars of the case, talking about the Washington family and the multiple incidents of harassment. Jake was glad he'd reported each incident. Now, there was a record of everything. Jake also recounted exactly what happened with Frank Harper.

The cop wrote everything down, mentioning the Northsiders gang and crimes associated with them fell under the jurisdiction of some special task force Jake had never heard of. The cop said he'd file a report, and that someone from the task force would be getting in touch with Jake in the next day or two.

Jake didn't want to explain everything again and said as much to the cop. At this point, the whole thing was just exhausting.

"No, don't worry," the cop said, indicating the paperwork he was holding. "The task force will have a copy of my report. If the Northsiders end up being behind this, and the family is dead, the task force will add more charges."

Jake nodded. He hadn't heard anything about a gang task force, but it was probably because it was happening in Dayton and not in Cooper's Mill.

Jake thanked the cop when they were done and headed back to his truck. He had to maneuver carefully to drive away. Two other firetrucks had arrived after him, blocking him in. At one point, he had to drive over a thick water line and hoped it didn't do any damage to the line or his tires. McGinty, the woman firefighter, saw him and waved him on, pointing him in the right direction.

He drove past her. "Thanks."

Parker nodded in her helmet. "Those four-inch lines are sturdy. You're fine."

Once he was free and headed for the highway, Jake got out his phone. After talking to the fire department and the cops, Jake decided he needed to call Frank. He had started this mess, and some part of Jake wanted the man to hear it from him. Frank's screw-up had cost the Washingtons their lives.

CHAPTER 10
The Call

At some point very early Monday morning, Frank woke with a start, jerking up in his chair. His shirt was soaked with sweat and his head was pounding. The TV was on, showing some old movie he didn't recognize. The sound was muted, but the soldiers on the TV were scampering across a wooden trestle bridge, setting explosive charges. He thought it looked like the old film *Bridge over the River Kwai*.

Frank looked around for the remote but he didn't see it anywhere. Frustrated, he stood and wavered, putting his hands out to steady himself.

His phone had been ringing. He remembered that much. The clock on his cable box read "3:18 a.m." Frank got down and crawled around on the floor, looking under the couch, but the remote was nowhere to be found.

"Screw it," he said and stood, staggering toward the kitchen. He passed a painting on the wall, the only piece of art in his sad apartment. It was brown and green and vaguely shaped like a house, with a roof and grassy lawn. The subject, a farmhouse, reminded him of the country home where those kidnapped girls had been held. The painting was by a man named Hochstetter. Frank had bought it on his first trip to Ohio. The painting always reminded him of what it had been like to be a real investigator.

He was hungry, but his fridge was in a sorry state—it looked just like one of those refrigerators you saw in movies about sloppy bachelors. His was even more sparse—beers in the box they'd come in, some pickles in the door, and an old carton of milk laying on its side. And a thing of bacon in the "meat" drawer. That was it. No leftover takeout and certainly nothing he could prepare, even if he had been in the mood.

He got another beer, but hesitated and put it back. He only had the two left, cans of swill that were nonetheless better than nothing. Frank could get more tomorrow, but these would have to last the rest of the night. It was a sorry state of affairs—a few months ago, he'd been living the high life, buying a car and helping his daughter pay for her son's preschool. Now he stared into his fridge and wondered if you could make a meal out of just pickles and bacon and BBQ sauce.

Out of the corner of his eye he saw his iPhone and remembered someone had called. He closed the fridge and picked up the phone, touching the screen.

ONE MESSAGE — JAKE DELANCY.

"Christ," he said. "Just what I need."

He put the phone down and walked back into the living room, standing at the floor-to-ceiling windows that looked out onto downtown Birmingham. At night, it looked like a smattering of jewels. Funny how the nicest part of his apartment was the view to the outside.

Frank leaned against the window. The cold felt good on his face, bracing. Pure.

He didn't want to talk to Jake, and he didn't want to hear any more messages. He knew he'd left that family high and dry.

Frank shook his head and looked down at the floor near the window and saw red footprints. He looked around, confused, and saw more—two dozen all over the wood floor, circling his couch. He followed them and found the broken bourbon bottle. He lifted up his feet and checked. One of them had a good-sized gash on it and a piece of glass sticking out of it.

"Oh, Christ." How could he cut himself that badly and not notice? Frank went into the bathroom and sat down on the toilet seat and dug the glass out, wrapping his foot.

He looked at the bottles by his sink. Five different prescription bottles, all for Oxycontin. He'd emptied them all, long ago, and refilled them from "alternate" sources. The Oxy numbed his pain, energized him, and buffered him from the outside world. When mixed with alcohol, it often made him feel like he had some kind of manic, sedate superpower. He could work for days at a time, eating little and accomplishing much. Or he could sit in front of the TV for days.

He resolved to skip his next few "doses." He needed a good, solid day at work. Collier had been watching him like a hawk lately.

But the phone was nagging at him. Finally, Frank shook his head and limped into the kitchen, his foot wrapped in a towel, and got his phone to retrieve his message.

"Frank, this is Jack Delancy. Sorry, Frank. Um, I've got some news that…well, they're dead. The Washingtons. All of them," Jake continued on the message. "I just left the house. It's a total loss. Fire. Arson, they think. Everything burned."

Oh Christ, Frank thought.

Oh Christ.

The kitchen started spinning. He grabbed the counter. On the message, Jake was quiet for a moment and Frank thought maybe the message had ended, but Jake came back on.

"The fire department said the doors were chained from the outside. Someone locked them in and set the house on fire."

Oh God.

"I don't...I don't even know what to say," Jake said, talking to himself, it seemed. "I was just over there earlier today—I was going to relocate them tomorrow. Or today, I guess." Jake sounded confused, and the next part was so quiet, Frank could barely hear what he said.

"They had a kid and everything."

The message ended. The phone went silent.

Frank had stuck his nose in and gotten those people killed.

No, Frank reminded himself. He was a cop, or an ex-cop. He was supposed to stick his nose in where it didn't belong. But he hadn't been there for the follow through. He'd threatened a gang and then left. And now a family was dead.

Frank's eyes landed on the broken bottle on the floor and that desire, the horrible endless need for a drink, suddenly washed over him. He staggered under the weight of it. His need for a drink was a tidal wave of black water, filled with loneliness and guilt and pain that threatened to push him over the edge.

The beer was in the fridge. The flask of what was left of the bourbon was in his coat, and it took everything he had to not empty it all down his gullet. The only thing that made it possible was the fact that he knew he had something better, something that would erase the pain.

But first, he had to know more.

He fumbled with his phone and pulled up the web browser, finding the website for the *Dayton Daily News*, the local paper. It was the third story down: "Overnight Fire Claims Three Victims, Doors Chained." He clicked on the link and read the story, his heart pounding. It was a sketchy, first-draft story by probably the only reporter awake. Dayton FD had responded to a house fire late Sunday night, finding a one-story home engulfed in flames. Firefighters broke down the chained front door but were unable to search the home due to the spreading fire. The fire captain spoke to a reporter at the scene and called the fire suspicious.

"For anyone to make it out of there, they would have had to have left within moments of the fire starting," the captain said. "Dayton PD are treating it as a homicide."

Homicide, Frank thought. A shiver went through his body.

Calling it a homicide investigation meant the cops were probably looking for the Northsiders gang members to speak to, including the young man Frank had chatted with in that titty bar. That also meant the Dayton PD would be calling Frank for more information. There was no getting around this now.

First, he'd made it worse. Now, he'd made them dead.

He shook his head and plugged the phone back in and walked carefully to his small bathroom. He sat on the toilet and looked at the bottles. When he was using Oxy, all the guilt and anger just floated away. Oxy meant forgetting all about the flooded St. Bartholomew's hospital and the bodies floating in the darkness. Frank never had to think about his ex-wife Trudy and how he'd treated her, or how he'd abandoned Laura and missed half of her life.

Oxy meant he never had to think about running across slippery ice while a sniper shot at him, or getting shot in the back by a lying police officer.

Frank opened one of the bottles and took out a pill and popped it into his mouth, swallowing it dry. He was still a cop and knew that if anyone ever wanted to search his house, it would be better if the drugs he was using at least "appeared" to be legitimate. The ruse wouldn't stand up to much scrutiny, of course—all the prescriptions were expired, and yet the bottles were full.

He made it to his bed before the pill kicked in. The rush washed over him, warm. Smoothing him out, flattening him against the dirty sheets. The waves of heat reminded him of lying on the ground, tied up in a dirty field, black smoke and heat and sparks drifting in the sky over his head.

The room grew warmer and a sheen of sweat broke out on his face and arms. Frank knew it was coming. The blissful depths. The silence of the mind. It was coming for him.

And he was glad.

CHAPTER 11
Same Shit Different Day

Five hours after taking his pill, Frank was dressed and sitting in his car in the parking lot at work.

It was nearly 9:00 a.m. and he felt like shit. He had absolutely zero interest in going inside the ABI building. Couldn't he just sit here in his Camaro and start sipping from the flask and stare out the side of the parking garage?

Last night's message played in his mind. Frank checked the *Dayton Daily News* website again, but there were no updates on the fire. Frank hoped the family had somehow managed to escape, but that seemed more and more unlikely. Smoke inhalation was bad. If they'd somehow managed to get out, they would have turned up at one of the area hospitals.

Or maybe the family was taken from the house by the gang before the fire. Killing them at another location made a lot of sense—it was easier to control.

Frank's mind raced at the possibilities, the aftereffects of the Oxy. Sometimes, it made him sleepy; other times, it made him think better. Now his mind wandered down all the corridors of possibility, searching for answers. He didn't need to feel bad about them dying. All he needed was to figure out what to do next. That's why going to work would be a pointless exercise. There was really no point. It would be the same as yesterday, and the day before that. The officer at the front desk would check his badge and weapon and repeat his mantra, "same shit, different day." Frank would smile and try to resist the urge to pick up his weapon from the metal detector and shoot the man in the face. After smiling and nodding at the man's joke—which, by the way, NEVER got old—Frank would take the elevator up to five, get off, and set his things on his desk. Frank would say something snarky to his partner, Detective Murray, about Collier, their boss, and they'd have a laugh. Then Frank would sit down at his desk and sigh and stare at the pile of cold cases. Stacks of brown folders, smelling stale and yellowing around the edges. Each would probably remain unsolved until the ABI "retired" the case. Ironic that they used the word "retired"—it sounded a lot better than "unsolved." Or "unsolvable."

It was an exercise in futility, one Frank repeated every day. Open the files, try to figure out some kind of new angle to take, come up with little or nothing, close the files. Rinse and repeat. And to make matters even more exciting, Frank's boss would realize that Frank had shown up to work. Collier would somehow manage to take time away from his eight-hour shift of playing solitaire on his computer to come out of his office and yell at Frank for a while.

His favorite line was to call Frank and Murphy his "ladies" and treat them like whining women.

Frank finally undid the flask and took a tiny sip. Ten High Blended was the least-expensive bourbon he could find, but the liquid danced on his tongue for a pleasurable moment before he swallowed it.

Guilt edged in from the perimeters of his mind. Frank shifted uncomfortably in his seat, wishing he could stop thinking about the Washingtons. No one deserves to die in a fire. Frank had half a mind to put the car in drive and just head north to Dayton. His anger at the Northsiders was palpable, like a fire racing through him. Chaining the doors? Did they know the Washingtons had a kid? He should just start driving north, begging in gas stations for change to buy food and gas. He could drive straight up to that ratty strip club and find the kid with the fancy Civic. Squeeze his scrawny little neck until he squealed.

Or his head popped off, whichever happened first.

If this were one of those stupid cop dramas on TV, the police would have learned about the arson plans and stopped it just in time, catching the arsonists setting the fire and saving the family. Or, better yet, the house would be on fire and the cops would rescue the family as the house burned around them. There needed to be a great action scene for the trailer, right? The black family and a friendly white cop running across a clean-cut, grassy yard just as the blazing house exploded behind them.

But this wasn't some TV show or dumb movie. It was real life. The family had died. Burned alive, the criminals probably cackling outside with laughter.

Frank gripped the flask tighter, strangling it. When the last of the bourbon was gone, he'd wander inside and get to "work" on those cases. Open them up, read some old and depressing details that filled each folder, and do some cursory Internet searches to see if there was any information out there that could further the case. Not that it ever worked. He was just wasting time, a hamster on one of those wheels.

He tipped up the flask and the last few drops drizzled out and into his mouth. He shook it, but nothing else came out. Empty. Like his prospects.

Frank Harper pulled his jacket around him and stuck the flask under his seat. He climbed from the old Camaro and locked it, then trudged reluctantly toward the building he hated.

CHAPTER 12
Mayor

Dayton's mayor passed through security, smiling and nodding at the familiar faces of the men and women who guarded the lobby of City Hall.

In his mid-forties, Roy Denton was dressed in one of his trademark suits and stood a foot taller than anyone else in the lobby. He'd made a name for himself in college basketball before blowing out his knees. He was naturally friendly and shook hands with a visitor before taking the elevator to the fifth floor, where his offices and those of the city council and his special task force were located.

Like many mayors before him, Denton had come into office facing challenges—budget deficits, tax problems, a crumbling downtown infrastructure. Dayton had a shrinking tax base and a growing poor population, straining the city's coffers. Long ago, most of the middle class and wealthy had moved to the outlying suburbs, and it was difficult for cities like Dayton to pay for all the needed urban services. It was a challenge just keeping the public transportation running on time.

But Denton had run on one issue, and one issue only: doing something about the drugs. Heroin and cocaine and crack had been a huge problem since the mid-2000's in Dayton, but in the last few years it had exploded. Crime had put the city back on its heels. Without a change, Dayton's crime situation threatened to spiral out of control.

He ran with that in mind—he would do something or die trying. It didn't hurt that he was a smart, articulate black man. Dayton had a long history of electing strong African-American mayors. The full faith and support of the local Democratic Party certainly didn't hurt.

But that wasn't why he'd won.

Denton was certain he'd won because, for the first time, voters saw in him a chance to make a "dent" in the crime rate. That had been his slogan, in fact. His posters and commercials had all played on the "dent" in his name: "No one else can make a 'dent' in crime like 'Denton'" was his big one. It was hokey, but his advisers loved it. And it worked. Voters loved alliteration and rhymes—it made things easier to remember.

The elevator finally dinged and the doors slid open with a long rusty wheeze. The building was in dire need of repairs. Someone got stuck in the elevators on a weekly basis, it seemed, but Denton was focused on other matters. He would make a difference in the heroin epidemic, and no money would be spent anywhere else until he saw some progress. His first decision as mayor had been setting up the task force.

Denton exited the elevators and made his way down the hallway, passing his own suite of offices and those of city council. He waved at his secretary. "I'll be back after my 9 o'clock."

He moved down the hall toward a set of doors on the west side of the same floor. For decades, this suite of rooms had been used for private meetings with groups of visitors or donors to the mayor's office. He smiled at the guard, who held the door to the DAHTF open for him.

The massive room was crammed with desks and lamps and four large white boards along the walls. To his right, the northern third of the room had been subdivided into several small offices and interview rooms. Double-doors led off the south side of the room to the administrative offices. Even early on this Monday morning, officers and task force members were working, taking calls, and coordinating their efforts with other local law enforcement agencies, including the FBI's Cincinnati field office.

Ahead of him, on the western side of the room, was a large conference room. Denton could see a small group of men and women gathered around a table. He walked in and greeted them, including Dayton PD's Chief Craig and various members of the task force staff, along with one of the administrative assistants taking notes.

Sergeant Roget, the task force leader, kicked things off by recounting yesterday's raid, including the quantity of cocaine and other drugs seized. Denton had been notified of the event but was eager to learn more.

"And we took five into custody, but one was killed last night in holding," he said, glancing up at Chief Craig, a burly black man with graying hair.

Denton turned to the chief. "What?"

Craig nodded. "A mix-up with the paperwork," he said casually. "It happens."

"It shouldn't," Roget said quietly. "The kid was ready to testify."

"I saw the paperwork," Craig leaned forward. "It came from this office. You want us to start doubting everything that comes out of here?"

Denton put his hands up. "Okay, let's not start in again. Chief, this is one of the reasons I started the task force. There are too many holes in your organization. I know you won't argue with me on that."

Chief Craig started to say something and then thought better of it.

Denton turned to Roget. "But you can't expect them to ignore paperwork from this office, Tom," he said. "Sounds like your people have their wires crossed. Work with the chief and figure out what happened, okay?"

Sergeant Roget nodded and continued with his brief, going over the information gleaned from his short interview on Sunday with the impressionable gang member. "He gave us some names, and we're following up on those."

"Good job," Denton added.

"Based on what we know of the Fifth Street Runners, it's at least a third of their product," Roget continued. "I'm telling you, the more we're out in the communities, the more people are going to want to help us. People want this crap off their streets—and the people peddling it."

"I agree, Chief," Denton said, looking at the other men and women around the table. Most of them worked for the mayor—he'd hand-picked everyone on the task force. It was distinctly separate from the DPD and for good reason. "It's important to remember, every success gets us closer to what I promised the people. We must shut down the major trafficking groups, and make it too costly—in people, transportation, and lost product—for gangs and others to base their operations here. They need to shut down or take that stuff somewhere else."

While he was speaking, he saw the heads nodding and knew he was on the right track. Denton had always been good at reading people, even back in the day. He'd been the only kid in his neighborhood with a paper route—three, actually—and he'd learned early on which customers were good and which ones were trouble. People complained about missing papers or refused to pay on time or came up with an amazing array of excuses when he came around to collect.

He'd learned early on how to read people—and he'd been smart enough to let his manager at the newspaper know. "Oh, yeah, those people aren't gonna pay on time," little Denton would say. It wasn't that he was a snitch. He just didn't want to be left on the hook for the eight dollars a month that the paper ran. Letting his boss know made them part of the same team. They were both getting screwed by the bad customers, so it wasn't little Roy Denton vs. The Paper. That was important. He learned early to never piss off the people who give you the means and opportunity to make money or grow your influence.

Looking around the table, Denton could tell they were all on the same page, at least for now. He had given Roget the resources to prosecute a "war," and the chief and the rest of the DPD were told to back off. It had been messy at the start, but things were improving.

Chief Craig nodded. "Your group is making good progress," he said, pointing at the central white board in the front of the room. It listed the names of the local gangs involved in the drug trade, along with all the pertinent information the task force had on each group, including things like the leader names, top "activities," and sources of income. Areas of the map were color coded to show each gang's approximate area of influence. They were all into drugs full time, and most of them ran other operations like prostitution, loan sharking, and protection.

The mayor listened as Roget outlined the extensive number of follow-on tasks. The officers scribbled down their assignments while the admins wrote everything down for the record.

Denton relaxed and listened, adding very little to the rest of the conversation. It was enough for him to be there, to nod along and offer his support. After everyone had their assignments, the meeting broke up and those around the table stood and went back to their desks. Denton walked out with Chief Craig.

"I know, I know," Craig said, putting his hands up. "You were right."

"Really?" the mayor said, smiling. "You're finally going to admit it?"

"Your task force is making a difference, that's for sure. And keeping it separate from my department was a good idea," he said, the reluctance obvious in his voice. "But I'm still pissed at you for taking some of my best men and women."

The mayor smiled. "You'll get them back, soon enough."

"You think?"

"Yeah," the mayor said. "Like I said from the start, this is just temporary. I have no interest in having my own separate police force." It had been a bone of contention between them from the start. They walked out to the elevators together and Denton shook his hand. "Thanks, Dan."

Denton turned and smiled as he walked into his own offices and was immediately surrounded by his staff. It was Monday morning, and there was a lot to do.

CHAPTER 13
Boss Fight

"You were late. Again."

Frank was sitting at his desk on the fifth floor, flipping through case files and trying to decide which one to work on next when his boss, Tim Collier, walked up to his desk.

"Yes, sir. Sorry about that," Frank said, concentrating on enunciating each word slowly. The last thing Frank needed was Collier realizing he was half in the bag.

"I know you don't think these cases are important, but I do," Collier said, waving a hand at the stack of brown case files piled on Frank's desk. "And Murray thinks they're important, too. Don't you, Murray?"

Frank glanced over at Murray, the only other person in the Cold Case division and the closest thing Frank had to a partner. Murray and Frank got along, probably based on their mutual hatred for Collier. But Murray was no idiot. And he needed his job, just like Frank did.

"I do think they're important, sir," Murray answered, nodding. "We're making some good progress with a few files—"

"Thank God," the man said, shaking his head. "Frank's good at working cases when he's here," Collier said, his voice louder than it needed to be for the three of them to hear it. "But he's always off, running around in Ohio. Solve any murders this weekend, Frank?"

Frank shook his head and concentrated on not slurring. "No, sir."

"Well, you look like shit, I have to say," Collier said. "And it sounds like you solved the case of 'who murdered the twenty-four pack!' Are you drunk on the job?"

Frank shook his head and said nothing.

"You do remember we have a dress code around here, right?" Collier said, brushing his hand down one arm of his shirt sleeve and stopping to remove an invisible piece of lint.

"Yes, sir."

Collier looked down at Frank's desk and the piles of cases. "Like I told you last week, when you work hard, you get results. And those closed cases make us all look good. But I'm not approving any more vacation time for you for a while. Last October, you were gone for three weeks."

Frank knew he shouldn't, but he looked up at him. "I got shot. I apologize if that inconvenienced you—"

Murray looked away as Collier's face turned red.

"I know you were shot, Frank. I talked to that guy in Ohio. But last month, you went back to Ohio and disappeared, right?"

"I was involved in an investigation—"

"What do you call these?" Collier yelled, slapping his hand down on a stack of files. "These are all your investigations, and they're going nowhere. Why do you need to go to another STATE for things to work on? It looks like you have plenty to work on right here," Collier said. "Or maybe you don't want to work here anymore."

Frank shook his head, ignoring the way it made the room spin.

"Yes, sir, I do want to work here." Even if it was just for his room and board, he needed this job. "I'll be on time the rest of the week."

Collier glanced at Murray. "Wow, did you hear that? He's going to be ON TIME every day for the rest of this week. Murray, call the newspapers and let them know."

Murray simply nodded.

Collier leaned over Frank and lowered his voice. "Frank, you're a good guy. And sometimes I give you shit. But seriously, between the way you look and the way you smell, there is no way you're getting anything productive done."

Frank looked at him but didn't say anything.

"If I were a nicer boss, I'd give you the day off to get your shit together," Collier said. "I'm not that kind of boss. I need you to sit here today and make some progress."

Frank nodded. The man might be a prick, but he was right.

Collier turned and walked back into his office, closing the door behind him. It was quiet for a few minutes, both Frank and Murray shuffling papers and tapping at their computers.

"Jesus," Murray whispered.

"No, he's right. I'm barely keeping it together. Maybe concentrating on some work for a while would be a good thing."

Murray nodded, then started to say something and hesitated. "Have you...have you been drinking this morning?"

Frank didn't know what to say, so he didn't say anything. Murray was like any other cop—he knew how to hold his liquor, and he was the first one out the door when they went out for drinks after work.

"Okay," Murray answered. "Just...just be careful, okay? If you left, I don't think I could handle Collier on my own," he said, smiling and turning back to his own piles of folders.

Frank rested his hands on his desk and tried to figure out where to start. If this were a movie, he'd have some amazing epiphany that would tell him what to work on first. Instead, he decided to write down the things that were bothering him.

On the ride in to work this morning, the people on the radio had been talking about how people made "to do" lists the wrong way. Most people wrote down a list of the things they needed to do. But the "expert" on the radio said you needed another list: things that were bothering you. He said both lists were important, but the "to do" list was perpetual—you were probably going to be adding things to it for the rest of your life. Once everything on the list was done, you would think of more things to do.

The "issues" list was different—it included all the things in your life you wanted to resolve. Issues that needed fixing so that you never had to worry about them again. Issues that were bothering you, hanging over you, making life difficult. And once things were crossed off the "issues" list, you didn't need to worry about them again. The guy on the radio said that by writing things down, you let your mind be free.

Frank grabbed some paper and started an issues list. Some of the things that were bothering him were sensitive, at least to him, so he wrote in code or used short phrases that would probably be meaningless to anyone else.

- **St. Bart's**
- **Family and fire and Jake**
- **Atlanta Box**
- **Missing Laura and Jackson**
- **Medication**
- **Family of Russians**
- **Work**
- **Ben Stone**
- **Future**

Under each item on his list, he added a few more details. Some of them were easy to think about, and he jotted down related ideas on how to work on the items. Others he had no idea what to do with, so he just added a few nouns to clarify, an abbreviated mind map like the kind he used sometimes to map out case details to get the big picture.

Next, he made a list of things that he needed to do. Most of them were related to his days here in Birmingham, and at the top of the list he wrote "source." He needed to figure out what to do about his Oxy supply. And he needed to start weaning himself off the stuff. It was the only logical thing to do, really, or he was going to wind up dead. Or fired.

The rest of the list was basic stuff, like "clean apartment" and "make progress at work." The guy on the radio said the best to do lists were full of actions, like "join a gym," instead of unspecific goals, like "get in shape." Frank tried to write down specific actions he could cross off. Feeling better, he numbered both lists, organizing the items and rewriting each list in order of importance. Not surprisingly, the Washingtons were top of mind for him. Frank shook his head and pocketed the lists. His mind felt better, clearer. He grabbed the first case file from the tallest stack, opened it up on the desk in front of him, and got to work.

CHAPTER 14
Club Meet

Tavon was waiting for the others at Riley's, killing time. He was still sickened over what had happened last night. Watching that house burn in his rearview mirror had changed something in him.

He sat back in one of the large cushioned couches and watched the current dancer go through her moves. It was pretty early in the day—just after 2:00 p.m.—but there were already five or six men in the club. At least Tavon had a reason to be here. He couldn't imagine having nothing better to do with your time then sit in a strip club on a Monday afternoon and watch some girl grind a pole.

Tavon sipped at his drink. Free drinks and free food were a nice perk of meeting here. The Northsiders needed places to work besides the headquarters, and bars and clubs made sense. Lots of people were coming and going. But strip clubs were different. Equal opportunity hangouts. It was like the races could get over their seeming mutual hatred of each other if tits were involved.

There was motion by the door. Tavon turned to see Rubio and Gig walk in. Gig, their boss, was an older black man in his mid-forties, muscular and confident. He came over and sat down next to Tavon while Rubio headed for the bar.

"How you, man?"

Tavon nodded, looking at Gig. "Fine."

Gig leaned over so he could be heard over the loud music. "I know you didn't wanna do it. Rubio told me. But it had to get done. Dragon's orders."

Tavon didn't say anything.

Gig went on. "Sometimes blood has to be spilled. You need to toughen up, little man. Lots worse things are gonna happen before all this shit is over."

That got Tavon curious. "What do you mean?"

"We in a war, man. Starts any day now." Gig glanced at the woman on the stage and then looked back at Tavon. "The task force is hitting people hard. Shutting down all the little operations all over town, or running them out. Keystone is all dead, and the Swifties all went to

Chicago. Hear about that raid Sunday? Took out a Fifth Street lab."

"Fifth Street—they used to own most of downtown."

"Yeah, I know," Gig said. "Now they don't own shit."

Rubio joined them, setting three drinks down on the end table between the couches. He pushed one of the drinks in front of Tavon.

"No hard feelings."

Tavon accepted it and sipped while Gig looked at them.

"Where's Slug?"

They both shook their heads.

"I need you guys to run some stuff to Piqua tomorrow night," Gig said. "Pickup is here. Big run, so watch your back." Gig looked at them both and waited for them to nod.

"Gotcha," Rubio said. "And that fire—it happened the way you wanted, right?"

Gig glanced at Tavon.

"Yeah. Too bad about them people, but with Fifth Street moving that way, we had to get control of the neighborhood."

Tavon stared at the table between them. "It was a family."

Rubio started to say something sharp, but Gig cut him off.

"I know. But, like I said, shit happens. You guys warned them plenty. And then that old cop comes in here and tells you to leave them alone. We don't need that kinda attention. It sucks, but the Dragon said make a statement, so we did."

Tavon listened and nodded. He wasn't happy about it and might never be. But Gig was right, at least about the cop in the Camaro. That guy had looked like he could get mean if you backed him into a corner. And the task force was really squeezing things. Security was tighter than ever at the mall, and no one went in or out without some serious scrutiny. It explained why they were having more meetings in places like this.

Rubio was talking and Tavon wasn't paying attention.

"...and we're ready. If there is trouble on I-75, at least between here and Troy, we've got options."

Gig was nodding along and looked at Tavon.

"That's smart, setting those up like you did. What gave you the idea?"

"What idea?" Tavon said.

Rubio cursed. "I was telling him about our exits."

Tavon nodded. "Not sure if they'll all work, but we've got at least four, just in case."

"Okay, last thing," Gig said. "You gotta keep our people loyal, especially if Fifth Street or the Bowling Boyz come in here and try to undercut our rates. I don't tell all my crews this, but I trust you guys."

"Thanks, Gig," Rubio said. "What about those Chinese in Bayline? I heard they were running girls."

"Yeah, I heard that, too," Gig said. "See, this is what I'm saying about protecting our territory, Tavon," he said. "People see weakness and move in. It's just one guy, I forget his name, but he's running six or eight girls now out of the back of his restaurant. Not competing with anyone yet, really, and his girls are all Asian. But that's how it starts. Business goes down, and Johns start asking questions about our prices and shit. Hit up these businesses," he said, handing Rubio a list. "They're all paid up, so just let them know we're collecting monthly now."

"Yup," Rubio said.

"And find Slug and get him to work," Gig said, standing. "We all need to be ready. The Dragon says a war is coming. And the Dragon's never wrong."

CHAPTER 15
Admin Staff

The task force offices took up a good portion of City Hall's fifth floor. The main room, known as the bullpen, and the surrounding offices took up most of the space, but the southern portion hosted several other rooms, including a large one given over to the administrative staff.

Connected to the elevators and galley through a short hallway, the admin area held nearly a dozen workstations grouped around a large central table full of paperwork and other documents to be processed. Adjacent to these offices were several storage rooms filled with boxes of task force paperwork, reports, and other documents. One locked room held evidence that was collected for ongoing and future prosecutions.

The core members of the admin staff were a tight-knit group of four older African-American women on loan from the mayor's office. They had worked together for years and moved over as a unit when the Mayor was elected and started his task force. Shayla and Tammy had been there the longest, starting with the office back in 1997 and coming up on fifteen years for each. And while the mostly-female staff came and went, staying for varying lengths of time, it was this group of women who kept things moving.

Tammy Wayne was at her desk in the center of the room, telling another one of her stories. Not all the women worked the same shifts, but everyone had heard most of her stories.

"...and I'm like 'boy, you better not be taking me in there,'" she said, pointing out the door with her long, curly fingernails.

Shayla leaned forward in her chair and took a donut from a half-empty box on her desk, her considerable bulk making her chair groan. "Did he? Did he take you in the restaurant?"

"Well, you know, he stopped the car right in front, just like he owned the place, and parked," Tammy said, waving her arms. "I was like 'I'm not getting out,' but he came around and opened the door for me."

"Oh, that's nice," one of the other women spoke up, a young black woman named Jada. "I love it when they open doors for you."

Tammy nodded. "Yeah, it's nice, but then I get out of the car and I'm thinking 'this place is a dive. I ain't eating here.' I mean, you girls know that part of town, right? But he takes my arm and leads me inside, and it's not too bad. I heard it was nasty, but the place got fixed up, I guess. Dinner was good. Damn good. Then he said he had a surprise for me."

Jada leaned forward toward Tammy and smiled. "His dick?" the young woman asked.

Tammy and Shayla both looked at her, groaning.

"Jada, that's nasty," Shayla said. She finished the donut and wetted her finger to pick up the crumbs from the pile of paperwork on her desk. She looked at Tammy. "What'd he give you?"

"Well, after dinner, he just sat back and says, 'How much you think that meal cost?' I didn't know what to say. Like, did he want me to pay? Tammy never pays for nothing."

"That's right," Shayla agreed.

"You never pay for nothing? Then how do you—" Jada started to ask, but Shayla shushed her.

"So, he says 'it's free,' and I'm like 'what do you mean it's free,' and he says 'it's free, cause I own the place."

"No," Shayla said. "That's amazing."

"Yup," Tammy said. "He bought it and fixed it up. Didn't tell me or nothing. Now he's got like four restaurants."

Jada looked at Shayla and made a face. "Sounds like your dream man, huh, Shayla?"

"What?" Shayla shook her head and stood up. To Tammy, it looked like levitation—it wasn't really standing up as much as it was getting all her parts to move upward in concert. Shayla burst into tears and leaned on the desk for support, then shuffled off to the bathroom, grabbing another donut on her way.

Once Shayla passed out through the doors, Tammy looked at Jada.

"Damn, you don't make fun of a sister's weight. That's just not right."

"She's an eff-ing whale," Jada said. "I don't know how she gets around."

Tammy leaned in. "She's been working here since you were in diapers, girl. And she's my friend. If you want to keep on working here, put a lid on that shit."

Jada nodded and went back to work, tackling another stack of folders. There was plenty of work to keep them all busy, and new stacks of reports and documents to process were always appearing, as if by magic, on the central table, which was marked with a large sign that read "Incoming."

Tammy turned back to her work, carefully arranging the papers on her desk. Some people thought her nails were obscenely long and hard to care for, but she didn't care. It was part of her look, and she liked it. And the men seemed to like her look as well. She was out there, dating and hitting the scene, while these other women were whining about their men or sitting at home and getting fat like Shayla.

Tammy was worried about Shayla. Jada wasn't wrong—Shayla was getting bigger, to the point where she was starting to have serious medical issues. It wasn't healthy to be that big, but a lot of sisters were "big boned," as the saying went. Or BBW, "big beautiful women." That was fine—some men liked their ladies with a little meat on their bones. But Shayla had a LOT of meat on her bones. Tammy could drop a few as well, if she had to, but she liked where she was at. Shayla, on the other hand, was getting huge. Tammy might have to say something soon, or have Dottie say something. Dottie had been the last of the senior women to join their little group, but she was the best at helping people get along. Dottie knew how to get people talking and how to get people to agree. Maybe it was because Dottie was older, or because she had a daughter and granddaughters, but she knew how to get people to talk to each other and work things out. There had been a lot less bickering and fighting in the office since Dottie came along.

Tammy wished Dottie was here this morning, but she wasn't in until 2:00 p.m. Maybe Tammy should talk to her, see if she could say something to Shayla about the weight.

Rosanna was the last of the four senior admins and was sitting at her desk across from Tammy. Rosanna was a knitter and very quiet—she almost never got involved when Tammy was telling one of her dating stories. But Rosanna was a good worker—she'd joined the mayor's office in early 2002, just after 9/11 and those crazy months when the cops and the mayor's office were freaking out about security. Tammy liked Rosanna but didn't know much about her. It was weird, knowing someone for nearly ten years and still not knowing much about them.

The doors opened. "Rosanna, you finished with that report?" It was Sergeant Roget, walking into the room with Shayla.

Tammy smiled at him—she wouldn't mind taking the sergeant home with her one night—or a long weekend—and find out what made the burly man tick. But everyone knew he was spoken for.

Rosanna looked up. "The transcript from the interview?"

He nodded, and she handed him a manila folder. "Just finished it."

"Thanks," Roget said, flipping through it for a second. "This looks great," he said, smiling at Tammy on his way out.

"Don't get any ideas," Rosanna whispered to Tammy as they both watched the sergeant leave. "I seen that look."

"What look?" Tammy said, acting shy. "I ain't given him no look. And I have no idea what you mean."

Jada joined in. "You like him?"

"She better not," Shayla said, picking up another donut from the open box on her desk. "That one's already spoken for, you know." Shayla turned back to her computer.

"Nah, I'm good," Tammy said to Jada.

Jada leaned over and lowered her voice. "I heard you've banged like half the cops here. Is that true?"

Tammy paused before answering. Rosanna glanced up and smiled as Tammy made the new girl wait, pretending to work. Then she looked up at Jada.

"Damn straight, girl," Tammy said, sending the room into giggles.

Chapter 16
Williams

Collier came and went. Murray and Frank kept their heads down, working. The man was in one of his moods and both of them knew enough to keep off his radar. Well after lunch time, Collier came out of his office and walked over to the two of them.

"I'm going for a late lunch. I want you ladies sitting right here when I get back. No wandering off to a strip club, Frank," Collier smirked. Collier knew the whole story of what had happened up in Dayton a month ago and liked to twist the knife. "And Murray, close at least one case while I'm gone. Think you girls can manage that?"

They both nodded and said nothing. Collier turned and got on the elevator and waved as the doors closed.

"God, what a prick," Murray said quietly. "I can't close cases from the 1970s," he said, pointing at an ancient-looking folder wrapped in several rubber bands. "There's no DNA, no trace evidence. All the witnesses are dead."

Frank looked up and nodded. He had a headache, but Frank needed this job to cover his expenses.

Expenses. That was what he was calling illegal drugs now. Go to the bank, get crisp twenty dollar bills. Find the dealer on Tomany Street and trade the money for more Oxy. The dealer called his crisp twenties "yuppie food stamps," whatever that meant. Maybe because they were straight from the ATM, clean and unwrinkled? Frank chaffed at the term. He'd earned that money—it wasn't a handout from the government.

Some part of him knew he should wean himself off the drugs. It was so clear, so obvious when he was thinking straight. But that didn't happen a lot lately.

Frank pushed his chair back and stood. He needed to walk around, clear his head.

"I'll be right back," he said to Murray, who made a face.

"You're not leaving the building, are you?" Murray sounded genuinely concerned.

"No, no, just running down to Four," Frank said. "I need to talk to Williams."

Murray nodded and went back to work.

Frank took the stairs down one flight, pausing in the stairwell and leaning against the cold concrete wall. He'd gotten dizzy, standing up, and breathed slowly, in and out, for forty breaths before heading on down to the next floor.

Mack Williams worked for the Alabama Fire and Arson Bureau. Frank had met Williams on a case several years ago, and they had become fast friends.

He found Williams sitting at his desk in yet another confusing scramble of cubicles. Whoever invented the cubicle farm should have been sentenced to an eternity of working in one. Williams was a huge man with a bald head and a short goatee. Some of the people in the office called him Marsellus because he looked just like the Ving Rhames character in the movie *Pulp Fiction*.

"Hey, Williams," Frank said as he walked up.

Williams looked up and took off his headphones. "Hey, man. How you doing?"

"Not great," Frank said. He pulled a chair over from another cubicle and sat down. In a few minutes, he'd recounted the information he had on the fire and the Washington family. Williams sat quietly, listening, only taking his eyes off Frank long enough to jot down a note or two. Frank helped him draw a rough diagram of the house, the exits, and the reported location of the fires.

"Have you heard of arsonists chaining people inside like that?"

Williams thought about it for a moment, then nodded.

"Twice. Both gangland hits. These guys didn't know what they were doing—you run the chain through the door handle, not the screen door handle. Those screen doors are cheap—a good kick or two and the hinges bust. A real hard-ass would have done it to the inside door, assuming it had a handle with a loop."

"Could they have escaped?"

Williams shook his head. "I don't know. Maybe. But those gasoline fires burn fast. Maybe if they were already awake and ready to run," he said, pointing at his drawing.

Frank sat back and looked at the diagram, thinking about the fire. "You know, I think that's the most I've ever heard you talk at one time."

Williams nodded. "Yeah, I got excited."

Frank nodded. "They're looking for the bodies. Say they don't find any?"

"Wouldn't matter," Williams said, shaking his head. "Heat like that can erase everything. People think we find a whole skeleton in a burned-out place like this. Most times we find little bone fragments, if anything.

Depending on how long it burned and how concentrated the fire was. Small spaces, high heat—turns into a crematorium."

Frank looked at his friend and wondered what made the guy tick. He'd known Williams for years. In fact, he was one of the people Frank talked to the most, and yet he knew very little about the man. Williams was good with cars; Frank had asked Williams to check out his new Camaro before he'd bought it. But Williams was quiet; he didn't have a lot of friends around the office. On the rare occasion Frank was invited along for a beer at some bar after work, Williams was never there.

Sometimes people teased Williams about losing his soul. In *Pulp Fiction*, the Marsellus character is trying to procure a briefcase with a glowing object inside. Some Internet theorists said that briefcase held Marsellus Wallace's soul.

"And you agree with the arson call?"

Williams nodded. "Yeah, makes sense. I'd have to see the scene photos to be 100% certain, but the chains on the doors makes it a done deal."

They chatted for a few more minutes and then Frank thanked him and headed back upstairs. In the stairwell between floors, he rested again, sitting and leaning against the cold concrete wall. He could hear the wind gusting outside even through the cinder blocks. There must be a storm going through. He had gotten used to working out in the world: ten years with the military, then nearly twenty out on patrol, driving around, talking to people. Even when he'd made detective in the New Orleans PD, he was still out in the field more often than not. Maybe sitting behind a desk just wasn't in his DNA.

Frank felt two conflicting urges: he didn't want to get back to work until his headache backed off, but he didn't want to be away from his desk if Collier returned. Frank doubted the man ate. Maybe he was off getting a mani-pedi or something.

CHAPTER 17
Interview

Jake knew he wasn't in trouble. But just being walked through City Hall by a cop and led through the door that read "Dayton Area Heroin Task Force" made him feel like he was under investigation. The place was impressive—he'd seen lots of people working in the main room before the cop held open the door of a small interview room.

"Thanks for coming down. I'm Sergeant Roget," the man inside said, indicating a chair for Jake to sit in. After closing the door, Roget sat across the table from Jake and spread out a file on the cold metal table. "I just wanted to go over a few things related to the fire."

Jake nodded. He wasn't used to dealing with cops. He'd had a few run-ins before, of course. Everyone did. He'd been working on homes and renting out apartments long enough to have a few disputes with contractors or tenants, some of which inevitably led to calling the police.

"You okay?" the sergeant asked, and Jake realized he hadn't said anything since they sat down.

"Oh, sorry. Just thinking about that family." Jake rested his left arm gingerly on the metal table in front of him and tried not to move it much.

Roget nodded. "It says here—this is the initial report you gave—that you were there the day before, talking to them?"

"I'd decided to move them," Jake said. "Because of the threats. I had it all arranged."

"Hmm," Roget said, making a note. "Did anyone else besides you and the family know they were vacating the premises?"

"No," Jake said, thinking about it. "I don't think so. Just the people at the truck rental. Why?"

"Just standard questions," Roget said. "And the threats—they had been getting worse?"

Jake nodded.

"Rocks through the windows, stuff like that. Then a bullet a few nights ago. Not sure when."

Roget jotted it all down.

"After Frank talked to them and the guy at Riley's, things calmed down for a while," Jake added. "But then they got worse."

"Frank Harper, that's the ex-cop?"

"Yes. I asked him to help out on a couple things when he was in town last."

"Is he a certified private investigator?"

"No, nothing like that," Jake said, hoping he wasn't getting Frank in trouble. Actually, screw him. "He was assisting the CMPD on a case, and I thought he could help me."

Roget nodded and took out a blank piece of scratch paper. Jake saw him write down CALL CMPD RE FRANK HARPER on the paper and set it aside. "And after Mr. Harper spoke to one of the gang members, you say things calmed down."

"For a bit," Jake said. He went on to describe in more detail the events that took place between Frank talking to the gangbanger and the fire. "I was moving them to a hotel, temporarily," he said. In this cold room, sitting at this metal table, the whole tale just sounded pointless and sad.

Roget finished writing down what Jake said, then took the piece of scrap paper and added CALL FRANK HARPER to his list. Jake wondered how that conversation would go. Good, probably, if the sergeant caught Frank when he was sober. Otherwise, the call would go to voice mail and not likely be returned.

"Anything else you can think of that might be pertinent?"

Jake thought about it.

"I've...I've never heard of people chaining the doors. Is that normal?"

Roget shook his head.

"Not really. But the gangs are freaking out because of our task force. We've been putting a lot of resources into shutting them down. We've closed a few gangs, forced others out of town. The rest are fighting for territory. The Northsiders are still the strongest gang, and they were sending a message—to the other gangs, of course, but also to their own soldiers. 'Stay loyal' or something bad might happen to you. Or your families."

"It's just sad," Jake said.

Roget nodded. "You were helping the family out, though. Most people wouldn't. Thank you for trying. Another twenty-four hours and they would've been safe."

Jake nodded, agreeing. There was nothing else to say.

Roget closed his folder and stood, opening the interview room door and holding it open for Jake.

"By the way, what happened to your arm?"

While they walked out, Jake told Roget what happened with the Russians. Jake's story ended with Frank Harper getting the Russians to pay Jake for his work.

"This guy sounds like an idiot," Roget said.

Jake looked at him. "I got paid."

"Yeah, but he's reckless," Sergeant Roget said. "The fight with your Russians—someone could've gotten killed. Escalating things with the Northsiders—going into their club like that—nobody does that. It's like sticking your hand in the hornet's nest."

Jake thought about it as they passed through the main task force offices. He saw lots of white boards with maps and names written on them—gang names, mug shots, photos of graffiti. These people were taking their job very seriously.

"This is the kind of thing that works," Roget said, waving his arm around. "People working together, gathering evidence. Solid police work. This Mr. Harper of yours sounds like a fool—he's lucky he didn't get himself killed."

At the elevator doors, Jake stopped and Roget shook his hand.

"Thank you for coming down—if I have anything else, I'll call you. Or call me if you have any updates," Roget said, handing Jake his card.

"Will do," Jake said as the doors opened. He got on and nodded at the sergeant and pushed the button that said "1." The doors closed, and Jake thought about what Sergeant Roget had said. Frank was lucky—he hadn't gotten himself killed.

He just got a family killed instead.

CHAPTER 18
Breakfast

Tavon had nothing on the schedule for Tuesday until the run to Piqua that evening, so he slept in. Slug and Rubio usually handled the details—where the pickup was, who it went to, if they were receiving cash or not. Tavon concentrated on showing up and making sure all the cars were well maintained.

For now, he was crashing at his mom's place, a small home in Vandalia. It was well away from the Northsiders' territory in Dayton. He lived with his mom and his three sisters. It was weird, living at home again, but now, more than ever, his mom needed the help.

He got up and took a shower and then went back into his room and tidied up. He didn't like living in squalor and kept things tidy most of the time, even though he was out most evenings, running product or helping with the books. Gig was giving him more and more accounting work, another way that Tavon had found to make himself useful to the gang. It was interesting, seeing how the gang made money, watching certain areas of the business grow while others didn't do as well. Things had gotten crazy lately—with the task force taking out several other gangs, the Northsiders had only grown more powerful and profitable. The police crackdown had actually helped, as crazy as that sounded.

His room now tidy, Tavon went to the safe on his dresser and spun the dials, putting in the combo. Only he and his mother had it. Inside there were several guns, a stack of papers and handwritten notes, and about $40,000 in cash, stacked up in bricks against the back of the safe. The money had come from side deals or had ended up in his hands through one means or another. None of it was owed back to the Northsiders—he wasn't stupid enough to steal from his own gang. He supposed he could if he wanted to, and get away with it, but doing the books probably only got you so far. Tavon figured making cash disappear in large quantities was nearly impossible. And he'd seen people killed for far less.

The Northsiders were a gang, of course, and did some seriously shady shit, but they had taken him in and given him a family when things had gone south in his life. But Tavon was glad to be back with his own family.

It had only taken a tragedy. A few weeks ago, Talisa, his youngest sister, had been raped and beaten and left for dead. She had been a vibrant young woman. Now, she spent nearly all her time in her room, recovering from her injuries. And crying.

On some level, Tavon blamed himself. If he'd been around more, maybe he could have prevented it. He liked to think that he could have been walking home with her, or given her a ride. But things could have gone just as badly, or worse, with him there. That was the way things went in gang territory. Bad shit happened.

Tavon had moved back home after that. Everyone had been devastated by what had happened—it was the kind of crime that happened to someone else. Not Talisa, and not three blocks from home.

Tavon had ended up back in his old room in the attic, a cramped space he'd always loved. She'd never approved of him joining the gang, but he and his mom had reconciled, probably mostly as a way to put the arguments behind them and get on with the task at hand.

Talisa had been beaten so badly she was barely recognizable. After three full weeks in the hospital and five expensive surgeries, she was home and recovering. It would be a long and painful process.

Tavon also wanted to be back at home in case those fools came around again.

The gangs in Vandalia were light-weights. He'd asked around and found out who had attacked Talisa. Tavon got their names and gang affiliations and passed them along to Gig. But if he got his chance, Tavon would settle the score on his own.

Tavon took out one of his guns and some cash and locked the safe behind him, then left the attic, climbing down the ladder to the second floor. He tapped on Talisa's door to say good morning. As usual, there was no response, so he continued on downstairs to the kitchen.

"Morning, son," his mother said, standing in the kitchen. She was a wide woman, dressed in her work clothes, already wearing her Sam's Club name tag that read "Lucinda Walker."

Tavon hugged her and turned to his two sisters—Minnie and Shawnda—and greeted them as well. It looked like the three women were in the middle of a discussion.

"Looks like you guys are planning something. Bank robbery? Art heist?"

His mom shook her head. "More hospital bills."

"I thought we paid them all off," he said.

"Hospital, yes. Home care three days a week, no. It kicks in next week, $600 a week. That's with the Medicaid."

Tavon whistled. It wasn't a small expense, even though he had enough upstairs to pay for it for years. "Don't worry about it—I've got it covered."

She gave him a look, a mixture of "thanks" and "you know, I still don't approve of where your money is coming from." He ignored it, smiling at her.

"How's she doing?" he asked, nodding up the stairs. "I knocked but she was sleeping. That's good, right?"

Shawnda, his older sister, spoke up. She was a large young woman, and when she spoke her lips and cheeks moved in a way that made it hard to concentrate on what she was saying. "I heard her crying all night," she said. "I don't think I can take it any more—"

"Shawnda!" her mother said. "Have some empathy."

Shawnda nodded and closed her mouth with a "click."

"Don't worry about the money, momma," Tavon said. They'd made an agreement when he moved back in: she would pay for the house and other expenses, and he would cover Talisa's bills and anything else she needed. He was sure his mother knew where his money came from, but she didn't ask too many questions. "As long as you're safe," she'd said at the time. "That's all I care about."

Tavon and his sisters and mother talked for a few more minutes while he made himself some eggs. Minnie and Shawnda both worked at Wags, a dog grooming place in Vandalia. His sisters hoped to save enough money to open their own dog grooming place sometime in the next year.

Tavon's mom announced she had a date coming up, drawing shrieks from the girls and an "oh, gross!" from Tavon. He smiled—it was nice, the four of them standing around, chatting. It was too bad Talisa was stuck in her room upstairs. Her broken pelvis was on the mend but it would be weeks before she could start physical therapy. The doctors weren't sure if she would ever walk again.

After breakfast, Tavon said his goodbyes and headed out into the cold. It was another brisk day, the sharp wind cutting into his face and wriggling up under his jacket. He pulled his coat tighter and removed the fabric cover from his Civic, stashing it in his trunk. He always covered his car, especially in the winter. The extra hassle every time meant that he never had to scrape ice from the windows or wait for his car to warm up enough to run the defrosters.

Tavon read the sheet of notes from Rubio. "Prep cars for tonight" was listed first. There were no special notes or anything on what they were delivering, so he didn't need to swap out the shocks or anything.

Getting in, his car started up with a hearty rumble. Tavon looked back at his home with a smile and headed off to work.

CHAPTER 19
Tuesday Briefing

Tuesday, just before lunch, Sergeant Roget was back in the upstairs conference room, waiting to brief the mayor and other members of the task force. But he was conflicted—he had a lot to cover in this meeting, but he was still pondering Sunday night and the death of his informant. It had been a brutal scene, and Roget partly blamed himself. The young man had been "accidentally" transferred to the general jail population. It couldn't have been an accident—the timing was just too perfect. And no one saw anything, of course.

The paperwork was sketchy, too—he'd gotten copies. There were no date or time stamps and the signatures were illegible. But they were the right forms, sent over from the offices of the task force.

He shook his head and set the papers aside. Roget was the only one in the conference room. He liked to be early for meetings and sat at the wide table alone, organizing his thoughts. He'd also brought in the large, full-color gang map from his office, setting it up on an easel by the windows that looked west out over Dayton. He tried to bring props and graphs to any meeting he hosted—anything for people to look at. If they were looking at charts, they weren't looking at him.

He didn't have a problem speaking in small groups; it was really only when he had a lot of faces looking at him that he got nervous. The whole thing was silly, he knew, but there seemed no getting past it. It had started in high school and gotten worse ever since. Hawkins had helped with it somewhat, but the sweaty palms and quivering facial muscles returned every time he had to talk in public. It had even affected his career at the Dayton PD.

Roget ignored his anxiety for now and set out his folders. Yesterday's interview with Delancy had been interesting. The fire was in a Northsiders neighborhood. Roget remembered the house, a production lab for the Northsiders for at least a year. They'd stored and packaged coke and heroin there, along with making meth, Oxy, and Molly, also known as ecstasy or MDMA.

Roget's task force had raided them last year and shut down the place. According to the records, the house had foreclosed and was sold to

Delancy at auction. The man had fixed it up and rented it out through Section 8, the local housing authority. And the Northsiders had been back around, bothering the family. But why? It didn't make a lot of sense to Roget. This was Dayton, Ohio. Abandoned houses were a dime a dozen.

There was a bustle of activity out in the bullpen and Roget looked up to see the mayor and several other people entering the conference room, including Patricia Hawkins and the Dayton police chief, Dan Craig. Behind his back, people called him James Bond—he shared a name with the actor who played the famous character.

Behind them, several others followed them into the conference room, including the Dayton fire chief and an unwelcome face, the local FBI liaison from Cincinnati. Last into the room were Dottie and Jada, two of the admin staff. Dottie was in her late fifties and very smart. Roget had only talked to Jada once and hadn't been impressed—she seemed only interested in her phone. Dottie and Jada sat at the far end of the table and prepared to take the meeting notes. Roget saw Dottie's McDonald's cup on the table next to her—the woman took her Diet Coke everywhere.

The rest of the attendees took their seats and Denton offered them all coffee. The mayor was obsessed with coffee and making his meetings comfortable and welcoming.

Roget started, recounting the updates since yesterday. He covered more results from Sunday's raid, including a list of the sizable amount of drugs and lab property they had seized at the Fifth Street production house.

"Damn, son," he said, smiling at Roget. "Nice work. Glad to hear all of that stuff is off the street."

Roget nodded, not looking around the room. Too many eyes on him. "Thanks, sir. It was a group effort."

After that, Roget continued, hurrying to get through his list of topics before he started twitching. He covered the house fire, describing the victims and summarizing the information he'd gleaned from interviews. He mentioned Frank Harper, and how he'd confronted one of the Northsiders gang about their harassment of the Washington family. When he was finished, Roget paused and glanced around the table furtively. "Anyone have any other information on this fire?"

Chief Craig nodded. "Well, it's like you said. We'd been getting reports about harassment for a while and passed those along to you guys," he said, nodding at Roget and the mayor. "I spoke to Captain James from the Dayton Fire a couple hours ago—it was definitely arson."

"Thanks, Chief," Roget said. "I'll get a copy of the fire report?"

"I already asked them to send one over," the chief said.

"Can I get a copy of that, too?"

Roget turned and looked—it was the FBI liaison, Ted Shales, seated at the far end of the table next to Dottie. So far, the kid had added exactly nothing to the investigation. In Roget's opinion, this kid—he didn't look old enough to be an agent—had absolutely no idea what he was doing. Shales always sat at the far end of the table like he was barely in the meeting, and spent most of his time checking his phone. But the mayor had brought him in to cover all the bases, insisting that Roget give him an office. Roget hated catering to the Feds. Of course, it might help to have them around to scare up some resources if the shit ever hit the fan.

"Sure, no problem," Roget smiled. "I'll walk a copy over when I get mine."

"Thank you," Shales said. "I've got a few resources that might be able to help with the investigation."

The chief looked at the mayor and then back at Shales. "Well, it sounds like the fire department has a handle on that. They have a good arson team."

Shales nodded. "Okay, no problem. I'll just pass along the report. Sergeant, can I also get the notes from the Delaney interview?"

"Delancy."

"What?"

The home owner? His name is Delancy."

"Right," Shales said, jotting it down. When he wasn't bent over his phone, the kid took notes on pocket-sized yellow pads, the kind you got at an office supply store. "Got it. Delancy. Also, I worked with Mr. Harper on a case last year."

Roget looked up. "Really?"

"Yes. Do you remember the kidnapping case up in Cooper's Mill? Daughter of a city councilman?"

Most of the people around the table nodded—the case had been local news for months.

"What did you do?" the mayor asked.

Shales leaned forward. "Chief King looked for my expertise on kidnapping cases, and also had me pull relevant cases from federal databases to see if there were any connections to other similar crimes in the area. I also brought my expertise in criminal behavioral patterns and helped configure the roadblocks and street closures to stop the kidnappers when they retrieved their ransom."

"I thought the kidnappers escaped with the ransom," Chief Craig asked.

"Yes, that's true," Shales said, moving around in his chair. "I had everything set up, but the kidnappers knew the town well. They slipped out through the back of a store and avoided the roadblocks. And they had a cop helping them."

The kid might be an idiot, Roget thought, but at least he didn't have a paralyzing fear of speaking in public. The others nodded, following along.

"From what I can tell, this Harper sounds reckless," Roget said. "He stuck his nose in and ended up making it a lot worse. If he hadn't confronted the gang, maybe none of this would have happened."

"I'm not sure of that," Chief Craig said. "From what you said, it sounds like the Northsiders were getting restless."

"As for Harper," Shales added. "The man had some interesting techniques, to say the least. He found the farmhouse where the girls were being held."

The mayor turned to Roget. "So, more raids coming up?"

Roget nodded. "After the production lab was destroyed on Sunday, anonymous tips came in on the location of their other lab. They apparently only have one production location left."

Roget passed around a handout on the last Fifth Street lab and got feedback on the neighborhood. He could have looked it up and gotten the same information from filed police and fire reports, but real-time sharing of information around a table like this was better. You got more than just the facts. Chief Craig and Captain James both knew the area and talked briefly about the location.

"It's a good plan, Sergeant," the mayor said, glancing at this watch. "And after this lab, Fifth Street will be done?"

Roget nodded. "Yeah, we think so. Their numbers will be so low, they'll get absorbed into another group. Probably the Northsiders."

The mayor nodded. "Who are we hitting next?"

Roget got up and went over to the map, which showed the ever-shifting locations and neighborhoods controlled by the gangs. He usually kept this in his office where he could study it. The map read like a who's who of gang crime in Dayton.

"We've done a good job of identifying where the gangs are and who controls what. We've made some great inroads on the Fifth Street Runners, Triangle, and Angel Face. The Swifties and La Chupacabra have pulled out of Dayton completely, as far as we can tell," he said, pointing at the list of gangs on one side of the map. "And we think last week's raid shut down Keystone. The few remaining have joined up with other gangs," he said, glancing around the table. Most of the heads were nodding.

Chief Craig leaned forward, looking at the map. "We've had a lot of activity in the triangle over the last week," mentioning the Triangle gang's home turf.

"Probably reacting to our raid. We'll hit them again, this week or next. And we got another tip yesterday on the North Boyz, up on north Salem near Clayton. They're looking to move south to fill in the Fifth Street gaps." It was like a house full of roaches—kill one, and three more popped up in its place.

"Concentrating on the south and central areas of Dayton was smart," the mayor said, turning to look at Chief Craig. "We needed to reduce crime as much as possible, especially near those new apartment buildings near Dragons stadium."

He was referring to the Dayton Dragons, the local minor league baseball team, which operated a popular stadium downtown near the river. New apartment buildings were going up in the area, along with a pair of old buildings that were being converted to apartments and condos. One of these, the old Mendelmann's building, would hold nine floors of upscale condos, some with awesome views of the baseball stadium and the river beyond.

The mayor had been right—the middle class and millennials were starting to move back into the Dayton core, and with them new restaurants and a growing art scene. The Oregon District had proven that downtown Dayton could sustain a popular restaurant and bar scene as long as the proper amount of policing was applied. Folks just wanted to walk around and not get mugged. "Make 'em feel safe," the mayor would say, and "they'll spend the money." It was hokey but true—and that meant driving the criminal elements out of the downtown area and away from places like the Oregon District or the Dublin Pub or Urban Crag, the new wall climbing place on Clay Street built inside an old church. By keeping the crime down, people moved in and fixed up the old places. Tax receipts went up, and the city could afford more cops.

Chief Craig nodded. "I can speak to the progress. I had two developers in my office this morning, moving up their plans to break ground on another condo development. They read in the paper about the dropping crime rate and figured it was time."

"Where are they looking?" the mayor asked.

"Somewhere over by Fourth, by the new pubs." A pair of new pubs had opened in the area, spurred by Ohio's recent overhaul of their alcohol laws.

"That's good," the mayor said. "We're looking at that area for more growth. If they call you again, have them contact my office so we can schmooze them a little. Anything else?"

Roget shook his head, and the meeting broke up. The mayor and others left, talking loudly, and Roget gathered up his handouts. Jada, the younger admin, walked over.

"Can I have an extra of those for the report?" Jada asked. "I need to include them with the notes, and the FBI guy will probably want extras," she said. "He's always losing stuff."

"Sure, no problem," Roget said, handing her the spare copies. "Just shred what you don't need."

CHAPTER 20
Piqua Delivery

Tuesday evening, Tavon met Rubio and Slug at Riley's, parking next to their matching Civics and going inside.

"Hey, what's up," Rubio said when he saw Tavon enter. He and Slug had been watching one of the girls dance, wending her way around the metal pole that stood in the center of the wide stage. "You get all that work done today?"

Tavon nodded. He'd been asked to make some collections on his own, and he had, trying to earn his way back into Rubio's good graces.

"Yeah, no problems," Tavon said, handing Rubio an envelope. "We ready? I need to check the cars."

"Go ahead," Rubio said, nodding at the girl on stage. "Slug's fascinated. We'll be out in five."

Tavon went back out into the cold. He didn't mind winter so much, except when the sun went down and the temperature dropped twenty degrees in a matter of minutes. If he'd known it was going to be this cold, he would have worn a warmer jacket.

He popped open Rubio's Civic—he had keys to all three—and climbed in, starting it up. The stereo blasted rap music. He turned it down and listened to the engine while he studied the instrument panel, looking for warning lights. He also double-checked two buttons he'd installed in the car's dashboard: one read "Stealth" and the other "Boost." Both were lit, indicating they were operational.

"Stealth" was just a fancy word for a "Police" mode, a setting that turned off every light inside and outside the car. Most cars had running lights, trunk lights and bright red brake lights. If you were trying to get away from the cops, you had to pull into a parking lot and turn everything off. Sometimes even that didn't work: on some newer cars, lights stayed on for a while even after a car was turned off.

He'd read about the "Police" mode somewhere: the cops did it on their cars so they could sit in parking lots with their engines running and no lights on. On the road, "Stealth" mode for Tavon's cars made them ghosts at night, nearly impossible for cops to see.

The "Boost" button controlled a small Nitrous system that Tavon had installed in each car that gave a temporary boost to the car's speed. It added another thirty or thirty-five miles per hour, but only for twenty seconds. This mode had its limits—it could only be used twice before the whole system needed to be recharged.

On a whim, Tavon put the Rubio's car in drive and took it out onto the street, going up and down Dixie in front of the club. Everything seemed fine; the car handled well, and the engine purred. Tavon returned to the lot and parked, repeating the same procedure with Slug's civic. He drove it for a few minutes, finding nothing that gave him pause. The steering was loose, the way Slug preferred. Tavon smiled, remembering the note Slug had written to Tavon once, asking for the steering to be "loser," spelling it wrong. When he got back to the club, Slug and Rubio were waiting out front. He pulled in and stopped near the front doors.

"We good?" Rubio asked. He was carrying a metal suitcase, one Tavon hadn't seen before.

Tavon nodded. "Yeah, just checking the cars out. Everything looks good."

Leaving the club, Tavon and Slug followed Rubio north on Dixie, heading for the highway. They passed a strip mall and an abandoned grocery store. Continuing north, they got to the highway and merged onto the flat, wide interstate.

Here, I-70 ran due east and west. Heading east, they were traveling in the direction of Huber Heights and Columbus. Behind them, the highway headed west to the Ohio border and Indiana. Being close to the border made it easier to run stuff over into Indiana. Rubio kept his speed low, just under the speed limit, and Slug and Tavon fell in behind him.

Signs appeared for the big interchange of I-70 and I-75, which ran north and south. The interchange was under construction and a huge mess—the workers were always changing the lanes around, making it hard to predict when to get over. The Civics merged and took the new cloverleaf down and around and headed north on I-75. Behind them, the lights of Dayton faded and soon disappeared.

Tavon put on some classical music, another habit the Northsiders gave him shit about. He often heard other members listening to loud EDM or rap to get their blood pumping before going out on a run. But Tavon liked his music mellow, especially when he was trying to think. He had too much on his mind to have his thoughts competing with someone screaming about "bitches and hoes."

They headed north, staying under the speed limit. The three matching Civics, with their low fairings and LED underlighting, were enough of a draw already. Changing lanes too often was just another way to get the wrong kind of attention. Rubio was smart enough to know this.

Whenever they ran product, the first rule was always never get pulled over. If you saw those flashing lights behind you, it was already too late. They passed exits for Vandalia and Cooper's Mill and Troy. The wind picked up, gusting, almost pushing Tavon's car into the other lane. He held the wheel tight as they took the exit for Piqua. Rubio headed into downtown Piqua, which ran along the river, parking on the street in front of a small club called Water's Edge. Tavon parked nearby and got out, locking the car. To his left, he noticed the dark smudge of the nearby river, running through the darkness.

Inside the club, the place was hot and sweaty. It was packed with a bunch of white folks, all drinking and dancing under a spinning disco ball to some song by Maroon 5. Tavon and Slug waited by the bar while Rubio went into the back with a big bouncer and a nerdy guy that looked like he might be the club owner or manager. And then Tavon and Slug waited, bored. This happened a lot. Rubio would go into a store or a club and "chat" with the owner. Sometimes it was protection money or a payment on a loan. Often Slug went with Rubio for muscle and Tavon waited, alone.

Things were looking up and had been for at least the last year. Even with the task force squeezing business, things in Dayton had improved for the Northsiders. The Dragon had a very specific plan for them. Whoever he was—and no one ever saw him, except for the Council— the guy had completely changed the way the gang did business. Before he'd come along a two years ago, the Northsiders were like any other gang. They sold drugs, buying them from some source in Cincinnati or Columbus and selling it on the streets of Dayton.

But the Dragon had changed things. He'd patterned the new version of the Northsiders after the Italian mob, creating the Council and organizing the gang. He'd even insisted that every person in the gang watch a particular list of gangster movies. Sure, the movies were fiction, but you learned how the old mobs made their money—different businesses, like drugs, gambling, racketeering, running girls. Each part of the business supported the others. When one did good, they all did good. And running bookies and girls was a new thing for a black gang in Dayton, and some of the customers, especially whites and Hispanics, weren't sure how to react.

Having the drug business set up and running made it easier to expand into other areas. Again, they were following the mafia lead. The whole idea of "multiple streams of income" was new to the streets of Dayton.

It also gave the gang a bigger mission. They started providing other services to the community beyond sponging off the community's addictions. Running a book and taking bets and paying them out to winners raised the gang's visibility. How could it not? Before, all you went to the Northsiders for was blow and Molly. Now, you could also bet on the horses, get a temporary loan and even find "companionship" when you were lonely. It helped bring more people around, and it helped with recruiting.

Tavon watched the Piqua clubgoers dance to one pop hit after another and wondered how much money was being spent in this club tonight on drugs. People needed to take the edge off, like Stimpy used to say. Tavon did some rough calculations in his head—three hundred people in here, a hundred were either high or on their way to get high. That was at least three grand, depending on their drugs of choice, just tonight. Thirty grand over the course of the week, assuming business doubled on the weekends.

Another ten minutes went by, and Tavon passed the time watching the people casually getting high. He'd seen at least ten people popping pills. One woman was doing white lines of powder right at the bar, and he could see several people passed out on couches and in the dark spaces around the dance floor.

He was also watching the DJ. He'd never been into dance music, but it was interesting to see the young Asian woman behind the equipment. She wore a huge pair of headphones but didn't seem to use them much; they hung off the side of her head, almost like they were part of a uniform or something. The woman bounced along with the tunes, though, and was clearly enjoying what she was doing. Plus she was cute. She blended the songs together or faded one in as another was wrapping up, keeping the mix going. He wasn't sure how she did it, but the DJ timed it so the beats from both songs overlapped, keeping the dancers moving.

Finally, Rubio came out of the back office, followed by the bouncer. Rubio smiled, signaling at Slug and Tavon to head for the door.

"We good?" Slug asked over the music.

Rubio nodded, carrying the same metal briefcase he had going in. When they got outside, Rubio stopped them. "Okay, we're good," he said, glancing at the case. "We're heading to the mall," he said, using the code word for the Northsiders headquarters.

"Really?" Slug asked. It was rare—usually the mall was off limits to runners and anyone low in the organization.

Rubio patted the case. "Yup, Gig wants this cash right away."

Minutes later, they were merging back on the highway, headed south toward Dayton. Tavon was following behind Rubio and reached over, tapping at his phone and starting the "Waze" app, which showed sightings of police cars. He also turned on the CB radio mounted in the dashboard and flipped it to the local Miami County police band. Between the two of them, they did a great job of showing recent locations for local cops. The police band was good to listen to anyway, even just to get a sense for what the cops were dealing with at any particular time. If there was a fire or high-speed chase, it quickly grew into a full-on conversation between the police and other local emergency crew, like firefighters and EMTs.

South of Troy, a car merged onto the highway. It seemed like nothing at first, but Tavon noticed the car looked like a late '90s Taurus, a favorite of police departments. He texted Slug and Rubio and told them. The new vehicle stayed even with Rubio and Slug, who were traveling together, and then slowed and got in Rubio's lane behind him.

Tavon was maybe an eighth of a mile back, keeping watch. It could be a cop or a rival gang, looking to run Rubio off the road and take the payment. Both options were bad. Another car joined the group—this one merged on at Cooper's Mill. It also dropped in behind Rubio and stayed there. Tavon texted them again. The drivers had few options but if this was a bust they needed to know about it soon. Tavon had set up "exits" but they were few and far between. In fact, they were just passing one near a Cooper's Mill gun store.

"We busted?" he texted to Rubio.

"No clue," Rubio texted back.

Tavon waited. It was Rubio's call.

"There's an exit at the big interchange," Tavon responded, knowing that Rubio knew what he meant. "Remember?"

A few seconds later, a text came back—this one a group chat to Tavon and Slug. "Yup, taking our exit," Rubio sent. "Split up on 70, lose the pricks, head home. I'll make the delivery."

Tavon nodded and texted back: "OK." At least they had a plan. Strangely, there had been no talk at all on the police band.

He accelerated, moving up behind the two cars giving chase. He could see they were both Tauruses and the vehicles were both black and had no markings. The only way to tell them apart was by the license plate. One vehicle was behind Rubio, the other behind Slug. The two black cars accelerated and the police lights came on at the same time, splashing the snow and trees and road around them with piercing red and blue lights, colors designed to disorient and confuse.

But instead of slowing down, Rubio and Slug accelerated, pulling away from the cops, who sped up to match their speed. Rubio and Slug weaved in and out of traffic, staying together, changing lanes and darting around each other and the few other cars that were out on this snowy evening. Tavon followed the two cop cars at a distance, looking for other cops and waiting his turn.

The chase quickly reached speeds of nearly a hundred miles an hour. The cars raced south, zipping past the exit to Vandalia and the airport, the last exit before the I-70/I-75 interchange.

Just past the off-ramp, Tavon backed off some more. There were no cars merging onto the highway from Vandalia, so it looked like these two were it. Rubio and Slug were a hundred yards up, quickly approaching the interchange.

Tavon's phone rang. He reached over and answered, put it on speaker, then laid it face down on the shelf in the dashboard.

"Ready?" It was Rubio. "Slug, you go west, Tavon east."

"Yup."

Slug chimed in. "Me too."

"Now."

Slug and Rubio hit their "Boost" buttons at the same time, and Tavon saw their cars leap away, racing ahead and moving beyond the reach of the police car headlights. Tavon stayed back, saving his "Boost." For now, he followed the cops at a safe distance and staying out of their lanes.

When the nitrous was gone, Rubio and Slug were a quarter-mile up on the cops.

"Okay, stealth," Rubio said over the phones.

It wasn't really a stealth mode—everyone knew that. This would never have worked against the military, for instance, or against anyone who had a helicopter with a searchlight at their disposal. Still, it always made Tavon feel like Batman.

Up ahead, Rubio and Slug's cars simply disappeared. With no headlights or brake lights shining, and with no overhead streetlights, the cars were impossible to see.

Behind the cops, Tavon he stayed in his lane, dropping back further and letting the light from the cop cars guide him.

"Tavon?"

"Yeah, Rubio, I'm here. Both cops are still following you but they've slowed."

"Good," Rubio said. "I'm stopped in the middle of the interchange. Our exit worked great."

The cop cars ahead as they approached the interchange. One cop went west, the other east. Tavon slowed as well and took the east-bound ramp at seventy, a good twenty miles faster than recommended. But the Civic was designed to corner, and it hugged the road without the slightest skip.

Just beyond the merge, he punched the brakes, swerving onto the frozen shoulder, slowing down. There was nothing ahead but the highway, stretching off to the west. He could see the cop car accelerating away and used the reflected red and blue lights to slow and stop on the shoulder.

Then he gingerly steered off the shoulder and down into a ditch beside the highway, holding his breath. There was always a chance the cars would get stuck in the mud, or that they wouldn't be able to get far enough off the road and the top of the car would be spotted by a passing cop. But it was so damned cold—and had been for weeks—that Tavon judged the mud and dirt of the shoulder to be as solid as pavement. His car hugged the ground, and Tavon heard the plastic fairing scraping and dragging at the snow and dirt. Bad for the car, but good if you didn't want to get caught. He had spent countless hours driving the highways between Troy and Dayton, looking for safe places like this to pull off.

Parking, Tavon toggled his "Stealth" switch. His car went dark, and parked like he was off the shoulder, he was all but invisible in the night.

"Okay, I'm good," Slug came over the phone. "Just left the highway in Huber, near the Walmart. Cop went on down the highway."

"I'm on the shoulder west of the interchange," Tavon added.

A minute later, three more cop cars raced past Tavon, the sirens blaring and the lights flashing in all directions.

"Three more just passed, heading west," Tavon said.

"Good," Rubio said. "I'm waiting. Hanging up now—text me when you get home." The line went dead, and Tavon flipped his phone over and turned off the screen.

Rubio had the trickiest part. His "exit" was the most difficult to maneuver—but done correctly, he would be scot-free. If everything had gone according to plan, Rubio would have raced ahead, then slowed quickly and driven off the shoulder in the middle of the interchange, leaving the road completely and driving over the hard-packed mud and snow, positioning the Civic behind one of the huge concrete supports that held up the three-level interchange. There were several of them, but Tavon had identified the two that were the easiest to get behind and large enough to block an entire car. Done properly, it was likely the cops would not see him, especially if they entered the interchange going at least sixty, as he had done. The interchange was under construction and pieces of equipment were always moving about, making the location more confusing. The hardest part was slowing down rapidly in the allotted space and exiting the offramp. Tavon had practiced it several times, and it had not been difficult.

CHAPTER 21
Blackout

At some point late on Tuesday evening, Frank woke up on the floor in his own vomit.

He was lying on the floor near the floor-to-ceiling windows. It had gotten dark out. He remembered sitting down to watch some TV, but now the TV was off. He pushed himself up onto his side and coughed, spitting out a wet mass. Throwing up and passing out were a bad combination.

Frank didn't remember much about yesterday. He'd had a fight with his boss at work. But he didn't remember the rest of the work day, or how he got home. Somehow, he'd found his way back to his apartment. He didn't remember what kind of state he'd been in when he was driving. Or today. Had he gone to work?

The blackouts were getting worse.

He lay on his side for a few minutes, panting and coughing and trying to remember.

Frank vaguely remembered being on Oxy at work. It had energized him, allowing him to work on several cases at once. That was today, right? He vaguely recalled typing, his fingers on the keys. He remembered using the computer and printing out sheets and more typing. He remembered reading reports and filling out requests for DNA evidence. Follow-up interviews. It was all a blur. The Oxy either sent him into a tizzy of epic proportions, allowing him to work for days without sleep, or left him passed out on the floor.

After a minute, he rolled onto his back, away from the vomit. It reeked of bile and acid. He put his face on the cold floor and looked at his hand. It was close to his face and he regarded it as if he were looking at his right hand for the first time. Wide knuckles, hair just below each one. Nails that needed trimming. A tiny cut, nearly healed, the last of the deep defensive wounds from his fight with a family of Russians. They said wounds on the hands healed the fastest, but that was bullshit. They took forever. Scabs got knocked off.

The Russians. What a hoot that had been. A fight with knives in an unfinished kitchen. Lots of impromptu weapons sitting around. A great use of his close-combat skills and Krav Maga, something he never got to use anymore. It was a shame—when he was in good shape, and sober, he could be a force to be reckoned with.

He looked around and saw suddenly, with clear eyes, just how bad his apartment had gotten. It looked like the apartment of a junkie. Crap everywhere, spilled food and drink. Piles of pizza boxes, even though he was only ordering enough for himself. How long had it taken to make three piles of pizza boxes?

He'd gotten that family killed, his latest epic screw up. He'd been spiraling downward for fifteen years. Katrina had nearly killed him, and he'd never really recovered. Or maybe Katrina had killed him. Maybe what happened in St. Bart's had killed him. And he'd been dying ever since. And taking people with him, apparently.

After St. Bart's, the New Orleans PD had insisted he talk to a shrink. It hadn't helped. He never told the woman what really happened in that flooded hospital. He'd never told anyone, and doubted he ever would.

Trudy had stuck with him for a long time, but after Katrina, she'd had enough. Frank had withdrawn into his cave and she'd filed the papers and fled with Laura. And who could blame her? If she'd been around, he would have dragged her down, too. They say that happens when you help a drowning person.

Even Laura wouldn't understand if she knew the whole story. She thought he was having trouble with the alcohol. Imagine her learning he'd become an enthusiastic fan of Oxycontin.

But it wasn't his fault. He'd gotten shot, and the meds had run out. His back still hurt, and the doctors were unsympathetic, saying he needed to wean himself off the pain meds. Well, the Oxy dealer over on Tomany Street didn't agree. And, when you were dealing with medicine, weren't you supposed to get a second opinion?

CHAPTER 22
Cemetery Gates

Rubio drove around for another hour or so, killing time. He knew not to go straight back to the mall—protecting their headquarters was job one. The Northsiders worked hard to make sure few knew about their primary base of operations. Another edict from the Dragon—the man was obsessed with "operational security," as he called it.

After the cop car raced around the on-ramp and passed him, Rubio waited another ten minutes before starting his car. He'd maneuvered his car across the muddy track that separated the two off-ramps, then took the rest of the ramp that led from east-bound I-70 to south-bound I-75. Getting back on the ramp, he remembered to switch off "stealth" mode so other drivers would be able to see his lights.

Rubio got off at the first exit at Miller Lane, a popular shopping and dining area that boasted nearly thirty eating establishments, along with a Sam's Club, Walmart, and Staples. At the top of the off-ramp, he turned right. He passed a group of restaurants—Red Lobster, Panera, Smokey Bones, and others—and pulled into the Hooters parking lot, turning off the car.

Rubio sat quietly in the car. He watched the vehicles that entered and left the parking lot, waiting to see if any of the drivers glanced in his direction or checked his plate. No one did.

Occasionally, he looked at the restaurant. Through the windows, he could see groups of customers and the busty waitresses who were waiting on them. He saw how the attractive women smiled and pretended to be interested in the customers. It was interesting how much a woman could pretend if it meant money in her pocket.

That kind of thing had always pissed him off. Why were women so fake?

Inside, one of the waitresses laughed at a customer's joke and ran her hand down his arm. She was leaning over, showing off her huge tits. There was no mistaking—she was touching him to get a larger tip. And leaning over like that—no woman did that unless she wanted attention. Rubio doubted the joke was that funny. As long as she faked it good enough, and faked being interested in the customers, she could walk away with cash.

Sometimes women disgusted him. They were gold diggers, begging for money. Some were no better than the homeless men by the highway, the ones with the signs out that said "hungry - need food." But instead of cardboard signs, women used their tits and asses to beg for attention and money.

Rubio went back to watching for cars coming and going from the lot. None of them seemed interested in him or his car. He waited for another ten minutes, then started the car up and drove away, heading back south on Miller Lane. Without signaling or slowing, he turned suddenly into the Panera lot.

No one followed.

He looped around and drove back out onto Miller Lane, heading north, passing the Hooters and turning into the parking lot of a Chinese buffet. He repeated the same actions again, parking and watching for cars, although this time he wasn't distracted by women in the windows.

Rubio passed the time by checking the suitcase he'd brought out of the club in Piqua. Inside he found stacks of cash, counting them out. $20,000. He counted the money three times out of sheer boredom.

Ten minutes later, and satisfied he wasn't being followed, Rubio started the car again and moved on. He had an idea and drove through several parking lots, ending up at Walmart. He avoided passing directly in front of the store—they had cameras—and circled the parking lot, finally spotting what he was looking for—a lone young woman, walking across the lot by herself.

Rubio drove his car toward her and slowed, lowering the passenger window.

"You okay, girl? Need a ride?"

She glanced up at him—she was in her twenties and looked high. The young woman's eyes were dark, her eyelids drooping. She was carrying two plastic bags filled with chips and beer.

"Ah, yeah, no thanks," she said, not stopping. She nodded ahead. "My boyfriend's in the car."

He glanced over at the dark cars in the lot. Most had snow on them, and none were running.

"Really? Sitting in the cold, waiting on you? My ride is warm—you like it?"

She nodded and stopped, her eyes sliding along the exterior of the Civic.

"Oh, hey, look what I got," he said. He pulled open the glove compartment and pulled on a hidden lever. One of his air conditioning vents tipped open and he reached inside, pulling out a clear bag. Inside he had bottles of pills, a small bag of marijuana, some one-hitters and rolling papers for weed, a wad of cash and several small clear bags filled with white powder. He held one of bags of coke up for her to see.

"You gettin' low?"

She didn't seem offended. Not by the fact that a stranger was talking to her in a cold Walmart parking lot or that he assumed she was a druggie. The young woman only looked at the bag and nodded.

"Yeah, I could use a ride. I was gonna take the bus," she said, nodding at a bus stop on the far end of the snow-covered parking lot.

Rubio unlocked the doors. "Get in."

She pulled on the door and it lifted straight up. She made a face while ducking out of the way.

"Here, check this out," he said, patting the briefcase. "Full of cash."

She climbed in, putting her bags on the floorboard. She glanced at the briefcase but only had eyes for the coke. "Can I have that? You got more?"

He smiled. "As much as you want," he said. "Where'm I driving you?"

She pulled the door shut and took the bag. She opened it gingerly and tasted a tiny amount from the end of her finger.

"Clayton, if that's cool."

She poured out some of the bag onto the briefcase. She used her fingernail to push the coke into three thin white lines, careful to keep it all together.

"Yeah," he nodded. "That's cool."

He put the car in gear and drove. She took out a rolled dollar bill and sniffed it all up with practiced ease. She sat back and pinched her nose, then wetted her finger, dabbed up the remains of the coke lines, and rubbed it on her gums.

"We'll take the long way home," he said to her. "If that's cool."

She nodded and settled back into the passenger seat, already checking out.

Rubio turned west, heading past a McDonald's onto Dixie Drive. He glanced over—her eyes were closed, passed out. He started looking for a private place to park, turning north and cruising for a few minutes before spotting a large cemetery. He pulled off, finding a place to park away from the road, under a dark patch of trees. Rubio put the car in park and looked over at the girl.

"Hey, you okay?"

Nothing.

"Hey, girl," he said loudly, shaking her leg.

"You okay?"

He took her face in his hand and slapped her. Once. Twice. Hard enough to wake her if she were asleep—or pretending to be asleep. There was no response.

He glanced around and didn't see any other cars. Leaving the car running, with the heat blowing, Rubio got out of the car. It was dark outside, with a few lights around the perimeter of cemetery gates.

He went around to the passenger door and pulled it up, then leaned inside and hit the "Stealth" button. He rolled her over onto her back and propped her head on the cushion that separated the two front seats. He wasn't ginger with her—Rubio wanted to make sure she was passed out before he got started.

CHAPTER 23
The Itch

Frank's back and head ached. Oxy made everything better or made everything hurt. When it wasn't masking the pain or dulling his senses, it came back with a vengeance. But when it worked, it was amazing.

Frank made his way to the bathroom, scratching his arms again. Everything itched: arms, legs, chest, and belly. The itching came and went, along with the sweats and the headaches, but sometimes the itching was infuriating. It felt like ants crawling on him. Frank ran his nails along his arms and chest, scratching until his skin was pink and tingling. Sometimes, he scratched and scratched to the point where he started bleeding. Yesterday, he'd been digging at an itchy area on his side and realized his finger was moist. He'd stopped and realized he'd dug a hole in his side and hadn't even noticed it.

Frank took a leak and then leaned over the sink, washing his face and hands and running water through his hair. He didn't look good. His eyes were sunken, making him appear crazed and deadened at the same time.

He looked down at the bottles by the sink, estimating how many pills he had left. How long before he needed more? Oxy was cheap and easy to get around here. Hillbilly heroin, people called it. He rattled the bottles and found two empty. The other three held probably 30 pills total. Three a day meant 10 more days. Of course, three a day was low. Frank smiled and popped another one and walked into the kitchen. In a few minutes, the warm feeling of completeness washed over him, happy and welcoming. Frank didn't need anyone else. He could just do his thing, chill, go to work, come home, relax.

He didn't need to worry about Laura or Trudy or those people up in Ohio. It would all work out. Frank had plenty to worry about down here. But first, he needed a drink. The last time he'd run out of alcohol, he'd doubled up on the Oxy. It had been fine, but not as good as combining it with alcohol. Frank pulled the fridge open, but the beer was all gone. He checked the freezer for a forgotten bottle of bourbon or vodka stashed in the back, but it was empty. He went to the cabinets, even checking under the sink, but there were no beers to be found. No stashed bottles of stronger stuff. He'd ransacked the place earlier, accidentally breaking off one of the cabinet doors.

The flask. Frank went to his bedroom and found his clothes from Monday in a pile on the floor next to the bed. He dug through the pockets and found the small metal flask and pulled the stopper and tipped it up to his lips.

Empty.

CHAPTER 24
The Salem Mall

A few minutes later, Rubio was done. He rolled off the girl and stood up, pulling his pants up. Rubio smiled as he closed the door, then went around to the driver's seat, climbing in and turning on the radio. Rubio directed the car back out onto Dixie Drive and headed south, passing the McDonald's again and turning west when he got to Needmore. He glanced over at the girl, passed out and naked from the waist down. She was a slut, and a druggie, and got what was coming to her. She probably traded drugs for sex all the time, and that's exactly what had happened. Honestly, she was probably 100% fine with it. In fact, when she woke up, he'd tell her what happened. She probably wouldn't care. The only thing she would care about was where was the next hit coming from.

She'd make a fantastic addition.

Rubio went west on Needmore, passing Main and turning north on Salem. This was Trotwood, a town that was down on its luck, as people liked to say. Stores were always coming and going—a Walmart would open just as a Kmart was closing. It was really nothing more than a collection of strip malls and old homes and the Salem Mall, or what was left of it.

Right in the center of town, the Salem Mall had been a major retail hub back in the 1980s and 1990s. Located at the intersection of Shiloh Springs and Salem Avenue, the mall had been a shopping destination for north Dayton and the surrounding counties.

Opened in 1966 on the site of an old farm, the Salem Mall was the first enclosed mall in the Dayton area and attracted thousands of shoppers every day to the Sears and Rike's anchor stores, the Liberal supermarket, theaters and the dozens of smaller stores tucked inside the sprawling two-story complex. The mall soon expanded, adding a JCPenney and a new food court to replace the closed supermarket.

But by the late 1990s, the mall had fallen on hard times. A series of crimes in the parking lots scared away once-loyal suburban shoppers. Businesses started having trouble making rent and closed. Two national retailers left in 1998, and the theater and several restaurants closed soon after, leaving Sears as the only remaining anchor. With fewer businesses and more crime, fewer shoppers visited. It was a vicious circle, one that seemed easy to prevent: hire more security. Put in a curfew. Keep out the loiterers and make it a safe place for people to shop. Add more lights to the parking lots and offer escorts. It wasn't rocket science.

The mall closed for good in 2004. It was slated for demolition when the city of Trotwood stepped in, buying the empty mall and surrounding lots for the princely sum of one dollar. They hoped to redevelop it, putting up ten-foot barbed wire fencing around the mall and the expansive, cracked parking lots that surrounded it. But without tenants, the mall quickly fell into a state of disrepair. To many, the mall had gone from an expensive and sad eyesore to something that looked like a prison compound.

Rubio turned on Shiloh Springs and approached the guard shack.

Trotwood was forced to hire an independent security company to ensure the building was secure and to keep out the riff-raff. It was only years later that the Northsiders, using money from their drug operations, purchased the security company.

Rubio stopped at the guard shack located just south of where the old theaters used to be. A guard walked out and approached.

"Can I help you?"

The guard looked impressive—he was a huge, muscular black man with a bald head. He carried a mean-looking rifle pointed at the ground, and wore a uniform that read "North Side Security." The guard's eyes roamed the exterior of Rubio's Civic, then looked inside and took in Rubio and the revolver sitting in Rubio's lap and the coke-stained metal case and the passed-out white girl.

"Just making a delivery," Rubio said.

"Password."

"The pearl is in the river."

The guard nodded, turning and going back inside the shack. The gate went up, and Rubio drove through. The city of Trotwood had no idea the security firm they had hired to guard the derelict mall was a front company operated by the Northsiders.

Rubio turned right and drove around the mall, passing the old Sears with its ornate column signs, one for each letter. Most of the old mall entrances were blocked off and sealed up. He drove around the back and parked near one of the few open entrances, still lit up with the words "Salem Mall" in white, arching over the door. Rubio noticed there were at least another forty or fifty cars in the lot.

He went around and dressed the girl, then pulled her from the vehicle. Rubio grabbed the metal case and her bags of chips and beer. She struggled along, leaning on him but stumbling, half out of it. Rubio got them to the doors without slipping on the ice. Another guard stopped him outside the mall doors, and Rubio had to give the password again. Once the guard knew he was supposed to be there, he offered to help. Rubio shoved the white girl toward him, and the guard caught her.

"She's had a rough night," the guard said.

Rubio nodded. "Yup, looks like it."

The three of them went inside. The area between the inner and outer doors had been converted into a guard station, and Rubio nodded at another guard waiting behind a screen. The Dragon was serious about security—every time Rubio had been here, the place felt like a fortress. Rubio had to pass through a metal detector and hand over his gun and knife for inspection before getting them back.

Inside, the mall was quiet, clean but still outdated and aged. It had been painted and maintained in the years since it closed, but nothing could update the architecture or the old maroon brick floor that Rubio remembered from when he used to come here as a kid. Many of the store signs remained up and dark, right where the stores had been located. As Rubio and the guard made their way through the center of the mall, he read the names off out loud: Hot Tropics, Bath 'n Body, Izzy's, an old Merlin's.

Inside, most of the empty spaces were dark, with their metal gates pulled down, giving the place the look of a ghost town. Inside some of the spaces, Rubio could see old display racks and counters, as if the stores were just waiting for someone to show up in the morning and start stocking the place, ready to open.

This part of the mall was two stories, and he looked up at the high ceiling and the second-story shops, all dark and quiet. A huge palm tree grew in the middle of the mall, the top branches brushing against the glass roof fifty feet above them.

Two guards approached, and Rubio greeted them. They both wore "North Side Security" uniforms.

"Here, I brought you guys some snacks and a new recruit for the Harem," Rubio said, nodding at the girl and handing them the bag with beer and chips. "Keep her warm for me until I get back, okay?"

The guards smiled and nodded at each other. "Dude, nice. When you coming back?"

"Who knows," he said, pushing the girl toward the guards, who caught her.

They all laughed at the joke—the young woman would be a permanent resident for as long as the gang wanted her around. They called it the Harem. Rubio knew they had a half-dozen women here, drugged up for entertainment purposes or to bribe members of other gangs to join. It was hard to say no to joining the Northsiders when you got free X and a turn with a coked-up white girl.

Gig came out of the one of the larger central spaces, a storefront that had been converted into office space. Rubio saw desks and phones and cubicles. Above the entrance, the sign read "Foot Locker" in large letters.

"You're late," he said, tapping his wrist.

Rubio nodded. "Yeah, I texted you."

"I know, I know," Gig said. "I'm just giving you shit. Come on."

Gig turned and passed the Foot Locker, leading Rubio to the next storefront. "It went okay, though, other than the cops?"

"Yeah," Rubio said, following. "That club in Piqua was packed—they're running a good crowd. On the highway, we picked up a tail. Strange thing—they weren't using the radio to coordinate."

"That's weird." They turned into a "Build-A-Bunny" store and walked through the open gate, where they were stopped by two guards.

"Delivery," Gig said, and the guards waved them through. Gig and Rubio passed into a large room—the former store had been converted into their bank. The front half of the room was full of tables and counting machines, and the back half of the room was taken up by a massive walk-in vault, its thick metal door standing open and guarded.

At the other tables, men were using counting machines and stacking large quantities of money, wrapping them with paper bands.

"Wow," Rubio said under his breath.

"Yeah, I know. You like our vault?" Gig pointed at an open table. "Sit."

They sat, and Rubio handed over the case. Gig opened it and started taking out the money, opening the bands and arranging it on the table. Each counting table held a counting machine and a tray that held rubber bands, sharpies, paper envelopes, and paper bands for wrapping stacks of bills.

"When we were on the highway, we split up and lost our tails," Rubio continued, watching Gig count. "Those Civics are working out."

"Tavon knows what he's doing with those cars," Gig said. "You did good, Rubio. Slug?"

"Yeah. He was good."

"Tavon?

Rubio looked at the table. "He's wavering. I can see it in his eyes. He's down with the selling and moving, but every time we have to muscle someone, he gets uncomfortable. Won't be long before he refuses an order."

Gig nodded, counting off a stack of $20 bills and wrapping a paper band around them. The machine did the work, counting and verifying the bills—all Gig needed to do was stack and wrap. Each bundle of $20s was labeled with a band that read "$1,000."

"If Tavon ever bails, it would be a loss to the gang. Tavon's smart and good with numbers," Gig said. It also went without saying that he knew far too much about their operations.

Rubio glanced around and then back at Gig. "You don't need to have him popped. He's a good kid. Just not on jobs where we have to get pushy."

Gig nodded. "After what happened to his sister, I can't blame him. But if he's gonna be on a crew, you have to be able to do what needs to be done, right? I think getting him off the streets might be a good first step. Some people can't handle blood, others don't like guns. You know how it is."

"I know," Gig said, counting the stacks as the machine finished with the contents of the case. "$20,000. Good job."

Rubio nodded. "Thanks. But his hesitation could get somebody hurt. Without some stern words, he's gone."

Gig nodded. "Actually, I've got an idea on how to fix it." Gig lifted the stacks of bills and put them in one of the paper envelopes, then wrote the amount on the outside and took it over to the vault, handing it to the guard. Inside the vault, Rubio could see shelves piled high with stacks of money. The guard had Gig initial something on the envelope, then initialed it himself and went in.

Gig walked back over and grabbed the metal suitcase. "Ready?" He headed back to the entrance, setting the metal suitcase on a table near the door with a dozen other identical suitcases. Rubio followed him back out into the mall.

"I found you guys a new girl," Rubio said.

"Good," Gig said. "I was getting tired of the other ones," he said, laughing.

"How many you got?"

"Not sure," Gig said. "Three or four."

"Well, tonight makes it five." Rubio looked around. "This place is huge," he said.

"You never had the tour?" Gig asked.

Rubio shook his head. "Nah, only been here a couple other times."

"Well, we'll get you a tour next time," Gig said. "I gotta get back to work. When you and the others are in next, I'll walk you around."

"I heard you guys have an indoor shooting range," Rubio said.

Gig nodded. "Yeah, we'll get you out there next time."

"Thanks, Gig," Rubio nodded and headed toward the exit. He wondered how many people they had working in here—he could hear industrial sounds and lots of people talking to each other. The place was massive and well-guarded—he'd seen several guards since coming inside. The cops might raid this place someday, but if they ever did, they'd take some serious losses.

CHAPTER 25
Thursday Stand-Up

Thursday morning was cold and overcast over Cooper's Mill, a small town in southwestern Ohio just north of Dayton. Winters in Ohio could be unpredictable—this morning, the sky was a solid layer of bruised gray clouds that threatened snow.

Deputy Peters, one of the younger members of the Cooper's Mill Police Department, struggled with his half of a heavy dry-erase board. His cousin, Chief Jeff King, carried the other half, backing through the front doors of the Cooper's Mill police station. Lola, the receptionist, held the door open for them.

"Thanks, Lola," Deputy Peters said.

"Not a problem," she said, smiling at them.

Peters turned and backed down the hallway.

"Here, that's good," Chief King said. They set the board down in the hallway right outside Jeff's office, which looked out onto a sea of cubicles that took up the better portion of a large room lined with windows on one side. Through the windows, Deputy Peters could see rows of trees and the back of the local grocery store.

"What do you need this for, Jeff?"

Jeff smiled at Peters. "We can always use another whiteboard, right?" He turned to Lola. "Can you get everyone together for the stand-up?"

Deputy Peters glanced at his watch—it was nearly 10:00 a.m., time for the station's informal "stand-up" meeting to get everyone up to speed. Larger departments did shift changeover meetings, with updates passed along every eight hours at the start of each of three shifts. But the Cooper's Mill PD was smaller and usually only needed one daily briefing.

Deputy Peters walked around and reminded the staff and the officers to gather in the common area. He liked working here in Cooper's Mill, and especially liked working with his cousin. Jeff treated him like an equal, even though Peters hadn't been on the streets long. The academy had prepared Peters for being a cop, and now he was learning the ins and outs of investigations from Jeff and Detective Barnes and others on the force.

He was still a beat cop, obviously, so most of his time involved pulling over drunk drivers or investigating domestic abuse cases. But, more and more, he'd been getting pulled into longer-term investigations. And people were even starting to ask his opinion on things.

A lot of it came down to the two cases he'd worked on with Frank Harper. The ex-cop had been in town visiting family and had gotten involved in two cases in Cooper's Mill over the last six months. Harper was unorthodox, to say the least, but working with the gruff old man had given Peters some unique insights on case work. Both cases had their own twists and turns. In October, Peters had been shot. Even now, in late March, he was still feeling the lingering aftereffects of the gunshot to his shoulder. His surgeries and physical therapy sessions were all over, but he still got twinges of pain now and again.

With a few minutes to spare, Peters went to get some coffee from the galley. While speaking to Lola, Peters misjudged the amount of coffee in the pot and managed to spill some on his hand, singeing it.

"Jiminy Christmas Trees!" he said under his breath, wiping away the spilled coffee and cleaning up the mess.

"What was that?"

He looked at the Lola. "Nothing. I just burned myself."

"No, I know that," she said, handing him a paper towel. "What was that about Christmas trees?"

He smiled at her. "Don't make fun," he said. "You know I don't like to curse."

She smiled and walked out. "Damn straight. Me neither," she said.

Peters shook his head. He wasn't one to curse, and chastised others for doing so. He was always trying out new versions of words that sounded like he was emphatically not cursing. And people replied in kind, relentlessly making fun of him by going out of their way to curse in front of him.

But he knew why people cursed—there was something cathartic about saying words, loudly or quietly, to express how you felt. His mother would never approve, but maybe that was why so many people did it. Sometimes, Peters felt like he was holding back the tide.

The meeting was already going when he arrived, holding the coffee out away from his body. Peters found a wall to lean up against and listened to his cousin update the staff gathered in the common room.

"...with their mayor. The task force is making a lot of progress, and that's a good thing," King said, looking around. "But other departments are seeing what we're seeing—increased activity, especially to the south."

He pointed to a board with a large map of Cooper's Mill on it. Peters could see the historic downtown on the right, the "uptown" area nearer the highway on the left, and then the straight, wide line of Interstate 75, the busy north-south thoroughfare, on the left edge of the map. Jeff was pointing near the bottom, where Cooper's Mill and Miami County rubbed up against the northern edge of Montgomery County.

"We're seeing more activity down here, including that meth house you guys closed down two weeks ago." Everyone nodded soberly at the mention—it was the first drug production facility found in the vicinity in twenty years. "There have been more overdoses in the last six months then I've seen in years. We need to keep an eye out for anything suspicious, obviously. Strange cars, people who look like they're uncomfortable."

He went on, reviewing what they were to be on the lookout for. Mostly it was illegal or unauthorized use of property, like barns and homes where the owners weren't around a lot. Drug users often wanted privacy to get high. And thefts had increased exponentially as people stole money or anything that wasn't tied down to support their habits.

"One other thing," Jeff said, wrapping up the stand-up. "We had another car chase up the interstate Tuesday night, and I didn't hear the details on it until yesterday. Two or three matching Honda Civics, possibly involved in a drug sale. Driving at high speeds and heading south."

"South?" Stan, one of the beat cops, chimed in. He was always itching for a fight, a dangerous trait in a cop. "I thought they were running product north?"

Jeff shrugged. "Looks like they were returning from Piqua to Dayton. Piqua patrol saw them leaving a club and followed them to the highway, then called in help from Troy. Stayed off the radio—lately, Troy cops have been using their personal phones to coordinate, fearing the police bands were being monitored. The suspects did that thing again where they speed up, switch off all the lights, and disappear."

This had happened a few times, now—Peters had heard about this trio of Hondas that could seemingly evade police cars at night. There was something going on here.

"Any ideas?" Jeff asked, looking around. A few people speculated that the cars were being driven up into the back of a truck, or pulled off the side of the shoulder. Others argued those techniques wouldn't work, especially in the snow. Shoulders and the dirt near them were notoriously soft. Any cars pulling off into the snow and dead grass would sink up to the hubcaps.

Peters wasn't sure—with enough planning, anything was possible. "Eyes open," Mr. Harper had told him once. Keep your eyes open and your mind open. There were always possibilities.

CHAPTER 26
Basement Lab

On Thursday morning, the Dayton Area Heroin Task Force carried out another raid, this one of a lab in the basement of a home on Weathers Street. It was purportedly the last location for the Fifth Street Runners, serving as headquarters and a production facility. Three days of planning went into the raid, including securing an observation post on the target location.

Roget and Hawkins led the raid, this time simulcast to the rest of the task force leadership back at headquarters. Mayor Denton and Chief of Police Craig watched a live feed from the body cameras of Roget and Hawkins as they and a dozen other fully armed task force members raided the rickety old home just before noon.

The raid was a success—thirty-four pounds of coke, weed and Molly, plus a small amount of flakka, a frightening new street drug. They also found a ten-pound container of fentanyl, a scary new synthetic opioid that drug cartels and some gangs were starting to add to heroin that make the drug even more addictive.

Thirteen persons were arrested at the crime scene, all either in leadership positions in the gang or making drugs and packaging them for sale in the lab. All in all, it was a good raid. The mayor was pleased when Roget gave his post-action report.

After signing off from the live feed, Roget and Hawkins spent another two or three hours at the location, walking through the home and scouring it for details that others might have missed. All the suspects were removed and taken to Central, with explicit orders from Roget that they be held separate from the general population. No one was allowed to move any of them without speaking directly to him.

"It was a clean raid." Hawkins said as they walked through the house, kicking over broken furniture and picking at the bullet holes that riddled the old wallpaper.

Roget nodded. He'd been quiet since signing off from the live feed to the mayor and chief of police. She could tell there was something bothering him. He had that half-dazed look on his face when his mind was going a mile a minute and couldn't figure out what to work on next. She loved that look. That meant his brain was close to solving a problem.

"What are you pondering so hard, Bigfoot?"

He looked up at her and smiled. "Sorry, just thinking."

Hawkins picked up a framed picture from the mantle and held it out to him with one of her gloved hands. The photo showed a picture of the St. Louis Arch standing over a wide river. A silver casino boat was moored on the opposite side of the river—the side of the boat read *Margaret*.

She showed it to Roget. "This looks recent. Was there a family here?"

Roget shrugged. "Not sure. The paperwork says the house was foreclosed. Fifth Street was using it for a while. Before that they were still part of the East Dogs."

She pointed at the photo. "From St. Louis?"

He looked at the framed photo and shrugged. "Yeah, I guess," he said.

She pulled the frame off and flipped over the photo. It read "NEVER FORGET," and was signed by someone named "Shotgun" Pope. She put the photo and frame into an evidence bag for later study.

Hawkins looked at him and bit her lip. "What's wrong, Tom? You've been so quiet, ever since Monday."

He looked at her and started to say something, then decided against it. "I don't know. I need to clear my head. Can we get lunch?"

She was taken aback. He always kept things at work very professional. They were keeping the fact they were dating very quiet. They never walked out together during the day, and he NEVER asked her to lunch. Sometimes they'd meet, but they never arrived or left together. They went out on the weekends, of course, but maintained separate homes and vehicles.

Once, last year, she'd stayed over at his place for the evening and they'd been running late the next morning. Roget offered to drive her to work, something they never did. She'd reluctantly agreed—there just wasn't enough time to get back to her place, get her car, and make it to work ahead of an important briefing. They'd ridden in together and Tom had pulled into the underground parking structure and found a spot far from the elevator doors. And just as they were getting ready to climb out, a car came around the corner. It was the mayor. She'd ducked down like a teenager on a clandestine date. Roget had watched the mayor drive past and waved.

"It's clear," Tom had said with a smile.

She'd sat up and punched him hard on the shoulder. "That's not funny. Either we're telling people, or we're not. I don't like hiding in your car like we're in high school and making out in the parking lot."

Tom had nodded, agreeing. She'd gotten out and walked inside, watching for other cars, and Tom had followed her inside, keeping his distance. It had mortified them, and since, they'd decided to keep it very quiet.

These thoughts raced through her mind. Something was wrong, very wrong. Tom was conflicted, and she knew that couldn't be good.

"Sure. But we should meet, right?" she asked, hinting that they should try to keep up the charade as long as they could.

He wasn't looking at her, his mind elsewhere. "Oh, sure, that's fine," he said, missing her entire point. "3:00 p.m. Carillon Park, by the bell tower."

She looked at him. "That's a weird time for lunch," she said, but Roget had already turned away and left the room.

CHAPTER 27
Rudimentary Staircase

Someone was banging on something. A door, it sounded like.

Frank woke up and looked around. He was on the floor again, sprawled out. His left arm hurt. He couldn't tell where he was. He blinked and it took him a minute to recognize what he was looking at. The stripes and round hole didn't seem familiar. He turned and looked up and saw the refrigerator door handle. He was in the kitchen, lying on the floor and looking at the bottom of the fridge. The floor was cold.

More banging, louder this time. He couldn't tell where it was coming from, and didn't really care. His arm still hurt. He squeezed his hand into a fist and realized he was lying on his arm.

He tried rolling onto his back but he couldn't move. Frank's chin and cheek were pressed against the linoleum. He remembered he had another arm and used it to reach out above him. He reached out to find something to push on. His hand scrabbled around but felt nothing.

"Frank, you in there?"

Someone calling his name. Was it a man or a woman?

Frank stopped moving his arm so he could think. Someone was at his apartment, looking for him. Calling his name. It didn't sound like Laura, the only person he really wanted to talk to. But she was ashamed of him. Because he'd killed a family. Burned them up. She would never forgive him.

He rolled hard, flopping onto his back. Maybe it was his dealer, or the clerk at Tammy's Liquor Store. His left arm was free now, and Frank could move the fingers. The blood rushed back into it, burning with pins and needles.

"Ow," he said to no one. "Ow, that hurts."

More banging. On a door, it sounded like. Not his dealer, or Trudy. Not Laura, not Ben Stone, not Joe Hathaway, shooting at him from far away. Not any of them.

He found the corner of the fridge and grabbed onto it, pulling himself across the floor. Away from the voices. He didn't want them to find him. They were angry.

"I don't care," the voice came again, quieter. It sounded like a conversation, although one voice was indistinguishable.

He ignored them. The only thing that helped was his pills. He remembered most of them were in the bathroom, but one bottle was on the kitchen counter. By the phone. So high up. He could see the counter and the four drawers between him and the top. Maybe he could pull them out and form a rudimentary staircase. Just enough for him to climb up. Another pill or two or ten would make it better. He needed them in his mouth, needed to feel the gritty, chalky taste as he chewed them. All the alcohol was gone so he'd doubled up on the Oxy and it had changed things. Changed him. He struggled to pull the bottom drawer out, then crawled toward it.

The jingling of keys.

Key sounds were sharp and had a funny edge, like the clinking of piano keys or lightning. The keys led to a door being opened and two people suddenly standing over him, neither of whom he recognized. They yelled at him but Frank ignored them—he was busy. He'd gotten the bottom two drawers open and was climbing his "stairs." One hand on each. No problem. Using his feet to push himself up. At the top of the stairs would be the bottle of Oxy. Both of the people sounded angry, saying things about him and to him that he didn't understand. One of the voices belonged to a friend of his, a black man he'd seen many times before but didn't recognize. Frank knew the guy was nice but right now he was in the way and Frank pushed at him angrily. The top of the counter was all that mattered, like climbing a mountain. The other voice belonged to a woman he'd seen around the building. She held a big ring of keys and it suddenly occurred to Frank that she was like a god. She had access to every room in the building, bathrooms and everything. She could walk in on anyone at any time without knocking. The power. She could go through every room in the building. What if she came into his place and into his kitchen and took the bottle on his counter? He wouldn't like that at all. The voices were shouting again and they were mad at him for some reason. He was just minding his own business, looking for his medicine. Maybe later he'd take Trudy and Laura to that new Six Flags amusement park they had just opened up south of New Orleans. It looked amazing in the pictures. Laura had been begging to go. And after that they could drive down into the French Quarter and go to Café Du Monde. Trudy loved the beignets, and the coffee was outstanding, with just a hint of chicory. Du Monde was just across from Jackson Square and fifty feet from the mighty Mississippi. He loved to grab an outside table and just watch the people pass by, tourists and locals alike.

He didn't like that these people were yelling at him. Frank just wanted to rest. He let go of the drawers and slid aside and felt himself hit the cold floor again.

The man's voice was coming into focus.

"Frank, get up," the man said. His name was Williams.

Frank looked at him from the floor. "Williams?"

"That's right," the man said. A woman got down on the floor to yell at Frank some more, and he recognized her as the landlady. Williams said something to the landlady, who shot Frank a look and turned around and left. Williams turned and looked at him.

"Jesus, Frank," Williams said, getting Frank up off the floor and leaning him up against the counter. At least Frank could stand. Yesterday, all he could do was travel between the kitchen and bathroom and television. He'd passed out at some point while watching a late-night show on DNA analysis.

"Hey, Williams."

The man shook his head. "You look like shit, man. And Collier is pissed. You didn't come in to work this morning. Came by to check on you. You want to get fired?"

Frank shook his head. "No, it's Sunday."

"Thursday."

"Christ," Frank said. He had to get to work. Things were shitty enough with Collier. "I overslept," he said, standing and stumbling out of the kitchen. "I'm just not feeling well," he said, louder than he needed to. "Give me three minutes. I'll be ready to go," he shouted and walked away, going into his bedroom and locking the door.

It was a lie. Frank could take three hours and not be ready to go, or interested in going, but that was beside the point. He started getting dressed, and heard Williams wandering around the apartment, probably noticing the pizza boxes and trash everywhere. They were hard to miss.

"You got a junkie living with you now?" Williams called from the other room.

Frank suppressed a smile and a snarky comeback. Wouldn't do any good. "Nah, it's just been a rough month."

Williams laughed. It sounded weird from two rooms away. "Looks like a rough year."

You have no idea, Frank thought. He finished pulling on some pants and a shirt from a pile on the floor next to the bed, then went back out to the bathroom to wash his face and brush his teeth. His movements felt slowed down, like he was slogging through mud. He needed a shower but it would have to wait. While he was in the bathroom, he pocketed the Oxy, all five bottles. Apparently, he'd imagined the one in the kitchen. He shouted to his guest. "How'd you get in?"

Williams laughed again. "Your landlady. She wanted to call 911. Thought you OD'd or something," he said.

Frank opened the bathroom door, stumbling out into the living room. Williams was standing near the windows, looking out at downtown.

"You driving?"

"Hell, no," Williams said. "Not unless you're Miss Daisy," he said, turning. "All the same, I'll follow you to work. After we get some coffee in you."

CHAPTER 28
The Washingtons

Jake Delancy was driving through Cooper's Mill, headed home from a job, when his phone rang. He didn't look at the number—it was probably Frank calling back. Good, he thought. The man should be wallowing in guilt, the same as me.

"Hello?"

There was static on the phone. "Mr. Delancy?"

"Yes," Jake answered. The voice didn't sound familiar, but it was probably one of the cops involved in the fire investigation. He'd been talking to a lot of cops over the last few days.

"Mr. Delancy, it's Markeys," the voice said quietly. "Me and the family are fine."

Jake sat up straight and banged his left arm on the door, sending a sharp pain down his elbow and shoulder. He cradled his phone and kept talking, one eye on the road ahead, looking for a place to stop.

"You're alive? Your family is okay?"

"Yes, sir," the voice came back. "The Northsiders showed up that night, burned the house down. But we got out."

Jake didn't know what to say. "Wow. I mean—that's great. Everyone's okay?"

"Yeah. We was scared, so we went to a hotel. Took a bus across town, stayed under a different name. Listen, sorry about your house."

"It's fine," Jake said. "I'm just relieved. I'll call the police and let them know you guys—"

"No, sir, you can't do that," Markeys said.

"Why?"

Markeys was quiet for a minute.

"The cops were no help. And we barely got out. Only 'cause they were real loud when they were getting ready to set the fire. If you tell the cops, the Northsiders will find us. We gotta hide for now."

Jake didn't know what to say. He slowed and turned into the CVS parking lot, stopping his truck.

"You can't tell no one," Markeys continued. Jake could tell the man was scared. "There's a lot of people at this hotel. Too many. We're taking a cab up to Troy to a hotel there."

"Okay, stay safe," Jake answered, not sure what else to say. "Call me when you get settled."

"Actually, if you don't mind, I'm not gonna do that, Mr. Delancy," Markeys said. "We're all scared. Right now no one knows we ain't dead. We wanna keep it that way for a while."

"Okay," Jake said. "But call me if things change."

Markeys was quiet for moment. "That's fine. I'll be in touch when I can."

Jake wished him luck and hung up, deep in thought. He pulled back out onto Main, heading downtown. He crossed the train tracks and passed into the historical district that made up the heart of Cooper's Mill: the shops and restaurants and Victorian homes that lined either side of the street all the way to the canal. The old flour mill stood at the edge of town, an old wooden structure painted red and standing four stories tall. It was perched next to the remains of the canal that had once powered the mill to grind flour for the Cooper Flour company. The mill was so important, the town ended up being named after it.

Jake turned up Second and parked in front of his house. He put his coat on and climbed out of his car, walking up to the sidewalk. If he didn't tell the cops, Jake was covering up the fact that they were alive. Could he get in trouble for that? Was that technically "obstructing" a police investigation?

Jake opened the front door and set his things down, heading into the kitchen to pour himself a drink. His thoughts remained on the Washington family as he wandered through the house, wondering how he should proceed. Tell the cops or keep it from them?

CHAPTER 29
Carillon Park

Three hours later, Deputy Sergeant Hawkins left the office and drove to meet Roget. It felt weird, leaving to meet him without any idea what he wanted to talk about, but she trusted him.

The tall concrete bell tower of Carillon Historical Park loomed over the snowy park, the bell ringing just as she arrived. Behind her, the parking lots were torn up—some kind of construction was going on. She found him next to his car, looking up at the tower.

"Tom? You okay?"

Roget turned to her and smiled. "Yes. You still wearing your vest or your cam from the raid?"

She shook her head.

"Good," he said. "Can I have your phone?" She handed it over. He tossed it and his phone into the front seat of his patrol vehicle, then locked the car. "Come on." Roget started off across the snow-covered grass in the direction of the bell tower. Hawkins followed, confused.

They walked in silence for a few minutes. She looked around to enjoy the momentary quiet. Their lives were often filled with so much chaos. It was nice to have a moment where nothing was happening, where nothing was expected to happen.

"What are they building back there in the parking lot?"

He shook his head, distracted. "Not sure. I heard maybe a restaurant or a brewery."

The park was located next to the wide Miami River—beyond, she could see the towers of Dayton hulking in the snow. Closer, directly across the river, she saw the University of Dayton Arena, which shared an expansive set of parking lots with Welcome Stadium, where the UD football team played. It was beautiful out here, crisp and quiet, with no sounds other than the passing vehicles on the roads on either side of the expansive park. She could even hear the river ice cracking.

They were half way across the snowy field before he started talking again.

"I've got a bad feeling," he said quietly.

She had questions, but she knew Tom. She knew he needed to talk at his own pace, and asking questions would just derail his thought process. She respected him, both as a partner and as a cop.

"Go on."

He glanced at her. "You can't say anything, okay? To anyone. I mean, literally anyone." His eyes told her he was serious—he'd obviously been thinking about this for a while, whatever it was.

"Okay, Tom. I won't. What's going on?"

Tom looked up at the bell tower. "Beautiful, isn't it?"

She nodded and agreed. They were quiet for a moment, just walking toward the base of the massive tower. The ground sloped up as they got closer to the tower. She waited, giving him time.

"I think...I think there's a mole," he finally said. "In the task force. Or something. The information is getting out."

She glanced at him and kept walking.

"What makes you think that?"

"I'm not sure," he said. "I mean...we're making progress, right? We're knocking down gangs or scaring them right out of town. Three are gone and today we got Fifth Street."

"It's remarkable, really," she agreed.

"But my informant from that last raid got stabbed in the belly and died on a dirty floor."

She knew he was upset about that—he was blaming himself.

"That wasn't your fault, you know."

"I know. I know." He stopped as they got to the base of the tower. It stretched up into the air high above them, and a wide circle of concrete ran round the four-cornered base.

"It's not just my informant," he continued. "Other things...they don't add up."

"Like what?"

He walked off to their right, circling the base of the tower.

"That family on Eckhart Street, the ones from the fire?"

She nodded.

"There were no bodies," he said, looking at the tower. "No bone fragments...nothing to say they were actually even there. What if it was a fake-out, to get us to look at the Northsiders? I feel like we're being played."

"I don't know, Tom. The fire chief said people die in fires all the time, and sometimes there are no remains. Depending on how hot the fire burns, right?"

"Yeah. And another thing—don't you think the anonymous tips come in too easy? We just sit back and wait for the tips to roll in. You've worked other cases. Ever had the public so interested in helping?"

She followed him as he walked down the hill.

"I guess the gangbangers are always going to rat on each other, right?" she said. "I mean, the street code doesn't apply to other gangs. 'Snitches get stitches' only means your own people, right?" she said, quoting the number one rule of the streets.

"Why don't we ever hear anything about the Northsiders? I mean, except for that house on Eckhart Street, there's been nothing. They're the biggest gang around," he said. "You'd think we'd hear more about them than any other gang."

"Well, the Northsiders are gaining territory, that's for certain. With all the pressure on the other gangs, they've probably picked up members, too."

Roget shook his head. "They're making out great. So far, they've only gained strength. We need to move on them."

"I agree," she said. Hawkins wasn't sure what he meant, but too much power in anyone's hands was a bad idea, in her opinion.

CHAPTER 30
A Couple Weeks Off

Frank Harper sat at his desk at work, ignoring the throbbing pain in his head. He had the medicine for his pain in his pocket, but he didn't dare take any. The prescription had run out long ago, and CVS couldn't help him. They'd take one look at the old empty bottles and laugh at him.

Or, more likely, they'd report him.

Frank was keeping his head down, working quietly. The headache made it hard to concentrate, but he had three different case reports laid out on his desk, making it look like he was extra busy. Every time he heard Collier coming, Frank would pick up his office phone and start talking to someone, as if he were following some all-important, half-forgotten lead. At one point, Collier, unimpressed with Frank's mess of reports or phone conversation, interrupted Frank.

"See me before you leave today."

Frank nodded and placed the phone back in its cradle. He was convinced the only reason the ABI had a cold case department at all was so they could honestly tell the families involved in these cases that someone was "still working" on it. Technically it was true: if a case file was on one of their desks, or in the stacked file cabinets around them, then it was being "worked on." To save face, Frank would need to solve a case today, preferably in the next hour. Of course, that was impossible—these cases had gone unsolved for decades for good reason.

Detective Murray sat at his desk, ignoring Frank and quietly working on his own stack of hopeless cases. He turned from his desk and looked over at Frank.

"Anything?"

Frank shook his head. "You?"

Murray held up the folder he was working on. "Nothing, but this is one I keep coming back to. You have those too? This one—I don't know. It just feels like it's one phone call away from being solved."

"Yeah, I have those."

Frank stood up and headed towards Collier's office. Might as well get this over with. The door was open, so Frank knocked and walked in.

Collier's office was immaculate, the walls festooned with pictures of

Collier with famous people: the mayor, the governor, three congressmen, half the city council. And famous Birmingham people: Emmylou Harris; Tammy Wynette, who got her start in Birmingham; four with singers from American Idol; and someone named Amber Benson, an actress from that *Buffy the Vampire Slayer* TV show.

Collier's desk was spotless—it looked like he never did any actual work. Probably the only thing he wrote on the desk was lists of reasons he hated Frank Harper. Frank sat down in the chair opposite Collier and waited.

Collier looked up from his desk, straightening a pile of papers, and got right to it.

"I need you to take some time off, Frank."

"What do you mean?"

Collier looked at him, his gaze cold and unblinking. "Look, I can't fire you. Union, and all that. If I fire you, it goes before the board and wastes everyone's time. But I don't think you want to be here, Frank. I don't think you want to work on cold cases, and your closure rate shows that. So I'm suspending you, effective Monday. Take a couple weeks off and get your act together. That's an order."

Frank didn't know what to say.

Collier continued. "And...lately, you've looked bad, Frank. Disheveled, I think the word is. And, on more than one occasion, you've come in drunk. I can't have that."

Frank sat back in the chair. "I'm having...some issues. Should I use my vacation time?"

"Actually, no," Collier said. "Sorry to say this, but I need to document the problem before taking any other action. The two-week suspension will go on your records."

"I'd...I'd prefer to just take a vacation," Frank said quietly. It sounded like he was begging, which he was.

Collier looked around the room, then back at Frank. "Do you want to be here, Frank?"

Frank was taken aback. He'd expected to get reamed out, but Collier was being thoughtful. And respectful, for the most part. Frank hesitated at the frankness of the question. The rote answer was "Of course, I love it here, I love everything about this place," but Frank paused, and the pause lingered between them.

Finally, Frank spoke.

"I don't know, sir. I enjoy the cold cases, but they aren't as fulfilling as they used to be. I don't know why. Probably because the principles are deceased. Literally no one cares about the closure of some of our cases except us."

Collier leaned forward. "I can tell you're unhappy, Frank."

Frank nodded, not sure what to say. He'd never heard Collier talk like this.

"I'd prefer there be nothing ugly on my record. Sir."

Collier nodded. "I get that. And I know I pick on you guys," Collier continued. "Sometimes I'm just as frustrated as you. Dusty cases and people dead for decades can't compete with rescuing kidnapped girls. Or car chases."

Frank looked up at him.

Collier smiled, another rarity. "Don't think you were the only one to notice, Frank. When you came back with that gunshot wound and your Ohio stories, you looked ten years younger. Ten years happier. I envied you. And there is no way to put that genie back in the bottle."

Frank didn't know what to say. The man was right—even wounded, and on pain meds, and limping around, he'd never felt more alive than after solving that kidnapping case last October. He hadn't felt like that in years, not since before Katrina.

Something had changed in that weird moment in his daughter's apartment, when she'd been recounting how scared everyone in her town was about the kidnapping. Frank had told her that the local police had asked him to help. The look of pride on her face was like sunshine, something he hadn't felt or seen in a long time. And her anger when he said he wasn't getting involved? She'd practically shamed him into helping.

"I can see you thinking about it," Collier said. "Just that makes you smile. You don't need to be stuck here, not unless you want to be stuck here." He thought about it and nodded. "Take the suspension for what it is: two weeks, starting Monday, for you to get back on track. Do something about the drinking. And your appearance."

"I will," Frank nodded, his head still throbbing. "I will."

Collier took a deep breath. "Just figure out what you want to do. Working on these cases might be filler for you, but I'm starting to think you retired from the field too soon, my friend."

Frank walked out of Collier's office, unsure of how to proceed. Murray asked him quietly about the conversation, but Frank had no idea what to say so he didn't say anything. It was like finding out the evil monster from the horror movie turned out to be the crucial thing at the end that saves everyone.

Frank had a lot to think about.

CHAPTER 31
Dinner and A Delivery

Thursday was a lazy day, the kind of day Tavon liked.

He slept in until past noon, hung out with his sisters, and sat with Talisa for an hour or so, listening to her read some poems she was working on. Talisa's injuries left her bedridden, but it did Tavon's heart good to see her doing better, even if she rarely made eye contact any more.

After a while, he went downstairs and helped his other sisters make dinner. His mom was running late and they were going to surprise her by having dinner waiting when she got home. Tavon also spent some time going over the family finances, leaving sticky notes on the various bills to let his mother know which ones to pay first. He'd been working with her on her credit cards and the mortgage. He also paid a stack of Talisa's medical bills and left his mother the statements.

Tavon figured his time with the gangs was short lived—hell, everything to do with gangs was short lived. He'd seen so many promising kids come and go. Most ended up in jail, or in the ground, ten toes up.

Dinner was nice. Their mom came home from Sam's Club, tired, and Tavon and the sisters presented her with enchiladas and a sweet cornbread and beer. She was very pleased, even though she had to head out to her second job in a little while.

Tavon asked her why she still worked two jobs when he was there and his two sisters were still bringing in money, but she didn't answer. Sometimes, his mom kept her opinions to herself, but it reminded him of what he'd been thinking earlier, about how his time with the gangs was limited. He had this time only to make his money, sort of like how they say a football player's career on average lasts just four years. Some went longer, for certain, but it was too easy to get hurt. A career-ending injury at 23 or 24 meant that, at least in the NFL, you had to get paid up front. That's why they paid players so much. Unless you were a kicker, your time in the NFL was limited. His mom had the same mindset—she had a limited amount of time when she had the energy to work two jobs. Might as well burn the candle at both ends.

Plus, there was Talisa.

Tavon's mom was worried about her, obviously, but she was probably also concerned about Tavon and how long he'd actually be around to pay her bills. Mothers like his had to be pragmatic—there was no retirement waiting for her.

After dinner, Tavon and his mom headed off to their night jobs. His paid far better, but hers was far less dangerous. She worked three nights a week at Tim's Donuts, a hole-in-the-wall donut shop in Vandalia that was famous in the Dayton area. They walked out together and stood outside in the cold

"Mom, I just wanted you to know I paid all of Talisa's bills."

She looked at his and stopped. "Thank you, son."

"And there's more," he said. "I don't want you to worry so much." He told her there was money in the safe for Talisa's treatments, enough to get her through the last surgery and all her physical therapy.

She smiled, and he could tell a weight had been lifted from her shoulders. After a second, she hugged him, their breath making cold clouds in the night air.

Tavon, Rubio and Slug had two deliveries tonight, one south of Dayton in a new development called Austin Landings on the southern edge of the metro area just south of the Dayton Mall. Developers were throwing up stores and office buildings as quickly as possible, and with that came people. And more people meant more customers for the Northsiders.

Tavon spent most of the night on autopilot, following Slug and Rubio and thinking about his sister and the Northsiders. If this was a real gang, like those in the movies, then he and some of his "homies" would have tracked down the guys that jumped Talisa and killed them. But it didn't work that way, at least not in this gang. This was business. Hell, he was surprised they didn't have little business cards to hand out.

Tavon had brought along his guns in a hidey hole behind his dashboard. He loved the idea of hiding stuff in obvious places. His gun safe in the Civic was inside the A/C control panel. To access it, you had to turn the A/C all the way to cold, put it on minimum output, and hold down both defroster buttons, allowing the panel to tip forward. Inside, he had room for several handguns and stacks of cash. All he kept in there right now was a small stack of 100s that someone had "lost" along the way. He'd fashioned similar hidey holes in the other Civics.

Tavon wondered what had come out of that house fire. He'd read in the paper about the investigation, but hadn't heard anything about it lately. If there was a triple homicide, you'd figure the cops would be all over that. Maybe they were getting paid to look the other way.

After making their pickups and deliveries, Rubio led them to the

Salem Mall. Tavon hadn't been there more than a few times, mostly to work on cars, so this was a rare treat. The mall always made him sad. It seemed like such a waste, a big beautiful space, reduced to nothing but an empty shell.

Tonight, from the outside, it looked deserted, with only a few cars coming and going. The Northsiders parked around the back, behind the tall fencing that ringed the empty mall. As far as anyone could tell, the only people working in and around the mall itself were the North Side Security staff members.

Tavon followed Rubio and Slug around the back, parking and heading inside together. The trio got frisked at the front door, turning in their weapons before being allowed inside. Security was tighter than before, Tavon noticed.

The interior looked like he remembered, but there were definitely more people around. Men and women were pushing hand-trucks loaded with boxes up and down the hallway leading to the old JCPenney.

The guards walked the three of them to the front of the old Foot Locker—the sign was still lit up—and Rubio asked for Gig. Tavon noticed that someone had gotten the indoor fountain going, and it really sounded like a mall now. A private mall, just for their purposes. It was a good thing they didn't tear the place down—it would be a shame if the only thing left of this place was a dirty open lot.

Gig came out and greeted them, then lead them under the Foot Locker sign. They walked down a long hallway; all vestiges of the old store had been removed and replaced with office spaces. None of the doors had names on them, only numbers. Gig led them to 307 and went in. His office was nice, with room for a desk and a small couch and two other chairs. He gestured for them to take a seat.

"I wanted to chat about your deliveries. Austin Landings went well?" Rubio nodded.

"Good. Rubio said you guys needed a tour, too, before you head out again. We can swing that, but first things first. Things are going really well, and we're going to have you do more runs, so the number of pickups is going to drop. We got other people for that. Cool?"

Rubio nodded. Slug and Tavon knew better than to say anything. Rubio ran their crew and made the decisions.

Gig turned to Tavon, surprising him. "Tavon?"

He looked up. "Yes?"

"I also wanted to thank you for your help with the books. The Dragon's impressed—if he was here tonight, I'd introduce you." That was high praise. Almost nobody besides the Council got to meet the Dragon. "I also brought up your particular problem with the Dragon, and he said I could move on it. Things are going to be happening in that direction soon."

Tavon was confused. "What problem?"

Gig looked at Rubio. "You didn't tell him?"

"Nah, I didn't want to get his hopes up," Rubio said, turning to Tavon. "You know those Vandalia guys that jumped Talisa? They ain't long for this earth."

Tavon looked from him to Gig, swallowing. He had no idea the gang was considering stepping in on Talisa's behalf. He'd assumed they might give him permission to retaliate, but figured he'd be on his own from there.

"Seriously?"

"Yeah, we're authorized to move on them," Gig said. "You passed along all the info to Rubio, and he gave it to me. We are going to handle it, though. You can't be involved, you're too valuable. Should happen in the next day or two. But we'll get you in a car nearby so you can watch. Good enough?"

Tavon's head was spinning. While he wanted to take out the thugs himself, this was smarter. And they were giving him a chance to see it with his own eyes. He nodded, unsure if he should say anything.

"Good, good," Gig said. "The Dragon will be happy. Rubio, you got that stuff from tonight?"

Rubio reached into his pockets and took out two large envelopes. "Yup. I marked on the envelopes where they're from. And that dry cleaner near Riley's is getting lippy again."

Gig nodded. "Yeah, I heard," making a note on one envelope. "I'll take care of it. You got time for another run tonight, after a little R and R? Take about three hours."

Rubio looked at the rest of his crew. "Guys?"

Slug and Tavon nodded.

"Good," Gig said. "This should go quick. See the guy outside—Mikey P. He knows you want a quick tour and some time with the girls. Tell him you're doing the Columbus run and he'll get you set up. Cool?"

"Yup, no problem."

Tavon followed them out, his mind racing.

Mikey P., a huge guy that looked like a black Captain America, quickly walked Rubio and the others around the interior of the mall, showing off the highlights. The old Sears on the eastern side of the mall was huge—in fact, the auto parts area was just one small part. He'd only ever seen that auto service area. Turns out they used the rest for storage. They had a shooting range near where the old theater used to be, along with an ammunition and weapon service shop.

Rubio whistled under his breath. "Wow."

Mikey P. continued. "Back that way is the old Rike's—nothing much down there except the old Gap and Banana Republic, where we keep folks we need to hang on to. Some contractors broke them up into a bunch of cells. Good sturdy locks. Once in a while we need a place to hold folks, right?"

They were ramping up production, using a large portion of the old JCPenney. It had been separated into "clean rooms" with floor-to-ceiling plastic sheeting. Noxious fumes from the production spaces were vented through pipes that ran up and out through the roof of the store. The production lines ran twenty-four hours a day, churning out product for half of the Midwest.

They continued walking and ended the tour at the Harem. It was an old Lane Bryant and, inside, the lights were dimmed. Tavon could see beds and couches spread around a group of TVs. Some guys were playing video games on one of the televisions, while on another, a man and woman moved under a sheet. The woman looked drugged. Tavon could hear yelling, followed by a slapping sound.

"You coming?"

Rubio and Slug were headed in. Tavon shook his head. "Nah, I'll pass."

"Whatever, man," Slug said, shaking his head, and they turned and disappeared into the dark store.

Tavon wandered the mall, killing time and thinking about Talisa. A half-hour later, he saw Slug and Rubio come out and they met up with Mikey P. again near the JCPenney. Other delivery crews were picking up product and meeting with handlers to find out where the stuff went and if payment was due. Tavon saw at least two other groups, picking up and dropping off.

Tavon didn't pay much attention. He was still thinking about Talisa and those women the Northsiders had for "entertainment." It didn't sit well with him.

For the second delivery of the day, Rubio collected three hefty packages of coke, one for each Civic, to deliver to a location in Columbus. Back in their cars, Tavon fell in behind the other Civics and followed them without much thought. His mind was on what would happen to Talisa's attackers. Thinking about them being "dealt with," thinking about the opportunity for him to watch. Once again, the Northsiders were taking care of their own.

Rubio and Slug handled the Columbus drop while Tavon stayed outside with the cars. It was not a club this time but what looked like an abandoned house in a seedy residential neighborhood of southern

Columbus. It reminded him of the house on Eckhart Street. While he was waiting, he saw another car pull up and stop outside the home. Four men got out. Tavon recognized two of them from the Salem Mall. Hitters, sent in to take out rivals. One of them scanned the parking lot and gave Tavon a casual wave as the other three stood around the open trunk of a car. Tavon didn't need to be a genius to figure out what was going on—they were picking out weapons.

He breathed a sigh of relief when Slug and Rubio came out a few moments later, passing the hit crew and exchanging nods before getting into their Civics. As the trio departed, Tavon strained to get look in his rearview mirror. He saw the hit crew approach the house before it passed out of his sight.

CHAPTER 32
Working Hard

It was Friday morning at 8:42 a.m., and Frank Harper was sitting at his desk at work, clean-shaven and ready for duty, just like a good drone. Murray and Collier weren't even in yet. How was that for being punctual?

Murray usually ran late on Fridays for some reason, and Frank had forgotten. Lately Frank had been coming in at weird times, all dictated by the whims of his dosage the night before. Last night, after getting home and processing the strange conversation he'd had with his boss, Frank had come to a realization. Oxy wasn't the problem. He was the problem. Frank knew that he was restless and conflicted about his job at the ABI. Heading off to Ohio and getting involved in exciting cases would have that effect on anyone who was ostensibly retired. It made perfect sense.

What Frank needed to do was get excited about the work he was doing, not wander off in search of excitement. The ABI needed him and these cases needed him. Frank knew he was probably the smartest investigator around, and the victims trapped inside the brown folders on his desk deserved his attention. They needed the smart Frank, the alert and awake Frank.

Now he was at his desk, wired and ready to work. Frank couldn't stop cold turkey—didn't want to. Frank liked the Frank with Oxy in the mix. Most of the time, it made him smarter, calmer, better.

Frank had Googled it last night and found that one fourth of a tablet was enough to keep a high most of the time without the worst of the effects. It was called a "maintenance dose," just enough to keep him happy and content, spread out over enough time for it to not trigger withdrawal. Last night and this morning he'd tried one fourth of a pill, and it seemed to work better. He felt awake and alive, but without the shaking hands. Maybe this would keep the blackouts away. And the webpage said that, after that, he could taper off over time.

Maintenance dose. That sounded good. Sounded like he was taking care of business, taking care of himself. It would also stretch out his stash for a long time.

Frank set aside his coffee—some nasty swill from a fast food restaurant. Not nearly good enough to be called "premium coffee," as the cup suggested. Premium coffee, in his mind, came with beignets and a sidewalk view in New Orleans.

Frank dug back into a case from yesterday, a quadruple homicide. Maybe Collier would lift the suspension if Frank closed a case or two. Or maybe Frank should just take the two weeks off and head to Ohio. It seemed the more he thought about the Washingtons, the angrier he got. Maybe, if he headed north, Frank could track down the people responsible.

CHAPTER 33
Time to Confess

Jake had no idea what to do.

The Dayton PD was still calling regularly with updates on the burned house and the homicide investigation. And where earlier he'd been glad to hear from them, and glad to know someone was working the case, now he was actively lying to them.

They called again on Friday morning for more questions about the Washingtons—how Jake found them, how long they rented from him, etc. It was the same questions, over and over, but by different people. He always directed them back to the original police report he'd given the night of the fire, and the interview the next day.

Jake was careful not to lie. But the family wasn't dead. He'd moved them to a nice hotel in Columbus. Troy was just too close, so he'd convinced them to move. On the drive, Markeys told Jake the story again, but in more detail this time. Markeys had heard the gangbangers outside the house the night of the fire. He'd already been on edge and couldn't sleep. The Northsiders had been there twice in the previous twenty-four hours, and Markeys had gotten mad and called the cops to complain. Who knew what kind of shitstorm that would start, so Markeys was already awake when he heard the three low rumbles of the Civics approaching the house.

Markeys had already packed a couple bags and put them by the front door, just in case. After seeing the Northsiders park up the street and gas cans being removed from the trunks of their cars, Markeys knew what was coming. He'd gotten Denise and Noah downstairs, keeping them quiet, then grabbed their bag from the front door, taking care to avoid the windows. He'd heard the chain being applied to the doors. Once the fire began flickering out on the front lawn, Markeys used his baseball bat to pry open the back door.

After that, they'd run out, carrying their baby and their bags, and disappeared down the dark alley that ran behind their home. They walked six blocks in the night and caught a bus to a nearby hotel.

Jake had gotten them set up in the hotel in Columbus and driven home in silence. Now, as he paced his house, nervous. He was lying by omission, but the Washingtons were adamant—no one could know where they were. They were scared for their lives.

What if something happened to them now? What if the gang members tracked them down and killed them? Would Jake be held accountable? Jake had to talk to someone. The cops in Dayton seemed untrustworthy. Frank Harper? No way—he'd gotten them all into this mess. The local Cooper's Mill cops? He wasn't sure. Could they be trusted? And were they obligated to tell the Dayton cops?

Jake had no idea. But he knew he needed to talk to someone. Jake needed advice, and had a sudden thought—Rosie. She might be able to help. She was smart and had a great head on her shoulders. She could at least listen to him and keep his secret. And more importantly, give him advice on how to proceed.

But they'd never—he'd never had a conversation longer than three or four minutes with her.

He dialed the number from memory before he had a chance to chicken out.

"Ricky's," a familiar voice yelled over the din in the background.

Crap, what was he thinking? It was Friday right before lunch and she was probably slammed.

"Hi, is Rosie there?"

"You got her. Can you speak up?"

"Yes, sorry," Jake said louder. "Rosie, it's Jake. You guys slammed?"

"Not too bad," she said. "Hang on." Jake heard the phone being set down, then another extension picked up and the original phone hung up. "Nah, just some loud guys talking about the election. It's still six months away, and these guys are already worked up. So, whatcha need?"

Suddenly he was incredibly nervous. This was a mistake. She couldn't help him, and would think he was a coward for asking for help.

He decided to plow on anyway.

"I've got a situation. Well, I'm kinda worried about something. Something big. And I need to talk to someone about it." It all sounded so vague when you said it out loud.

"Um…okay," she answered. "Sounds like an excuse, but I'll bite. What is it?"

"Can we talk in person? Have you eaten yet?" He looked at the clock on the wall—it was nearly noon—and rolled his eyes. Of course she'd probably eaten ahead of her lunch rush—

"I could eat," she said. "And you're buying. O'Shaughnessy's. Ten minutes?"

"Yes," he said, hoping he didn't sound too desperate. "Thank you. See you there. And thanks."

"No prob," she said and hung up.

Jake hung up the phone. Rosie was strange, so casual and friendly. Did that mean she liked him, or was it just a by-product of her co-owning one of the most popular bars in town? Of course barmaids and waitresses were nice. They wanted you to think they liked you. That's how they made their tips, he assumed.

Jake pulled on his coat, careful with his arm for once, and left his house, locking up behind him. O'Shaughnessy's was on the corner of Second and Main—he could see the restaurant awnings from the front porch of his house.

He arrived a minute later and spotted Rosie seated at one of the five tall tables that ran along the exposed brick wall that ran the length of the building opposite the long, wooden bar. There were already two men standing by Rosie's table—she looked amazing in her T-shirt and jacket and jeans. She always drew attention, no matter where she went.

She turned and smiled when she recognized Jake, waving him over. As he walked up to the table, the other two men left. They both looked dejected.

"Thanks for meeting me," he said, sitting down.

"Wow, that sounded formal," she said, making a serious face. "Are we about to discuss international monetary policy, Mr. Delancy?" She smiled and waved at the bartender, putting up two fingers. Seconds later, two cold bottles of beer appeared at the table, delivered by Spence, the bartender.

"Sorry, I don't think I'm going to be very good company," he said, picking up his bottle and sipping at it.

She started to make another joke and then stopped and looked at him. "Hey, seriously. Are you okay?"

He nodded, setting the beer down. "I've gotten myself into a situation, and I don't know what to do."

"Are you pregnant?"

Jake shot her a look and felt a smile on his face for the first time in days. "No, nothing like that." Jake took a deep breath and started talking. As weird as the situation was, he liked talking to her about it. She asked good questions and paid attention. She was free with her reactions, something Jake appreciated. He hated it when he was talking to someone and you couldn't tell what they were thinking.

"Geez," she said, sitting back as their food was delivered. While Jake had been talking, she'd ordered them some food and was now picking at a plate of waffle fries. "That's wild."

Jake nodded as he watched Spence head back toward the bar.

"I know," he said. While he'd been talking, he'd slowly peeled the label off his wet bottle of beer. "I just don't know what to do."

Rosie squirted some ketchup on the edge of the plate and dipped a waffle fry in it, then sipped her beer. "Well, the way I see it, you've got two options."

He waited, but she didn't say anything. "What are they?"

She looked around and then leaned in closer, conspiratorially. "You could tell King. He's a good sort, and can keep a secret. Last year, he kept a lid on things when Charlie went missing. He was smart and careful—my sister said he would have figured it out a lot sooner if it hadn't been an inside job."

"I don't know," he said. "Chief King was completely fooled. Doesn't that speak to his intelligence?"

She shook her head, and Jake noticed how the long strands of her blonde hair fell on her shoulders. She was wearing a silly knit cap that looked great on her. "Nah, he's a smart guy. It was just that the other guy was great at pretending to be someone he wasn't."

"Two options, you said," he repeated. "I'm guessing the other one is to call Frank Harper?"

"No, I wouldn't do that," she said while shaking her head. Rosie's hair moved in a way that was very distracting to Jake. "I wouldn't tell him a thing. No, your other option is to tell no one. Except me, of course."

He was confused. "Um, why?"

She leaned closer. "Then you'd have to keep calling me to talk about it."

He was confused and then understood and felt flushed. "Oh boy," he said again, sounding like a five-year old. "It wasn't...that wasn't why I called. Seriously, I just needed someone to talk to. You're always so flirty with everyone—"

It was out of his mouth before he could stop it.

"What?" She made a face, leering at him. "Flirty? Are you saying I'm some kind of slut or something?"

Jake started to panic and put his hands up and nearly knocked the beer off the table. "Oh, no, I'm sorry. I didn't mean anything like that. I'm not saying you're flirty...I just meant that you're so nice to people, and you're nice to me. And I would love to hang out but I can never tell if you're flirting with me or what is going on."

She stood, angry. "I'm not a slut, Jake Delancy," she said forcefully. "I'm not flirty, not with everyone."

"I'm not saying that," he said. "I just wanted to talk to you. You're the only person I wanted to talk to about this," he said, scrambling for words. "It's just that...in the past, sometimes it seemed like you wanted to hang out, and then I'd see you chatting with other guys and it seemed the same with them—"

She was taller now, standing, and she stepped closer. She smelled good. "Excuse me? I might be a tad flirty with a few people sometimes, but there is a difference. I tend to be friendly and happy most of the time."

"No, it's my fault," he said. Leaning over him, she was somehow beautiful and angry and scary all at the same time. "I just like talking to you."

She nodded.

"Good, me too. And there's a big difference between being flirty and hitting on someone." She leaned over and kissed him, full on the mouth. The kiss lasted at least a week, it seemed, and then she pulled away, smiling. "I don't hit on everyone," she said quietly. "I flirt with people I like. And I am now officially flirting with you, in case you can't tell."

He smiled and put an arm around her, pulling her close. "Good," he said, and kissed her back.

Chapter 34
Suspended

"Okay, I'm heading out," Frank said, standing in Collier's doorway. The maintenance dose had kept him going all day, balanced and even.

His boss looked up, then waved him in. Frank was a little disappointed that Collier hadn't dropped by his desk at some point during the day, but Frank sat down. This was it—Collier had probably wanted Frank to put in a full day's work before canceling the suspension.

"Good, good," Collier said. "Have you given any more thought to what I said yesterday afternoon?"

"Which part?"

Collier smiled. "I want you to be happy here, Frank. I mean that. I might pick on you and Murray sometimes, but I'm just trying to create a work environment where success is rewarded and failure is not," he said, emphasizing the last few words and raising his voice so that Murray could hear it as well. "But if you're not happy, we're not happy."

Frank nodded. He'd hoped Collier would cancel the suspension, but it sounded like it was still on. "I do have a few things I need to take care of, and I'd enjoy another visit to see my daughter," he said. "That's what I was planning—if the suspension stands." He let the words hang out there for a moment, giving Collier another opportunity to change his mind.

"I think that would be good for you, Frank," Collier said. "Take some time with your daughter. See if you miss this place," he said, pointing at the door.

Frank stood, unsure of how to proceed, but Collier didn't seem to notice. "Okay, I'll let you know."

"Thanks," Collier said, not looking up.

Frank walked out of Collier's office and back to his own desk, his hands already starting to shake. Murray had snuck out while Frank was in talking to Collier. Frank's mind raced—he hadn't brought any extra Oxy in with him and wanted one right now so bad that he felt the bile rising in his stomach.

He walked quickly to the bathroom, passing the elevator and just making it to the stall in the men's room before he threw up. The panic seized him. He needed to get out of here, get home, get his dose. Or stop at Tammy's and get alcohol on the way. It was the only place left in town that let him run a tab.

"Frank, you in here?"

He stood, startled. "Yeah, be right out."

Frank heard the door shut. He hadn't recognized the voice. He opened the stall and looked out, but there was no one there. Frank flushed and crossed to the sink and washed his hands and face and felt a little better, then pulled the bathroom door open and walked out in to the hallway.

Williams was waiting for him, leaning on the wall and checking his phone. He looked up. "You okay, man?"

Frank nodded, lying. "Yeah, something I ate."

Williams nodded and didn't acknowledge the lie. "Look, Murray called me—he's worried about you. Said you got suspended for two weeks. That's not true, is it?"

"Yeah."

"Hmm."

"Collier doesn't appreciate it when I don't show up for work."

Williams whistled under his breath. "What you gonna do?"

"Well, I was hoping he might be kidding, but he wasn't," Frank said, shrugging. "I think I'll head up to Ohio, see my daughter. And look into that arson case I showed you." Frank had a sudden thought. "Why don't you come along? I could use your opinion on the fire." Suddenly, Frank didn't want to go alone. The blackouts were scaring him. What if he had one while driving? Would he wake up in Cooper's Mill, or at the bottom of a ravine with two broken legs? With Williams along, Frank might have a better chance of controlling his urges.

Williams thought about it. "Hmm. That's an interesting idea, but I can't take the time off. I got that cruise coming up this summer."

Frank nodded. It was a dumb idea anyway. "Okay, just thought I'd ask."

Williams nodded. "Hey, lay off the booze for these two weeks, okay? You're looking pretty rough lately."

It was literally the first time Williams had ever asked Frank to do anything. He was the closest thing Frank had to a friend, and now the man was begging Frank to get on the wagon, at least for a few days. He didn't know what else to say, so he nodded and patted Williams on the shoulder as he walked away.

CHAPTER 35
Production Labs

Friday was a busy afternoon and evening for Tavon and his boys. The trio was tasked with accompanying a huge semi down to Cincinnati. They navigated the traffic and driven in a group, one ahead of the truck and one behind, and the third, usually Tavon, trailing by a half mile, watching for surveillance.

The truck made its way to the southern edge of the city in good time, ending up at a dock-side warehouse surrounded by other unmarked warehouses that overlooked the river near the Bengals stadium and downtown Cincinnati. Tavon watched workers unload twenty wooden crates at the loading dock. Each of wooden crates was big enough to hold two refrigerators, and each was unloaded separately by forklift. Whatever the Northsiders were delivering, it was big.

After Friday's delivery, they all returned to the Salem Mall to celebrate. What they were celebrating, Tavon didn't ask. It was weird, getting invited to the mall twice in the past week. Rubio said they were getting to be "insiders" and to go with the flow. But watching Rubio and Slug wander off to the Harem to abuse those imprisoned women made him sick. Tavon kept his opinions to himself.

He wandered up to the drug production area and watched the workers. They had laboratories for meth and MDMA production, which shared space with coke and heroin prep rooms, where the product was cut and repackaged for street use. In other smaller labs, the gang worked to create counterfeit versions of over-the-counter drugs.

It all looked like a real-life episode of *Breaking Bad*, but on a much larger scale: individual clean rooms made of plastic sheeting hung from the ceiling, creating a dozen sealed off spaces. Inside, tired-looking men and women in gloves and masks labored over boiling pots and long metallic tables, creating products out of chemicals. Others were purifying product or packaging it for sale or using hand trucks to carry boxes of products out to the loading dock on the west side of the mall.

Gig found him and they chatted for a while as they watched the men and women work. Gig didn't pressure him to visit the Harem; instead, they talked about the production process. Gig walked Tavon through the products they were making on-site or preparing for sale: cocaine and heroin for local distribution; MDMA, better known as Molly or ecstasy; and fentanyl, the new synthetic drug that Tavon had only just started hearing about. It was an opioid added to heroin that make the drug even more addictive.

"You heard of flakka?"

Tavon wasn't sure. "Maybe. Something new out of Florida?"

Gig nodded, pointing at one of the smaller labs off to one side of the JCPenney. "It's a synthetic marijuana. They call it the 'zombie' drug. Starting to get popular, so we're starting to make it so we don't have to buy it from Mexico."

Tavon listened, wondering how many lives the products in this room would destroy. He kept his opinions to himself, though, and pointed out a few simple cost-saving ideas right off the bat to appear helpful. Tavon needed to stay on Gig's good side.

CHAPTER 36
The Drive Up

A few hours later, Frank bundled up some dirty clothes into his raggedy suitcase, grabbed his bag of toiletries and "medicine," and headed north.

He'd decided to get to Ohio as quickly as possible by driving up Friday evening. It was a seven-hour drive in the dark, but Frank preferred driving at night. With the Oxy, it was no big deal—he'd be awake and alert the whole time with no issues. But it would make for a short night. Even if he got in around 2:00 or 2:30 a.m., it would still mean a long nighttime drive. Frank didn't mind—he was alone with his jazz and blues CDs and his thoughts.

The trip in his old Camaro, carrying him through Louisville and Cincinnati and finally through Dayton, passed uneventfully. The old car drove well, smoothly purring through the night. Frank was wide awake—he'd taken a fourth of an Oxy around 6:00 p.m. and took another at midnight. He was good to go. Maintenance dose.

Frank spent most of the drive thinking about the Washington family. Thinking about what he'd said to them and what he'd said to that gangbanger in the strip club.

He got in around 2:00 a.m. He'd kept the pedal down the whole way. That, along with the Waze app on his phone, which showed him traffic conditions and the recent locations of police cars and speed traps, let him fly.

Frank exited the highway at Cooper's Mill and saw the familiar sights—the Honda dealership, the sign pointing to the 'Downtown Historical District,' the fast food joints clustered around the exit. He smiled, thinking about his last trip up a month ago—he hadn't expected to be back so soon.

Neither had other people. He'd called ahead to get a room, and also spoken to Laura. She seemed surprised at the suddenness of the trip, but when he explained about the Washington family, she understood.

Laura was giving him those one-word sentences that meant she was ticked off at him, probably because he hadn't returned several of her calls. And telling her the truth—most nights he was passed out—wouldn't go over well. Frank had also called Jake and Chief King, but they hadn't picked up. He left messages with both. Maybe people didn't miss him as much as he missed them.

He pulled the Camaro into the snowy parking lot at the Vacation Inn, passing the squat outline of the darkened Tip Top Diner and wondering how early they opened.

Frank climbed from the car and gathered his belongings and headed inside. He woke the dozing kid at the front desk. For some reason, it was always the same young man working when Frank came in. The kid sounded like a rat, but he got Frank squared away with a room on the second floor.

Once inside, Frank went to the windows first. This room faced to the south, and he could see a massive snow-covered field that lined the highway to his left. Together, the road and the field stretched off into the cold darkness.

He unpacked a few items before showering. It was his first shower in a while and it felt good just standing under the hot water. Frank needed to make an early start if he was going to talk to everyone he needed to. Someone had to be looking into the arson investigation.

Later, when he was dry and dressed for bed, Frank stood by the window and stared out at the blustery night sky. Wind blew from right to left, carving patterns in the snowy field. He left the curtains open for the sunlight to wake him. He watched the flakes fall and skitter across the glass and wondered what the hell he was doing in Ohio.

CHAPTER 37
Recruiting

Early Saturday morning, Tavon met up with Rubio and Slug again. Lately their schedule had been crazy: deliveries every day, sometimes twice a day. Today they were assisting with recruitment, showing off the three Civics to interested youths to gather more recruits for Sharps and Bones, two members in charge of growing the Northsiders' ranks. Tavon answered questions about the cars and let some of the kids sit in the driver's seat. A few got to rev up the engines.

New recruits were pouring in—with other gangs being eliminated, plenty of people were lining up to join. Kids loved the idea of belonging to something, and making money helped. Times were hard, especially in places like Dayton. Employment was down, and jobs and money were harder and harder to come by.

It was no wonder the lure of gang life was so powerful, especially now that the Northsiders were on a roll. Everyone wanted to be on the winning team. Tavon could see the allure—it had drawn him in as well. It felt good to be part of a group. And, in a break from tradition, the Northsiders were accepting members from rival gangs. The Dragon had decreed that all were welcome, following a little-known rule with the Italian mafias that allowed other "made" men to switch allegiances. Of course, those from other gangs had to "buy" their way in, proving their worth—and loyalty—by carrying out specific jobs.

In the new Northsiders, everyone was welcome. There was plenty of money to go around.

CHAPTER 38
Gang-Related

Frank got an early start Saturday morning. Something about being back in Cooper's Mill filled him with energy. It was either that or the Oxy he'd washed down.

Breakfast was at the Tip Top Diner, as usual. The ladies remembered him and squealed when he walked in. He thought about calling Laura to let her know he had arrived, but it was still early.

Instead, he headed to the Cooper's Mill Police Department, but was disappointed: no active members were working today, and no one was scheduled to be in until Monday. Only Lola, the receptionist, was there, and she was only in until noon when her shift ended. They had the front desk manned every day from nine to five, even on weekends, but all the police officers on duty Saturday and Sunday were busy out on patrol.

Frank asked Lola to have Chief King call him. And, seeing no one else was around to discuss the case, he left.

Frustrated, he turned the Camaro south. He thought he might have trouble finding the exact location, but it was seared into his brain. When he made the last turn, Frank saw the blackened hole where the house once stood and his hands started to shake. He needed to hold it together, at least long enough to walk the crime scene and get a sense of what had happened.

Frank parked his car on the street and walked up the driveway. They'd had a car, right? He couldn't remember. He walked up the narrow walk to where the front porch had been. The whole place smelled like a campfire. Fires were weird—much of the house had been destroyed, but there were still portions that seemed undamaged. In one corner, a wall stood and he could see the wooden studs and drywall. A brick fireplace remained in another corner, the chimney ending awkwardly half-way up.

He stopped where the front door would have been and studied the footprint of the house. It looked like it had burned quickly. He wasn't an expert, like Williams, but he'd been involved in enough homicides by fire to know what to look for. The remnants of the second floor lay scattered atop what was left of the first floor. Snow-covered wooden beams and chunks of broken ceiling littered the lumpy, melted carpet.

Frank stepped off the porch and circled the house, avoiding the large patches of dirty ice and looking for anything out of the ordinary. The back door led to a small fenced backyard, the far gate standing open. The houses on either side had been damaged by the fire. Frank continued around the perimeter of the house, feeling like a criminal returning to the scene of the crime.

What did he expect to find here? The family, trapped under a loose piece of drywall, miraculously safe and sound? Coming here was pointless, other than allowing him to put a physical description to the tragedy.

The other thing that struck him was the lack of sound. Other than the muted sounds of the neighborhood around him, the burned-out remains of the house were as silent as a tomb.

Frank shook his head and walked back out to the street. With all the snow and ice, it was impossible to tell anything about how the fire started or spread, other than what Jake had told him that first night over the phone.

There was nothing here for him.

He started up the Camaro and left, driving the neighborhood, looking. There were nicer neighborhoods and run-down ones, and street after street of homes with families and used cars in the driveways. Not a great place to live, or grow up, but not as bad as what he remembered of Baton Rouge. If the gangs—and the cops—would just leave these people alone, they'd probably be fine.

On one street, he found a group of officers and three squad cars, lights spinning lazily in the early morning cold. He parked nearby and walked up, greeting a cop standing near a roped-off portion of the snowy street. On the pavement, Frank could see part of a chalk outline, white lines on dark pavement. At the far end of the sidewalk, another cop was putting down those little yellow plastic tents, the ones with the numbers on them, and taking pictures. She was marking the location of several bullet casings.

"Can I help you?" the male officer said.

Frank nodded. "Yeah, just wanted to talk to someone about that house fire over on Eckhart."

The cop nodded and took out his notepad. It seemed every cop carried the same one, a thin pad designed to fit in the back pocket of their uniform. He took down Frank's information but looked up when Frank gave his address in Birmingham.

"Yeah, I know," Frank said. "I'm just in town to help out with a situation."

"You a cop?"

"Used to be. Helped out the Cooper's Mill PD on a couple things last year."

"P.I.?"

"Nope, not yet."

The cop sighed, putting away her notepad. "Well, that fire's being worked by the DAHTF, so they're the ones you want to talk to."

Frank nodded and glanced at the chalk outline. "Will do. Drive-by?"

"Yeah," the cop said. "Maybe."

Frank looked at the arrangement of the scene. "The bullet casings should be in the street. If they came from a car. Looks like your shooter was on the sidewalk, shooting out into the street."

The cop looked at him and smiled. "Yeah, that's probably right."

Frank waited for him to say more, but an awkward silence fell between them. Frank let it lie, waiting for the cop to fill it. People hated silent moments. But the cop didn't take the bait. Frank looked around at the rest of the scene and got the hint.

"Okay, well, thank you," he said, walking off. He got back in his car and noticed the cop had his notepad out again, looking at Frank's car. Probably getting the make and model and license.

That would be another reason to be an official private investigator. If he was going to continue poking his nose into things like this, it would be nice if he were afforded at least a modicum of respect and cooperation from the police. Telling them he was a member of the public or an "interested party" wasn't going to get him very far.

Frank started his car and drove away, stopping again two blocks over, out of sight of the police. He Googled the address of the task force; it was located in the same building as Dayton's mayor. He should talk to them, give them his version of the events and threats that led up to the fire. He only hoped he could be helpful, though he was unsure what information he could add that the cops probably didn't already know.

But he had one more stop to make on the way.

CHAPTER 39
Stained Glass

Jake woke in a better mood than he'd been in in weeks.

His lunch yesterday with Rosie probably had something to do with it. Kissing her in the restaurant had seemed like the culmination of a long, difficult climb, one that he hadn't even realized he was making. And it had felt so natural, like they'd been dating for years.

He got up and got on with his day, still thinking about the kiss. She'd just leaned right in there, hadn't she? He smiled until he remembered his conundrum with the Washington family.

He walked out into the hallway and around the corner into the upstairs bath. He'd been planning on knocking down a wall between the bath and largest bedroom to make a master suite, but he just hadn't gotten around to it yet. It was always the same—his time and effort went into maintaining his other properties, or it got diverted into a hobby. He was restless, and he knew it, but that also meant being surrounded by half-finished projects.

Rosie was right—he didn't need to decide right now. No one besides Jake knew where the family was, and the hotel in Columbus was paid up for two weeks. And he'd gotten them a burner phone for emergencies.

He went downstairs, passing an ornate stained-glass window on the landing. He stopped and admired it for a second. It really looked good. He should remind himself to be more confident in the future, like with Rosie. The glass panel had taken time and effort and expense to repair, but now it looked amazing.

Jake descended the wide staircase and crossed the cold foyer. His house was a hodgepodge of finished and unfinished projects, worked on between 'real' jobs. The stairs and foyer were a perfect example: the glass was fully restored and looked beautiful, and the staircase and paneling had been meticulously refinished. But he hadn't gotten around to repairing the radiator in that room yet, so the foyer was always cold in the winter.

He made a cup of coffee in the kitchen and then walked into his dining room, another half-finished room. The paneling looked great, but instead of a light or chandelier over the wide table, nothing hung from the ceiling but a thick wad of wires. He had several floor lamps standing around the perimeter of the room, all hooked to one switch that hung from the south wall, attached only with a thick piece of electrical tape.

A large white-board, hung on the east wall in his dining room, listed his ongoing personal and house projects. Half the board was taken up with punch lists of things to be repaired or replaced in the old house. He'd bought the place two years ago with the idea of flipping it. The idea had been to buy a new place once a year and work on it between paid projects.

Below the white board was a wide sideboard stacked with folders and files from his past and current paid projects and jobs for other people. Those were the jobs that brought money in, so those took priority. But he was free this Saturday, and he was excited to tackle a few jobs around the house. The list had sat, mostly ignored, but now he felt a sense of urgency. The living room was in good shape, as was the kitchen. But other parts, like the downstairs bathroom, were a complete mess. The water wasn't even running in some parts of the house. Things needed to be tidier around here if he was ever going to invite Rosie back here for a nightcap.

CHAPTER 40
Impromptu Breakfast

There was a knock at her door. Hawkins, not expecting anyone, was wearing nothing but her robe. She found her piece and stood beside the door.

"Who's there?"

"It's me."

She knew that voice and smiled, pulling the door open.

"You're not supposed to be here, sir," she said. "You're my super-hairy boss. Am I in trouble?"

Sergeant Roget smiled back. He seemed to be in a better mood today. "Yeah, busted. I order you to let me in."

She blocked the door. "You need a warrant."

"I'll give you my warrant," he said, reaching into his front pocket. "I think I have it right here…"

"Oh, you're nasty," she said, standing aside and letting him in. "I'm just finishing a late breakfast—want some coffee?"

"Yeah, that would be nice."

He followed her into the kitchen. Her apartment was on the smallish side and the kitchen was the best room, airy and bright in the mornings. Roget took a seat at the table in the corner, where her breakfast was already laid out, half finished.

"I don't want to interrupt," he said, pointing at her food. "Go ahead and finish. Coffee?"

She nodded and sat, pointing at the pot. "It's hot."

They hadn't been dating long and were still working through the awkward phase of being in each other's homes. It was weird when she was over at his place, and it was still strange when he was here. They had both been single for so long, they had their set patterns. A new person coming in was like a rock thrown into a shallow pond—the ripples and waves could be disturbing.

They could also be fun.

He made a cup of coffee, searching for the sugar instead of asking. She smiled. He kept opening cabinets and drawers.

"Over the sink," she said, nibbling at her eggs and toast.

"Thanks."

He came over and sat at the small table and his presence in her kitchen was cute and awkward at the same time and she loved it. It was nice having him in her space. It shook things up. She handed him part of the *Dayton Daily News*, and they read the paper together and sipped coffee and chatted about their week.

After a few minutes, she realized why he was here: he missed her. A warm feeling trickled through her, the feeling of being needed. Not as a cop, or as a fellow member of the task force, but needed for her, for who she was.

She smiled and finished her coffee. "So, any plans for the day?"

He sat back. "Oh, I don't know. As silly as it sounds, I need to go to IKEA."

"What? Really?"

"Yeah. Not like anyone really NEEDS to go to IKEA," he said with a chuckle. "But I got their catalog, and I want a new coffee table. They look like they have some nice stuff."

"Yeah, they do. Modern, classy. Not really a good fit with your apartment," she said with a grin. His place was decorated in the perennial-bachelor style, meaning it looked like every piece of furniture had come from the closing minutes of a garage sale. The couch cushions sagged, the dining room table was spotted and pitted and only had one chair. And nothing matched.

He looked up from the section of the paper he was holding. "Well, maybe it's time for a change. Want to tag along?"

She thought about it for a moment. "Yeah, that would be fun. I need to pick up a few things, too. Plus, I get to watch you shop—that should be a hoot. But I need to take a shower first. Mind waiting?"

"No, no, that's fine," going back to the paper.

She stood and cleared her dishes, then folded the hand towel and laid it on the edge of the sink. She turned to him—he was still seated at the table, reading the paper.

"Or you could join me."

He looked up and she was loosening the strip of fabric that tied the robe around her. It slipped from her shoulders and in a second she was naked.

He smiled and set down his coffee.

CHAPTER 41
Meeting at Riley's

Saturday afternoon, the trio met Gig at Riley's. Inside, contractors were rewiring the ceiling while a number of customers watched one of the dancers gyrate on the raised dance floor above them.

"New speaker system," Gig said when they asked about the contractors. "Gonna be bangin'."

Slug returned with their drinks and they started talking, leaning close to be heard over the booming dance music.

"Thanks for meeting me. Just wanted to see how that recruitment went today," Gig said.

"Good," Rubio said. "We followed Sharps and ended up doing six different locations. He probably got thirty or forty kids interested."

Gig nodded, then looked at Tavon. "Good, that sounds good. Hey, Tavon, I wanted you to know that we're still planning on that thing we talked about for your sister."

Tavon gulped, unsure if he should say anything. Instead, he just nodded.

"But things are going sideways right now," Gig said. "The Dragon called an emergency meeting for tonight—the Council is going to be there, along with me and all the other crew leaders. I'm not sure what's coming, but something big. So that other thing, for you, that's gonna have to wait a week or two."

Tavon nodded again, unsure of what to say. But it was clear that Gig wanted an answer. "That's fine."

"How's she doing?"

"Better. I'm paying the doctor bills to help out."

Gig nodded and reached into his pocket and fished around, taking out a wad of cash. He counted off $2,000 and handed it to Tavon. "Here. That should help."

Tavon pocketed the money. "Thanks."

"No prob," Gig said, turning back to the others. "Okay, keep on your toes—over the next week or so, things are gonna get crazy. Don't be surprised if we send you on more runs out of the area. Oh, and if I call or text any of you and say 'Head to Vegas,' gather your crew and lay low for a while."

They covered a few more items, including their schedule for the next few days. Gig said he'd let them know about the meeting tonight and if anything came out of it for them. Rubio was set up to make a large pickup on Sunday and then the three of them were scheduled to make another delivery to Piqua Sunday night. Gig also gave Tavon another stack of financials to go through, the third such stack this week.

The meeting broke up and Gig left. Rubio and Slug went to watch the dancers and drink even though it was barely noon. Tavon found his normal spot at the bar and was just digging into the stack of financials when a white guy walked into the club.

It was the old man from last month.

He came in, blinking at the change in light. It was a bright day outside, but they kept it dark in the club. The man looked over and spotted Tavon at the bar immediately.

Christ.

Gig had mentioned some stuff about him but Tavon had forgotten the details. Why was he back?

"Hey, buddy," the old guy said, sitting down at the barstool next to him and greeting Tavon like an old friend. "How you been?" he said without a smile. "You remember me? 'Cause I sure as heckfire remember you." The guy waved the bartender over and ordered a bourbon.

Tavon looked at him.

When it arrived, the scrawny old guy sipped at the bourbon before turning to Tavon.

"So, you guys burned that house down," he said matter-of-factly. "Killed that family, right? Burned 'em alive. Great work," he said, then lowered his voice. "I should shoot you right here."

Tavon felt his eyes go wide.

"Look, old man, I don't know who you are, or what you're talking about."

"Yeah," the man said, looking straight ahead and sipping at his glass. "You guys are all tough in groups. Get you alone, and you get forgetful. I'm Frank, by the way. Frank Harper. And I liked that family. Now, burning them alive—was that your idea?"

Tavon suddenly wanted to be anywhere but here. He knew to keep his cool, but good God he wasn't ready to deal with this crazy old guy today. They had enough going on—

"Thinking up an answer," the guy said, turning to Tavon. "That's nice. The cops will think it's nice, too. Should we go see them? I was just talking to a group of them. They're very interested in who torched that house. Your friends must be here. I saw all your cute little matching cars in the lot. We can all go for a chat together."

"Look, cop, we're all paid up," Tavon said quietly. "No need to come in here and try to shake us down for more cash."

The man shook his head and laughed. He actually laughed. "I don't care about your payoffs. Just you. And your buddies."

Tavon looked at him, waiting. The man's crazy eyes came to rest on the papers on the counter.

"And I'm interested in your 'gang,' the Northsiders. Inventive name there. What's this stuff?" The old man was looking at Tavon's sheets and reached to pick one up. Tavon snatched it away. In a flash, the old man was holding Tavon's arm in a tight grip.

"You don't want to do that," Tavon said, glancing around.

"Oh, no, it's fine," the old man said. "It's okay," he said, squeezing harder. "I can even do this," he said as he twisted Tavon's arm to the point of pain. It was only a slight movement, one of a fraction of an inch, but it somehow brought a tear to Tavon's eye. All the while, the old man was smiling. Tavon saw a familiar look in his eyes.

"You high, old man? Come around to see Stimpy for more Oxy? He's got a stash—"

The grip on his arm tightened.

"Stand up and follow me outside."

"Nah, I don't think that's gonna happen," a voice said from behind them.

Tavon turned and looked. Rubio and Slug were standing behind the old man. Rubio had a gun out, pressed against the old man's back.

The old man looked and the grip on Tavon's arm loosened by a fraction.

"Okay, old man, let's go." Rubio nodded, indicating he should stand up.

He seemed to think about it for a second, then smiled and let go of Tavon, reaching for his drink. He lifted it, finishing the bourbon and ignoring Rubio for a moment, then slowly stood.

"That stuff is expensive," the old man said, smiling. "Can't waste it."

Rubio led him outside, Slug and Tavon following close behind.

"Okay, okay," Harper said, backing away and putting his hands up. He looked at the three of them, and Tavon saw that Slug had his gun out now as well. But Harper didn't have that nervous look most people got when you pointed a gun at them.

To Tavon, the old man looked bored.

Tavon could also see a holster peeking out from inside the man's jacket and the butt of a gun. Would he draw on them?

Was this the moment where Tavon's life ended?

The guy was a cop. That much Tavon remembered. He glanced around and saw the rusty old Camaro—he remembered that, too. It was a mean-looking car, in good shape except for the wide patch of rust that spread across the hood like a smear. With the right equipment and some better tires, it could be a car to be reckoned with.

As it was, Tavon could outrace him in any of the Civics, even without the nitrous.

"You best be on your way," Rubio said. The gun was steady in his hands. "And don't come around here no more." The three of them were facing the old man, and Tavon got the sudden impression they were in some stupid western. Like they were going to have a gunfight in the parking lot of a strip club.

Tavon could tell the old man was trying to decide what to do. He wasn't a cop anymore, Tavon remembered. The guy was retired or something, but once a cop, always a cop.

After a long moment, Harper smiled and Tavon knew he'd made his choice. "Okay, no problem," the cop said, lowering his hands. He started backing towards the Camaro. "You guys—just remember, they were a nice family. With a kid. And you killed them. For what? Territory? Power?"

"Shut up, old man," Tavon sputtered suddenly. He didn't need more guilt.

Slug narrowed his eyes while following Harper with his gun. He always held it sideways, like they did in the movies. "Don't make me shoot you, old man."

Harper smiled and backed up against his car, then unlocked it and climbed in. He looked at Tavon for a second before starting the car, and Tavon wondered if he'd try to run them over. Tavon noted that the engine purred like it had been well maintained, possibly rebuilt.

The old man floored it, sending snow and grit and rocks up from the parking lot, spraying the three of them as he backed out, letting his growling engine have the last word.

Rubio and Slug ducked away, coughing. A large piece of gravel flew up and grazed Tavon's face, cutting his cheek.

By the time the snow and dust had cleared, the Camaro was gone.

Chapter 42
Nobody Home

Frank raced away from the strip club, his hands shaking.

"Christ!"

It had been childish, backing out of the parking lot like that. But it had thrown up enough snow and gravel to make the kids duck and allow Frank to get away without them taking potshots at him or his car. If they controlled the territory enough to pull guns on him in a public place and then stand in the parking lot with their guns out for everyone to see, they probably wouldn't hesitate to take out his back window. Or him, for that matter.

He drove south on Dixie Drive, assessing his options. Frank had hoped to catch one of the gangbangers alone at the strip club. Maybe question him. He'd seen all three of the matching Civics in the lot when he got there and wavered—it was a risky proposition, confronting them without backup or a warrant or anything. He couldn't even arrest them, technically.

It was probably the Oxy. Making him overconfident.

Yeah, that was it.

His mind was racing now. The gangbangers knew he was in town and asking questions. Would they make a move on him? Or Jake? It was hard to tell. They would likely go to their higher ups for direction.

Frank drove south, wending his way into Dayton and finally finding City Hall. It was a short brick building, six or seven stories tall, with large stone columns along the front flanked by concrete buildings on each side. There was no street parking, so he parked in the tall parking structure next door. It was a weekend, so the gate was up and parking was free.

A homeless guy was sleeping on the steps. Frank tried to go in, but the red front doors were locked. He knocked, but no one answered. After a minute, he only succeeded in waking the homeless guy at his feet.

"Aw, man, they closed."

Frank looked down. "This the mayor's office?"

"Yeah, man, they closed!" the man said.

Frank walked back to his car, frustrated. He Googled and found the address for the Dayton Police Department and drove over, parking in front. It was on the same street as the City Hall, two blocks down. A large sign out front read "Dayton Police Department."

Frank headed inside. It was set up like a typical police station—the lobby held a large seating area and a wide front desk for citizens to speak to officers. The place was nearly empty—only three or four people were in the lobby, and two of them looked to be asleep. There was a window for "Records" and another for "Traffic."

A young female officer was looking at him from the front desk.

"Can I help you?"

Frank walked over to the desk. "Yeah, I wanted to speak to someone with the heroin task force, if I could. I went by their office, but it was closed."

"Yeah, they're not open on the weekends. I can take your name and number and have someone call you on Monday, if that works."

Frank nodded and gave his information for the second time in two hours. "I have information about that house fire…just have them call me." He decided not to tell her about the Northsiders or his connection to the arson case. He wasn't sure if she'd see appreciate his willingness to help, or just throw in him a cell for good measure, in case he was a witness to a crime.

"No problem," she said, although she seemed curious. "What's your involvement in this, sir?"

"Oh, I was just looking into the situation for a friend," he said, keeping it vague. She looked at him like she had more questions, but at that moment the phone rang at her desk, and he took the opportunity to leave. "Thanks." He turned and left.

Frank needed to speak to someone in charge, not street cops or first-year's who were forced to man the lobby on a Saturday. Talking to the folks at the task force would be a good first step. He needed to chat with someone who knew the gang backwards and forwards.

Frank decided to head back to Cooper's Mill. He called Laura on the way, setting up breakfast in the morning. But he was getting antsy—he hadn't felt comfortable driving around with his 'medication' on him. Maybe a maintenance dose and a drink and a good meal would smooth him out.

CHAPTER 43
Timetable

Deep inside the former Salem Mall, a meeting was being called to order. Most of the council was already seated around the conference table, and Gig, arriving late, found a seat among them.

The Foot Locker served as the primary office space for all Northsiders "business." Most of the store had been reconfigured into offices, but the back quarter of the store had been turned into a large conference room. Lining the walls of the room were the relocated shoe display walls from the store, now displaying photos of members of other gangs that had been killed or captured and executed, along with rough diagrams of the other gangs' suspected organizational structures and areas of influence.

There was also a large framed photo of Mama Leonita, the head of the Luciano crime family. The Dragon idolized her, patterning the new Northsiders after her St. Louis organization, which had remained one of the most powerful crime families in the Midwest until it was destroyed by infighting. In fact, one of the two Luciano boys in charge of the family had killed the other, then himself been killed by his wife in a house fire.

They rarely all met like this. Two of the Council ran all the drug production and distribution for the gang. In doing so, they also tracked everything they could about the other gangs in Dayton and surrounding areas.

"We're sure about that?" Juice, Gig's boss, was saying to someone else. He ran distribution.

"Yup, it's all over the news, so it's gotta be true," Mr. Kingmaker answered. He was in charge of production. "On Weathers Street?"

Juice nodded. "Yeah, that's it. Their last lab. Jesus, with Fifth Street gone, it's just down to us and the North Boyz."

Another council member leaned over—the table was now nearly full, despite it being late on a Saturday evening.

"Don't forget the Triangle Gang," he said. That was Mr. Roosevelt, who oversaw the Northsiders' fledgling bookmaking and gambling ring. Most of the council members were dressed in suits, in stark contrast to the young men around the table, all dressed in jeans and T-shirts and sported varying amounts of "bling."

Mr. Kingmaker nodded as more men entered the room, filling up the table. Over twenty people sat around the table, including all seven members of the Council. Along with them, Gig and a dozen other crew leaders and higher-ups in the organization were present. Gig noticed that they all chatted quietly amongst themselves, with the gangbangers and council members keeping to themselves.

The chair at the head of the table sat empty, reserved for the leader of their group. But tonight, a conference call would serve in their stead.

At precisely 10:00 p.m., the phone began to ring.

Gig heard the voices around the table fall to a hush as Mr. Kingmaker, sitting closest to the phone, reached over and pushed a button on it. "Hello?"

"Yes, I'm here," the voice came over the speaker, sounding weird and distorted. It was impossible to tell anything about the speaker other than they could speak fluent English. "Are we ready? I'm assuming everyone is there."

"Yes, Dragon, we're all here," another of the council members spoke up. His name was Sausage and he was huge man. He wore several large rings on thick fingers that reminded Gig of little sausages. He served as *consigliere* to the Dragon and ran intelligence. Everyone always called him Sausage and now Gig knew why. "You are coming through fine."

"Good," the Dragon said. "Thank you all for coming. Please go around the table and introduce yourselves. It's rare we all get together."

Starting with Sausage, they went clockwise, introducing themselves. They were all either Council members or crew leaders. Each nodded, saying their name and place in the Northsiders' organization. Each council member ran their own part of the "business." Gig didn't realize, even as well-placed in the organization as he was, that they had branched out into transporting guns and other weapons.

When the roll call was over, Sausage leaned forward.

"That's everyone."

"Good. Okay, I know we all have other things to do, so let me get straight to the point. Because of this morning's raid on the final Fifth Street production facility, their gang has effectively been eliminated. Because the task force has just removed the last of our large competitors, we're ahead of schedule."

The others around the table looked at each other. Low murmurs surfaced as people leaned together to discuss the implications of the last task force raid.

The Dragon spoke up. "Sausage, who else is opposing us?"

The big man leaned forward. "Well, the North Boyz, really. The

Triangle Gang and Angel Face are about done—one more raid on each will close them down. And the Bowling Boyz are done."

"What about the East Dogs?" one person asked.

Sausage shook his head. "They fell in with Fifth Street, but then left town. The last five or six of them left earlier in the week, back to St. Louis, I heard," he said. When he shook his head, the extra fat around his neck jiggled.

"They still need to pay for what they did to the Lucianos," the Dragon said. "It's not relevant to our situation, but it's important to me. Send a team to St. Louis to eliminate the rest of them."

There was silence around the table. Sonny, one of the other council members, leaned forward. "Will do."

Sausage spoke up. "On the upside, we picked up a bunch of new customers from them."

The voice on the phone cut in. "Do we have an updated map?"

"Not yet," Mr. Juice said, glancing at Gig. Sometimes he had Gig help him with updating the maps.

"Okay, take care of that," the Dragon said. "The task force will soon turn their eyes to us. We have been able to deflect them well enough up to this point, but we're starting the next phase."

The room grew quiet again.

"Council, you know what comes next. Get started, and let's talk again on Monday. We need to make some progress on a few items first. Sonny?"

Gig knew Sonny ran the hitters, small squads of Northsiders that carried out the assassinations of other gang members. And, according to his introduction, he was also now running guns and explosives. Yet another lucrative market for the gang to be in.

"I'm here, boss."

"Okay, we're going to need that alternate location set up and ready, sooner than we planned." The voice on the other end of the phone hesitated, and Gig could hear the Dragon flipping pages, probably consulting his notes. "Middle of next week. We'll get the task force the information they need and plan for Thursday, the fifth." Gig saw several other people writing the date down.

"Already started. Um, how much are we talking about this?" Sonny said, glancing around the room. "Is this need-to-know? I could use more people."

"This is priority one," the Dragon said slowly, as if he wanted to make sure everyone at the table heard it. "Recruit anyone you need."

There had been a lot of changes for the gang over the last few months, and Gig was starting to see the big picture. Everyone knew they were expanding into other areas, consolidating control over geographical regions, rapidly growing the size of the organization. The Dragon was treating the gang like a business, patterning it after the old Italian mafia.

But Gig realized the Dragon had bigger plans. Once the other gangs were out of the way and they had a solid handle on the Dayton area, they would begin expanding out to Cincinnati and Columbus. That explained why his and the other crews had been making so many runs east and south.

The Dragon wanted all of southwestern Ohio. Maybe more.

The meeting ended after the Dragon handed out a few more assignments: production and distribution were to remain steady but security for both was to be increased. Prostitution and sex trafficking were to look into the Fifth Street Runners' operations to see if they could be absorbed. Recruitment was to be stepped up. And, lastly, some of Sonny's hitters were to shut down the fledgling prostitution ring in Bayline. Best of all, the Dragon promised that the days of the Dayton Area Heroin Task Force were numbered.

CHAPTER 44
Bob Evans

"Grandpa!"

Frank was waiting in the lobby of the Bob Evans and stepped outside when he saw Laura's car pull up. She saw him and waved and parked, and as soon as the car door was open and his car seat strap was off, little Jackson Powell jumped down from the car and ran full speed across the parking lot for Frank. He gathered the little kid up in his arms and hugged him.

"Hi, Grandpa! How you been?"

Frank smiled. "Good, Jackson, good. You?" He put the boy down. They chatted and waited for Laura.

"Hi, Frank," she said, smiling and hugging him. She looked good, Frank thought. Maybe the cold air made everyone look flushed and alive.

"Hi, Laura," he answered, holding her for an extra second longer than he really needed to. "Sorry I haven't been calling you back like I should," he said into her hair. It was easier to apologize if you weren't looking at the person.

She pulled away and nodded. "I'm just worried about you, that's all."

"Let's eat!" Jackson yelled, pulling at Frank's leg. "I want bacon!"

They headed inside and were soon seated. Within minutes Frank and Laura were enjoying a pot of coffee and Jackson was coloring a kid's menu.

"You're just up here to work on this case?"

Frank looked around. "Yes, and to see you guys. It's been on my mind a lot, and after Jake called me..." He trailed off and looked at Jackson.

"It's crazy," she said quietly. "And I don't really want to talk about it now," she said, making her concerns about Jackson overhearing them obvious. "But I'm glad you're up here. I'm sure the cops can use the help."

"Well, I'm not so sure about that," he said, picking up his coffee. "Yesterday was pretty much a waste."

"What happened?"

He recounted his frustrating Saturday, leaving out the confrontation with the Northsiders. "And there was no one at the task force office, so I ended up not really getting a chance to talk to anyone related to the case. I ended up having dinner alone in the bar at O'Shaughnessy's."

She smiled. "You should have called and come over."

He looked at her and then at Jackson, busy drawing. It looked like he was working on some kind of grid of dots. "Nah, I just needed to think," he said. "But thank you. How have you been?"

"Good," she said. "Better, actually. Things at work are going well. My boss is starting to give me more responsibility. And we had several stylists leave to go start their own salon up in Troy, so that was interesting."

"Trouble? Is that why they left?"

"No, no, nothing like that," she said. "Remember I told you that our boss can be slow with paying what she owes the stylists? Well, some of them got fed up and left. Banded together and started their own place. We'll see how that works out."

She went on to explain how she was helping out more around "A Cut Above," the salon in downtown Cooper's Mill. Frank loved listening to her talk, loved the way she moved her arms around as she punctuated the words, nearly knocking over her coffee when she got animated. He smiled and nodded and listened to every word with the intensity of an interview, as if this were the last conversation they would ever have.

Frank, sitting there in the Bob Evans, realized he'd never been happier. He should have seen Laura and Jackson as soon as he got to town, not put it off. Even with the dead family weighing on his conscious and the lapses in judgment he'd exhibited over the last few months and the fact that he was just asking to get killed by confronting the Northsiders on their own turf, he realized that it was all about this. This, right here. Sitting with his daughter, sipping coffee, and listening to her talk about her work. Or anything, really—she could be reading him a dictionary and he would have been happy.

The waitress came with their food, breaking the mood. But there, for one shining moment, Frank was happy. And Frank realized that for the last half-hour or so, he hadn't thought once about bourbon or what had happened at St. Bart's.

Or the Oxy.

CHAPTER 45
In Hiding

Jake drove carefully, with one eye on the rearview mirror. They were on the long, empty stretch of road between Dayton and Columbus, approaching the beltway around the latter.

"Are you okay?"

He looked over. Rosie was in the passenger seat.

"Yeah, just nervous, I guess."

She nodded, looking over at him. They were in his truck, and he suddenly realized how messy it was inside and wished he'd cleaned it. Of course, he hadn't expected her to come with him to Columbus. But once he told her about the trip, she had insisted.

"I can see that," she said. She was wearing a heavy coat and leggings and a very cute pair of boots. "You want to keep them safe, but you're worried if you're doing the right thing or not."

He nodded, looking at the road.

"So, what else can we talk about?" she asked cheerfully.

"Um...how's the bar?"

"Good," she said. "It's doing good. Times were rough there for a couple years, especially 2009. The downtown lost a few shops, as you probably know. But my business is as close to recession-proof as you can get. Ken and I are thinking about expanding, actually." Ken Meredith was her co-owner, a local who also ran the public access channel.

"Oh, really?"

"Well, you probably know we can get pretty crowded on Friday and Saturday nights."

He nodded.

"Well, I'd like to expand out the back, maybe add a patio. Like a party deck, with TVs and couches."

The exits for the beltway around Columbus came up, but Jake continued east into downtown. Traffic increased exponentially in the next few minutes as the tall buildings of the downtown loomed in front of them. "Could you use it year-round?"

"Yeah, we'd have to include heaters and all-weather furniture. Ken is worried about the zoning."

"Why?"

"People don't like the noise, obviously. We get complaints if the music is too loud after 11:00 p.m. This would probably make things worse. Even if the music is quiet, there will still be people outside talking."

"And that can lead to fights," Jake added.

"Yup," she said. They approached the downtown and she glanced over at him. "You think you're ready for this?"

"It just feels weird."

"I know."

They drove on in silence. He exited at the airport and drove to the hotel, parking in front. He had asked Markeys for an extra key so he could use the side door and avoid the lobby. Jake was wary of attracting any attention to the family. They took the elevator to the fifth floor.

Rosie led the way down the hallway from the elevator. He was more nervous than he thought. She got to the room first and knocked. He hurried to catch up.

"Why are you racing ahead?"

She smiled. "You need to get this done so we can go. I want you to take me shopping."

He was looking at her strangely when the door opened a crack. "Yes?"

Jake felt a flood of relief. "Hey, Markeys, it's me."

"Who's that with you?"

"A friend," he said, and she smiled at him and then turned to the door. "It's okay, Markeys. I'm Rosie, a friend of his. You guys doing okay?"

The door closed all the way, and Jake could hear the chain working inside. The door opened. "Yeah, yeah. Come in. Denise and Noah are at the pool."

They walked into the hotel room—it was nicely appointed, with two large beds and a separate sitting area with a flat-screen TV.

"Good, glad they're having fun," Jake said, realizing that he'd never known the little boy's name before this moment. "Everything else fine? Any trouble?"

"Nah, nah," Markeys said, sitting down on the couch and muting the TV. "Been a nice break, although we've been out for most of our meals. Hard to cook here," he said.

"Could you guys move to an extended-stay hotel?" Rosie asked Markeys, then looked at Jake. "You know, those have full kitchens. Might be nicer, depending on how long you're staying."

"Well, that's the big question, right?" Jake looked at Markeys. "When are we gonna tell the cops you're alive?"

Markeys shook his head. "The Northsiders want us dead. I don't know why, but they do."

"Or maybe they just wanted the house gone," Jake suggested. "We're not really sure about why they chased you guys out."

"They needed to make a statement," Markeys said. "That's what they kept saying— 'you guys need to get gone cause this is our house,' stuff like that. Most people are scared of them, but we weren't." He got quiet for a moment. "Guess we shoulda been. Almost got us killed."

The room was quiet for a minute. Jake didn't know what to say, and Rosie wasn't helping, sitting there smiling and looking around like she'd never seen a hotel room before.

"Anyway, I don't wanna call the cops," Markeys finally said. "I don't know how much trouble we'll be in, but I think a judge would understand. We're running for our lives here."

Rosie nodded, but Jake wasn't sure. "I hear you. I do. But I'm still worried about you. If the gang somehow finds out you're here—"

"They ain't gonna find out, unless you tell someone," Markeys said, looking at Rosie. "Don't need any more people knowing."

She nodded and looked at him. "I'm not telling anyone. Jake asked me for advice because we're really good friends," she said. Jake noticed the embellishment and tried not to smile. Was her comment just for Markeys' sake, or did she have a better opinion of their relationship than he did? Or, at least, a more hopeful one?

"We need a plan," he said, looking back at Markeys. "The cops are still calling me. And I got a message from Frank Harper—he's back in town and looking into the fire. He came up Friday night to poke around."

Markeys shook his head. "We don't want him around. Don't tell him nothing."

Jake started to say something but then closed his mouth. Markeys was right—the more people who knew the Washingtons were alive, the more trouble there would be.

"Okay, but you can't live here forever," he said. "Rosie's right. Why don't we finish out the week and move you to one of those extended-stay places next week? Saturday. Would that work? Then you'd be here five more days."

Markeys nodded. "Yeah, that would work."

"And we can go get you some groceries and stuff," Rosie added. "You gotta be sick of eating out."

They chatted for a few more minutes, working out the logistics. Rosie brought up a good point, expressing concern that going out to eat or to the pool too much might get them recognized. Jake was impressed with how helpful Rosie turned out to be. She had a knack for taking care of people, it seemed, probably from her years of getting drunk people home alive. How many people had she taken care of by arranging rides for them or getting someone to walk them home?

A few minutes later, Rosie and Jake were back in his truck.

"Thanks," he said.

"No problem. I could tell you were nervous."

"Do you think we're doing the right thing?" he asked, glancing back at the hotel in the rearview mirror. "Hiding them like this?"

"I don't see any alternative. Though, if you really want to cover your bases, you might want to talk to Chief King. Get his opinion on the matter. And then, if the shit really does hit the fan, you're covered."

That made sense, even if it felt like a betrayal of the Washingtons. "What about Frank Harper?"

"No, I'd leave him out of this."

Jake nodded.

"So, ready to take me shopping?"

He looked at her. "I thought you were kidding."

"Oh, hell no. You owe me for holding your hand in there," she said. "Let's go to that grocery we saw and pick them up some groceries. Then we're heading north to that big outdoor mall. I need new jeans."

Jake smiled and turned the truck around. He knew he would soon be buying her jeans, and he had absolutely no problem with that.

CHAPTER 46
Stimpy and the Mall

Sunday evening, April first, and he felt like a fool. Except for the nice breakfast with Laura and Jackson this morning, he'd been spinning his wheels all day.

Frank sat in his Camaro in the parking lot of Riley's, the engine running. People were going in and out of the club, but he didn't see any of the Civics or the three young men. Frank wanted another conversation with the bookish kid, the one he'd seen twice sitting at the bar working on what looked like financial statements. He got a studious vibe off that one—not like the other two, young criminals itching for a fight.

Clearly, they were a crew. With the matching cars and the way the two of them had 'rescued' the third, it wasn't hard to figure out. With those nice cars, they were probably runners, delivering people and product for the gang. It made sense—cops drove fast cars and could outrace most civilian cars. And that, along with things like the PIT maneuver and other techniques taught to police officers to end car chases, it was rare that a civilian could get the better of a cop.

But those little Civics might make it interesting, especially if they were outfitted with booster technology like nitrous. Frank didn't envy the cops chasing those kinds of drivers. Thank God Joe Hathaway hadn't been driving one of those little souped-up Civics last month, or Frank would have never been able to chase him down.

Someone had asked him if he'd felt bad about it. At the end of the car chase, Hathaway had been trying to outrun Frank and had taken on a passing train and lost. But Frank didn't feel bad. He hadn't caused the wreck. Joe had, first by trying to kill Frank and Deputy Peters with a long-range rifle, then when he fled the scene to escape. It made sense that Hathaway would run, and that Frank would give chase. And Hathaway could have stopped the chase at any time by pulling over and giving up.

No, Frank didn't feel bad.

If Hathaway had pulled over, he wouldn't have been in the wreck. And he wouldn't be in intensive care, awaiting trial for two murders and three attempted murders. The guy would answer for what he did, even if the trial had to be delayed for the defendant to recuperate.

Frank turned the Camaro off, frustrated. He hated sitting here in his car, wasting time. But the task force seemed uninterested in talking to him, or at least couldn't be bothered to call him on the weekend. He wanted to make some progress, now, right here. The Oxy in his system made him antsy, driven. He needed results.

He saw the dealer again. On a hunch, Frank climbed out of his car and walked over. "Stimpy, right? Remember me?"

The drug dealer looked at him and nodded, his face a mixture of panic and interest. "Yeah. Tavon said you're a cop." The skinny kid was wearing a light jacket. How could he stand to be out here in the cold?

Tavon, that must be the bookish kid's name. "Nah, not a cop. You got any Oxy?" Frank handed him $200. "Whatever that will buy."

He waited as Stimpy rummaged through his pockets. The guy was like a magician, pulling stuff out of a dozen places in his pants and jacket. Finally, he came up with a bag of white pills. Opening it up, he counted off ten and put them into another bag, handing it to Frank.

"Twenty bucks each."

Frank nodded and took the bag. "Fine. Where are Tavon and the others?"

"Dunno. Haven't seen them tonight."

"What's going on with the construction workers?" All night, Frank had seen people going in and out a back entrance, pushing wheelbarrows and carrying PVC pipes and wires.

Stimpy shook his head. "Heard they were adding some new rooms off the back. And a new sound system."

Frank frowned. It seemed like more than just that, but the kid probably didn't know anything. "Okay, last question. Northsiders work out of any other places than this?"

Stimpy started to shake his head and Frank dropped and spun, turning and kicking the kid's legs out from under him. In a flash, the kid was on the wet pavement, face up, and Frank was kneeling over him, a knee on the kid's chest.

"What were you saying?"

The kid was gasping. "No, I'm sure. I'm sure."

Frank reached down and rifled through the kid's pockets, finding the bag of Oxy and his wad of cash. "Well, you see, I don't believe you. So, unless you want me to take these off your hands, you're gonna tell me. Now."

"I don't know. I don't know."

Frank shook his head and took his gun out and put it in the kid's mouth. It was extreme, but hey, these were extreme times. The euphoria he felt in his system made Frank feel invincible. There was no way this stupid kid was going to stand in his way.

He tapped the end of the gun against the kid's teeth and suddenly remembered where he'd heard this before—Jack Terrington, the notorious serial killer from FBI Agent Noble's presentation, all those years ago at the FBI Academy. She'd said that the killer liked to put his gun in his victim's mouths and move it around, a blatant expression of power, sexual or otherwise.

Some part of Frank's mind recoiled at the thought. Was that what he was turning into? Someone who aped the actions of a notorious psychopath who had killed hundreds of people?

Frank took the gun out of the kid's mouth and put it under the kid's chin instead. "Okay, last chance. Tell me what I want to know."

Now that the gun was out of his mouth, the kid started talking. He mentioned three places: another strip club further up Dixie Drive, an old closed mall on Salem Avenue, and an old tire factory on Northpoint. They all sounded promising, and Frank stood, putting his gun away and pocketing what looked like at least 200 Oxy pills, the dealer's entire stash. And the wad of money.

"Hey, man, don't take all of—" Stimpy started to complain, but Frank ignored him.

Driving out of the parking lot, Frank felt great.

The club and tire factory turned out to be nothing special—he drove around them several times but saw little activity.

The old mall seemed a much better prospect. The place looked empty, but he saw cars coming and going. The place was ringed with a high fence and protected by security. He watched for a while, then finally just drove up to the front gate and rolled his window down.

A black man came out of the shack and approached the Camaro. He was employed by a company called "North Side Security." Frank wondered how many businesses on the north side of Dayton followed that naming convention.

"Can I help you?"

Frank flashed his ABI badge. "Yeah, just got some reports of a prowler, 10-14. Mind if I drive the perimeter, check it out?"

"Hold on a second, let me check." The guy turned and went back in the shack, and Frank saw him use a phone before coming back out. "We haven't heard anything, but feel free to do a loop around. Want me to come with you?"

Frank shook his head. "No, it's probably nothing."

The guard nodded. "Okay. There are a bunch of cars around back—a local dealership pays us to park extra inventory back there. Sometimes we get vandals, so let me know if you see anything."

Frank nodded and thanked him, then cranked the handle to roll up his window. He wished the Camaro had push button windows like every other car in the world. He drove straight ahead, clearing the gate area and turning right, starting a long loop around the mall. Across from the guard shack was one closed entrance to the mall, the doors topped by two large red arches meeting in the middle in a way that looked almost Asian or Polynesian. It included the word "Theater," but he couldn't see any more.

To the east was a massive Sears, with large pillars holding up oversized letters spelling the store's name. All the lights inside were dark.

Frank continued around the back, passing a closed automotive area. More expansive parking lots stretched behind the mall. The guard was right—there were at least fifty or sixty used cars lined up. But the mall itself was dark and appeared completely abandoned. There were no lights except for the streetlights of the neighborhoods that encircled the old mall. Frank wondered as he continued around the mall perimeter if the security company had people walk through on occasion just to make sure it was as empty as it appeared.

He continued past a large, darkened JCPenney store. The doors looked like they'd been sealed shut a decade ago and never opened since.

Frank got to the end of the JCPenney and turned left, heading south. More huge empty parking lots. This part of the mall looked to be two stories tall. As he headed south, he approached the back of what looked like a large home improvement store. He jogged to the left, staying inside the fencing that separated the Home Depot from the closed mall. Another right and he was back around the front. He pulled up to the guard shack and stopped.

The guard came back out. "See anything strange?"

"Nope, nothing. You get a lot of traffic in and out of here?"

The guy shook his head. "Nah, nothing. We just make sure no vagrants or anyone gets inside," he said, nodding at the mall.

"They gonna do anything with it? Seems a shame, just sitting there empty."

"I have no clue," the man shrugged. "Way above my pay grade, know what I mean? I heard they want to redevelop it, make it an outdoor mall. Who knows."

Frank thanked him and drove off, heading south. Another dead end.

He resigned himself to getting nothing done tonight. He could sit in an empty parking lot or outside this mall or the tire factory and see if anything came of it. Or he could enjoy the spoils of his encounter with Stimpy.

Frank decided on the latter.

CHAPTER 47
Guard Shack

"That's all he said?"

The guard was looking at Gig and shaking his head. "That's it, Gig. I swear. He just wanted to roll around the perimeter. He showed a badge, so I figured it was one of the cops on our payroll. But I didn't recognize him. That's why I called it in."

Thank God for that, Gig thought. The guard had called in a blackout, forcing the mall interior to go dark while the cop was investigating.

"It's good you did."

The guard nodded. "Yeah, the boss always said if there's a cop here wanting to look around, you let them in."

Gig nodded. It was standard procedure, and the guy had followed the rules.

"Tell me about the guy."

"Older white guy, definitely a cop," he said. "I didn't get a real good look at the badge but it was real, I know that. Said he was checking out a disturbance and used the right police code. Did a loop around in his old car. I told him there would be cars in the parking lot. I know you guys are really staffed up inside, so I gave him the line about the car dealership."

Gig nodded, shuffling his feet. It was cold out here, but the guard shack was only big enough for one person—one person, a computer, a phone, and a pair of shotguns. "You said 'old car.' What was he driving?"

"Old Camaro or Mustang. Not sure. Looked old, rusty, early '70s, I'd say. Black."

Gig had a sudden thought and pulled out his phone, flipping through old photos from a month ago. He found what he was looking for and held it up for the guard to see. "Like this one?"

The guard didn't hesitate. "Yup, that's it."

Shit.

Gig looked at the phone again and swiped until he found another photo from a month ago. Gig held up the phone again. "This the guy?"

"Yeah, that's him."

"Okay, thanks. Call it in if he comes back, or if you see him driving around the area. And leave a note for the other guards. Once they call it in, let him do the tour again."

The guard nodded and Gig started back towards the theater entrance of the mall, thinking. This was not good. The trio had attracted the attention of this cop. Rubio had called Gig earlier, letting him know the old man was back in town. He'd shown up at the strip club and would have dragged Tavon out of there if Slug and Rubio hadn't stopped him.

Gig knew the cop was up from Alabama or Georgia. He didn't remember the details. But he'd looked into it again this afternoon, pulling up all the old photos and information from a month ago. He had no authority up here in Ohio but looked to be working with local law enforcement. In fact, the guy had solved some kidnapping case last year. Now he was back, poking around. Was he working for the task force?

Under the wide, unlit red eaves of the former theater, Gig knocked and was let inside. He walked to his office in the former Foot Locker and called Riley's and Tavon, verifying what Rubio had told him.

Next, Gig went and talked to Sonny, who ran security for the complex as well as running guns and explosives for the gang. Normally, he wouldn't be in his office this late on a Sunday, but he was working on the big construction operation at Riley's.

Gig explained the situation, and Sonny said he'd pass it along to the mall guards and coordinate more closely with North Side Security, which only protected the parking lots and exterior of the mall.

After, Gig went to JCPenney and checked on production. They were angry for having to shut down for a few minutes. Some product might have to be destroyed, and Mr. Kingmaker was on his way in to oversee things for the rest of the night.

Gig walked back to his office. There was one more person he needed to call, and they would not be happy about Mr. Frank Harper nosing around. But at least the Dragon would have a definitive answer about what to do about the old guy.

CHAPTER 48
Curious

The next morning, Frank was out before 8:00 a.m., looking for answers. It was the first "official" day of his suspension, but he'd almost forgotten about the Collier situation.

Frank had woken up angry. The Northsiders had a death grip on this city, squeezing the life out of anyone and anything that got in their way. The burned-out home had gotten Frank off his duff and back up to Dayton—and although it might cost him his job, he was going to get to the bottom of this. The gang members were like roaches—they operated with impunity in the shadows, and he was here to shine some light to make them scatter. And his maintenance dose just made him see clearer.

This morning, he was cruising around in his Camaro. He'd already been to the scene of the fire again, tracking around in the fresh snow at 8:00 a.m., looking for clues. He picked through the burned wood beams and unburned wall studs but found nothing to advance the investigation.

He left the ruined house and found a place to grab some breakfast, a fast food restaurant he'd never heard of called Tim Horton's. Must be a northern thing—they didn't have them down in Alabama. But the food was good, crisp and hot, and the coffee was not bad. And the ten-pack of little donut holes really hit the spot, especially on a cold Monday morning like this.

Driving around on his own wasn't too smart. He knew that, even while he was doing it. His old partner Ben Stone had been killed doing the exact same thing—he'd been out following a lead and was ambushed and shot in a rainy alley in Coral Gables, Florida. Stone had been a crack shot, better than Frank could ever hope to be, but Stone's gun never made it out of the holster. In the end, his range rating hadn't mattered one whit. None of it mattered if you didn't take the appropriate precautions—and right now, Frank was rolling the dice. Some would call it reckless.

Frank drove past the old tire factory and the big empty mall again before ending up at the strip club. He parked on the street a half block down from the club. Too far away to see individual faces, but he would spot Tavon or his car.

He got a kick out of how the cops on TV did their investigations. They were always parked right outside the suspects house or wherever and never got spotted. They would chat with their partner for like five seconds and then the suspect would come out. Somehow, the suspect ALWAYS looked right at the cops, giving the audience a perfect view of them, but the suspects never spotted the cops sitting there in their cars. It was so silly. That wasn't how stakeouts worked. They were dull and boring. The suspects never came out five minutes after you arrived. Most of the investigators he knew kept a stack of magazines and crossword puzzles in their cars for just such occurrences.

Frank relaxed—based on his experience, this would take a while.

CHAPTER 49
Follow Him

Tavon watched as the old man parked a half block down from Riley's. Tavon slowed, not wanting to pass the Camaro and get spotted. He pulled the old Toyota he was driving into the parking lot of a Subway sandwich shop and parked where he could see the Camaro.

Gig had called very early this morning—the Dragon had ordered eyes on the old cop. It didn't surprise Tavon—the old man was involving himself in things that didn't concern him. Coming to the club on Saturday and questioning him? Tavon could understand that much. The family was dead, and the old cop wanted answers.

But things had escalated from there. The old cop had come back to the strip club again on Sunday and roughed up Stimpy, taking his Oxy stash and hurting his arm.

Then he had showed up at the Salem Mall, curious about the location.

The guard at the gate, following some procedure Tavon hadn't even guessed at, had let the old man make a lap around the mall in his rusty Camaro to look for a "prowler." But it also meant they'd had to temporarily halt all operations inside the mall and turn off all the lights, like a bunch of kids throwing a party at their parent's house. The old man didn't stay long, but it was still a huge problem.

Serious enough to involve the Dragon.

Tavon had driven to the mall and swapped his Civic for a beat-up Toyota borrowed from someone working on the production lines. Then he'd driven up to Cooper's Mill. Tavon found the hotel quickly. It was located right off the highway, and he recognized it from passing it on every trip he'd ever taken on this stretch of highway. Tavon wondered how the Northsiders knew what hotel the old man was staying at, but he knew better than to ask. Their gang was very well informed.

A few minutes later, he was parked in the lot of some restaurant called the Tip Top Diner, watching the Camaro. It didn't take long. Just before eight, the old cop had come out and climbed into his ride and driven off, getting onto the highway and heading south.

Ever since, Tavon had tailed him on a tour of Northsiders properties. First stop was the burned-out house, where the guy spent a few minutes walking around, looking at the ground and kicking over debris. Tavon had no idea what the cop might be looking for, but being back at the house made Tavon's stomach turn.

The Camaro led Tavon to the old Coviello tire factory. It too was fenced off and guarded by North Side Security.

After that, it was back to the Salem Mall. For Tavon, it was the second time in the past couple of hours. This time, the old man just drove around the mall using the residential streets that ringed the old mall. He could see the cop slow down and look between the homes, trying to get a view of the mall.

Tavon called Gig and gave him a report, and Gig instituted another blackout and lockdown just in case. No one in or out. It was a good thing—around the north side of the mall, the residential street, Bloomfield Drive, gave a really good view of the back of the mall. A straight shot right across the old parking lots. If there had been people coming and going from the entrance to the old JCPenney, the old man would have spotted them.

As it was, the place looked abandoned, as it should. The old man just continued his loop around the mall and then drove away, heading south.

Tavon followed him, relaxing. There was no telling how much damage the old man could do if he knew the Northsiders' entire operation was housed inside the mall. It had been a good strategy for a long time—as long as they kept the place secure and kept the prying eyes away, it worked. But keeping everything in one location was also a gamble.

Next, the old man drove south on Dixie, ending up back at Riley's, where he parked. Tavon sat back and relaxed. It was going to be a long day.

CHAPTER 50
Tipped Off

At the task force headquarters, it was just after 9:00 a.m. on Monday morning. Sergeant Roget sat at his desk, sifting through the weekend reports as he waited for the 11:00 a.m. meeting to start. He was briefing the mayor and others, but he had plenty of time to get through the pile of work he had in front of him.

One interesting item—there was a confession in Fango's murder. The kid had been stabbed in jail by his boss, a guy named "Poker" and one of the other gang members arrested in the same raid. "Poker" apparently thought killing Fango would somehow help protect his own identity. Roget made a note to add more charges to the gang member's file.

The other big news of the weekend was an anonymous tip that had come in on Sunday about the Northsiders. There had been a lot of speculation about their primary headquarters. There were two schools of thought—the old Salem Mall and the old Coviello Tire factory out on Northpoint. Both were located squarely in Northsiders territory, and both were guarded by the North Side Security company, an obvious front for the gang. During months of surveillance, the task force had seen people coming and going from both locations, but, so far, the task force had been unable to get anyone on the inside.

But a new piece of info had come in. Apparently, the gang was moving most of their major operations into Riley's, a good-sized strip club on Dixie Drive. It was smaller, and farther south, but it made sense— the location was closer to downtown. If the Northsiders were taking advantage of the power vacuum in Dayton and spreading south, moving their headquarters made sense. The rumor was they were moving their "administrative" offices into Riley's and expanding the tire factory with more production equipment. Roget wasn't sure. He had a couple beat cops out there this morning—hopefully, he'd get a report before 11:00 a.m.

Other news included a few hits on other gangs, including one in Columbus. The one on Thursday night had taken out an entire crew operating near the Columbus airport.

Another hit the next day essentially decapitated the Bowling Boyz, one of the last remaining gangs in south Dayton. Both of the Bowling brothers and five of their lieutenants were found shot up in three cars near the Dayton Mall.

He flipped through other reports. One was on the street drug quality in Dayton proper—it was apparently going up.

Another report, thicker than it needed to be, was from Agent Shales, who was looking into the financial structure of the Northsiders, Bowling Boyz, Fifth Street Runners, and other remaining local operations. Shales theorized the Northsiders were the only local organization who took the concept of "organizing" seriously. They were shifting roles and changing their structure, reportedly patterning it after the old-school mafia. Their newest leader, someone known affectionately as "the Dragon," was a fan of Midwestern mafia greats from back in the day, like Mama Leonita, a female Luciano crime family member who ran a notorious gang out of St. Louis in the '60's.

Great, Roget thought, putting the report down. Just what we need. Gangbangers turning into wise guys. And who picks these leader names? The mob was always run by someone called "the Chin" or "the Nose" or "Teflon Don." Roget thought they got a kick out of coming up with the silliest sounding names they could.

His mind drifted, remembering the long weekend with Hawkins. He'd shown up at her house on Saturday morning on a whim, prompted purely out of a sense of missing her. They had ended up in bed, then spent the rest of the day together, taking in IKEA and two other shops. They had an early dinner at the Cheesecake Factory before heading back to her apartment for another round between the sheets. It was, by far, the best weekend he'd had in a long time.

Roget felt guilty. He should be going through these reports and prepping for the meeting. But all he could think about was Patricia in that robe, standing by the sink. It had been bright in the kitchen and she'd taken her dishes over and then surprised him by untying her robe and dropping it to the floor. Jesus. Not that he was complaining. It was just that…that kind of stuff didn't happen to him. He was a rule follower, ready to get to work and knuckle down and take the slow and steady path. But she was more spontaneous.

He was starting to like spontaneous.

Dottie, one of the administrative staff, knocked on his open door, breaking his train of thought.

"Oh, hi, Dottie. Come on in."

She walked in and smiled. "How you doing, Sergeant? You look like you've got a glow about you. Get some sun this weekend?"

"Something like that. What you got for me?"

She handed him a sheet. "Couple reports, both on the same guy. A possible witness. Ex-cop, up from Alabama. He talked to some investigators on Saturday, then the front desk over at DPD."

"Thanks, Dottie," he said. "I've been waiting to talk to this guy."

She left as he looked at the paperwork—two standard reports, very short. It appeared Frank Harper was back in town. Sergeant Roget knew him as the ex-cop that stirred up trouble with the Northsiders over that family that had died.

One report from Saturday morning was from a drive-by near the burned home on Eckhart; the investigating unit said Harper stopped by and asked about the house and the investigation. A few hours later, the Dayton PD front desk reported Harper had visited, asking to speak to someone involved with the task force.

Roget stood and walked out into the main offices of the task force. He handed the reports to a junior police officer. "Call this guy and see if he can come in."

The officer nodded. "Will do."

Roget went back to his desk, trying hard not to look over at Hawkins' office. Sunday she'd come over to his place. They'd assembled furniture together, then had a late lunch and watched some TV. It was just so easy—they got along so well, and she was just so great to be around. And surprising. That thing with the robe. Wow.

But he was waiting for the other shoe to drop. Surely, at some point, she'd turn out to be like all the other women he'd dated. She'd start making demands. Start listing off the things he needed to change about himself to make them happy. Clean this, organize that. Stop doing this, start doing that. Listing off the things that he did that disappointed them.

But for now, Roget was approaching this relationship in a different way: he was just going to live in the moment, and see what happened.

CHAPTER 51
Lab Equipment

An hour later, his cell phone rang. Frank set down the book he was reading and answered.

"Frank Harper."

"Hi, Mr. Harper? I'm with the Dayton Area Heroin Task Force. We received reports saying you were interested in discussing a few 'items related to the Eckhart Street fire.'" Frank could tell it was a young cop, reading from a report. "Would you be available today, say 1:00 p.m.?"

"Absolutely," he said, not taking his eyes off the strip club. "I can be there. Who should I ask for?"

"Oh, just check in downstairs and they'll send you up."

Frank said goodbye and hung up. Nice to see the folks were finally back to work. Hope they had a great weekend, he thought sarcastically.

He adjusted his position for the hundredth time and continued to watch the strip club from down the block. More construction people, going in and out. Trucks pulling up, furniture being removed, other boxes going in. Lab equipment and stainless steel tables. Frank could make no sense of it, other than the Northsiders were putting considerable effort into it.

It was boring, watching the club from down the street, but that was fine. Police work was boring sometimes. That's another thing the cop shows always got wrong. Or, they didn't really get it wrong—they just cut out all the boring "in-between" parts and showed you only the exciting bits. They never showed a guy sitting at his desk for four hours, filling out paperwork until his back was sore. They never showed cops sitting in their cars on a stakeout that led to absolutely nothing but frustration. If you went by the cop shows, every stakeout and every search had a 100% chance of success. It did the police a disservice, Frank thought. It made police work look so easy: you showed up at a house, you bang on the door, there's an exciting chase and at the end there's a tackle. Why is there always a tackle?

They never showed the nerves before a raid, or opening ten or fifteen different doors, sweeping the room with your weapon and flashlight, searching for people in the bed or under it. Frank figured if they showed all that on TV, people would change the channel.

But that was what cops did, every day. It wasn't all shoot-outs and car chases and "a-ha" moments during interviews where the suspect suddenly, inexplicably confesses to the crime. It was more like those two-parters, the ones where it's ten minutes until the end of the show, and they still haven't caught the criminal and the viewer starts to wonder "what if this is an episode where they don't solve the case in exactly one hour?" and then the screen cuts to "To Be Continued." The viewer's heart sinks from that lack of closure.

Being a cop was like seeing that "To Be Continued" sign every hour of every day for your entire career.

There were dangerous criminals you'd remember in the back of your mind from cases from a decade ago. Would they pop up again? And there were those cases that bothered you forever, both solved and unsolved. You wonder if the evidence had been handled differently? Was it tainted? Did we convict the right guy?

And there were cases you never solved, like the kid in the box. Frank thought sometimes it was the lack of closure that washed out so many cops. It was impossible to not get frustrated.

CHAPTER 52
Keowee Street

Tavon waited with the old man at the strip club for over an hour. By the time the Camaro drove away, Tavon's back was killing him. He was not made for sitting still in one place for a long time.

Tavon expected the car to head north, maybe head back to the Salem Mall. Instead, the car went south on Dixie toward downtown Dayton. They passed over the river—Tavon made sure to hang way back—and continued south as Dixie Drive became Keowee Street. They passed into downtown and then the old man turned into a parking lot next to the Dayton PD. Unsure of what to do, Tavon decided to keep with the tail. He circled the block and parked where he could see the parking lot exit.

He called it in, and Gig said things were under control. Somehow, Gig already knew the old man was at the police station. Gig said Harper was being interviewed by the task force. Tavon was to wait and follow him when he left.

Tavon waited, flipping through a magazine he'd found in the Toyota. He wished he'd known he was going to be bored all day—he could have brought along that stack of financials and other paperwork he was supposed to be reviewing. As it was, he'd wasted the hours catching up on news on his phone and perusing the same issue of *People Magazine* over and over. The only interesting article was about a pretty Hollywood starlet who was in rehab again. Over the last few years, her career had taken a nosedive. It looked like she was just barely hanging onto the bottom rung of "fame."

He sighed, glancing up at the parking structure, and got on his cell phone to check his messages and waste some time on Twitter.

CHAPTER 53
Interview

The 11:00 a.m. meeting had gone well. Some of the local chiefs of police were there—Dayton, Vandalia and Cooper's Mill—along with the mayor and Agent Shales. At the end of the table, Tammy and Patty from the admin pool sat in to take notes.

They spent much of the meeting discussing the tip that had come in on the new Northsiders headquarters. Roget had gotten a report back from two street cops who were surveilling Riley's; they reported construction workers and moving trucks around the building.

"Why move south?" the chief of police for Cooper's Mill asked.

Chief Craig leaned forward. "We think the Northsiders want more control of the south." He turned and looked at Roget. "Were they behind the hit on the Bowling Boyz?"

"We're not sure, but it certainly looks like it," Roget said, looking down at his sheets. He hated making eye contact in meetings, even with people who were his friends and co-workers. He could just feel his cheek starting to twitch. "They ran south Dayton, especially that area around the mall. They had been spreading south to Austin Landings, but it looks like that's over."

The mayor tapped the table. "What about these hits in Columbus? That concerns me. I just got off the phone with the Columbus mayor, and he's pissed. He thinks our increased interdiction has pushed our gangs on them."

"It's possible," Agent Shales spoke up, interrupting before Roget could answer. "But it's more likely they are spreading influence and taking over new locations, not moving." He looked around the table. "If they're following the mafia pattern, as I outlined in my report, they are just growing. Not moving."

"Who?" the mayor looked at Shales and Roget. "The Northsiders?"

"It looks like it," Roget said. He pointed at the maps on the wall. "Moving their HQ will let them keep a closer eye on the downtown area. Taking out the Bowling Boyz and, if they were behind it, that crew operating near the Columbus airport—it's all a sign of expansion. Aggressive expansion."

"With less competition," Craig said. "We're helping them."

"No, not really," the mayor said. "It looks like that now, in the middle of the operation. They're growing, others are shrinking, but we're working our way up the food chain. Concentrating on the little players first—"

"Most of which are gone now," Chief Craig interjected.

"Right. You're right, Dan," the mayor said, tapping the table again for emphasis. "We're going after them next."

The rest of the meeting went well—the task force had a plan. Deputy Sergeant Hawkins would pull together an assault plan for both the mall and the new headquarters. A raid on Riley's was tentatively planned for the middle of this week, depending on further intelligence gathering.

Agent Shales decided to talk about his report some more, and Roget was fine with letting him ramble. Shales talked about the Dragon, the shadowy leader of the Northsiders, and how there were no pictures of the man. It was a good report, but the kid just didn't know when to stop talking. After a few more minutes, the mayor stepped in to wrap up the meeting.

Roget grabbed some lunch from the cafeteria in the basement and brought it back to his office so he could update the color-coded gang maps. They got redrawn weekly, although lately they'd been redrawing them more and more frequently.

"Sergeant, your 1:00 o'clock is here," one of his junior cops said, leaning into the door of Roget's office. "Harper, from the fire. I put him in the conference room—Hawkins is there, and Shales wanted to sit in, too. And Dottie's in there to take notes."

Roget nodded and stood, grabbing some files and heading to the conference room. Frank Harper was already seated, making chit chat with Shales. They obviously knew each other. Roget walked in and sat, doing the introductions. The ex-cop from Alabama looked tired and thin, as if he'd seen a lot of bad road in his life. Roget got the immediate impression the old man was overextended—he had bags under his eyes, and slouched at the table like he hadn't slept in days.

Dottie was pouring coffee for everyone from the coffee cart. "Sergeant, do you want coffee?" Dottie asked. Roget nodded as Dottie finished pouring a mug for Harper, handing it to him.

When she was seated again, Roget got started. He began by covering the police report on the fire on Eckhart Street. Harper interrupted a few times with clarifications and more information, including a little more background on the Washington family and the owner of the home, whom Roget had interviewed last week.

"They seemed like a nice family," Harper said. Roget got the impression the man blamed himself for their deaths. His hands were shaking slightly, like he was nervous.

"Why did you confront the gang member at the strip club?" Hawkins asked, leaning in. "It says here that Delancy hired you to 'look into things.' Warning the Northsiders off seems like an escalation."

Harper nodded. "Yeah, I guess it was. But I don't like seeing people getting pushed around." His answers were short and to the point. He sounded like a cop. "I realize it was a mistake."

The guy had an annoying habit of looking down at the table. Roget was getting a strange vibe—there was something here that he couldn't put his finger on.

They continued through the report, ending up with Harper's discussions with the beat cops on Saturday. Roget had Dottie find one of the arson investigators, and the man sat in for part of the interview, covering some of the more detailed information.

Harper was smart—that much Roget could see. He asked a lot of good questions of the arson investigator and shared what he'd seen at the house. A few times, the discussion got too technical. Harper and the arson investigator got off on a tangent about accelerants and pour patterns, and Dottie had to interrupt several times to ask for clarification.

"Did you find anything else interesting at the house?" Agent Shales asked.

Harper shook his head. "Not really. I was looking for where the fire started, or where it seemed to be concentrated. I have an associate who investigates fires," he said with a nod to the other arson investigator in the room. "He told me what to look for."

Roget looked at the man's eyes—they were bloodshot. It seemed like, at times, he found it hard to focus. One minute he'd be talking to one of them, and then the discussion would just dry up—

Roget realized what it was.

"Good, good," Roget said, putting up his hands. "I think we've got everything we need. Anyone else have questions for Mr. Harper?"

Hawkins and the others shook their heads.

"Good," Roget said. "Mr. Harper, if you don't mind, I just have a couple more questions for you, but I'd like to finish the interview on my own. Would you guys mind stepping out?

Hawkins and the others nodded, curious, and stood. They said their goodbyes to Mr. Harper. Dottie, at the far end of the table, stopped taking notes. "Me too, Sergeant?"

"Yes, thank you," Roget said. Dottie gathered up her notes and pens and Diet Coke and pulled the conference room door shut behind her. He waited until the others had left and the door closed before continuing.

"Are you high right now?"

Harper turned and looked at Roget. "What?"

Roget looked him in the bloodshot eyes—they seemed to vibrate slightly. "I think it's cocaine, or maybe Oxy. Your eyes are bloodshot, and the whole interview you were fidgeting like a junkie."

Harper looked away. "I'm here to help you, and this is what you're asking? If your cops had protected that family instead of ignoring all the threats—"

"Are you on any medications right now?"

Harper looked down at the table. "I was shot in the back in October. I'm sure you know that, if you've read my file. I reinjured myself last month. I have a doctor's prescription for Oxycontin, not that that's any of your business. Are we done here?"

Roget resisted the temptation to end the interview right then and there.

"No, there are a few more things we need to discuss. Like your interactions with the gang. Have you interacted with them since you've been back in town?"

Harper was reluctant to answer, and the rest of the interview was awkward and more combative. Roget didn't think Harper's answers could get more succinct, but he was proven wrong. By the time he started asking about what Harper had done in the past two days, Harper was down to one-word answers.

Like a criminal.

"Anything else you want to tell us, Mr. Harper?" Roget looked at the man. His hands were in his lap now, or he was sitting on them to keep them from shaking.

Harper looked up at Roget. It looked like he wanted to say something, but then decided not to.

Just as well, Roget thought, and thanked him for the meeting. Roget shook his hand—it was clammy and wet—and stood, heading for the door. Shales was waiting outside the conference room—probably to chat. Good, he could walk Harper out.

Roget was done with him.

CHAPTER 54
BK

An hour later, the old man came out of the police station and got into his car and headed north, back to Cooper's Mill. Tavon followed. The man went to his hotel for a while, and came out around dusk and drove to a young woman's apartment. He was greeted by the woman and a little kid. They hugged him, and they all went inside. Tavon texted Gig the information, including the young woman's address.

He got a text back: "Dragon says we're grabbing him tonight. Crew will meet you at hotel at midnight."

Tavon nodded. It also meant he would be here or at the hotel for several more hours. He was starving. Taking a risk, Tavon ran to Burger King for food and a bathroom break—they had passed one on the way—and was back in a few minutes.

The Camaro was parked right where it had been.

CHAPTER 55
Garlic Bread

"Grandpa, do you like garlic bread?"

Jackson was smiling and waving a piece of bread at him.

Frank glanced at Laura, who was smiling as well. "I do. Are you done with that one?" he asked, pointing at a half-eaten piece on Jackson's plate.

Jackson shook his head. "No way!"

Frank grabbed a piece from the serving tray and stuffed it into his mouth and making a dinosaur face at the boy. A hunk of garlic bread shook from his mouth and fell into Frank's lap, and Jackson laughed like it was the funniest thing he'd ever seen.

Laura looked at him. "I'm gonna make you clean if you get it everywhere."

He smiled. "Sorry. But I just love it SO MUCH!"

Jackson giggled and went back to his plate of lasagna.

"This is really good, Laura," Frank said, his tone much quieter. "It's been a long time since I had home-cooked lasagna."

"Well, I don't know about home-cooked," she said. "I use that no-boil lasagna. It's just so much easier."

"It's really good. And the garlic bread is CRAZY!" he growled, making a face at Jackson.

They enjoyed the rest of the meal in relative peace, and there were few other outbursts by what Jackson began to refer to as the "garlic bread monster." It was an enjoyable meal, his first in a while.

That interview with the task force had made him angry. Here he was, spending his own personal time, driving up from Birmingham to help them try and catch the people who murdered the Washington family, and they were asking him about his medical needs? It was infuriating. Sure, he'd popped an extra Oxy on the way into the interview to stave off any pain. He was doing it for them so that he could sit in the interview for as long as needed. It wasn't like he was taking Oxy for fun.

"You okay, Frank?"

He looked up at Laura. "Yeah. Just thinking how good this stuff is. Love it." He could tell that she knew he was lying, but she let it slide.

She was getting better at reading his moods.

After dinner, they cleaned up the dishes and retired to the small living room to watch the news. Jackson ran off to play in his room and Laura joined Frank on the couch.

"Now we can talk," she said. "So, why are you really up here, Frank?"

Jackson was playing loudly, the pleasant sounds of a kid giggling and having fun.

"I'm working this case," he said. "That family died."

"I know that, but there's nothing you can do," she said. "It's a horrible tragedy, but they were living in a gang-infested area AND in a house that the gang thought was theirs, for some reason." He'd told her enough of the story to hopefully quash her interest. But she was a Harper. Her brain had been working the problem even if it wasn't her problem. "You threatened them, and yes, that was stupid. But what happened—you can't fix that. So why are you really here?"

"I wanted to see you!" he said, smiling. "Isn't that good enough?"

"Sure, it's good enough," she said quietly. "Jackson loves seeing you, and so do I. But there was no planning, no mention that you were coming."

She turned and muted the TV and looked at him, waiting. She had no idea what she was doing, but he was pleased, on some level, to see her using his trick on him. The silence stretched out into awkwardness, and she didn't say anything.

He couldn't take it anymore.

"I got suspended," he said finally. "From work."

She nodded. And she didn't seem surprised. He wasn't sure what hurt more.

"I figured," she said. "Your boss must be pretty tolerant. Last time you were up here, you checked out for a whole day, remember? Missed a meal with us, one that Jackson had been looking forward to. You doing the same thing to him? Disappearing for days at a time? You need to get yourself right, Frank. You need help."

He didn't look at her. He suddenly found the swirl pattern of her thread-bare carpet fascinating. He knew he was struggling with it. Frank would crawl in the bottle for days at a time, but, even at his worst, he could still function. He could still get around, do his work, take care of what needed to be taken care of. Mostly.

Now, things were different. The Oxy made him feel powerless and powerful. It either made him feel like his insides were burning with energy and purpose, or it knocked him on his ass. He could get so much done when he had his medicine—like the drive up here. Focused, watching the road with wide eyes, never a thought of sleep. He felt like he could see a hundred miles in every direction and detect cops and speed traps from miles away. He'd varied his speed and watched the Waze app and slowed when he spotted an area that looked like it could be a speed trap. Then he'd make up extra time, going ninety or a hundred in the long flat spaces.

He'd felt so driven. As long as he had a quarter- or a half-pill in his system, he was flying high. Sometimes it backfired, like in that interview today. The cop had seen Frank's eyes, maybe even noticed his hands. For some reason, he couldn't keep his hands still.

Sitting on the couch, looking at the carpet, Frank's hands started to shake again.

Laura looked down at them, then placed her hands on his.

"Don't worry, we'll get through this," she said. "We're family, and we need to start sticking together. Not flee every time something bad happens," she said, and he wondered if that was a subtle backhanded swipe at her mother, who'd left Frank and taken Laura away when his post-Katrina phase had been at its worst.

Actually, his post-Katrina phase had never ended. His actions were still dictated by bourbon and memories of the National Guard. Memories of him, floating in brackish water, grabbing at the broken ceiling. Things, awful things, bumping against him in the water.

They talked for another hour. He told her about his suspension and troubles at work, and it felt great, telling someone. He didn't tell her about the off-prescription Oxy, making it seem like he was still following doctor's orders. He just couldn't look in her eyes and admit that.

She went off to get Jackson ready for bed. Jackson ran out in his night clothes and hugged Frank goodnight. Frank smiled and helped tucked him in, and then he and Laura said goodnight. It had been a long and exhausting day, but he tried to be present and in the moment with her, sharing at least some of what was on his mind. She told him again that he needed help and that she would be there to help him if he wanted it.

He drove back to the hotel, his mind buzzing. There was a soreness, a kind of sharp dull pain that crept in from the sides of his mind when he went too long without his dose. He hadn't had anything since heading into the interview at 1:00 p.m., and it was now after 9:00 p.m.

As soon as he got back to his room, he popped a maintenance dose and downed some bourbon to stave off the approaching headaches. He just didn't want to deal with them. He felt the Oxy coursing through his system and sat at the desk in his hotel room, drinking and writing down notes on the case. By midnight he was passed out, sleeping like the dead.

CHAPTER 56
Fire Alarm

Tavon watched from his borrowed Toyota, waiting.

He was outside some woman's apartment, and the old guy was inside, apparently having dinner. After, Tavon followed the old Camaro back to the hotel by the highway. It had all been one huge circle, all around Dayton, to end up right back where he'd been 12 hours ago.

According to Gig, the Northsiders had considered just taking the cop out, but a dead cop brings too many questions. But a cop who got frustrated and left town on his own? The last call with Gig was a conference line with him, Tavon, Rubio, and Slug. They discussed the plan for the evening, and Rubio and Slug signed off to get the needed equipment. Around midnight, they'd head up and meet Tavon in Cooper's Mill.

Until then, Tavon had the same job he'd had all day—keep a close eye on the old man.

Slug and Rubio arrived in Rubio's Civic at about 12:15 a.m. They pulled up and parked right next to Tavon's borrowed Toyota in the Tip Top parking lot. Tavon was tired, sipping from a cold cup of coffee he'd gotten at the McDonald's across the highway around 10:00 p.m., an hour after the old man had left the young woman's house and returned to the hotel. Slug and Rubio got out of the Civic and climbed into Tavon's car.

"You doing alright?" Rubio asked. "Gig said you've been following the guy since this morning."

Tavon nodded, yawning. "Yeah, long day. I was sitting in this parking lot this morning at 8:00 a.m., and now I'm back here."

"This shouldn't take long," Rubio said, showing them what he'd brought: three Tasers and a length of rope. "Knock him out, tie him up. Slug, you drive him to the mall in this car, Tavon you follow in my Civic. I'll get the man's Camaro and all his stuff."

Tavon nodded.

"Okay," Slug leaned in from the back seat. "But how we gonna know what room he's in?"

Rubio looked at Tavon. "That's the only part we have to figure out.

Gig said roll with it, make it look like the old man left in the night. Any ideas?"

"Not really," Tavon said. "I tried to watch for his lights but didn't see anything. He could be in a room on the other side."

"There's no cameras on the exits except the front door," Rubio said. "But the side exits are locked—you need a room key. We went past the front doors. It's one young guy behind the counter."

"Could be others, or a security guard."

Rubio looked at the hotel. "Doubt it. Look at the place. Not fancy enough for cameras on all the doors. I doubt they have a guard."

Tavon had a thought. "Fire alarm?"

"That might work," Rubio said, thinking about it. "But how we know which door he'd come out? Or grab him up with everyone around? Plus, it's supposed to look like he left, taking all his stuff."

"Let's just jump the front desk, get them to give us the room number," Slug said. He was always the first to suggest violence. "And they could give us a key, too."

"What about the cameras?"

"Delete 'em. Or take the computer or tape or whatever they store it on," Tavon added. "What about the person at the front desk?"

Slug smiled and waggled the Taser in the air. "Ah, it's just not his night, I guess."

Tavon shook his head. "Gig said the old man's supposed to be checking out, right? Like he bailed. If you knock out the clerk, they'll call the cops when they wake up."

"Could take the clerk with us," Slug said.

"Nah, then two people are missing."

They thought for a few minutes more, discussing several ideas, then circled back to Tavon's fire alarm idea. "If he comes out, he'll have his room key, right?"

"Nah, they don't put it on there, Gig said. So people who lose their key don't get visitors."

They talked about it for a few more minutes and came up with a plan with the best chance of success. It would require some timing, but if they did it right, no one would get hurt.

Ten minutes later, the three of them were ready to go. Slug and Tavon were stationed at either exit—the hotel was one building, with exits on the ground floor at either end. Rubio was just outside camera range at the front doors. And after all the planning, an opportunity presented itself: as Tavon was getting ready, a hotel guest came outside for a smoke. Tavon texted Slug and Rubio to wait, and when the guest stepped back inside, Tavon ran and stuck a rock between the door and the jam, keeping it from locking. He waited a minute, texting the others to get ready, and then opened the door. There were no guests in the hallways and no cameras, as far as he could tell. Tavon walked ten steps down the hallway until he saw the first sprinkler, then flicked the lighter Slug had given him and held it up.

A moment later, the alarm went off.

Tavon ran for the exit, doors opening behind him. He stood off to the side and watched as, over the next ninety seconds, twenty or so guests trudged out into the cold, pulling jackets and coats around them. Most gathered near the exit door, not wanting to venture out too far into the night. The alarm continued to sound. Tavon had his Taser ready to go but didn't see the old man in this group.

Four minutes later, a fire truck arrived out front—red lights flashing and lighting up the night. An EMT also showed up, and Tavon was getting worried. There were too many people out here milling around. Too much was happening.

Rubio texted them both: "No security system. Must be fake. Room 212." Rubio's job, while the others watched for the old man, was to wait until the guy at the front desk exited the building with the guests. Then he was to sneak in the front door and do two things: disable any security system and figure out what room Harper was in.

The siren went silent, and guests started trudging back inside. Tavon started to panic. He got a group text from Slug: "Got him. Tased and on the ground between two cars."

Tavon walked around the parking lot and met Rubio in front of the hotel, by the Civic.

"We good?"

Rubio nodded. "Yeah, fake cameras, I guess. I got the room number, then went in the office behind the front desk. There was a laptop but nothing on it about security, and no camera setup like they would have with a dedicated system. Anyway, the kid was drinking a Coke and had left it behind, so I poured it on the laptop. It shorted out and stopped working."

"Nice," Tavon said. "I'll follow you."

Rubio drove his Civic around to the east side of the hotel and Tavon followed, avoiding the EMT and firetruck and the cop car that had arrived.

They found Slug on the far side of the hotel. He waved them down, pointing at the ground. Tavon drove the Toyota over and stopped as close to the cars as he could. Rubio and Slug appeared, carrying a prone figure over. Tavon held the back door of the car open. Together they got the old man inside—he was out cold.

"It was easy," Slug said. "Walked right up behind him. He might be drunk or something. He was havin' trouble walking."

"Okay, you guys go," Rubio said. "Tavon, drive my car back to the mall for me. Slug, you drive the cop. Stop at the next exit and tie him up good. And tase him again if he wakes up. I'll wait until things die down. Then I'll go back in, get the guys stuff and leave," he said, digging through the pocket of the old man's jacket and pulling out the key card. "Meet me at the mall."

Tavon didn't have to be told twice. He switched cars, following Slug as he slowly circled the lot and got on the highway, heading south. They stopped in Vandalia, and Tavon watched as Slug got in the back and tied up the old man.

They all met at the mall an hour later. Rubio had waited until the cops and firetrucks were gone, then used the key. He cleared out room 212, taking the car keys and clothes and everything he could find. He piled everything into the Camaro and drove it to the mall, parking it inside the Sears Automotive.

Even the most prying eye wouldn't find that car.

Chapter 57
A Metal Chair

Voices drifted around him. Frank felt groggy, out of it, as he heard more voices coming out of the dark.

"You got him trussed up good," one person said.

Another person laughed. Frank squinted his eyes, looking down at a floor. His face hurt and his chest was killing him. All he could see were his bare feet on the concrete.

"Gig said to be careful."

The first person grunted. "Okay. Wake him up."

"I'm already awake," Frank grumbled.

He heard people back away, and then a cold splash of water crashed across his face. Frank spat the water away as he blinked and looked up.

There were two black men in front of him, young guys, dressed like gangsters. T-shirts, jeans, baseball caps. One was crazy skinny, the other rippling with muscles. They were in what looked like an abandoned building. Dark lighting, high ceilings, and the place smelled musty.

Frank looked down. He was tied to a metal chair, rope looped around his chest and arms. Each leg was tied to one of the chair legs. He wiggled but there was no budge in the ropes.

The young men watched him in silence.

"What do you want?" Frank asked, spitting again.

The muscle guy smiled. "Nothing. Nothing." He turned to the skinny one. "Imma get Gig." He walked off into the dark and the other kid got a ratty chair and sat down to watch Frank. He sat ten or twelve feet back. Wary. At least they were scared of him.

"What am I doing here?"

The guy shook his head and took out a magazine from his back pocket. "You're waiting to meet the boss, Mr. Harper," he said, glancing at a nearby table. Frank turned and saw three tables to his extreme right. On the closest table were Frank's personal items from the hotel: wallet, shoes, keys, phone, belt, along with something that took him a second to recognize, his suitcase and briefcase.

"Looks like you checked me out. Hope you paid."

Next to those items were his guns. He noted his guns had been unloaded, the bullets standing on their ends next to his weapons. There was also a small stack of papers—it looked like papers from his glove box.

"Look, you need to let me go," Frank said quietly. "You have no idea who I know or how many people are going to come looking for me. I was just talking to the task force today."

The kid looked up from his magazine and smiled at Frank. "Yeah, we know. We had people outside that building for an hour, waiting."

"Your people were tailing me?"

"Look, Mr. Harper, you kept coming around. Now you're going to be here for a while. Might as well relax."

He wondered what that meant but let it go as the kid went back to his magazine. Instead, Frank busied himself.

The ropes were tight. He clenched his fists and released, hoping to grow the gap around his wrists, but the thick ropes merely stretched with his efforts. His shoulders and chest would not budge either, and his legs were secure as well. His feet were on the ground—he might be able to lean forward and slam the chair down on the ground. The metal wouldn't break, but it might snap the rope. Either would draw a lot of attention. He'd have to wait.

Frank looked around. They were in some old retail space—the florescent light banks and ratty drop ceiling were a giveaway. The wall behind the kid was covered with that striped, slatted wall covering that stores used to display pants and shirts and shelving to hold merchandise.

The floor was dirty old concrete, open except for collections of boxes and clothing racks. To his right, he could see a hallway lined with doors. Beyond he could see an enclosed interior space and what looked like stores on the other side of a wide opening. One of them displayed a broken "Auntie Anne's" sign, half of it missing.

They were in that closed mall.

Frank smiled. In the '80s and '90s, malls were for shopping. You took the family and wandered around the enclosed interior space, shopping in the stores and walking past the sparse indoor plants.

The food courts were always his favorites. Where else could you find ten or twelve different "cuisines" all facing the same seating area? And it was Darwin at work—survival of the fittest. There was always a Sbarro, KFC, Taco Bell, and at least two Asian restaurants, where the workers always held out samples of bourbon chicken. Why did they all do that? It sounded like some kind of Asian customer-service pact. Every mall Frank had ever walked through, he'd been "greeted" with people pointing toothpicks at him, each dangling a piece of brown meat. It was like something one mall restaurant had discovered once that worked to increase sales, and then it got passed along through the

Chinese restaurant grapevine.

His mind was racing. Frank tried to calm himself. It had been hours since his last dose.

He heard movement off to his right and several people entered from the mall. The muscled kid came back with four others, including a taller, older man. This had to be Gig. Who thought up these names?

Frank looked at the older man, ignoring the others.

"Why am I here?"

The older guy smiled and glanced at the others. "Wow, he is eager to get started, isn't he?" The others nodded along. Gig walked closer to Frank, shooing the skinny kid out of the chair and draping a jacket over the back of the chair. He picked up the chair and brought it closer. Very close. When he sat, his knees brushed against Frank's.

"I'm Gig. You're a guest of the Northsiders," he said quietly.

"I figured. Love what you've done with the mall. It's a real fixer-upper." Frank leaned closer. "Why'd you kill that family?"

Gig smiled. "Okay, let's get right into it. I heard you're not the kind of guy that likes chitchat."

Frank narrowed his eyes.

"They were in our house. We owned it, and had used it for several years—flop house, production lab, lots of things. We gave them the opportunity to move out. Several opportunities."

"But then you killed them."

Gig nodded, slowly. "Yes, that's what we do to folks who don't listen," he said, speaking as if he were speaking to a child. "We can't have people thinking we're weak."

"Great plan," Frank said. "The house is gone—you can't use it for a stash house or anything else now. So, what was the point?"

"The point, Mr. Harper, is fear," Gig said slowly. "When we say something's gonna happen, it's gonna happen. Then people do what they're told."

Frank looked around at the others. "What do you want with me? I know all the cops, and I'm working with the task force. They will be looking for me."

"We know. And now that you're here, you'll be interviewed by us. If we don't learn what we want to know—well, we have a specialist coming in just to talk to you," Gig said quietly. "Either way, you'll stay here with us and tell us what we need to know. And you'll be out of the way. You have a tendency to show up where you're not wanted."

Frank felt the hair on the back of his neck stand up.

"The Dragon has plans," Gig continued. "But you can't be a part of them."

The task force guys had mentioned this mysterious Dragon guy—ran the whole gang. Frank was surprised that these people were talking about him so freely.

"You really should let me go," Frank said. "They will find me," he said, glancing at his effects.

Gig followed his eyes. "You mean the phone?"

Frank didn't answer.

Gig turned to the skinny kid behind him. "T-Bone, is that true? Will the cops know where Mr. Harper is by the phone signal?"

T-Bone shook his head. "No, Gig. They disabled all the location stuff when they picked him up. Pulled the SIM card and everything. It's not pinging any cell towers."

Gig turned back to Frank. "You see, Mr. Harper, we're not idiots. We may look like a bunch of gangbangers to you, but we know what we're doing."

Frank looked up at Gig and they stared at each other for a long moment. There was nothing else to say, and Frank's head was killing him. Taunting Gig wasn't working. And these kids seemed loyal. Frank would have to think of something else.

After a minute, Gig smiled and looked at something behind Frank, nodding slightly. Frank heard the shuffling of feet and realized that someone had been standing right behind him the whole time, silent as the night. Pain flared in the back of his head and the world swam for a minute and then everything went black.

CHAPTER 58
Warning

Harper's head slumped over.

Gig waited a minute before saying anything. It was just after 4:00 a.m. in the mall, and there were no sounds but the drip of water from some distant pipes and the howling winds outside.

"He out?"

Sonny leaned around Harper and slapped the old man's face a couple of times. Sonny, another senior member of the Northsiders, had a scar that ran across his jaw and another near his right ear. Sonny's boots jangled when he walked—he always wore a pair of cowboy boots.

"Yup, he's out."

Gig turned to the others. "Ignore what I said to him—he is dangerous, and should be treated as such. No one is to speak to him. Is that clear? He is not your friend—he's a cop. The worst kind of cop—a curious one."

The six youth nodded in unison. Sonny walked over and stood next to Gig, crossing his arms.

"Good. Now, you're going to keep him fed and watered. When he needs to use the restroom, two of you will take him," Sonny said, nodding at the hallway of doors that led out to the mall proper. One of the small, closet-sized cells had been converted to a bathroom. "Untie him, with two of you covering him, one gun, one Taser. Let him do his business and tie him back up. Same for when you feed him."

The group nodded.

"And remember—we're trusting you guys," Gig said, waving at him and Sonny. "Tiny, you're in charge," Gig said, speaking to the muscled kid. "You've all done good work in the past. We wouldn't trust this job to just anyone. It might not seem like a big deal to you, babysitting some old white guy, but it's important to us. And the Dragon."

The younger kids exchanged glances.

"And Gig wasn't lying," Sonny continued. "They are bringing in Gebhuza to question him." At the mention of the name, the younger men went quiet, looking at each other.

"The old man stays locked up, either in this chair or in a holding cell," Gig said, pointing at the hallway of doors. Tiny, T-Bone, any questions?"

The skinny kid shook his head. "We got this."

"Okay, take shifts, rotate in and out, two watching, two relaxing, two sleeping next door in the Gap. And no visiting the girls," Sonny said. "I'm serious."

"And no one gets within ten feet of him, except for food and bathroom breaks," Gig said, pointing. "Don't let his druggie appearance fool you—he's a martial arts expert. T-Bone, bag up all his stuff but leave it on the table. We'll throw it all back in the Camaro. Text us every six hours, day and night. Whoever's on duty, send me and Sonny an update with a photo."

Gig turned and looked at the slumped-over Frank Harper.

"Big things are happening, boys," Gig said to the room. "Soon. But this guy could bring down the Northsiders," he said, then looked at each of the six young men in turn. "What you do here and over the next few days could save the gang," he said. "And don't get me wrong. If he escapes, we're all screwed. And Tiny, I guarantee you and the others will pay the price. You hear me?"

Tiny and the others nodded.

"Good," Sonny said, looking at them each in turn as they glanced up. "Remember, nothing else matters. Don't disappoint us, or the Dragon."

CHAPTER 59
Plots and Plans

Wednesday morning, Sergeant Tom Roget was sitting in his office, going through the overnight reports and moving forward with the last of the Fifth Street Runners. His desk was a mess, littered with papers and files. A corner of his desk was taken up with a stack of manila folders containing the personnel files on every person on the task force. He'd come in early and taken them from his locking filing cabinet, reviewing them all over the past two hours. There were no clues in the folders as to who might be working against the task force, but he'd come up with a short list of people to investigate further.

He hated the idea of someone on his team betraying their work, but he couldn't ignore his gut. Little things—strange coincidences, wildly successful raids, the "anonymous" tips that appeared like manna from heaven—just didn't add up. And his cop mind kept trying to build a case for a mole in the task force.

Even though his informant had been killed in custody, Roget was still able to prosecute the case against the others captured in the raid. The county prosecutor had come over on Tuesday and they'd worked out the charges for the men captured in the production lab. If convicted, they would all be going away for a long time—possession with intent to distribute carried long sentences in Ohio.

He looked at his desk and shook his head. The problem with being in charge of an operation like this was that there were simply too many things for him to look at. There would never be enough time in the day, even with him handing off piles of work to Hawkins and others. In addition to the personnel files, this morning he had already reviewed:

- **the ballistics report on the Bowling Boyz homicide—the report was inconclusive as the weapons used didn't match any prior crimes;**

- **the final typed transcript and report on Frank Harper's interview from Monday—just seeing it left a bad taste in Roget's mouth;**

- **a report on the hits that took place last week in other parts of the state—these were troubling, as it looked like tensions were flaring in Columbus over the dead crew;**

- **more paperwork from another raid they'd done three weeks ago—two prisoners were still awaiting formal sentencing;**

- **and yet another updated version of Agent Shales' financial report on the local gangs—the report got thicker with each new version.**

He put a sticky note on each item, either assigning it to someone else for follow-up or sending it along to Dottie and the other admin staffers to file away for safe keeping.

When he was done, Roget pushed back from the desk and looked at the whiteboard on the wall in his office to review the raids they were planning over the next few weeks.

The big item was the planned raid on the new Northsiders HQ. Hawkins had gone through all the surveillance and come up with a solid plan that left little to chance. She wanted to hit the place on early Sunday afternoon to grab up as many Northsiders as possible.

Four days.

It had been a calculation, from the start, to work on other gangs first. The mayor had been adamant—get the crime numbers down in the urban center, especially in those places ripe for redevelopment.

He glanced around the office. Roget had been trying to keep things a little closer to the vest ever since he'd gotten the inkling there might be a mole. It seemed to be working. A few raids over the last month or so had been carried out without broadcasting the location ahead of time. In one case, a surprise raid had netted a small drug storage location run by the Northsiders, the task force's first real and only damage to the group.

CHAPTER 60
On a Bender

Laura parked her car in front of the Cooper's Mill police station and headed inside. There was a snowstorm threatening—she'd heard it would be a bad one, but hopefully the last major one of the year. But it was Ohio, so you never knew.

She'd never been in the police station before and was surprised to see just how small it was. The walls of the lobby were dedicated to displays of past famous crimes from the local area. For some reason, one of the display cases held a small kid's pedal car.

"Can I help you?"

Laura turned and saw a woman, a thin brunette with a pair of striking cheekbones. The sign in the window said "Reception." Laura walked over.

"Hi, I need to speak to Chief King or Deputy Peters, whichever one is available."

"No problem," the woman said. "Can I ask what it's about?"

"My father's missing. Frank Harper."

The woman's eyes went wide.

"You must be Laura," she said, standing up. "Frank's mentioned you," she said, shaking Laura's hand. "I'm Lola, by the way."

Laura shook her hand, surprised. "Nice to meet you."

Lola picked up the phone with her other hand and dialed. "Chief, Frank's daughter is here to see you. Can I send her back?" A second passed, and then Lola nodded. "Gotcha."

Lola buzzed her through a large, unmarked door. She met Laura on the other side and walked her down the hallway and into the police station proper. Inside the main room, several rows of cubicles and desks took up the main floor. Through a bank of large windows in front of her, Laura could see the back of the Food Town grocery store.

A young, gangly cop came up to them. "This is Deputy Peters," Lola said.

"Nice to finally meet you, Ms. Harper," Peters said, shaking her hand. Laura recalled her father had mentioned the deputy when discussing the local cases he had worked on. "Mr. Harper talks about you all the time, you and little Jackson."

"Oh, it's nice to meet you," she said. "But it's Ms. Powell."

"I thought Frank said the divorce went through," he said, looking confused.

"Oh, it did, I just haven't gone back to Harper yet," Laura said, smiling. "I've been putting off changing all my accounts and credit cards and such."

An older man came out of an office and walked over to the group. Lola pointed him out. "Oh, Ms. Powell, this is Chief King."

King shook her hand as Lola excused herself. "Well, we finally get to meet the woman Frank's always talking about. He's not staying with you?"

She shook her head, suddenly concerned that they knew less than she did. "He's been gone for two days. We had dinner Monday night at my place. He was supposed to come over yesterday, but he didn't," she said.

Chief King and Deputy Peters gave each other a look.

"I know what you're thinking," Laura said. "And I'd be lying if I said I wasn't considering it, too. I checked at Ricky's and O'Shaughnessy's—no one has seen him. And he's not picking up his phone, either," she said, waving her phone. "I called the hotel, but they wouldn't give me any information."

Chief King looked at her, biting his lip. "He was supposed to call me yesterday—I left him a message. Ms. Powell, I hate to say this, but I assumed he was off on a bender."

"Did he check out of the hotel?" Deputy Peters asked.

Laura shook her head. "I don't know." She looked at Chief King. "I know he was really upset. That family dying in the fire...has really affected him. It's not good for him to be alone," she said, hoping they understood what she meant.

Chief King looked at her. "Or maybe he went and did something stupid. How much do you know about the situation?"

She rattled off what Frank had told her, mostly about the Washington family and how they had been threatened repeatedly and the cops had done nothing. She realized what she said and then emphasized it was the Dayton cops and not the folks here. Did they all work together? Had she just offended their friends? Laura had no idea how these things worked. She wrapped up with Frank's interview with the task force.

King waited for her to finish. "Sounds like you know more than we do," he said. "My worst fear is that maybe he took the fight to the Northsiders."

"That would be stupid," Laura said.

"He was in a stupid mood," Chief King replied curtly. "At least his voice mails were. Okay, let's not get excited—he's probably sleeping it off in his room. Deputy, can you run over there and roust him?"

Deputy Peters nodded. "Sure, boss. Just let me grab my coat—I think it's supposed to snow."

"Can I go with him?" Laura asked as Peters walked away.

King looked at her. He thought about it for a second, then nodded. "Actually, yeah. That's a good idea."

He walked over to Deputy Peters, who was already a few steps away. King leaned over to speak quietly into his ear. "Take her with you. If he's not at the hotel, check the bars again," he said quietly. "And the liquor store."

CHAPTER 61
Gym Equipment

Tavon and the others sat at the bar at Riley's, waiting on Gig. It felt weird being back at Riley's so soon, but the old man was now a guest of the Northsiders.

The old man. Tavon wondered what had happened to him over the last 24 hours. They'd taken him to the Salem Mall around 2:00 a.m. Monday night/Tuesday morning. Tavon knew the gang was a criminal enterprise, and he had no problem with that. The gang might be moving in a new direction, but there was still plenty of stuff they were doing that was bad. Evil, actually. Holding those women at the mall like that, for the amusement of the men who worked there. Sex slaves, drugged out of their minds and used like a run-down piece of gym equipment. Every day, they were doing what those thugs had done to Talisa. Over and over.

Tavon squirmed in his seat at the thought of his sister's attack. And now, they were holding the old man? Tavon knew that, on occasion, the gang had kidnapped other gang members, holding them for ransom or to get information. But the old man was a cop.

Bad things were going to come from this, Tavon thought. Every cop in town would be looking for the guy. Would they think the old man just checked out of his hotel and went home?

"You okay, man?"

Tavon looked up from his untouched drink. Slug was across the corner of the bar, working on his third.

"Yeah," he shouted. "I'm good."

Slug shook his head and went back to watching the girl on stage.

CHAPTER 62
Front Desk

Deputy Peters offered to drive, and riding in the police car was interesting. Laura had never ridden in one before, and certainly not in the front.

Her side of the car was pretty normal, except for the laptop computer thingy attached to the dashboard that hung halfway over her seat. The dashboard seemed higher than usual, or the maybe seats were lower, she couldn't tell. But her side was uncluttered compared to the driver's side, overrun with extra buttons and equipment, some mounted right over the air conditioning vents. By the driver's door, a big handle stuck out to direct a spotlight affixed to the driver's side exterior.

Deputy Peters got in, banging his knee on the door jamb. "Better buckle up."

"It's like a mobile command center in here, huh?"

Peters nodded. "Yeah, sorry. Let me get that out of your way."

He reached over and swung the mounted computer over towards him to make room. In doing so, he almost knocked over a glass bottle of Snapple in a cup holder near the steering wheel. It would have tipped over if she hadn't reached over and grabbed it.

"Thank you," he said. "I'm always doing that."

"No problem," she said and buckled her seat belt. Along with all the normal controls, there was an extra panel down the middle with what looked like a CB radio and other communications devices, along with a bank of four open cigarette-lighter holes. "What are those for?"

Peters looked over. "Oh, yeah. Lots of our older equipment uses those lighter chargers."

"But nobody smokes. It's funny that's what people use lighters for now."

He nodded and they started off. The sky was darkening—bad weather was coming in. Peters glanced up at the sky as they exited the police station and turned right on Garber. He passed the McDonald's and Subway and the BBQ place before ending up back at Main, stopping at the red light.

"Do you like being a cop?" Laura asked.

He looked over. "Oh, yeah. Sometimes it's stressful," he said. "And I'm not a big fan of the guns," he said, pointing up. She glanced up and didn't realize there was a rack of shotguns and handguns locked into a mount on the ceiling. Each gun was latched in with a separate three-digit lock. How could she have been inches away from all these weapons and not notice?

"Wow," she said. "Good thing those are locked up."

"Yeah. Some departments started mounting them to the ceilings because it cut down on people trying to break in and get weapons. They're hard to spot up there, although that meant all the seats had to get lowered," he said. "Sometimes I feel like I'm sitting right on the road."

The first few flakes were starting to fall from the sky when they arrived at the Vacation Inn a minute later. Deputy Peters parked right in front, and Laura started to say something when she remembered she was in a cop car. They were probably used to parking where they liked. Just as they were leaving the car, Peters got a call on the radio. He nodded at her. "Go on in—I'll be right there."

She nodded and went inside. She'd never been to this hotel, even though Frank had stayed here the other times he'd come to town. She'd offered to put him up, but he would not allow it. She couldn't tell if he was respecting her space or just preferred to come and go as he pleased. It was probably the latter—he'd been on his own for a long time. Frank was very set in his ways. She doubted he'd ever live with anyone again in his life, or settle down and get remarried.

Frank was happy on his own.

The lobby was sparsely decorated, with some furniture and a rack of brochures for local attractions, some of which she'd forgotten. Looking at the rack of literature, she suddenly felt guilty: it had been too long since she'd taken Jackson anywhere fun, like Charleston Falls or a Dragons game. She needed to remember to focus on him more. On a whim, she walked over and grabbed brochures for a few places she'd never been, like taking a ride in a biplane at WACO Field or visiting the Dayton Art Institute. And she took fliers for a few places she had been as a reminder that she needed to revisit, like the fun Dalton Farms out east of town where you could pick your own strawberries and pumpkins. Jackson would love that.

Deputy Peters entered, nodding at her. "Sorry about that."

They walked over to the front desk. A young woman was doing her nails and looked annoyed at the interruption. A soap opera played on a large TV in the lobby.

"Can I help you?" she asked in a way that made it clear she wasn't interested at all in helping.

Deputy Peters nodded. "Yes, we're here to check on a guest," Deputy Peters said, thumbing in Laura's direction. "Her father. We'd like to see if he checked out."

Laura gave Frank's name to the woman, who looked it up.

"Well, he didn't officially check out," the woman said. "Housekeeping reported earlier no answer at the door. Let me call," she said, then dialed. After a few moments, the woman hung up. "There's no answer—the guest has probably left."

Laura shook her head and looked at Deputy Peters.

"He would never just check out and leave town without telling me first. And I know what you're thinking, you and the Chief."

Deputy Peters looked at the young woman behind the counter. "Can we see the room?"

The woman nodded and gave him a key. "That floor is being cleaned now."

Laura nodded and followed Deputy Peters to the elevator. They rode it up and exited, and she followed him down the hotel hallway. The carpet was threadbare in places, and one light at the end of the hall was burned out.

They knocked, Laura suddenly nervous. What if he was here and just passed out? Or what if he'd drunk himself to death?

There was no answer. Peters pushed the door open and entered, and she followed. There was no Frank, just a hotel room. It hadn't been cleaned yet, but there was nothing of Frank's in the room. All his stuff was gone. The bed was unmade and all the towels were used.

"Well, he's gone," Deputy Peters said, rummaging around near the window and looking behind a stuffed chair for any clues.

Laura walked over to the television. A cabinet next to the TV held a coffee maker and a small mini-fridge. On a shelf above, there was a tiny microwave that looked barely large enough to cook a frozen burrito.

She leaned over and opened the fridge, looking inside, then stood up, pointing.

"Well, if he was on a bender, I don't think he'd leave this behind."

Deputy Peters gave her a look and walked over. At the back of the fridge was a half-full bottle of Knob Creek bourbon.

"He always drinks it cold," she said. "I know, it's weird."

Deputy Peters shook his head. "It doesn't make a lot of sense, does it?" He looked around the room again and shrugged. "Maybe he forgot it," Deputy Peters said. "Sometimes, when he's...been drinking, Mr. Harper forgets things."

They spent another few minutes searching the bathroom and under the bed. Laura went through the trash containers—one in the main area and one in the bathroom—but found nothing of interest. It made her feel dirty, searching through stuff that her father threw away, but she didn't know what else to be do.

She finally shook her head. "I don't know. It looks like he packed up and left, and his car is gone." She looked down at the carpet. "But it just doesn't make sense. What do we do now?"

Deputy Peters shook his head. "I better call the chief."

CHAPTER 63
Payback Time

It was another half hour before Gig showed up for their meeting. Tavon had a lot of time to think about Talisa's rapists and the "entertainment" at the Salem Mall and the old cop and what they might be doing to him.

Tavon had heard the gang was bringing in some guy that specialized in torture.

Gig walked in and joined them, waving them together so he could talk to them over the music. Before they got started, Tavon handed him another stack of paperwork. Gig had him trading stacks now every time they met. On these recent documents, Tavon was to search for anything that might indicate if someone in the gang was stealing. While he was at it, Tavon was also looking for ways to improve their efficiency.

"Sorry I'm late," Gig said to them. "Things are crazy at the mall." He looked around the club. "They haven't started out here?"

"What you mean?" Slug asked.

"They're rehabbing this place," Gig said. "There's been construction people in the back since the weekend—adding rooms. Supposed to expand out here, too, and add more space and another bar. They built almost an entire lab downstairs in three days and stocked it with outdated equipment and some product."

Tavon didn't even know there was a downstairs. "Why?"

"We're expanding," Gig said, smiling. "That's what we're telling everyone, in case anyone asks. We need another HQ to replace the mall."

"What's happening with the mall?" Slug asked.

"Nothing," Gig said. "Don't worry about it. Okay, I have two runs for you guys today, one to Austin Landings and another to Cinci. Don't come back between—just take what you need when you go to Austin Landing and head to Cinci after. You heard about the Bowling Boyz?"

Tavon shook his head, but Slug nodded. "Dead, last week," he said, looking around at them. "Someone took out the whole crew."

Gig nodded. "That was us. Our hitters, the same guys you saw in Columbus. And we're stepping in to pick up their dealer network. I need more product down there," Gig said. "The guy in charge—Tangle—is cool. He switched over to us, but he might need a little muscle. See what he needs help with, collect our cut, make the delivery."

"Yup, got it," Rubio said, writing it down on his yellow pad. "What else?"

"Then head to Cinci. We're doing a big hit. Need you there for backup. Should go smoothly—if not, you might need to drive some folks out. Sonny's hitters might need to split up if things blow up. That happens, you each take one guy and swing south into Kentucky, drive around for a few hours. Take your time getting home. Sonny would rather his hitters get back to Dayton tomorrow or Friday than get arrested."

Slug and Rubio nodded. Tavon wasn't sure what all of that meant, but Rubio would know. Tavon could ask him later.

Gig turned to Tavon. "One other thing. You know that thing we're doing for you?"

Tavon nodded. It was hard to forget.

"It happened," Gig continued. "Sorry about that. I know I said you could be there, but things went south on a buy. Those two guys won't be bothering anyone now."

Tavon wasn't sure what to say. He wanted closure for his sister and revenge for himself. But it was good to know the punks were dead.

"How'd it happen?"

Gig smiled. "Thought you might ask. Painfully. It was a buy, and they were there providing muscle. Did a shit job of it. People grabbed for the money, somebody pulled their piece, and before you knew it, both got shot. Bled out. I got some pictures from before the cops showed up to investigate."

Slug smiled and put his hand down by his crotch, grabbing himself. "The cops can investigate this."

Gig laughed and continued talking. "I'll send over pictures."

Tavon nodded. "Thanks," he said, but he wasn't sure if he really meant it or not. And the idea of seeing pictures of his sister's attackers made him feel uneasy.

"I know it's a lot to think about," Gig said. "Show your sister the pictures, or not. But they're dead."

Tavon nodded again. It seemed like all he ever did now was nod. Nod and keep his thoughts to himself.

CHAPTER 64
In Hiding, Still

Jake was chatting with the Washingtons in their hotel room in Columbus, discussing the headline in the Columbus paper. He'd brought it for them to read, in case they hadn't heard about it on the news. And it had happened less than ten miles away from the hotel.

"Gangland Slaying Kills Eight."

"They're saying it's the Northsiders," Markeys said, pointing at the article. "Why they in Columbus?"

Jake shook his head. "I have no idea. And because you're all supposedly dead, I can't call the Dayton task force folks and ask."

He grew quiet for a minute, glancing over at young Noah, who was watching a cartoon on the TV. "I don't know what's going on," Jake said quietly. "Maybe the Northsiders are just expanding their territory, like the writer of the article is saying. Or they could…they could be looking for you guys," he said, mouthing the last few words so the little boy wouldn't hear them.

Denise shook her head. "Nah, nah, they think we dead," she said quietly. She looked at Markeys. "You said they weren't never gonna be looking for us."

"I don't know what's going on, any more than Mr. Delancy does," Markeys said, pointing a thumb at Jake. "It could just be a weird accident. But if they're around here, we have to stay inside."

"I'm considering telling just my local cops," Jake added. "They could protect you."

Markeys and Denise both shook their heads. "Nah, that's worse," Denise said. "If they don't already know we're still alive, the cop's'll tell 'em."

"What did Mr. Harper find?"

Jake looked at Markeys. "I have no idea. I know he's back in town but I haven't talked to him. I'd guess doing some investigating on his own."

"'Investigating, you say?" Denise asked. "I think you mean makin' trouble."

"Yeah, that's Frank," Jake said.

"Then we should stay as far away from Dayton as possible," Denise said, making her point again. It was hard to argue with her.

They sat in silence for a minute. All Jake could hear was the heater blowing and Noah's cartoon on the television. The room smelled like trash and old take-out. They had to be getting sick of eating out of Styrofoam containers.

"Look, I don't know what's the right thing to do," Jake said again. "But if you want to stay, we'll keep you here. But I need to tell someone. Just in case," he said, glancing at Noah.

"In case of what?" Markeys asked quietly.

Jake looked at him. "I don't know. If anything happened to you guys…"

Denise shook her head and looked at her husband. "Won't he have to tell the task force?"

"I don't know."

CHAPTER 65
BOLO

Laura stood in the police station with her arms crossed, looking at Chief King.

"So, where is he?"

The chief had no idea what to tell her.

"I assumed…" he began and then stopped. "Drunk?"

She looked up at him. "For two whole days? Drunk, but sober enough to check out of his hotel room—and leave behind his bourbon? I haven't heard from him. If he went back to Birmingham, he would have called me."

"That's strange," Peters said.

"No shit," Laura replied, earning another disapproving look from Peters. She hadn't figured out yet that Peters hated cursing.

Frank Harper was a fly in the ointment, a bad penny. He could make things better, on occasion, or spin things out of control. It was hard to guess what was going on in that man's mind: half of the time he was like a shark, cruising around, looking for trouble. Or a drink.

But he'd never gone off the grid like this. "His car is gone, too?"

Laura nodded. "And security cameras at the hotel are fake, so there's no video of him leaving. But I can't believe he'd leave that bottle behind," she said. "It's expensive…and he's not exactly rolling in funds."

King and Peters nodded.

"Deputy, anything else from the front desk clerk?"

Peters looked at his yellow pad, the same kind that King used, and read off his notes, including the name of the clerk and her recollections. "She said all indications were he checked out. They had a smoke alarm go off there Monday night, which required the hotel to be emptied. CMPD, the fire department, and EMTs responded. False alarm," Peters said. "The situation was resolved without incident, and all the guests returned to their rooms."

"They checked to make sure everyone was accounted for?"

"No, they didn't," Peters said, looking at his notes. "Sorry, I didn't mean to imply that."

"Then just stick to the facts."

"Okay, sir. The front desk clerk said the guests returned to their rooms."

King nodded. It was a fine distinction—"all the guests" versus just "the guests." He had been working with Peters to be more precise. "You understand the difference, right? Using the word 'all' in there makes it sound like they did a head count or something. You can't make those kinds of assumptions."

Peters nodded.

"What about the bars and the liquor store?"

Peters shook his head. "No one has seen him since Monday."

King looked back at Laura, wondering how much Frank had told her about the work they had done together. Would he have shielded her from the close calls? Frank had very nearly died, burned alive in that brush fire field last October. Did Laura know about that? How much did she know about Joe Hathaway and the incident on the frozen lake last month? Did she know that someone had planned to murder Frank and Deputy Peters, sending them through the melted ice and into a watery grave in Trapper's Lake? And when that didn't work, Hathaway had sat with his long-range rifle and tried to pick them off on the ice. Did she know any of that?

Chief King was used to working around cops. They routinely held back vast portions of their daily lives—the frustrations, the constant danger—from their wives and children. Partly it was about the investigations and the need to keep the information close. Nothing could end a cop's career faster than sharing something about an ongoing investigation with a family member and then having it splashed on the evening news or Facebook. It could end a career, or seriously hamper a criminal investigation. Or both.

But cops kept information to themselves for other reasons. They didn't want their loved ones to realize just how closely law enforcement walked that line. Every day they made a thousand life-or-death decisions. Every traffic stop for a police officer was potentially his last.

It was the one thing civilians didn't understand.

King felt like asking his civilian friends "remember that time you got pulled over last year and you were so nervous and your hands were shaking? Cops go through that heightened level of stress. But for them, it happens dozens of times every day."

No wonder so many cops drank so much. Or put a gun in their mouth.

But Chief King got the impression Laura was made of sterner stuff. She'd marched in here and stood with her hands on her hips and demanded they do something about it. Laura wasn't going to let up no matter what he told her.

She sounded like a Harper.

King looked at Peters. "Hit the bars in Vandalia and downtown Troy. See if anyone's seen him. Or if he had a drink on the way out of town. I'll put out a BOLO."

Laura looked at him. "What's that?"

"It's a 'be-on-the-lookout-for' notice, a way to have the locals looking for the car without entering it into the national database yet," King answered. "Can you go with Peters?"

She shook her head.

"I'm already late picking up Jackson." She looked at Peters. "But can you drive around down by that strip club in Dayton? Frank told me about his dust up with the gang members. I can't believe he did it, but he said on Sunday that he was heading back down there to look for them. He wanted to question them about the house fire."

King looked at Peters. "Did you know about this?"

"No, he didn't call me. You?"

King shook his head. "I knew he was back, not what he was up to. I don't like him off running his own investigation."

Laura nodded, and King realized she knew what he was talking about. Frank had told her a lot, evidently. "Maybe you'll find his car," she said.

Peters and Laura left, walking out together. King watched them go and wondered where Frank Harper had gotten himself off to. If you were going on a two-day bender, why check out of your hotel? Maybe he was taking the long way back to Birmingham. Maybe he was dead in a ditch somewhere. Maybe he'd wrecked his car. The BOLO would help with that. If not, King would put something out nationwide.

It was a few hours before Chief King heard back from Peters. King was home, making himself dinner and settling in to watch some TV when his cell phone rang. He checked the number and answered.

"Hey, Floyd."

"Hey, Jeff," Deputy Peters answered. They always used first names when they spoke off duty, a casual attitude that wouldn't be appropriate at the office.

"Find anything on Frank?"

"No, nothing," Peters answered. King could hear the frustration in his voice. King had been working on Peters, teaching him how to manage his frustration about the job. What was the old adage about police work? Three steps forward, two steps back?

"What about the strip club?"

"Nothing," Peters said. "They're doing some kind of construction— taking stuff in and out. Furniture, too. I didn't see his car, but I went inside and had a look around. Nobody had seen him. You think he's headed back to Alabama? Would he go without telling his daughter?"

"I don't know," King said, telling the truth. "I'd think he would call one of us to say he's leaving. Or Laura. Anything from the BOLO?"

"Nothing yet. I'm at the office and will send it out again. Should we go national?"

King shook his head before realizing he was doing it. "No, not yet. I'll do it in the morning if we don't hear anything overnight. Who's on duty tonight?"

Peters related the names of the Cooper's Mill PD who were on duty overnight and tomorrow morning.

"Okay," King said. "Let them know to be on the lookout. And, before you leave, can you call the task force and tell them? This time of night, you'll get a junior officer. Give them the details to pass along. Someone will find him."

Peters was quiet for a second. "I just hope they don't find it at the bottom of a ditch. With Mr. Harper in it."

"Yeah," King said. "Me too."

CHAPTER 66
Road Win?

The drug meet near Austin Landings went well. Rubio and Slug and Tavon met up with Tangle, their new contact, in the parking lot of a brand-new Kroger.

Actually, the whole area was new—the planners were still marking out areas for construction. A pair of new office buildings stood in the grid of fresh roads, while a large shopping area was finishing up construction closer to the new interchange with I-75. This was going to be a huge development when it was finished, but right now it looked strange: roads that went nowhere, street lights standing over empty fields.

The Kroger was done, though, and they met in broad daylight, parking close to each other. The buy went down without a hitch. Tangle, a big white dude, seemed to have no problem working with his new Northsiders bosses. Slug and Rubio asked if he needed more muscle, but Tangle said no. He'd hired on a few new guys to keep the distributors in south Dayton in line. They were all reporting to him now, and he was eager to keep the product moving. Bowling Boyz or no Bowling Boyz, there were people out there that needed their coke and heroin. Tangle wanted no disruptions in service.

Over the course of their conversation, Tangle made it clear there was no love lost between him and the Bowling Boyz. He was glad they were dead and happy to be working for "new management." Rubio agreed and told the man to call if he ever needed a hand.

The meet wrapped up early, so Tavon and the others grabbed an early dinner, and then headed south to Cincinnati. Rubio took the lead, the Civics winding their way along I-75 south until they exited near the riverfront, turning west. Tavon recognized the area from last week. The cars wound around the waterfront area, and Rubio stopped in a parking lot down the street from the warehouse from last week. Rubio got out and waved them over. It was starting to get dark and a light snow was coming down, settling on their cars and the roads around them.

"What are we doing?" Slug asked when the three of them met at Rubio's car.

"We wait," Rubio said, checking his notes. "They're having the meet now. We'll see how it goes."

They went back to their cars. Tavon got on his phone and read the news, looking into the incident in Columbus. It certainly sounded like two rival gangs fighting for territory, but Tavon knew it was more than that. The Northsiders were spreading, taking out competitors. Grow or die. Branching out to Columbus. And he was in a dark, snowy parking lot in Cincinnati. Were they spreading in this direction as well?

The Dragon was certainly ambitious.

Two hours passed without incident. Tavon started his car every few minutes to warm it up, then turned it off to conserve gasoline. Rubio texted a few times, keeping them in the loop on what was happening. Apparently, he was talking to someone in the warehouse.

The explosion came without warning.

One second, Tavon was scrolling through stories in the *Dayton Daily News*, reading about a new factory that was going to be built up in Cooper's Mill. The next, a deafening roar shook his car, and a blinding flash of light off to his left made him jump.

The warehouse they had been watching erupted in an orgy of red flames. Pieces of the building rained down around Tavon's car. A huge hunk of metal crashed in the parking lot less than a yard from his car. He started the car and was putting it in gear when he got a group text from Rubio.

"WAIT."

Another explosion followed, and then another, and another. Tavon watched, staring at the building a block down, wondering if anyone could make it out of there alive.

He saw two figures through the darkness approaching the cars.

Tavon picked up his gun and glanced at Rubio's car. Rubio was watching the approaching men as well. Did Rubio have his gun out? Were these Northsiders or someone else? If this was a gang war, Tavon didn't even know the name of the gang they were fighting.

Two figures approached, one helping the other. Rubio climbed from the car and shouted something at the approaching men. They answered him and Rubio lowered his weapon and ran to the guy carrying the wounded man. It seemed Rubio knew them.

Tavon got out and ran over. "What's going on?" He could hear the fire crackling down the street.

"He's hurt," Rubio said. "And they've got company."

Tavon looked up. More figures were approaching from the direction of the fire.

The injured man, blood on his face, looked at them. "There are more dead, back in the warehouse. Sonny said not to leave them."

"Too late," Rubio shouted as Slug joined them. "Slug, Tavon, get him into my car," Rubio said, pushing the injured man onto them.

The injured man was wearing jeans and a black jacket. There was a huge, jagged piece of glass sticking out of his stomach. They dragged him to Rubio's Civic and Tavon opened the passenger door. He was lowering the seat when he heard a weird coughing sound and something metal ricocheted off the hood of his car. He heard a thin "plink" from the brick wall behind him. Another piece of metal from the explosion?

"Get down!" Rubio and the uninjured shooter dropped behind the car, pulling weapons.

Two more bullets ricocheted off Rubio's car as Tavon struggled to push the passenger door up. He'd always opened the slide-up doors from a standing position and found it much more difficult to open from below.

It didn't help that his hands were covered in blood.

Tavon heard a rattle. Automatic weapons fire. He got the door open and pushed it up, and Slug leaned over and helped Tavon get the injured kid into Rubio's passenger seat.

There was another rattle, and several bullets hit Rubio's car. Tavon wondered if the doors were strong enough to repel bullets.

"Slug, Tavon, get out of here," Rubio yelled. "Split up and head home. Slug, take this guy," Rubio shouted, pointing at the uninjured shooter next to him.

"Gotcha," Slug yelled and grabbed the back of the man's coat, dragging him backwards to the other car.

Tavon got a few shots off, covering Slug until he and the other guy were in their car and driving away. More figures were appearing in the dark, outlined against the fire that now engulfed the entire warehouse and threatened to spread to other warehouses nearby.

Rubio looked over at him. "You, go!"

Tavon didn't wait to be told twice. He ducked around Rubio's car and ran to his own car, climbing in and starting it up. With one glance at Rubio—the man was already in his own driver's seat, starting the car—Tavon pulled away.

Ten minutes later, Tavon drove, his hands shaking.

The entire warehouse was destroyed, and probably dozens of people were dead, including some Northsiders. There were bullet holes in the side of his Civic. One had grazed the hood of the car, leaving an ugly black and silver streak from left to right along the flat hood.

Tavon took the highway north. Gig had said to head into Kentucky and take a long loop around before heading back to Dayton, but Tavon was too scared. He just wanted to be home, back in his attic room with his safe full of cash. When he calmed down, he texted Gig using the vaguest terms he could think of.

The response that came back wasn't vague at all.

"Come back."

He went north, passing through the northern suburbs of Cincinnati, then crossing the 275 beltway that ringed the city. Tavon was shivering even though he had the heat cranked.

CHAPTER 67
Prep Time

"You want us to get him up?"

Gig looked up from his paperwork. Who ever thought there could be so much paperwork involved in running a gang?

Tiny was standing in the doorway—he ran the team in charge of Harper. Tiny worked for Sonny. Sonny and Gig had been put in charge of overseeing Harper's captivity, and assigned Tiny to manage things like food, water, and bathroom breaks.

They'd had the old man for four days now, and the ex-cop hadn't told them anything interesting or useful.

"Get Harper into the chair," Gig said. Half of the old Banana Republic was taken up with the open area in the middle of the store, where they "questioned" rival gang members. The floor was concrete and easily washed down. It was common for guests to lose blood. Or limbs. And, on the rare occasion when they put someone down, it was the perfect place. There was also a back entrance to bring people in—and take bodies out.

"Gotcha." Tiny left the doorway of Gig's office, leaving Gig to his thoughts. He wasn't really sure why they were holding the old man. It seemed like it would make more sense to just kill the guy, but the Dragon and the Council wanted him questioned further.

No one outside the mall knew where he was. In fact, the cops weren't even suspecting foul play yet. Gig had seen the printout of the nationwide BOLO that had gone out on the car Thursday morning. The cops would never find the Camaro, parked inside the old Sears Automotive service bay.

Gig found the BOLO printout and scanned it again, just in case. They had the make, model and VIN on there, along with a good description of the old man, but nothing on it about him being in danger. Most BOLOs went out on suspects or "persons of interest," folks wanted by the cops for questioning. He guessed they'd used a BOLO instead of a "missing persons" report because Frank was law enforcement. Usually the cops sent out a missing-persons report or an AMBER alert, depending on the age of the victim. It was a good thing the Northsiders were tapped into the local law enforcement computer systems. This let them get copies of every alert or report that went out.

Gig smiled and put away the printout. None of the few people looking for Harper had any idea where to look.

Gig wondered if Harper would ever tell them what they needed to know, or if he'd die under the questioning.

CHAPTER 68
Hard Times

Frank was awakened by another splash of water. These people had no originality.

"Wake up," Tiny said.

He'd been here for four days, as far as Frank could tell. He thought it was Friday morning, based on his rough count of the number of mornings he'd been awakened by cold water. Before, he'd been tied to a chair in an open space, an old store. Two days ago, they'd moved him to this closet-sized room. It was tiny and driving him insane.

"Come on, let's go."

The guy named Tiny picked Frank up and walked him out of the small room. A tall guy, whom Frank had nicknamed "Lurch," stood off to the side with a Taser pointed at Frank. They always worked in pairs.

Yesterday, except for feeding time and for bathroom breaks, he spent the whole day in the little room, and the claustrophobia was overwhelming. Frank cried and pounded on the walls. When he wore himself out, he would lie on the floor and sleep with his legs curled up. There wasn't room for him to lie flat. Frank was going through his own personal hell. Four days with no Oxy and no alcohol. Four days. Trapped in a tiny room the size of the elevators he'd avoided for years.

All he knew for certain was that if he ever got out of here, he was gonna kill someone.

The first day, they'd beat him in the middle of the old Banana Republic. But the lack of Oxy was twenty times worse than the beating. He could feel the Oxycontin leaving his system, draining away to nothing. It was like his blood was running away.

The pain came first.

It was followed by the shakes, and then his mind began to feel off kilter, untethered from reality.

And that was just day one. Every day since had been worse, an exercise in pain management, and not in the way he'd been doing for months. Now, he had no crutches to help, no "maintenance" doses to push back the pain. But he could have taken the pain, and gladly, if that was all there was to it. The pain in his back and sides was nothing compared to the gnawing inside his skin. He felt like he was crawling with bugs.

Frank alternated between sweating and getting chills and shaking and scratching his skin raw. He imagined each day was the worst, but then the next day would come along and prove him wrong.

Frank shook his head and flushed. There was nothing in the bathroom to help him escape. He'd checked, over and over. Frank washed hands and ran water over his face and through his hair. He looked in the mirror and didn't recognize the man he saw.

Frank thought about Laura and Jackson, two of the few people in the world who might miss him if he were gone. Would anyone else care? Who would come to his funeral? Maybe Williams, or Detective Murray. Maybe the local purveyors of alcohol would attend out of mourning— losing their best customer would be difficult for anyone.

Maybe a few people from Birmingham or Cooper's Mill or Baton Rouge, where he grew up. But not many. Only a few people would care if Frank ever made it out of this place.

Frank looked in the mirror again. It was one of those cheap metal mirrors that couldn't be broken, or he would have shattered it days ago. Grabbed a piece of broken glass and attacked his captors. Anything to break up the monotony and distract him from the scratching, which led to bleeding and more pain.

He knocked on the door and Tiny opened it, letting him out into the hall.

Frank had assigned all the guards names—he'd heard a few, like Tiny and T-Bone, and invented names for the rest. They talked to him when they brought him food and let him out to use the bathroom. But they rarely said a word, to him or each other.

Tiny walked him into the main room, and "Lurch" followed close behind with a Taser. Tiny sat him back in the familiar metal chair and tied him up. Frank hated this chair.

When Tiny was done, "Lurch" handed Tiny his Taser and leaned over Frank, double checking the ropes on his arms and feet—these guys might be gangbangers, but they knew how to truss up a prisoner.

Frank's arms and legs and chest were rubbed raw by the ropes. The only way to keep them from hurting was to sit perfectly still. When he was in the chair, Frank had nothing to do but doze off. Or stare off into space and think about the Washington family. At least he was paying for what he'd done to them.

He stared at the back of the old Banana Republic and the double doors that led out. He'd seen people going in and out of the backroom— did it lead to a back door?

There were a few signs that the Northsiders' were novices at holding prisoners and interrogating people. The rotating team of kids guarding him was one sign—kids were restless and got bored too easily. The Northsiders should have been using adults to keep watch over Frank. Adults knew how to sit for hours at a time without losing focus. These kids were used to running and playing at being bad asses, dealing drugs or knocking over local stores. They weren't used to sitting for hours at a time, trying to find something to occupy their minds. Frank also noticed that the kids were constantly reaching for their pockets. They would grow bored and absent mindedly reach for their phones, then scowl when they realized the phones weren't there—apparently, they kept them in another place.

The only other gang member Frank knew by name was Tavon, the kid from the strip club, and the other two guys in his crew. Frank had kept an eye out for them, but had not seen them around. Bit he got a sense of activity all around him, with people coming and going. Sometimes he could hear sounds of equipment and machinery.

And, at night, he heard the laughter of men and the sobbing of women.

Tiny and "Lurch" left Frank and went over and sat down in their group of chairs clustered around a TV and Xbox setup. He could tell they were all as bored as he was, but no amount of talking or sharing had gotten any of them to open up. All they did all day was spend endless hours watching him and playing some shooting game called "Call of Duty."

Gig and another guy named Sonny ran Frank's guard detail, as far as Frank could tell. Tiny and the others reported to them.

On day two, Gig had returned and questioned Frank about his dealings with the task force and about his career and his family. Frank told him mostly everything—there was no point in holding back about the task force, not that Frank knew much. It had gone on for hours. But he kept some things back. No way he was going to give them any information on Laura or Jackson, although they already knew where Laura lived. Apparently, they had been following Frank for some time.

Gig also asked about the other members of the task force. Who they were, where they lived, stuff that Frank couldn't possibly know. He answered truthfully when he could. Gig recorded the whole conversation on his phone. After Frank answered every question, Gig stood and smiled and had Tiny and two other guys beat the crap out of Frank. By the end, Frank was spitting up blood and in more pain than he could remember. After, they dragged him back to his room and threw him inside.

That was Wednesday. Thursday had been better—they'd left him alone with his shaking hands to scratch himself and stare at the walls in his little closet.

How today would shape up was anyone's guess.

Frank looked up at Tiny.

"What are we doing now? I'm bored."

"We wait."

CHAPTER 69
Arrival Time

Gig finished his work and closed the large report, standing and carrying it out of his office. The kid, Tavon, had been useful, even before that craziness on Wednesday night with the hit in Cincinnati. Gig had been giving Tavon reports and stacks of inventory numbers for a while, having him investigate where they could be more efficient. And the kid had suggested several improvements.

Gig was carrying the drug production ledger, a large printout of an Excel report used to track how much of each illicit drug the Northsiders were producing each day and in which location it was being produced. The Northsiders were making so much product, it was hard to track it all: raw materials, production staff levels, cooking times, equipment, maintenance, and even break times were tracked in the spreadsheet. Quality levels were tested; new variations on standard products were tested; and, as with every chemical process, there was some small amount of waste. But Gig was happier now—he'd been tasked by Mr. Kingmaker to examine the process, and Gig had something concrete to discuss with him.

But that meeting would have to wait until later in the day. This morning was already busy—the torturer was arriving.

Gebhuza was known in many circles. The man was a legend, able to extract any information from any person. Gig shivered at the stories he'd heard about the man's methods—he employed every one known to man, and had even invented a few of his own.

Gig made his way to the vault, passing between two guards and the counting tables that ringed the room. He walked into the vault and put the production report where it belonged, on top of several similar reports. The reports were highly sensitive and kept under lock and key, just as the corresponding computer files were password protected. Anyone who acquired these reports could see just how the Northsiders were handling the drug side of their business, which was, by far, the most profitable business the gang pursued.

Gig turned and left the vault, nodding at the guards. He made his way out into the mall, passing the Harem and other darkened storefronts. They had plenty of room to expand, if necessary. And with all the territory they were acquiring, it wouldn't be long before they would need more offices and production labs, including offices to manage Cincinnati and Columbus and Toledo. Soon after, they'd be large enough to challenge the major gangs in Chicago. The Dragon had a dream, and it didn't end with the Northsiders controlling all the drugs and gambling and extortion in Dayton.

Gig walked around to the theater entrance. They kept two of the screens operational; it was good for morale. Sometimes they showed Denzel movies or old gangster films. The Dragon had screened *The Godfather* again for the Council only a few weeks ago.

Gig passed through the theater lobby, which smelled like popcorn, and spoke to the guard by a pair of red doors that led outside. These doors were usually kept locked, of course, but today they stood open, chilly air and gritty snow blowing inside. A half-dozen other men also waited by the open door.

"Are we ready?" Gig asked.

The guard nodded. "Yep," he said, nodding at the group of men.

Gig nodded and waited. He was a few minutes early and spent the time in a group text with Rubio and Slug and Tavon, checking in after Wednesday night's insanity. Tavon had returned first, followed by Rubio and Slug, who had driven their charges back to the mall. Sonny had been there and grilled them about the warehouse explosion.

Apparently, everything had gone to plan, right up until the death of several Northsiders. Six of Sonny's best shooters had gone to Cincinnati to "talk terms" with the Hive, the gang that ran most of the docks and waterfront areas in southern Cincinnati. Earlier in the week, the Northsiders had sent the Hive a substantial shipment of five large crates of drugs and drug samples. Ostensibly, the Northsiders were "trying out" to become the Hive's new suppliers. The Hive was getting most of their product from the Mexican cartels, and a local supplier might cut costs.

However, the Northsiders weren't interested in becoming their supplier. The bottom half of each crate delivered to the Hive's warehouse had contained a hidden cache of explosives. The plan was to get the shipment inside and then detonate the explosives remotely. They hoped to take out a good number of the Hive's leaders. Unfortunately, it turned out that the Hive used some sophisticated jamming equipment, which blocked any incoming signals.

The Dragon ordered Sonny to send in men to manually trigger the bombs. The meet to "talk terms" was a cover. After the Hive's upper management gathered, Sonny's men triggered timers in the clandestine explosives and started the negotiations. They waited until there were only minutes left, then excused themselves from the talks to "discuss our options."

Of the six Northsiders shooters, only one made it back to the mall alive. Some of the Hive's men made it out of the warehouse and chased the Northsiders. It was fortunate that Gig had sent Rubio and his crew.

There would be repercussions for the Northsiders' move on the Hive. But the Council and the Dragon would know what to do.

Gig finished texting as a limousine pulled up. The doors opened and several men got out. One held the door for another man, who climbed slowly out of the limo and looked around, straightening his tie. The man looked ancient, at least in his eighties, but moved with a fluid grace.

"So, this is Dayton," the man said, unimpressed. His nearly impenetrable Caribbean accent made him difficult to understand. "It's cold. No wonder I never been 'ere before."

Gig smiled and shook his hand, as did several members of the Council, on hand to greet the legend with the long, gray and black dreads.

"Welcome, sir," Sausage said, the Jamaican's hands disappeared inside the council member's huge fists. "We're so glad you could travel up on such short notice," he said. "You do us a great honor."

The Jamaican nodded. "Well, it's nice to be greeted with such words," he said. "Is the Dragon here yet?"

"Not yet," Sausage said. "Later."

"Very good. Please have someone get my bags," Gebhuza said, waving a hand at the long black car. "It's been a long drive." The man turned and started inside, followed by the members of the Council. Sausage began explaining the mall and their usage of the space.

Gig nodded at two of the waiting guards. "Get his bags. And follow us."

CHAPTER 70
Shaking Time

Frank sat in the chair and waited, trying to stay still. Every movement scraped his skin.

He had spent most of the last four days thinking. Thinking about how he'd gotten into this mess and how he'd allowed himself to be drawn into this turf war between the gangs and the cops. He made lists in his head—things he wanted to do if he ever escaped, places he wanted to go. Continuations of those silly lists of things that were bothering him back in Birmingham. How silly and simplistic that seemed now. He'd been worried about his job and where the next hit of Oxy was coming from. How much to take and when.

The alcohol—well, he'd always struggled with it, even back in his Army days. But he'd been able to tame it in the past. There was that time after his partner Ben Stone had died. Frank had climbed on the wagon for nearly six months then. Oxy was different. It had dug into him, claws and all. And now he was paying the price.

In a rare moment of lucidity, Frank resolved to study his current situation as dispassionately as possible, like he was watching one of those cops shows. He tried to look at it like a puzzle. He was a captive of the Northsiders. Could he solve it, or would he die trying? Sitting in the chair, waiting, Frank made another list. This one included all the Northsiders he could identify:

- **The three gangbangers who drove product were Tavon and Rubio and some big, muscular guy. What was his name?**

- **Frank's six guards, swapping in and out, were T-Bone and Tiny. Frank had named the others "Lurch," "Reebok," "Dancer" and "Prancer." They all carried guns and Tasers. They played too much of a game they called "Call of Duty," whatever that was.**

- **Tavon's crew worked for Gig.**

- **The guards worked for someone named Sonny—Frank had no idea what he looked like.**

- **And they all worked for some guy called The Dragon. Ohhhh, scary.**

The shakes were back. The Oxy had made everything better for a while, but now the pain was coming back. Payment in full, a loan to get rid of the pain. Now the loan was due, plus interest. His eyes swam as he looked around. He needed to be thinking about other things. He needed to ignore the pain and the way his skin crawled, ignore his shaking hands. He needed to think about escaping.

He was in the Salem Mall. That much was easy. It was a building and he was in it. And now he just had to get out of it.

All the kids carried cell phones, but each made a point of leaving them next door in the abandoned Gap store. This had apparently been a Banana Republic—Frank had seen a few discarded signs on the trips to the bathroom and back. The only time he saw a cell phone was every six hours, when one of the kids would come in, take a photo of him, and then text it to someone. Frank assumed it was for Gig, but maybe the messages were going out to someone else. Was Frank being held hostage? Were they negotiating with the task force for a ransom or something else? Frank had no clue.

Frank had driven around north Dayton, looking for trouble. An insane attempt to close the case by himself. And trouble had found him. What had he been thinking? No one knew where he was. No one had his back. Just like Ben Stone, driving around parts of Miami alone, trying to break a case wide open. And Ben had paid with his life.

Frank hadn't been this stupid since St. Bart's.

NO.

No, he was not going to think about that. It was better to think about almost anything else. Not St. Bart's. Not the little kid in the cardboard box. Not the bodies floating in the water.

His mind screamed and his skin crawled, and he could think of nothing other than how much he wanted one of those stupid little pills or just a tiny pull from his flask. The flask that was still in his car— he'd refilled it with the Knob Creek, a splurge to celebrate his trip to Ohio. He'd sipped at it while driving around Dayton, checking out the Northsiders' locations.

His car.

Was it still parked at the hotel? Or had they brought it here? If it was in front of the hotel, then people would think he was still there. Someone would have checked in on him by now and know he's missing. Someone would have called his phone, called his boss in Birmingham, tracked his credit card.

Laura. She had to worried about him. She'd probably talked to others—Chief King, Deputy Peters, maybe even Collier and Murray and Williams? Was anyone looking for him? Were they all out there driving around searching, or had they all chalked it up to an epic bender? Probably the latter. And he had no one to blame but himself. He could hear Chief King: "he's probably drunk himself into a stupor over that family. Frank's in a ditch, his car wrecked."

If the cops were looking for him, they'd put out an APB on his car. The Northsiders would have cleaned out the hotel room to make it look like Frank had left town, traveling the highways and byways with his bourbon and his little bag of white pills. Never to be seen again.

CHAPTER 71
Question Time

Frank looked up. There was a commotion in the hallway, and more guards came in, accompanied by Gig and a new gentleman. The new man looked like a caricature of a fellow from the Caribbean—a black man in his eighties, at least, with sunglasses and bright clothes covering his wide frame. The man also had the craziest dreadlocks Frank had ever seen—the thick strands were tied off with little ribbons, each a different color. They flopped around his face and moved likes ropey snakes, undulating over each other.

Behind him, a younger man carried an old, battered, brown suitcase done up with straps around it. Another man carried an orange extension cord and what looked like a metal wash-tub. The guards were talking to Gig quietly, but when they got close enough for Frank to hear, Gig shushed them.

"Mr. Harper, how are we doing?" Gig asked.

Frank looked at him. "Fine, thanks," his voice croaked. He'd been coughing a lot over the past four days and his throat was raw. "I could use a drink. Bourbon."

Gig nodded, his face nearing an approximation of concern. "I understand you've been shaking. DTs, I'm told. And I can see you've been digging and scratching," he said, nodding at Frank's self-inflicted injuries. Gig reached into a pocket and took out something, holding it up. It was the bag of Oxy that Frank had taken from Stimpy.

"Too much of this in your system. Am I right? I could get you some, if you cooperate."

"I'm bored," Frank answered, gripping the arms of the chair. Just seeing the bag made him start to shake.

Gig smiled and pointed at the old black man. "Good, then you'll like my friend Gebhuza. He's here to make your life more interesting."

Gebhuza nodded and set down his case and the tub, looking around at the furnishings. "Can you bring one of those tables over here?" he asked, his voice thick with a Jamaican accent.

Two of the guards cleaned one of the metal tables off and brought it over, setting it in front of Gebhuza. He lifted his case onto it and began unpacking things—towels, small cups and containers, a roll of tools, and another wrapped item that he set aside. Each item made a metallic noise as he arranged them carefully on the wide silver table.

"Where do you want the other one?" Gig asked.

"Right there, next to this table," Gebhuza said, making a motion with his hand. Gig directed the guards, who set a second six-foot-long metal table up next to the first one, making a "T."

"That's fine," Gebhuza said. "Can you prepare him? And I need that hose."

Gig pointed at one of the men. "Get the hose in here." He turned to the others and nodded. As a group, the guards walked over to Frank's chair. Three of them started untying his feet while two others pulled out their Tasers and pointed them at Frank. They untied him from the chair and walked him over to the table, laying him face up.

As he was being moved, Frank saw a crowd had gathered. There were spectators in the room now, at least twenty, seated on folding chairs or standing around.

The guards retied Frank, this time to the table. When they were done, he was strapped down tight, with only his head near the top of the "T" and free to move. Thick ropes ran over his legs and waist and looped down and around the metal table. Each arm was stretched out to his sides and strapped down as well.

Frank could see nothing but the ceiling of the store.

The ceiling, just like in St. Bart's hospital.

No, no. Not gonna start thinking about that. Not conducive—

Gig stepped up with a water hose and started filling the metal tub on the floor under Frank's head and Gebhuza was arranging a stack of thick, dirty towels on the table next to him and Frank suddenly realized what was happening.

They were going to waterboard him.

Oh, Christ.

No. Drowning, the feeling of drowning, would be even worse than coming off the drugs and the alcohol or being confined in that small room. He heard the water pouring into the metal tub and something inside him, some part of his mind, started screaming. The panic rose in him suddenly. He began squirming and kicking at the ropes.

"I think he figured it out," Gig said, laughing. Others in the room laughed as well, but Gebhuza said nothing.

Gig walked over and stood over Frank. "I need you to tell me everything you know about the task force."

"Well, it's a task force," Frank said quietly.

Gig smiled. "You're doing better than I would expect," he said. "Four days without Oxy. You should be screaming."

"Got any beer?" Frank croaked.

A smattering of laughs around the room. People thought he was funny. Or they thought what was happening was funny.

"Still making jokes, right up until the end," Gig said.

Frank looked at him. "This is far from the end, my friend."

Gig looked at him silently, staring down into Frank's face. "You think you are strong? You are not strong, old man," Gig said quietly, probably too quiet for anyone else to hear save Gebhuza, who continued fiddling with his tools, indifferent to their exchange. "You have not fought, or died, to build something great," Gig said.

"Great? Living in an old mall is great?"

Gig nodded. "It can be. We are building an army of—"

"Punks," Frank interrupted, speaking more loudly then he really needed to. "What do you think you are doing here? You're a bunch of kids playing grown-up. Running around, pretending to be bad asses and killing other kids over drugs or money or turf. It's pointless."

"I need to know why the task force brought you in."

"They didn't."

"You just showed up on your own?" Gig glanced up at someone else, then back to Frank. "The task force needed outside help. That's why the mayor brought in the FBI. Why are you helping them? What connection does the task force have with the Alabama Bureau of Investigation?"

"Jesus, nothing!" Frank shouted. These people were idiots. "I don't work for the task force!"

"Six weeks ago, you began investigating the Northsiders organization. You questioned one of our people."

"Yeah, about the fire," Frank said. "Not your gang operations or the drugs. I didn't know about any of that."

"Why the interest in the Washingtons?"

"JESUS CHRIST!" Frank screamed. It didn't make any sense. He'd been here for four days, and they'd already asked him all these questions. Many times. He and Gig already had several "discussions" while Tiny and the others beat him.

"I told you all of this a DOZEN TIMES. I was hired to scare off whoever was threatening the family. What does it matter? They're dead now."

Gig held up the bag of Oxy. "I can help you out. You just have to help me. Are you working for the FBI? You and Shales were colleagues on another case, correct?" Gig kept asking about why the task force had "brought Frank in," but Frank ignored him.

"No," Frank said. "The kid is an idiot."

"Okay, tell us about the task force leaders. Where do they live?" Gig continued with more questions, naming task force members from a clipboard he was holding, asking where they went in their off hours, where their spouses worked, etc. Frank had no idea, and said as much.

After another minute of not getting answers from Frank, Gig shook his head and waved the clipboard at him.

"This would go better for you if you were more cooperative."

"Screw you."

Frank heard a chuckle from somewhere in the room, followed by gasps.

Gig turned and his face grew serious.

"Oh, I'm sorry, ma'am. I didn't see you there."

"It's fine," a low, husky feminine voice answered, a voice Frank hadn't heard before. "I was just listening to Mr. Harper. Are we ready?"

Gig nodded.

"Yes ma'am. But I don't think he knows anything else."

Another chuckle, low and womanly.

"Yes, but let's be sure. Ask him."

The rest of the room went quiet when she spoke. Whoever this was, she commanded respect from the others.

Gig looked back at Frank.

"Okay, last question. Tell me about the interview," Gig said. "At the end of your interview, you spoke to Sergeant Roget privately for several minutes. Everyone else was asked to leave the room, and you and him talked about something. What was it?"

Frank was confused. How could this gang of thugs know such details about the interview? How did they know he and Roget had chatted alone?

"Tell me what you talked about," Gig said quietly. The room was silent except for the dripping of water. "With Sergeant Roget. Or else my friend can talk to you." Gig's eyes traveled to Gebhuza. "He will not be as polite."

Frank shook his head. "Nothing. We didn't talk about anything."

"Tell me," Gig repeated.

"He...he thought I was high," Frank screeched. "He wanted to know what I was on. I didn't tell him."

Gig looked away from Frank, in the direction of the old woman. Looking for instructions. He nodded and looked back down at Frank.

"I doubt he cared about your recreational habits," he said. "Tell me what you talked about. Did you discuss the upcoming raid?"

Frank didn't know what to say.

"Were you and he coordinating your efforts with the FBI?"

"I don't know what you're talking about," Frank said, the words coming out before he even realized what he was saying.

"It doesn't matter," the woman said. Frank strained to see her, but she was out of his visual range. "If he knows anything else, he'll tell us soon enough. Gebhuza, go ahead."

"Wait," Frank yelled. "Wait. What else do you want to know?"

Gebhuza approached the table, fiddling with a bucket.

"Okay, ask," Frank said, eyeing the black and gray dreadlocks. "ASK!"

Gig leaned back over him. "The head of the task force. Roget. Give me his home address."

"I don't know that," Frank said, telling the truth. "I don't know anything personal about them. You have to believe me. I am not working for the task force!"

The old woman spoke up. "Tell me when they will raid next, and where." The woman's voice was cold and clear.

"I DON'T KNOW!" Frank growled. "Besides, I've been missing for days. Maybe you noticed? I have no idea about any raid. And if I had, they would've changed their plans by now."

The room grew quiet. Frank could hear water running and dripping.

"Okay," Gig said and backed away.

A thick towel suddenly covered Frank's face. Held tight against him, it blocked out the light. Then water was poured onto the towel, ice cold water, cold enough to take his breath away. They held the towel tightly across his mouth and the water poured through into his mouth. The soaked towel clung to his face and nose and mouth and the cold water seared his throat and lungs. Frank sputtered but the towel made it impossible to spit the water out. Whatever he spit out was immediately replaced. More water came, and more, and more, flooding into his mouth and nose. Frank gagged and spat and gagged again.

Then the water stopped and Frank was gasping for air and spitting up water into the towel. They pulled the towel away and he convulsed, coughing as water came up from his lungs, burning like acid. He gagged and coughed for what seemed like hours, his eyes and throat and nose felt on fire.

"Talk to us, Mr. Harper," Gig reappeared over him. "Where do these men and women live, those on the task force? How many times have you met with the mayor? Where is the task force going next?"

Frank coughed and gagged again, his body starting to shake from the cold water. He had a sudden realization. People talked about how torture didn't work because the victims got so scared they said anything to make it stop. They made up stuff, tried to guess what the torturer wanted to hear. People would say anything to make it end. Frank understood that now, but he was too tired to invent anything. Images of St. Bart's and drowning crowded everything else out.

"I have no idea," he said when he was finally able to speak.

Gig shook his head and looked up in the direction of the woman. The room grew quiet. Frank heard the woman move in her seat, and then her reply came back. It sounded like the low, quiet knell of a distant bell.

"Again."

Chapter 72
Answer Time

The waterboarding lasted another two hours.

Gig and Gebhuza took turns asking questions. In between, Gig would walk over to the Dragon and speak to her, getting clarification or more questions.

In the end, Harper didn't tell them anything else. There was apparently nothing else to say. Harper had no knowledge about the mayor or his office or who on his payroll might be susceptible to bribery or coercion. Harper had apparently only been interviewed by the task force that one time and it was clear he didn't work for them.

Unless Harper was very good at keeping secrets.

It also seemed he had never met the mayor or most of his staff. And he had no idea where the task force members lived or where they spent their time off-hours. Not that it mattered. The Northsiders already had much of that information.

After two hours, the Dragon signaled for them to wrap things up with Harper. They began untying him and Gig watched as three guards dragged him back down the hallway to his little room. He turned to the Dragon.

"Do you think he told us everything?"

The Dragon nodded. "Probably," she said. "I assumed Roget brought him in to help. Maybe he did. I wasn't sure what they talked about at the end of the interview, but maybe it's true and Roget thinks he's a druggie. All the better for us," she said.

She turned to Gebhuza.

"Time for more?"

The old Jamaican nodded. "Of course, ma'am. I'm here for as long as you need me."

The Dragon smiled and turned to Gig.

"Bring in the next one."

CHAPTER 73
Hurricane Time

Frank lay on the floor of his store room, coughing. He had no idea how long the waterboarding had lasted. It felt like days. Days and days of drowning. And not just once, but over and over and over. Memories of St. Bartholomew's Parish Hospital flooded over him. The memories took hold, and the drowning then and the drowning now became conflated in his mind.

Now, curled in a ball on the wet floor of his closet, Frank Harper recalled every detail of what happened in 2005.

Hurricane Katrina had roared past New Orleans, destroying much in its path. The storm, threatening the downtown area, had tracked to the east at the last minute, sparing the city and striking parishes along the coast of Mississippi and Georgia. Entire beach towns were decimated, and the storm surge pushed water over six miles inland.

But the next day, August 29, 2005, brought the worst of it for New Orleans. The levees, built to withstand a direct hit from a hurricane, couldn't take the rising water around them. Levee after levee slowly breeched, one at a time, sending millions of gallons of filthy, contaminated water pouring into low-lying areas of 80% of the city, flooding rich and poor neighborhoods alike. Only the above-sea-level French Quarter and Garden Districts were spared. Reports of flooded homes and hospitals poured in, along with news of bodies and even cemetery caskets floating throughout the city.

Frank Harper and the rest of the New Orleans Police Department (NOPD) set up a temporary headquarters in a building next to the Superdome—the main police station, along with most of downtown, had been flooded. The NOPD was trying to control the massive and widespread looting while keeping in mind that many survivors were desperate for food and medical attention.

Ahead of the storm, 90% of the residents had been evacuated out of New Orleans. After the flooding, the National Guard took charge of the house-to-house searches, bringing along local PD to assist as needed. Frank was assigned to a small unit of National Guard, while other teams of cops and guardsmen searching for survivors on the east side of the city, the hardest hit.

Frank's group was clearing a block of flooded downtown buildings that included St. Bartholomew's Parish Hospital. Frank and the guardsmen were going door-to-door, looking for survivors or people who had decided to stay at home.

When they got to the hospital, the national guard went in first. Checking the hospitals and clinics in the area was a huge priority for the guard, both to look for survivors but also to secure the hospital facilities and get them reopened to care for the sick and wounded pouring into the Superdome.

St. Bart's was a large hospital, with six floors. The main floor was underwater, so they climbed from their boat onto a wide metal awning above the main entrance and made their way into the second floor of the lobby via broken windows.

The young guard leading the search party went in first. Once inside, they split into teams and used flashlights to begin a floor-by-floor search. Looters had made their way into some of the other structures, and hospitals and retail stores were prime targets for those looking for drugs.

The squad slowly searched the dark hospital. They found three people alive on the top floor and helped them get up to the roof for rescue. The guard called in a chopper and waited until the three women—a nurse and two patients—were plucked from the roof and taken to safety.

When the chopper was gone, the squad started back down, double-checking each floor of the dark hospital again. Frank banged on doors and looking inside operating rooms for any signs of habitation. It had been nearly thirty-six hours since the levees broke, but it was certainly possible that more people were still trapped.

They worked their way down to the flooded lobby, which was impassable. And that's when the argument started.

Frank told the guards that he wanted to keep searching. He was convinced there were more people trapped, especially on the first floor. He'd lived in New Orleans for years and knew how many people this hospital could hold. He also knew how many people had supposedly been evacuated. He told the guard the numbers didn't add up, and suggested they swim through as much of the main floor as they could to look for survivors. But the kid wanted to move on. Frank insisted on staying behind.

He remembered the young guard's words as if he had heard them yesterday.

"Okay. Just catch up," the guard had said.

Frank remembered standing on the second floor, near the broken windows that led to the boat outside. The rest of the troops had already gone out. Frank remembered watching the guard turn and climb back out into the sunlight, following the rest of his men.

Frank went back up to the third floor, searching for the pharmacy. They had passed it on the way down and given it a cursory glance, but Frank wanted to see if it had been ransacked by looters.

The gangbangers had surprised him.

They had been hiding the whole time the National Guard was searching, clearly trying to avoid a confrontation with men armed with machine guns. But when Frank walked into the pharmacy alone, he found five youths rummaging through the racks of medicine. They had broken open the cases and were scooping up bottles and boxes of pills, stuffing them into black leather satchels.

"What are you doing?"

They turned, surprised. Apparently, they had not expected anyone to return.

They opened fire almost immediately. No conversation, no talking, no negotiating. One turned and lifted his pistol before Frank had even known what was happening. There were five of them, and he couldn't watch them all.

Frank felt a fire explode in his shoulder.

He got a few good shots off as he backed out through the door, but by then they were chasing him, shooting, and all he could do was turn and run.

Frank raced through the darkened corridors of the abandoned hospital. It was a good idea he'd helped search this floor twice, already, or he'd have no idea where he was going. He headed for the three-story lobby in the front of the building. Frank thought he might be able to jump down into the water that flooded the main floor and escape his pursuers. As he ran, he turned and fired his weapon until it was empty. His left arm and shoulder felt heavy, useless. Blood ran freely down the front of his jacket.

They chased him, the black bags banging against their hips.

Frank was outgunned and outmanned and all he could really do at this point was escape. New Orleans was flooded, and the normal rules didn't apply anymore. It was the Wild West, each man for himself. There was no backup, no calling in reinforcements to race to his rescue. Even if he could somehow call the National Guard back, it would be too late.

Frank made it to the lobby and saw the railing ahead and gambled that the water below would save him. He tucked the empty gun away in his holster and vaulted the railing, bracing with his good hand.

For a second, he was in open space, falling through the lobby. He saw the water below and splashed into it, mercifully missing any submerged furniture. He flipped over in the water and kicked up to the surface, seeing the gangbangers up above.

They weren't stupid enough to follow. Instead, they fired down into the water at him.

Frank went back under and felt a strong current pulling him along. He surfaced twenty feet away, under an alcove. The water, running just below the low ceiling, carried him past a sign that read "Patient Wing." He bobbed along, struggling to stay afloat while also trying to avoid the low-hanging signs and broken lights.

That was when he saw his first body. An old man, his face sagging from his skull, floated past him.

Frank pushed away and grabbed at anything to stop his momentum, finding a loose bit of ceiling. The body slid past him silently in the water, looking much like a swamp alligators from his youth, the kind that hunted from just below the surface. He grabbed at the ceiling with his right hand and threw his heavy left arm up into a hole in the broken ceiling, cutting his arm on a jagged piece of exposed metal. It tore his skin from wrist to elbow.

He ignored the pain and held on.

The water was rising, brackish and dark. It was pulling him into a flooded section of the hospital. Going that way was suicide. His head was inches away from the ceiling and he held on for dear life. Trash floated past him—the clear bags they used for IVs, papers, clipboards, bottles of medicine.

Two more bodies floated past him, the toes green and swollen and rasping against the ruined ceiling. He suddenly felt like he was about to vomit.

Frank pulled himself up with every bit of strength he had, but his left arm and shoulder sang with pain. Water kept getting into his mouth—it tasted like a swamp—and he kept going under. Struggling, he moved slowly along, inches from the ceiling. The whole hospital seemed to be crushing down on him.

He made it another ten or fifteen feet, and there was more room between the surface of the water and the ceiling above him. He found a place to stop and breathed, in and out, trying to calm himself. To his left, he saw a set of double doors leading into another large room. If he could find a broken window or some other way to get out, he could avoid the lobby and the gang members.

He pushed his way through the set of doors, marked "Laboratory 9," and into a room filled with hospital beds and equipment. Some of it floated near the ceiling and some was still attached to the floor. Half of the room was a small lab, with unbroken glass reaching from floor to ceiling.

Inside the glassed-in lab, trapped inside the small room, at least five dead bodies bobbed on the surface of the water.

He looked at the bodies for a moment, wondering why the patients had been left behind. Finally, the tore his eyes away to figure out the layout of the room and determine where the outside windows would be. Frank made his way around the room, ducking under the rising water and looking through the murk for any windows to the outside. He felt the panic rising in him and ignored the tapping sounds of equipment banging on the glass walls of the lab.

Finally, he found a large window leading outside. Water rushed out of the broken window like a tide. Outside, he could see cars on a flooded street. The broken window was more than large enough for him to get out.

Frank went up to take another breath and started to push his way down under the water when the banging started again. Louder this time. He thought the banging was equipment hitting the glass wall. But the banging was very regular.

Too regular.

He turned and looked at the glassed-in laboratory one more time, A woman was staring back at him.

She was old and her eyes were sunken and desperate and she was rapping urgently on the glass.

Frank swam over to the glass and felt around, looking for a door or a button that would open the lab.

"Help me," she croaked. He could barely hear her through the glass. "Help me."

He nodded.

"I'm trying," he yelled. "I'm trying. Where is the door?"

She didn't seem to understand. He went around to the side and found what looked like a door—one of the panels of glass was designed to move. He pushed at a button that controlled the mechanism, pushing it over and over, but it wouldn't move.

"It won't open," he yelled. "Help me push it."

Again, she didn't seem to understand. She scraped at the glass with her hand and looked at him but otherwise did nothing.

He pushed on the door, but it would not move.

Another surge of water moved through the room, threatening to push him away from the glass. The water was rising, and the walls seemed to close in on him.

Frank looked at the woman. She seemed to be crying, her tears black, or maybe it was the brackish water splashing on her face. Another body floated next to her, and in his horror, Frank realized it was moving on its own. One of the hands was grabbing at her. A second set of eyes turned to look at him, these of a very old man.

"Get us out of here," the man shouted. The glass was thick, but it sounded like he was yelling. Next to him, another body lifted its head and hands started pushing on the glass door. It was another woman, younger, Asian, with panic in her eyes.

"Push the door! Push it!" She started pushing from her side, but it was no use. "Break it!"

Frank knew it wouldn't work but tried anyway. He found a fire extinguisher and shoved it against the heavy pane, over and over, but nothing happened. Underwater, he couldn't get it moving fast enough.

The water was rising. He only had inches of air between the surface and the ceiling. There was nothing he could do, and he was growing weaker by the moment. Blood from his shoulder and arm pooled in a slick on the surface of the water around him as he regarded the people inside the locked lab.

Finally, Frank shook his head.

"I'm sorry," he said.

They might not have been able to hear him, but each understood what he said. The old woman put a wrinkled hand up to her face. The other two began thrashing weakly in the water, slapping the surface and scrabbling at the thick glass. The old man yelled something at Frank, something about his doctor.

There was nothing Frank could do.

He turned and swam back over to where he could dive down and exit the hospital. Frank turned and looked at them, three sets of eyes staring at him. Blaming him for abandoning them, piling on enough blame to shadow him for a lifetime.

"I'm sorry," he said a final time. The fear overtook him, fear of being trapped in there forever. Trapped in a flooded hospital with those dying people.

Frank ducked under the water and swam out to freedom.

In moments, he found his way back to the metal awning that he and the national guardsmen had used to gain access to the hospital. He climbed up, exhausted. He'd been in the water for at least an hour, since jumping down to avoid the gangbangers. His shoulder and arm were numb and seeping blood.

A steady stream of detritus washed out through the broken windows of the hospital, and he found an unopened package of gauze. Opening it, he stuffed one end into the bullet hole in his shoulder, then wrapped the rest of the gauze around his arm and waited, listening for either another search boat or a low-flying helicopter.

Two hours passed before he saw a boat he could flag down.

They raced Frank and six other injured persons back a makeshift dock at the Superdome. The entire way, Frank babbled about the people in the hospital and how they needed to be rescued. He could hear his own voice and could tell he wasn't making any sense. No matter what he said, the medic leaning over him attending to his wounds just nodded. Obviously, the man thought Frank was delirious.

Frank woke a day later in the hospital. Lucid, and in much less pain, he flagged down the closest nurse and asked about the people in the hospital.

The young man had no idea what Frank was talking about.

"Laboratory 9?" Frank asked. "What happened?"

The young man shrugged and fetched a doctor, who walked over and looked down at Frank. She listened to him explain about the patients trapped in the hospital and then asked a couple questions before thanking him and walking away.

"She'll know what to do," the nurse said. He handed Frank some water. "She and the other docs have been dealing with so many dead, they'll move heaven and earth to rescue anyone still alive."

It took another two days before Frank learned what had happened. In that time, he pestered every doctor and nurse that came within twenty feet of him.

The people inside Laboratory 9 had died.

After Frank's insistent warning, a search and recovery team had been sent in. The entire hospital was searched. Evidence of a theft at the pharmacy on level 3 was found.

And on level 1, in one of the labs, a total of five bodies were recovered from inside a sealed isolation ward.

It made the papers, of course, but got lost in all the other news coming out of New Orleans in the wake of Hurricane Katrina. Dead bodies were recovered for weeks, months afterward. Some were found only by following the stench. Some were found in bizarre locations; many were found in attics and the top floors of multi-story structures, as the people climbed away from the rising water and then were drowned inside a structure they could no longer escape.

Ahead of the storm, people had been instructed to write their names and social security numbers on their arms in Sharpie. This unfortunate method was used to identify many bodies.

At a different hospital, a desperate nurse grew convinced that no help was coming. Agonizing over her patients and watching the water rise, she had used overdoses of morphine to euthanize five terminal patients in her care. She reasoned it was better than letting them suffer a slow and painful death from dehydration or starvation. She had no way of knowing the national guard was only hours away.

There were plenty of horror stories in the aftermath of Hurricane Katrina to go around. Whole families were lost in the flooding or washed out to sea, where they died in the unforgiving sun. Entire towns were scrubbed from the map, washed away by the storm surge. The entire Six Flags New Orleans park was wiped out. Ten feet of water rushed through it, killing dozens of employees and guards who had stayed behind after the evacuation to guard and secure the park from looters and thieves.

The five dead at St. Bart's Parish Hospital was a small story in a host of others. No one talked about it as a cautionary tale. Within hours, it had faded from most people's minds. Each horror was replaced with a new one. It went on for months afterward. There seemed to be no end to the number of dead that would be found, the count spiraling relentlessly upward.

But for one New Orleans police officer, those five dead people in St. Bart's were the worst thing to come from Katrina. They were people he should have been able to save, people who had seen him as a rescuer until he let them down. He was a weak man, unable to save people who couldn't help themselves. And wasn't that what he was supposed to do? Save people? He was a cop, for Christ's sake.

It was the eyes.

Frank remembered the eyes, even now in the darkness. Lying on his side on the wet floor of a tiny closet, a prisoner of a ruthless gang of thugs. He coughed, his throat ragged, and remembered the way those people in the isolation ward looked at him through the glass. He remembered the look in their eyes the instant they realized he was leaving them. The anger, the hopelessness, the dread.

Frank would remember those eyes forever.

CHAPTER 74
Planning Time

Gig hurried through the old mall. The meeting had already started.

He'd walked Gebhuza out to the waiting limo and seen him off. The infamous torturer would now make the long drive back to Florida. The man refused to fly and was driven everywhere, usually at the expense of those clients who could afford his services. When he got to Florida, Gig had been told that the man would take a boat back to Jamaica to await the next time someone needed his particular set of skills.

It was quiet in the mall. Usually there was no production on Friday or Saturday nights, but Gig missed the steady hum of the production lines and chatter of people working together. The mall was silent, quiet enough for him to hear the muffled moans and grunts coming from the Harem on the other side of the mall.

He got to the old Foot Locker and entered, walking down the hall, passing his own office. Gig entered the large conference room, the one with the walls lined with shoes and other displayed items, and found a seat near the Dragon.

"...and the staff?" The Dragon was asking a question of Mikey P., who ran the extortion and protection side of the business. The Dragon, sitting at the head of the table in the conference room, was dressed like a grandmother, wearing what looked like a dingy housecoat. Her hair was graying along the sides, and she was sipping from a large McDonald's cup. Gig knew of her penchant for Diet Cokes—the woman left a trail of empty cans and cups everywhere she went. She might look like the cleaning woman, but Gig knew that behind that simple visage was a woman of unparalleled mental complexity. She was easily the smartest person he'd ever met. Her mind was always running ahead of everyone else's in the room.

He'd worked with her often, especially over the last six months. Once, Gig asked her why she dressed like she did, and he'd instantly realized he'd probably crossed a line.

But she'd simply turned and looked at him. "Because I don't care how I look, Gig," was all she said. And the topic never came up again. When others asked him about her, he always said the same thing: she was too busy planning to care. Plus, only twenty people in the world knew who she really was. To the rest of the world, she was a simple old woman, a lowly admin in the Dayton mayor's office.

"Yup, they're good to go," Mikey P. said to the Dragon. "A few will have to stay behind, of course. The place has to look real."

The Dragon nodded. The old woman leaned back in her chair and glanced at Gig.

"Gebhuza?"

Gig nodded. "He left. One question—his payment seemed…well, less than I'd expected." Gebhuza hadn't taken payment in cash or drugs—instead, the man had picked out two young women from the Harem as his payment, including the new girl brought in by Rubio earlier in the week. Gig had seen to it that the young women were sedated and moved to his limo before seeing the Jamaican legend off with a wave.

"His payment is adequate," the Dragon said. "He owed me several favors. Now we are even."

The meeting continued, much of it revolving around the upcoming raid on Sunday by the task force of the Northsiders' new "headquarters" at Riley's. All the preparations were complete. Now it was just a matter of waiting.

"Last thing," the Dragon said. "After Riley's, we need to be ready to act quickly. Depending on the outcome, we'll need at least eight teams. Maybe twelve. And the device will need to be ready," she said, looking at Sonny and Mikey P.

"It's already ready, ma'am," Sonny said, swallowing. "I have it in my office. You can take it in whenever you like."

Mikey P. leaned forward, nodding at Sonny and Sausage. "We were talking. It might be better to take it in tomorrow or Sunday, when there are fewer people around. Then use the timer."

The Dragon nodded. "Yes, that's good. I'll get it tomorrow. Same as the ones for the Hive?"

"Actually, the yield is bigger," Sonny said. "More horizontal, too. It should do well."

"Okay," she looked around the table. "The teams. I need your best men, people. Your BEST. This must happen quickly and without hesitation. I'll give you the location information you need at the appropriate time," she said, thumping the table. "You'll pass it along on a need-to-know basis. We will only get one chance at this," the Dragon said, standing and looking around. "Mama Leonita would be proud. We're taking the fight to the very people who can stop us. The only people who can stop us. After this, no one will oppose us."

CHAPTER 75
Ready

Chief King wasn't sure what to do.

It was Sunday morning and he had plenty on his plate already, but he couldn't get Frank Harper out of his head. Gone six days, now. No one had seen him since Monday night.

He was on his couch, reading the *Cooper's Mill Gazette* instead of working on the department's budget. The numbers were due soon to the city government, and he had to make some cuts. King picked up his phone and checked. Still no messages. He shook his head and called his cousin Floyd.

"Hello?"

"Floyd, it's Jeff."

"Hey, Jeff. Having a good weekend?"

"Okay, I guess. But I'm worried about Frank. Anything come back on the BOLO or APB?"

"Nothing. Maybe he went back to Birmingham."

"Nah, I talked to his supervisor yesterday," King said. "No word down there either. I told him Frank left abruptly, but Collins, or Collier—I forget his name—said that Frank wasn't on vacation. He'd been suspended."

"Did you know?"

"Frank didn't say anything about it. Collins said Frank had been suspended for two weeks. Frank had been coming in to work drunk or possibly high. Painkillers or something."

They were quiet for a minute. King could hear some television show playing in the background at Floyd's house. It was loud—it sounded like a game show or something.

"It's not your fault, Jeff," Floyd said. "Mr. Harper's mixed up, that's all. He's a good man. He'll turn up."

King nodded again to himself. "I hope so. I hope so."

CHAPTER 76
Set

"We ready?"

It was just before 10:00 a.m. on Sunday, and every eye in the Northsiders' meeting room turned to look at the woman at the head of the table.

"Yes, ma'am," Sonny answered, pointing at the two large monitors he and Gig had set up near one wall of the conference room.

One monitor showed the exterior of Riley's from across the street. A streaming web-cam had been set up in the window of a liquor store catty-corner from the strip club. The grainy black and white feed showed the main entrance into the club and the front parking lot. It was early on a Sunday, but there were at least twenty cars parked in the two lots in front of and behind the club, cars brought in from the mall to make Riley's look busy.

The second webcam was from inside Riley's. This live feed showed the bar and the main floor of the club. On the screen, a young black woman danced on the stage for the few customers.

"Good," the Dragon said. "Task force?"

Gig had the feeling she already knew where the task force was, but Sonny told her anyway for the benefit of those in the room. "They're loading vehicles at their headquarters," he said. "We have a spotter outside the building. He'll follow them and call in when they approach. If they follow procedure, they'll arrive with three or four teams," Sonny said. "Two teams will go in the front door, one or two in the rear."

The Dragon nodded. "Anything for them to find?"

"We filled the office with false information," Gig spoke up. "And the underground lab has enough drugs to make it convincing."

The Dragon nodded.

"Good. Thank you, Sonny, Gig," she said, nodding at them before turning to the rest of the table. "While we're waiting, get me up to speed on the other items. Mr. Kingmaker, what do our numbers look like?"

Gig sat back and relaxed as Mr. Kingmaker walked the Dragon through their new production quotas, eager to impress her. They were ramping up production to satisfy the surge in customers, now that they had new territory in Columbus and Cincinnati to supply. Gig could tell the Dragon was happy from the look on her face and the questions she was asking. She was always digging for more information and for ways to make their operations more efficient.

She was also looking for leaders. There was no way she'd be able to be on the ground running things in Cincinnati or Columbus, or Toledo or Cleveland when the gang moved in that direction. The Dragon would need people she could trust, and Gig wanted to be one of those people. Desperately. He wanted more power, and more control, and getting out of Dayton would allow him to do that. Of course, as always, the Dragon would remain in charge, setting the tone and direction of the gang. But Gig wanted space to roam, virgin territory to explore and conquer.

CHAPTER 77
All Clear

Roget was watching out the front of the van as the vehicle moved up Dixie Drive, slowing as it approached Riley's strip club.

"Everyone ready?"

Hawkins and the others looked up at Sergeant Roget. They were suited, checking each other's gear. Roget stood by the rear doors, looking up at the others.

Hawkins nodded. "We're good."

Roget turned back to the driver. "Call it in."

Patrelli, fourth in command of the task force, nodded and slowed, reaching for the radio. "All clear. All clear. Van 1 ready. Form up in four minutes."

Roget couldn't see the other three vans, each full of his troops, but he knew they were out there. Two teams would enter the front of the strip club and one in the back. It wasn't exactly a stealth approach, like what they did at the production facility. It was late morning and anyone could see the four dark vans approaching the strip club. Five other cars full of Dayton PD officers waited nearby to form a perimeter around the club and detain and control civilians after the initial assault.

Roget checked his watch and nodded at the eight men and women in his truck, including Officer Patrelli.

"Let's go."

Roget opened the doors and swung down to the street. He held it open for the others, and Hawkins and other task force members climbed down and assembled on the side of the van away from the club. Roget went down the line, visually checking each person, ending with Hawkins.

"Okay," he said. "Here we go."

Hawkins waved at the other SUV parked a hundred yards away, and a figure in SWAT gear waved back.

Roget stepped out from behind the SUV and sprinted for the front door of Riley's. He could hear the others running behind him. Roget was first through the door, running into the darkness with his weapon out, pointing it around.

"Police!" he shouted. "Everyone out! Clear the building!"

Customers stood, shocked at the sudden arrival of dozens of men with automatic weapons. Tables of drinks tipped over as the customers made their way to the front door, streaming around the police. More task force members ran past Roget and Hawkins and headed backstage, where a group of strippers emerged, scared and pulling jackets around themselves.

"Let's go, ladies," Roget said. "Outside."

He watched as the customers and strippers all moved through the front doors that Roget and his team had just stormed. D Team waited out in the parking lot to process them. Roget ordered Hawkins and the rest of his team to search the interior of the club while he investigated the main floor, waiting for the rest of the civilians to be led outside. Roget stepped through a pair of doors that led to a backstage area, meeting up with Bellows.

"Anything?"

"Yeah, lots of office space and plenty of documentation. I have B Team collecting that now and arresting suspects. And C Team in the basement—they found a large underground lab and drugs. So far, no shots fired."

"Good," Roget said. "Tell them to search every room, office, and back stage area. Outside, gather the civilians and make sure no one leaves the parking lots until they've been identified and photographed, got it?"

Bellows nodded and grabbed his radio, passing the information along.

Roget turned and found the stairs down to the lab. He looked over the contents of the Northsiders lab: equipment, raw materials, and some product, packaged for sale. He also saw metal containers of acetone and Hypophosphorous acid, both of which were extremely flammable.

Hawkins came over the radio. "Sergeant? Other than the strippers and the bar staff, there's no one else up front."

"What about all the cars in the lots?"

"No clue. Want me to check them out?"

"Yeah. Take a couple guys, get all the plates from the cars out front and in back. See if any cars are open so you can grab their registrations and get the owners' names."

"Will do," Hawkins said, and the radio went quiet.

Something was wrong here, Roget thought. The place was empty, nearly, and there were a bunch of cars parked out back. What did it all mean?

CHAPTER 78
Live Feed

They waited, gathered around their televisions. The Council and other senior members of the gang watched the live feeds, including the one from across the street.

Gig watched the monitor and the Dragon, who was sitting at the front table and making notes on a clipboard. From where he was sitting, Gig could see it was the list of task force members he'd had during Harper's waterboarding.

"Our people clear?" Sonny asked. "I can't tell."

"It doesn't matter," the Dragon said. "When the entire task force is inside, blow it up. Not before."

Gig noticed that the only person in the room that didn't seem nervous was the old woman sipping from her McDonald's cup.

He had to hand it to her. The woman was fearless.

CHAPTER 79
Boom

Roget shook his head. Something was wrong here.

"Keep looking," he told the other cops still searching the basement. "There has to be more to it than this."

Roget climbed the stairs and walked back through the offices, but something was off. It didn't seem like there was enough stuff here to be the gang's new headquarters. It just didn't feel substantial. He saw tables and chairs and folding tables covered with spreadsheets and other paperwork, but it didn't look lived in. Maybe they were just getting set up and no one had actually started working here yet. The environment felt cold, antiseptic, like the lab downstairs.

Standing in the middle of the office area, he took out his cell phone and tried to call the mayor, but there was no signal. Roget turned back toward the entrance that his team had stormed less than ten minutes ago. Exiting the building, he passed the rest of A team, including Patrelli.

"Nothing up here except the DJ booth and the bar, boss," Patrelli said, following Roget outside. "We'll gather everything we can and label it before boxing it up." Roget put the phone up to his ear and looked at Patrelli. "That's fine. Make sure everything is accounted for." Patrelli turned to go back inside and the call finally went through. "Yes?"

"Mayor, it's Sergeant Roget," he said, walking farther from the doorway to get away from the noise of the cops interviewing the witnesses and staff. In the parking lot, Dayton PD officers were interviewing and photographing customers and staff that had exited the building during the initial search.

"There's something off, sir. I can't tell you what, yet," Roget said. "We have no explanation why there are so many cars in the parking—"

A massive explosion ripped through the building behind him.

The wall of flames boiled across the parking lot, rushing over him and the cops and people they were interviewing. The wave of pressurized heat threw Roget through the air at least twenty feet, where he impacted the side of a car and fell to the ground. Roget rolled onto his back, the wind knocked out of him. His phone skittered away across the pavement. A billowing cloud of white and gray smoke rose a hundred feet in the air, covering everything in a pall.

It took him a few moments to recover, his chest hurting. When he sat up, all Roget could hear was a ringing in his ears. His face and hands were scratched up. He rolled over and sat up and looked at the strip club.

It was gone.

He tried to stand, woozy. Smoke drifted around him, stinging his nose. It smelled like sulfur, or maybe cordite, a compact explosive. People were hurt, crawling on the pavement, trailing blood. He bent to help them as he made his way toward the club entrance—some were just in shock. Others were not moving, their eyes staring at the blackened sky. A woman, one of the dancers, staggered past him, her eyes blank. Half her arm was missing.

A bomb.

There had been a bomb.

Roget cursed and walked toward the front doors, or where they had been. Now the place had collapsed in on itself. It had all been a trap. Then he remembered.

Hawkins. She had been checking cars in the lot, getting license plates numbers.

He staggered around the front lot, looking for her. He checked the wounded and the dead but didn't see her. Turning, he angled to avoid the smoking hole where the strip club had been and limped into the rear parking lot. He looked down and realized his leg was bleeding—there was a huge gash on his thigh. He touched it and felt blood, hot and sticky.

Roget looked for Hawkins, stumbling through the smoke and the fallen men and women. He weaved around burning cars and wondered if any of them might explode. He should get people clear. But he only had one thing on his mind right now.

He finally found her, face down between two cars in the lot, thirty or forty feet from the explosion. She wasn't moving. He leaned over her and prayed silently to himself as he rolled her over.

She looked dead.

He leaned closer, feeling her wrists for a pulse and putting an ear to her mouth.

She was breathing, shallow, in and out. Ragged. Roget pulled her to him.

"Patty, Patty," he said. "Wake up, Patty. You're gonna be okay."

Her eyes flickered but did not open. And that was when he noticed the blood on her head. He felt through her hair and found it—part of her skull was concave, pushed in like a broken vase. His hand was bloody and for a moment he wasn't sure if it was her blood or his.

He looked around, desperate.

"I need help here! I need a doctor!"

CHAPTER 80
Step One

The explosion was enormous.

Gig and the others watched the devastation, cheering as the initial explosion took out what looked like dozens of people. The club itself was obliterated, as were dozens of cops and task force members. Unfortunately, some of the Riley's employees were caught up in the explosion as well, but that was the price to be paid. The Northsiders were finally fighting back now, making a real dent in the task force.

The others stood around the TV, watching and smiling. Gig turned and looked at the Dragon, who had started crossing names off the list on her clipboard.

"Our focus going forward will be anyone who survives, including the mayor and his staff," she said, calmly crossing names off as she listened to the video feed. "There must be no one left."

CHAPTER 81
War Movie

An hour later, the mayor looked around at the carnage.

The strip club was effectively gone, destroyed in a massive blast that had caved in the walls and thrown shrapnel—and people—thirty or forty feet into the air. All that remained of the club itself was a pit, a crater dug out by the underground explosives.

He'd arrived as quickly as he could, coming straight from church. Now he was walking through what looked like a scene from a war movie.

"Mayor, you shouldn't be here," one of the cops said. His badge read "Bellows." He was bleeding from a minor wound above his eye. "There could be more explosions."

The mayor shook him off.

"Who's left in charge, Bellows? I need to know what happened here."

Bellows blinked and pointed over toward a black SUV parked on Dixie Drive. "Sergeant Roget's over there. He's hurt but still in charge."

The mayor crossed the street, avoiding several large pieces of building materials that lay in the road. Police had the area surrounded and were directing traffic around the scene.

"Roget, thank God," the mayor said, pulling him into a hug before he realized the sergeant was covered with dirt and mud.

"Mayor, you shouldn't be here," Roget said. To the mayor, the Sergeant's eyes looked wild, like he'd been up for days straight.

"It's okay," the mayor said. "I need to see what's going on. I need to help."

Roget blinked, barely listening. "I'm trying to secure the scene. Bellows is coordinating the rescue efforts," he said, just as another ambulance raced off. "Can you help him? We're taking everyone to Dayton General."

The mayor nodded, thankful for something to do. "Tom, you're gonna be okay."

Roget nodded, his eyes flaring with anger. "This was a trap. They lured us in and set it off. Too controlled to be a lab explosion."

"It's okay, Sergeant. Let's get your men and women to safety, and then we'll figure out how to take out these people."

Roget nodded. There wasn't really anything else to say.

CHAPTER 82
Update

The first Chief King heard about the explosion was a *Dayton Daily News* text alert on his cell phone: "Large explosion reported in North Dayton, dozens of civilians and police injured." He flipped on the news and started making calls; within minutes he had tracked down the Dayton mayor.

The downtown drug task force had been attacked.

Chief King called the office and got Lola, who was covering the office phones. He asked her to call every officer, on or off duty, and have them meet at the station. A half-hour later, the police force of Cooper's Mill, Ohio, stood in the bullpen, along with the six on-duty EMTs and the city's fire chief.

King shared what he'd learned from the Dayton mayor: the task force had raided what they thought was the new headquarters for the largest local gang. It had been a trap—the building had been lined with explosives and detonated just after the task force entered the building.

"Jesus," Detective Barnes said. "How many are hurt?"

"Nine dead, so far," Chief King said, and someone in the room gasped. "Another dozen or more injured, some of them seriously. Sergeant Roget—he's the guy in charge—was thrown nearly twenty feet into a car. Concussion, fractured arm, leg wound."

"We heading down?" Peters asked.

King smiled. "Yeah, I just wanted to get everyone up to speed. The three of you on duty will stay here in town; the rest of us are heading down to help. If something happens here in town and you need backup, call me and the Miami County Sheriff's Office, and we'll work it out."

"This is crazy," Deputy Stan said. "Raids are dangerous enough. But to have people fighting back, actively planning the deaths of cops…"

King nodded. Nationwide, things were bad between cops and some groups, especially black youth. Over the last few years, there had been far too many incidents of unarmed black men being killed by cops. But organized, premeditated resistance against the police was something else entirely.

"Okay, let's go," King said, and the cops headed for the door.

Lola stopped King on his way out. "Anything you want me to do, boss?"

He nodded, swallowing. "Um, yeah. Let the 911 center know, and the Miami County Sheriff. They probably already know, but call them anyway. And Chief Wampler in Piqua."

She nodded. "Okay. Please be careful."

King smiled. "I will."

CHAPTER 83
Where is He?

Laura was really starting to worry.

It was Sunday evening, and she was just getting around to feeding Jackson dinner, a bowl of macaroni, while he watched a rerun of the Powerpuff Girls on TV.

But she couldn't relax. She paced in the kitchen, her phone in her hand. Who could she call? Chief King hadn't called back, and no one was picking up in Frank's office down in Birmingham. It was the weekend, of course, but she was growing desperate. No one had seen her father since Monday night. He'd been gone six full days now.

Desperate for answers, she called the only person from the Cooper's Mill PD that she had a cell number for.

"This is Floyd."

"Oh, Deputy Peters?" Laura said. "It's Laura, Laura Powell." It was hard to hear—there was a bunch of noise in the background.

"Hello, Ms. Powell. Sorry, I'm at an emergency situation. You'll have to speak up."

"Oh, can you talk?"

"Yes, for a minute. There's been an explosion in Dayton. We're down here helping with security."

She nodded. "Okay. Sorry to bother you. Have...have you heard anything on my father?"

"No, nothing."

"I can't stand this, not knowing. Any advice?"

"The BOLO came back with nothing. The nationwide APB went out Thursday." He stopped, speaking to someone else for a moment, then came back on. "Nothing back on that either. Here's Chief King," he said, then King came on the phone.

"Ms. Powell?"

"Chief?"

"Hi. Sorry, we're at a crime scene," he said loudly. "I wanted to let you know I called down to Frank's office on Friday, so they're on the lookout for him as well."

"Thank you for that. It sounds like you're busy. Anything come back on the credit cards?"

"No, but I'll call again in the morning," King said. She heard another siren in the background. "We have to go. I'm sorry—I saw your calls come through, but it's been hectic. Can you come to the station tomorrow morning around 11:00 a.m.? We can get everyone caught up then."

She said her goodbye and hung up. Peters was a good guy, as was Chief King. They all seemed to be genuinely concerned about Frank. But the days were starting to stretch out behind her, and now they were dealing with a new crisis. How long until their concern for Frank turned into a sad realization that he might never be found?

CHAPTER 84
Sit-Ups

Frank lay on the floor of the store room, coughing.

Early this morning, they'd beaten him again. Frank thought now they were doing it just for fun. It wasn't even the higher-ups—he'd seen and heard nothing from any of them since the incident with the Jamaican. Just the guards, in between matches of "Call of Duty." They'd tie him to the chair and take turns beating him.

Seven days. If he was correct, it was Monday morning, exactly a week from when he'd been taken. And Frank felt like he was going crazy.

He needed to get out of here.

The space was too small. Sure. That would have bothered him before. He'd hated small spaces since Katrina. That wasn't as much of a problem now. But Frank wanted to see the sky, see his daughter, talk to someone. Anyone. Frank wanted out. More than he'd ever wanted anything in his life.

And he wanted to stop thinking about St. Bart's. It seemed like the memories washed over him with frustrating regularity. Daily, hourly. Since he'd allowed himself to remember the whole story, the memories of St. Bartholomew's Parish Hospital kept coming back to haunt him.

Breakfast had come and sat untouched on the floor. He wasn't sure if they were putting anything in it or not to make him docile, so he'd started avoiding the food when he could.

Instead, he worked out. Again. First time today, but at least four times a day since last Friday and the waterboarding.

He needed to distract himself.

The endless push-ups and sit-ups filled him with the vibrating energy he'd missed in the hazy days of Oxy. His body was doughy and out of shape. He did the push-ups on his hands and knees as there wasn't room to stretch out. It had been a long time since he'd been on a regular routine, and it felt good. Slipping back into the familiarity was like putting on an old, worn coat. Frank counted in the dark, pushing up from the dusty floor, and tried to will the last of the alcohol and Oxy out of his system.

The gang members watching him seemed confused. He'd complained so much early on, especially those first few itchy days. Moaning and screaming and begging to be let out. Crying for a drink, and offering anything he had, everything he had, for one little white pill.

Maybe the waterboarding had broken him.

His spirit had been poured out of him like water from that rusty bucket. In between the questions from Gig and the old Jamaican and the mysterious old woman, Frank had ceased to be the old Frank Harper. He'd been reduced to a crying child, his simplest form. Now, it was Frank's job to build himself back up.

He flipped over and started on the sit-ups. He went slow, counting as he went. He used to be able to do two hundred before it started to burn. He got to sixty-two before it started to hurt. Frank pushed through it, rocking back and forth, counting under his strained breath.

"Sixty-three. Sixty-four," he gasped. It burned, a good burn he'd missed. Each sit-up hurt more than the last. But at least he wasn't thinking about St. Bart's.

Each sit-up was a delicious distraction.

CHAPTER 85
Confession

Chief King and his men were exhausted, having stayed at the Riley's explosion location well into the night.

Back at his desk in Cooper's Mill, he sighed as he went over the latest task force stats on the bad of paper in front of him: twelve dead, at last count. And sixteen wounded. Roget was hurt, and second in charge Deputy Sergeant Hawkins was among the most gravely injured: she had a serious head injury and was in a medically-induced coma.

And those numbers didn't even count the Dayton PD officers injured and the scores of civilians killed and injured. They didn't even have a good number on that yet.

King and members of the Cooper's Mill PD had provided security and backup at the crime scene and helped Dayton PD officers and their forensics staff sift through the scene, looking for evidence. Other departments provided security at Dayton General for the injured.

King looked down at his desk and found his yellow "PRIORITIES" pad, which listed his top-of-mind departmental issues. He also returned six calls from local and national media outlets—the explosion had made the news across the country.

He was starting to organize his thoughts when his phone buzzed. It was Lola at the front desk.

"Yes?"

"Chief, you have visitors: Jake Delancy and Rosie Miller."

"Hmm, I don't see them scheduled," he said, flipping to his calendar. "Walk-ins?"

"Yup. Want me to walk them back?"

"Yes, thanks," he said.

Jake and Rosie arrived in King's office moments later, and he directed them into the two chairs opposite his desk.

"Jake, Rosie, how are you?" he asked as he sat down. "To what do I owe the pleasure?"

King had been a cop long enough to tell when someone was nervous. Jake was nervous. He'd brought along Rosie for support. King wondered if they were dating.

"Um, thanks for meeting with me, Chief," Jake started. "I mean, meeting with us."

"So, you here to confess a crime?" King said, trying to relax the guy. It was a joke he often made with civilians. Many were nervous when talking to cops, but teasing them usually broke the ice. Not this time. Jake made a face, and King realized his joke wasn't far off.

"Um...I'm not sure, Chief. I think I've done something illegal," he said. "But I have a good reason."

"Now you've got my attention."

Jake glanced at Rosie for support. "You know about that house fire down in Dayton two weeks ago? The family that died?"

King nodded. "Yeah, nasty business."

"They're not dead."

King leaned forward, confused. "Wait, what?"

Jake started to say something but Rosie put her hand on his arm. "Hang on a second." She stood and closed the door. "Okay, go ahead."

They were worried about being overheard.

"The family escaped as the house burned," Jake said, detailing what happened the night of the fire. He said the family was his tenants and they got away, hiding at a local hotel until contacting Jake.

"So, they trust you," King said. He reached for a pad and started taking notes.

"They do. I'm here...I'm really just here for advice, Chief," Jake said, looking at the blank pad of yellow paper. "They are in a hotel in Columbus, but there was a gang shooting nearby. Same gang, the news said. Northsiders. They're worried."

King looked at Rosie. "How are you involved in all this?"

She smiled. "Jake asked me for my advice."

King looked back at Jake. "So, what do you want me to do about it?"

"Did I break the law?"

"Technically, yes. Tampering with an investigation. Obstruction, maybe. But any judge or jury would see that you did it for the family's protection."

Jake relaxed. "Good."

"As for their safety, I'd bring them here and put them under protective custody. Short of that, I'd leave them in Columbus for now. Did you hear about the Northsiders' operation yesterday?"

Jake and Rosie both shook their heads, and King quickly recounted what had happened. "The task force will be going after the Northsiders now with everything they've got, just as soon as they're healed up. For now, your friends should stay in Columbus, I think."

Jake nodded. "Good, good. I'll let them know."

"Can I get your contact info, in case anything comes up?" King asked, grabbing the notepad. They thanked him and left, and Jake looked a lot less worried then when he'd sat down. King shook his head and smiled. You never knew what people were going to get up to, did you?

CHAPTER 86
Conference Room

Riley's was gone, and with it more than half of his task force.

The mayor was sitting in a conference room at Dayton General, looking down at a report, hastily pulled together by Patrelli and Bellows, Roget's men. Both had been injured but working anyway.

The initial findings were clear: the building had been "renovated" over the past week. Walls had been added, power lines strung, loads of furniture and lab equipment were brought in. There were photos to prove it. But it had all been an elaborate trap.

Tom had mentioned there was a mole again, yesterday at the scene. He was injured and rambling, and the mayor had chalked it up to shock. But now the mayor was starting to wonder. Leaking the "moving our headquarters" information was now clearly bait. Riley's was a much easier target to hit then the old mall.

"You want something to eat, Mayor?"

The mayor looked up—he'd was waiting to meet with Roget. The hospital had lent the task force this conference room so Sergeant Roget could work. Dottie and Tammy were here as well. He saw Dottie holding up a donut from the box she'd brought in from "Tim's Donuts."

"You need to eat something, sir. It's chocolate glazed, your favorite."

He smiled and she walked it down to him. "Thanks."

Tammy stood and straightened her dress. "Anyone want something to drink?"

"Diet Coke, if they have it," Dottie said.

Tammy smiled. "I know, Dottie. Like you have to tell me. Mayor?"

"I'll take a water. Thanks, Tammy."

She left and the room grew quiet. Dottie was reading the same report as him. "So many people hurt and killed. It's so sad."

"I know."

"Sir, do you think the Northsiders are trying to kill every member of the task force?"

The mayor looked at her. She was clearly concerned. "I don't know, Dottie."

"I knew most of the people how died. Now…" her voice trailed off.

"I know, I know," he said, trying to comfort her. "We need to be there for their families. And we need to strike back. Hard."

She nodded at him and swallowed, dabbing at her eyes. "Yes, sir."

Tammy came back in with the beverages.

"All they had was cans, except for the water. Sorry, Dottie, I know you like bottles." She passed a water to the mayor and a Diet Coke to Dottie, keeping another bottle of water for herself.

As Tammy sat down, the doors opened behind her and Roget, Office Stevens and FBI Agent Shales entered. Roget looked horrible. His eyes were bloodshot, and his face was scraped and bandaged. His right arm hung in a sling.

"Mayor," Roget nodded as the three men took their seats.

The mayor noticed Roget was limping. "Sergeant, we can reschedule if you're in pain."

"I'm gonna be in pain either way," Roget barked. He looked at the table and spread his clenched fist out onto, breathing slowly, in and out. "Sorry, Mayor," he said quietly. "I've lost a lot of good men and women. And more are just barely hanging on."

"We're praying for them," Tammy said quietly. "Me and Dottie and the rest."

Roget looked at her. "Thank you, Tammy. Anything you can do will help." Roget turned to the mayor. "Should I start?"

The mayor nodded.

"Okay, well, things are looking pretty bad, if you want to know the truth," Roget said. "So far we've lost twelve."

"Oh no," Dottie said quietly. "I thought it was only nine."

Roget shook his head. "We lost three more overnight."

The room got quiet, and Officer Stevens leaned forward. "We also have sixteen wounded, all here at Dayton General. Nine are critical, including Deputy Sergeant Hawkins."

"I'm sorry to hear that," the mayor said to Roget. "We'll be praying for her."

Roget nodded and sighed loudly. The mayor knew Roget was close to Hawkins. There was nothing official, but Shayla had mentioned they might be seeing each other. It might explain why Roget looked like he was on the verge of tears.

"So, I'd say the task force is in trouble," Roget continued, looking at the mayor. "We're down to twenty-one healthy staff members, including the office staff. Dottie, Tammy, I hope you've been putting in time at the range. You ready to lead a raid?"

The women smiled and shook their heads in unison.

"I don't even like guns," Tammy said. "Too loud."

Dottie looked at her. "Me neither. Tammy, you couldn't shoot one if you had to, not with those nails." In any other situation, the people in the room would have laughed. But today, it just seemed sad.

"I'd like to hit back, take them down a notch or two," the mayor said quietly. "They knew you were coming. They planned for it."

Roget shook his head. "I don't need you to tell me what happened. But we're not in any shape to take them on."

Agent Shales opened a folder and set it on the table. "Montgomery and Miami County departments sent people to help, and Chief King brought staff down from Cooper's Mill. I've requested agents from Cincinnati. We should have a full team here on Wednesday."

The mayor nodded.

"We can't even cover this hospital without outside help," Roget said quietly. "At this point, the task force is on hold. We can't take the fight to anyone."

"Do you need me to call Chief Craig and get him to loan us more men?"

Roget shook his head. "I don't know, Mayor. Sure."

It was worse than he thought. Not the number of injured, or the extent of their injuries. It was Roget. He sounded beaten.

Shales looked at the mayor. "National Guard?"

Roget didn't even look up—he just kept staring at his hand, splayed out on the table.

The mayor looked at Shales. "Let me talk to the governor. Between them and the Dayton PD, do we have enough to hit them? And take them down?"

Roget shrugged. "Sure. But we won't be much help until my people are out of here," he said, looking up at the room and the wide windows that looked out over the snowy south side of Dayton. "We could hit the mall. I'm assuming that's what you want to do."

"They hurt us," the mayor said quietly. "We need to hurt them back."

Chapter 87
A Frank Discussion

At 11:00 a.m., Chief King joined Detective Barnes, Deputy Peters and Laura Powell around the big table in the bullpen. They got straight to the update from Peters—King had put his cousin in charge of the investigation.

Peters took them through the BOLO and APB updates, along with the report on Frank's credit card, which showed no activity since April 2, the day before he disappeared. Detective Barnes had subpoenaed Frank's phone records, but they hadn't come in yet. Hopefully they would tell them something about what had happened to Frank or even suggest a recent GPS location.

"I have talked to every single person I can think of," King said. "No one has any idea where he is." He recounted his conversation with Frank's boss down in Alabama. "And Laura, Frank was suspended for two weeks without pay."

She nodded, her face grim. "I talked to him, too. He promised to get back to me if Frank resurfaces."

Peters had also talked to others in town that might have run into Frank: the folks at Tip Top Diner, the hotel, even Monty Robinson and the others at the McDonald's coffee klatch.

The way King saw it, there were three options: Frank had gone back to Alabama, Frank had been abducted, or Frank had chucked it all and left, taking off on his own. Maybe he'd had enough guilt over the death of that family. Too bad he didn't know the family was still alive. King thought of mentioning it, but he'd promised to keep that information close to the vest.

Maybe Frank had taken off to California to search for Georgie, the last surviving member of the crew from last year's kidnapping case. Maybe it bothered Frank that Georgie had escaped with that duffel bag full of cash. It wasn't that far-fetched. Some of the bills had turned up in California, the place King suspected Georgie would flee to. Last year, weeks after the kidnapping, King had interviewed both girls who were held by the four-person kidnapping team lead by Cooper's Mill PD turncoat Sergeant Graves. Charlie Martin, one of the kidnapped girls, mentioned on several occasions the lengthy stories Georgie would tell her of locations in California: San Francisco, Alcatraz, Coit Tower, Morro Rock. Some of the places were so obscure, King had had to Google them before typing up his report. Georgie seemed to know the West Coast better than most. Charlie got the impression that Georgie and Chastity, his ill-fated girlfriend and partner in the scheme, had planned to head west as soon as the kidnapping was finished.

"I also talked to Frank's landlord in Birmingham," Laura said, bringing King out of his thoughts. "She was a real piece of work, but she took my information and promised to get back to me."

"I know we all started assuming he was drunk in a ditch somewhere," King said after another long silence. "Now, I don't know what to think."

Laura nodded. "I hate to say it, but doesn't it seem…doesn't it look like foul play might be involved? I mean, if not, his car would have turned up somewhere, probably parked at some shady bar."

"Even then, we would have gotten a hit back on the plate by now," Deputy Peters said. "Many larger metropolitan police agencies use automatic plate readers, vans that drive around town and scan and record every license plate on every vehicle they pass, including those in parking lots."

"What if he was in an accident?" Laura asked.

"Yup, even then," Peters answered. "Car accidents get reported back automatically. Even if he'd driven his car off into a ditch and wandered off, never to be found, the wreck—and the plate—would have made its way into the national police database by now."

Laura grew quiet. King could tell she was unsure of what to say next.

"I'm sorry, Laura. We've done everything we can. At this point, we just have to wait and see."

The meeting ended with an air of disappointment. Laura said her goodbyes and the officers went back to work on other cases, more pressing ones. Walking back to his desk, King wondered where Frank had gone? Was he an anonymous corpse somewhere, surrounded by white lines of chalk?

CHAPTER 88
Screaming

Two days later, Frank woke with a start.

The young woman was screaming again.

She'd been doing that, off and on, for the last two days. She was in what sounded like the next cell. Frank figured the gang kept girls for entertainment and locked them up when they got out of line. There was another girl nearby—for a while yesterday, they'd both been crying at the same time until someone yelled at them to shut up.

"Please," the young woman yelled, begging. "I'll be good. I promise." She screamed the first word, but her energy petered out. Frank was pretty sure he was the only person who heard her last words.

"It's okay," he said to the wall they shared. "You're gonna make it out of here."

He heard her sobbing. The walls must be thinner then he thought.

"I doubt it," she said. "I doubt it. Two of the girls—they just disappeared. Made the rest of us scared." Her voice was sluggish, slurred.

"They keeping you drugged? Something in the food, maybe?"

"What d'ya mean?"

"Never mind," Frank said. "Just get some rest."

There was no answer. She either fell asleep or gave up talking to him.

He figured it was early on Wednesday morning. It was amazing how regular the bladder could be. If you kept track, it was like your own personal clock. He'd been dreaming when the girl in the adjacent cell woke him. In his dream, he was driving a country road in his Camaro, happy and free.

Escape. It was all he'd thought about for the past four days, that and St. Bart's. But his prison was well-guarded, and the door was always locked.

Frank leaned back against the wall and scowled. He'd just been thinking about something. What was it? He'd been sleeping, dreaming. The girl woke him. He'd heard her crying, told her things would be fine.

How thick were the walls? Could they be sheet rock over plywood? Or just sheet rock? No, probably not, or anyone could kick their way out. Maybe they only kept drugged people here, like the girl. Would drugged captives be aware enough of their surroundings to even attempt escape?

He turned and felt the wall next to his face. It was smooth, painted. He rapped on it slightly and heard no hollow chamber inside the wall. It was thick enough.

What if he punched this wall right now? Would he put his hand through it? Or would he just hurt himself?

On a whim, he decided to try it. Picking a spot on the back wall, opposite the door, he pulled back and concentrated his energy. Krav Maga wasn't a discipline that highlighted power strikes, per se, but there were several different finger and palm strikes that concentrated power into a small area. Frank knew he was woefully out of shape. Would his hand and muscles remember the moves he'd forgotten?

Frank prepared to strike the wall and then stopped at the last second. What if he punched a hole in the wall? The guards would be here in two hours to let him out for his morning bathroom break and breakfast. They'd see the hole and move him to another cell. Probably beat him for his trouble.

Frank put his hand in his lap and thought about it. Could he get out of here? These were gang members. They weren't professional jailers, or people who knew much about keeping prisoners. They played video games all day long. Surely there was a way out, if he was smart enough to find it.

He just had to look.

CHAPTER 89
Hospital Breakfast

Roget woke up next to her bed.

She was asleep, the machines around her beeping. They were on the top floor of the hospital, and the sun was breaking through clouds and streaming in the wide windows. The nurse was pulling the shades open, sending bright light splashing across the room. Roget blinked and sat up.

"Wow, that's bright."

The nurse grunted. "Yeah, but I love this view. You can see halfway to Austin Landings," she said, her hands on her hips. "You should thank me for letting you stay. You know how many people get to stay round the clock for visiting hours? No one." The woman tidied up around Hawkins' bed and then looked at Roget. "You look terrible. You should rest. In your own room."

He looked at Hawkins in the bright light. She looked the same.

"Thank you for letting me stay." He glanced at the door.

"Don't worry," the nurse nodded. "Go, take a break. You've got like five cops just on this floor, and more in the lobby. I had to show my ID three times to get up here after I went out for a smoke."

"Okay," he said with a weak smile. He stood and stretched, then kissed Hawkins on the forehead and left the room. He didn't like leaving, but he had work to do.

Roget checked in first with the Dayton PD officers assigned to guard this floor. He also called in and talked to Bellows back at the task force for an update. After that, he limped around the top floor of the hospital, checking on his injured men and women.

Two more had passed away overnight, taking the total dead to fourteen.

Roget had to sit down when he got the news. Two others were still on the critical list, Hawkins and another. Three had been released, thank God, and nine still in the hospital for treatment.

Several of his people asked if he was leaving the hospital. He told them he was working out of the conference room at the end of this floor. His doctor said his concussion was healing well, but the arm needed another two weeks in the sling. He could move it and use it if he had to, but it hurt.

But before he got to work, he needed to eat. He took the elevator down to the basement and got some breakfast and the Dayton paper in the hospital cafeteria. He didn't have much of an appetite, but forced himself to eat the scrambled eggs and most of his bacon.

Roget read the paper's coverage of the explosion. People were still talking about it, apparently, and it had even made the national news. The task force had finally made the papers, and for all the wrong reasons: half of them were dead or out of the fight.

The future of the task force was really up to the mayor—it was his baby. He had pulled people from all over to make up the force, with half coming from the Dayton PD. Roget and Hawkins were both locals, but others had been recruited from Indianapolis and Knoxville. Bellows and Stevens were up from Florida. And now it didn't seem to matter.

He thought about Patricia, lying in her bed upstairs. Brain damage, the doctors had said. The swelling in her brain wasn't coming down, and he could tell the doctors weren't giving him all the facts. He had contacted her family, and her sister had flown in from Philadelphia and was staying at Patricia's empty apartment.

Roget wasn't sure what else to do, or how to feel, other than lost and confused.

Chapter 90
Brackets and Shelves

Frank crawled around the inside of the small dark closet, restless. He needed to examine the dark closet he was locked in. At least a search for a way out would keep his mind occupied.

First, he checked the door, sliding his hands along it. It was a standard door installed into this closet-sized room. The door opened out, so the hinges were on the outside, unreachable. He'd thought maybe he could unhinge the door by removing the little pins. Also, there was no light around the doorjamb, and the lock was operated from the outside. He wouldn't be escaping through the door.

He checked the floor, running his fingers along the walls where they met the linoleum floor. A rounded wooden strip known as quarter round had been installed around the perimeter. Frank was unable to pry it away with just his fingers.

Starting with the door side, he felt each wall, tapping and pressing. He pushed around the door jamb, looking for any part of the wall that was weak or had any give when he pushed on it. Nothing on the front wall—it was solid. He checked the side walls, although a hole in one of those might just lead to other cells. He toyed with the idea of trying to punch through the back wall, but any guard would see it the next time they fetched him.

Standing, he continued feeling around with his fingers, touching the walls and he stood, and found something on one side wall. A strip of thin wood ran across the wall, starting about halfway between the door and the back wall. The strip stuck out barely a half inch. Strange. It wasn't deep enough to hold anything. He had an idea and turned, feeling on the opposite wall. At the same height, he found another strip of wood. He felt higher on each wall and found more, one on each side, about a foot above the others. Anything higher was out of his reach.

There used to be shelves in this room. At some point, this small room had been used for storage, and the thin brads had held shelves.

Frank felt the brads, curling his fingers around one. Were they wide enough to climb? Or at least to allow him to brace himself? He didn't have the finger strength he used to, but the room was perfectly sized for him to climb the walls if he could find a hand or foot hold. He'd done that a lot as a kid, using his legs to brace himself in a doorway or narrow hallway and wiggle his way up to touch the ceiling. It always made him feel like Spider-Man.

Gingerly, he tried pulling himself up onto the first bracket, bracing with his feet on the opposite wall and pushing off.

His fingers sang from the effort, quivering. He was out of practice. There was a day, in his youth, when he could have balanced on his fingers without a second thought.

Frank growled and pulled himself up, eight fingers on the bracket. Off the ground, he put one hand up to the second bracket, a foot above the other, and pulled.

He swung a bare foot up and stepped onto the first bracket on the opposite wall. He used the other foot and his shoulders against the walls as a brace.

After a second, he was stable, and let go with the first hand, feeling up the wall while balancing himself. His fingers were screaming—most of his weight was on four fingers.

Sure enough, a foot above the second bracket was a third. How high did it go? There was only one way to find out. Frank started to pull himself up and heard the lock rattling.

Someone was opening the door.

He dropped down and came to a rest against the wall just as the door opened. Someone flicked the weak light on, and water was dashed over his head. He pretended that the water woke him and cursed.

"Breakfast."

They stood him up and turned him around to handcuff him. Usually he looked at the ground, half awake, but this time he studied the walls. It was just as he'd hoped—three strips of wood, painted white and blending in. Maybe the gang members didn't even know they were there. The third and final strips looked to be two feet or so below the ceiling.

Frank allowed himself to be dragged to the bathroom and then back to his cell, where his breakfast was waiting on a tray on the floor. A moment later, the door was locked and the light above went out. He wondered if they knew how unappetizing it was to eat in the dark.

Based on previous days, Frank guessed he had roughly four hours before they came with lunch. He ate his breakfast quickly and drank the OJ that came with it, then set his tray aside and got ready to climb again.

He started up the brads, climbing his way up and bracing himself on the second row, two feet below the ceiling. He felt along the ceiling and found the light fixture, the bulb still warm. Frank found a short chain and pulled on it. Nothing happened, so he pulled it again.

He ran his hands around the fixture, feeling where it was attached to the ceiling, and then felt the bumpy ceiling in all four directions until his fingers ran into the walls. He pressed up on the drywall, searching. He found a soft spot and punched upward with a fist into the ceiling. A part broke loose and fell to the floor, hitting with a crumbly thump. Another large portion disappeared up into the ceiling. The hole he'd made glowed with a dim, suffused light.

Frank stopped and listened. No one came to investigate.

He put his hand up into the hole and felt around. Everything he brushed against broke off and fell to the floor, small pieces of drywall breaking away and clattering down below. They sounded loud to him.

Frank moved his hand around. He felt a stud across the middle of the ceiling, the drywall and light fixture attached to the underside of it. He felt another stud above the rear wall. He reached up above that and felt nothing. Open space. Frank could even feel air moving through it.

After ten minutes at the top, he was exhausted. He wanted to climb up into the crawl space, but he needed a break. Frank gingerly climbed down, his hands and feet shaking from the effort. He'd managed to widen the hole big enough to fit through, breaking off larger pieces of the ceiling and throwing them up into the crawl space.

He looked up in the dark and could easily see the hole. It was easy to spot in the darkness. Frank hoped none of the guards would look up.

The fallen pieces.

Oh, God. He'd forgotten. Frank started feeling around on the floor around him. It was pitch black in the closet, as usual, but he was horrified, nonetheless. A dozen pieces of broken drywall littered the ground, some as big as his hand. Any guard opening the door would have to be blind to miss them.

What could he do with them? The room was tiny—there was no place to hide them. He was too tired to climb up and throw them through the hole—plus, how could he climb and carry?

He had an idea and felt the door in front of him and to the sides. The doorjamb stuck out an inch, then there was four or five inches of wall and then the side wall. He put a piece of drywall up and slid it into the space, flattening it against the wall and jammed it between the door jamb and the wall, using the meager light to see what he was doing. To see the pieces, a guard would have to step into the cell and turn around.

He found more pieces and jammed them into the space on either side of the door. The smaller pieces he broke up and scattered around the edges of the room, hoping they would just go unnoticed.

When he was done, Frank sat on the floor and relaxed for a few minutes, stretching and clenching his fingers and hands.

CHAPTER 91
Regional Planning

In another part of the mall, the Council was meeting again. The Foot Locker conference room was closed to everyone but the Dragon and the Council and a few select others. Gig counted himself lucky to be here.

They discussed the situation with the task force first: the body count was up to fourteen now. Two more cops had died overnight in the hospital. All the injured, including the two senior leaders, were at Dayton General, surrounded by round-the-clock security. And for the Northsiders, the bombing at Riley's had gone better than expected. The Dragon had nice words to say about Sonny and his team.

Next, the Dragon shared her plans for Columbus and Toledo. Cincinnati was nearly complete—with the Hive gone, and without a city-level drug task force, the Northsiders were having little trouble consolidating their newest holdings. The Dragon introduced a new council member, a Mr. Adams, a former Hive leader in Cincinnati. He had switched sides and was now overseeing the Northsiders' efforts to unify all the Cincinnati gangs.

"We're looking at another month, tops," Adams said to the Dragon, who nodded her agreement. He went on to discuss the general areas of Cincinnati and which groups still controlled which regions. With the financial backing of the Northsiders, Adams was confident he could consolidate them with few holdouts. Those, he said, could either be bought out or eliminated. "Take out a couple, and the other gangs will fall in line."

"Good," the Dragon said. "Here's how it's gonna work. Columbus is also getting its own seat on the council. I got my eye on a couple guys."

She turned to Sausage, her current consigliere. "Sausage, I'm also promoting you. You'll be spearheading our move into Toledo, consolidating the gangs there. You've got some great ideas. Make them happen," the Dragon said. Sausage nodded and thanked her—this was obviously not news to him. The others around the table congratulated him.

She turned back to the table. "Mr. Kingmaker will be promoted to my *consigliere* for Dayton," she said, nodding at the large man already in charge of production, using the old Italian word for advisor. "You'll need to promote someone to take your place."

Kingmaker nodded. "Thank you, ma'am. It's an honor."

The Dragon stood and began circling the table.

"Our next message must be sent loud and clear," she said. "Today's event still in the works?"

Sonny nodded, glancing at the clock on the wall. "They're already on their way, ma'am. It will be done in the next hour."

"Good."

Gig wondered at the sight of an old, black woman passing along orders to a room full of black men. Gig, for one, was glad to see it. The Dragon had a way of seeing what was coming down the tracks, instead of just focusing on what had already happened.

She stopped and looked around. "Are we ready for tomorrow? It's a big day."

Heads around the table nodded, including Sonny and Gig. They were both ready, or as ready as they were ever going to be for such an audacious plan. No one had ever really taken it to the cops before, not like this.

No one except for the Dragon.

"The device?"

Sonny spoke up. "It's ready, ma'am. We'll load it up in the morning and have it ready for you."

"Good," she said. "And don't anybody disappoint me," she said. "I don't like being disappointed."

CHAPTER 92
Crawl Space

Frank waited for lunch. The time stretched on, even more so now that he had things to do. Places to be. He sat by the door and listened to more crying. Around what he guessed was noon, he heard keys jingling outside. Frank backed away and pretended to sleep.

The light came on and the door opened, and it was Tiny, holding a tray of food.

"You need to use the bathroom?"

Frank nodded and stood.

"Whoa, hold on there," Tiny said, waving over another guard. They led him to the bathroom. Inside, Frank did his business, taking a minute to splash water on his face and rub it over his arms and legs. It was the closest thing he got to a shower, but it felt good, nonetheless. He also grabbed a thin wad of paper towels and put them down his jeans.

When Frank was brought back, he found the food tray on the floor of his cell.

"Okay, enjoy," Tiny said, and Frank exhaled. Tiny and the others clearly hadn't noticed the "improvements" Frank had made to his cell, or they'd be beating him senseless. "See you at dinner."

Frank nodded and stepped in and Tiny closed the door behind him, locking it. Frank looked up and saw the ragged hole in the ceiling just as the light went out.

Frank did the math: lunch was at noon, usually. Three hours and another bathroom break, unless he banged on the door to go sooner. Then three more hours and dinner around six. He had time.

But instead of getting to work, Frank sat on the floor and ate and waited. It seemed like an eternity. He listened as Tiny opened other doors and spoke to other "guests." Frank ate and set the tray aside, stretching his arms and legs. He felt like doing crunches or push-ups to get his heart rate up, but he didn't want to tire himself out.

When he could wait no longer, and there were no sounds from the hallway, Frank braced himself and climbed slowly back up to the top. It went quicker this time, his hand and feet learning where the brads were.

He stopped and listened again. Hearing nothing, Frank positioned himself and finally poked his head up into the crawl space.

It was much as he'd imagined, an open space above the store ceiling that stretched away into darkness on all four sides. The dim light showed studs running in parallel and, attached to those, the store's drywall ceiling. The studs ended at a thick metal girder, probably the "end" of this store and the start of the next one.

The crawl spaces above all the stores seemed connected, or at least these were. It made sense. When it came time to remodel, the interior space was easier to reconfigure. Or maybe this had originally been one store and they split it into two.

Light shined up into the crawl space in shafts, thrown up through holes or gaps in the ceiling. More light came from the direction of the front of the store and the mall itself through gaps around the signage. Eight feet above him, he saw a flat, concrete ceiling coated with white insulation, likely the roof to the outside world.

With his free hand, Frank began breaking off pieces of the closet ceiling, working his way to the stud. This time, he threw the chunks away to his right, into the dark crawl space. When the hole was big enough, he pulled himself up onto the wooden stud and rested his weight on it, grasping his hands and rubbing them.

Frank looked around and saw he should be able to crawl or walk along the parallel studs to the girder. Beyond, there might be roof access, or a way down into one of the other empty stores.

Frank looked back down into the small closet and wondered if he should just go now. It was smarter to wait, to go at night. Explore now, find the route, then come back to the cell. Do it for real when he'd have a ten-hour head start. As soon as they figured out he was gone, they would search the storeroom and find the hole, just like in that movie *The Shawshank Redemption*.

But it was so tempting to go now.

Frank turned and climbed up, standing on the studs. They held his full weight. He began stepping to the next stud, and walked awkwardly to the thick, metal girder. Based on what he knew about the layout of the store, it was the edge of what used to be the Banana Republic. To his right was the front of the "store" that faced the inside of the mall. That meant to his left was the common area, the area where he'd been waterboarded, along with the back of the store. Most shops in malls had back entrances, didn't they? For deliveries?

Frank turned left and walked on the cold girder. It was slippery with sprayed insulation. Halfway back, he stooped and lay down on the nearby studs and found a gap between the ceiling and a light fixture installed in the drywall.

Frank could see down into the store itself.

Tiny and T-Bone were relaxing in the common area, playing that shooting game again. On the screen, they were shooting guns and throwing grenades at other players. Beyond, Frank could see the open area where he had been waterboarded.

He stood gingerly and kept going. The girder ran to a dead end at a wall of cinder blocks. Frank leaned against them—they were cold to the touch. An exterior wall? More girders followed the wall, branching off in either direction.

He went left, assuming he was over the back half of the Banana Republic. He kicked something and found three large nails. He put them in his pocket—they might come in handy later.

Finally, near what he thought was the back of the store, he flattened himself on the studs to look down through the ceiling. It was a small room, an office with shelves on the walls. And a pair of doors standing open to the outside—the concrete outside sported a layer of thin snow. He heard men talking loudly.

The exit.

Frank put his head down on the drywall to think. He could break through the ceiling and be outside in ten seconds. But he'd have to fight his way past at least two men and get away. Frank was only wearing a T-shirt and jeans, no shoes. How far would he get? How many people would chase him?

And some part of him was nagging to return to his cell. Every minute gone was a chance that someone might come check on him for a bathroom break. They'd open his cell, look up, and it would be over.

Frank glanced back over at the dark hole, forty feet away.

Or he could go now. Take his chances, fight his way out. Take one of their coats and shoes.

Could he?

Frank didn't know what to do. His foot hit something. He turned and felt the flat surface and realized it was a half-sheet of drywall, four feet by four feet, it looked like, leaned against the back wall. That might come in handy.

Frank moved to another place where he could see part of the loading door. He could see two men outside—well, he could see their feet, at least. Frank listened for a minute. One dropped a cigarette on the concrete and stubbed it out with his shoe. They were talking about how cold it was outside and about some explosion somewhere.

This was his way out. He would go tonight, after dark.

He backed away from the hole and stood, finding the extra drywall. Frank lifted the piece onto his back and began walking, taking his time.

He made his way along the studs back to the girder, then back to the hole that led down into his cell.

Frank lay the half-sheet of drywall down on top of the studs next to the hole, breaking the edges off the half-sheet and forming a large circular piece. He climbed back down into the closet and braced himself, finding the walls with his feet. It was almost harder than climbing up—getting around the lip of the hole and down onto the brads was tricky. When Frank was stable, he reached up and pulled the rounded piece of drywall over the hole—it covered it perfectly—and then started down.

After a moment, he was standing on the floor of his cell. It seemed tiny compared to roaming the cold, open crawl space. He looked up—it was dark, as it should be. No light from the crawl space.

Frank checked the floor for broken pieces of ceiling—there were none—and sat down to think. He needed to plan.

Getting to the back doors seemed straightforward enough. But what next? It would be dark and cold outside. He would have no phone, no car, no way over the fences.

Frank remembered the parking lots and cars. He could try to find one that was unlocked and steal it, or he could carjack a driver. Then he'd have a car and keys and a way to get away. He'd be warm and dry and could drive right out the gate and be on his way.

It was the Frank Harper way—making it up as he went.

CHAPTER 93
Big Butter Jesus

Agent Shales and three other members of the FBI Cincinnati office rode in a nondescript Ford Taurus, traveling north on I-70 to Dayton. Shales was getting the others up to speed, reviewing the DAHTF's efforts to curtail gang and drug activity and the recent explosion that killed or injured half of the task force. They discussed the recent explosions in Cincinnati and Dayton, but from the looks on the other agent's faces, Agent Shales was boring them.

None of them noticed the boxy white van that had been tailing them since Cincinnati.

The agents passed an outlet mall and Trader's World, a huge flea market south of Dayton. Just north of Trader's World stood a fifty-foot sculpture of Jesus near the highway with his hands raised to the sky.

"What's that?" one of the agents asked, perhaps to change the subject from Shales' lengthy briefing.

"The locals call it 'Hug Me Jesus,'" Shales said, glancing around at his co-worker. "It looks like he wants a hug, right?"

The agent driving the Taurus spoke up. "That's the new sculpture. It replaced another one that burned down."

"What?"

"Yeah, it got struck by lightning," the driver said. "It was Jesus from the chest up, with his arms raised into the air. People called that one 'Touchdown Jesus' because it looked like he was signaling a touchdown. Other people called it 'Big Butter Jesus' because whatever the material they used to make it looked just like butter."

The boxy white van moved up alongside the Taurus and matched its speed.

"Struck by lightning?" one of the agents asked. "That's crazy."

The driver nodded. "I know, right? I guess God was making a joke. I mean, what are the chances of a huge statue being hit by lightning?"

In the next lane, a door on the van slid open behind Shales. One of other FBI agents noticed it immediately and started to say something. Three black men in the back of the white van lifted automatic weapons and opened fire at the Taurus, riddling it with bullets and instantly shattering the windows. The FBI agents' car, punctured by scores of holes, began to slow and drift to the left and into the next lane, nearly side-swiping another car. The door of the white van closed as the vehicle sped away. The agents' car drifted to the left and slowed before finally riding onto the shoulder and impacting the concrete barrier that divided the highway from the south-bound lanes. The car rolled, slower and slower, and finally came to a rest against the concrete wall.

Two other cars pulled off behind the wrecked Taurus. The driver of one got out and walked up behind the FBI vehicle. Once he saw the inside of the car, and the passengers slumped over the seats, he took out his phone and dialed 911.

Chapter 94
Up and Out

Every minute was like torture.

Actually, it wasn't, Frank reminded himself. Actual torture was much worse. He needed to stop using that cliché, now that he truly understood it. But the waiting was frustrating. The period of time from lunch to dinner seemed to drag on forever.

All he could do was plan his next few hours, over and over. He'd gone over every contingency in his head, but it was like that guy Sun Tzu said: plans were great but rarely survived "contact with the real world." Joe Hathaway had been big into Sun Tzu. After Hathaway was captured, Frank had picked up a copy of *The Art of War* and read through it. Some of it made sense, but most of it was just ruthless and cruel. It was about two things: striking first, before your enemies could, and assuming you were the smartest person in the room. Joe had been like that.

Finally, dinner came, along with a bathroom break. Frank went and did his business, returning quickly so no guards would have time to inspect his cell. He avoided glancing up at the ceiling and instead sat and started eating. The guard—this one Frank had nicknamed "Reebok" because of his shoes—locked him up, turning off the overhead light.

So far, so good.

He ate slowly, taking his time. It might be the last food he got for a while. Besides, now there was no hurry—he had ten hours until morning. They never checked on him at night, only letting him out if he asked for a bathroom visit.

Frank waited another hour before getting started. By the time he started up the walls, the place had been quiet for a while.

At the top of his closet, he slid the drywall aside and climbed out, pushing it back over the hole. A curious guard might assume he'd been taken out of his cell by another guard, perhaps for more questioning or a bathroom break. The cell wouldn't withstand a serious investigation, but it could mean a head start.

Gingerly, he crawled across the studs to the metal girder. It was darker now, much darker, and walking seemed reckless. He followed the same path as before, making his way to the cold, concrete block wall and finally the light fixture over the back room, where he'd seen the open doors.

Lying down, he scanned what he could of the room. Thankfully, someone had left the light on. He waited a minute, listening, but didn't hear anyone. Frank found a loose piece of ceiling near the light and slid it aside, poking his head down into the room.

The back room was upside down; shelves lined the walls, each full of boxes and other random stuff. He looked for shoes but saw none. He wasn't looking forward to walking around outside in his bare feet. From this different angle, he saw the back doors and a coat hanging on a hook on the wall next to them. He also saw a red ladder that stretched from the floor and up into the ceiling. How had he missed that? The metal ladder was attached to the wall. Maybe previous tenants had used it to access the crawl space, or maybe there had been a loft area up here at some point.

Frank pushed the ceiling tile back into place and crawled to the block wall. In the thick darkness, he found the metal rungs of the ladder. This part of the ceiling wasn't ceiling tile but a hinged wooden panel. Lifting it would allow him to take the ladder down into the room.

He looked up—the long ladder continued up through the crawl space and into a dark shaft topped by a metal panel.

Roof access?

Frank wasn't sure what to do now. The roof might let him work his way across the top of the mall and climb down to where there weren't any people. On the other hand, he knew the doors below led to the outside world.

Frank decided to take the door below. It was the known quantity. "Open eyes," his partner Ben Stone used to say. And it was clear this was the easiest and fastest way out. Besides, they might already be looking for him.

He lay down and lifted the access panel, laying it to the side. He leaned down and peeked around the corner. Holding his breath, he listened for any sounds, either in the mall or just outside. He was balanced on the edge of a knife—he was going too fast and taking too long, somehow both at the same time.

He slid around and climbed down the ladder, stepping onto the tile floor in his bare feet. Near the doors, he found the thick coat hung on a nail and put it on, then placed one hand on the mechanism that would open the door and paused.

Was it alarmed?

He pushed on the door handle.

It was locked.

"Christ," he said under his breath. He pulled and pushed on the door, then looked around for keys hanging on a nearby lock. Nothing. He checked the pockets of the coat. Still nothing.

Two options. He could wait in the ceiling for someone to take a smoke and sneak past them or knock them out. Or climb to the roof. Either way, he couldn't stay here.

He didn't like the idea of waiting.

Frank climbed back up the ladder and didn't relax until the hatch was back in place. The coat smelled like sweat and beer. He continued up the long ladder and prayed the roof panel wasn't locked as well. He got to the top and pushed on the door, but it didn't budge either. It was too dark to see anything. He felt around with his hands and found a latch on the inside of the door, the kind that swings and locks. He slid the latch aside and pushed again.

The door opened up and out. A blast of chilly air hit him, taking his breath away. Frank smiled and climbed out of the hole, ending up on the wide roof of the Salem Mall. He lowered the hatch behind him and stood for a long moment, hunched over, just breathing in the cold air. It was his first taste of the outside in over a week. The air felt crisp and sharp, like razors in his lungs. He breathed it in heartily, just the same.

Frank stared at his bare feet on the cold metal roof of the mall and stood slowly, looking around. To his left, he saw city lights. He didn't remember the name of the town. There was the Home Depot, built very close to the mall. It was separated only by twenty feet of parking lot and a twenty-foot chain-link fence.

In front of him he saw the north end of the mall and the back of the dark JCPenney sign. He remembered there were lots of cars parked around that entrance. To his right was Sears and, when he turned to look behind him, he saw the theater entrance and the guard shack beyond. In the distance, he saw the tall buildings to the south of downtown Dayton.

Okay, his new to-do list was very short. Climb down, get some shoes. Find a car, drive it out, and get away.

CHAPTER 95
Carjacker

Frank Harper hunched down between two cars and waited in the cold. His feet were numb and his legs hurt.

He'd nearly killed himself climbing down from the mall roof. He'd found an access ladder that ran down into a trash area, but near the bottom he slipped and fell the last three feet. His feet and legs, numb with cold, had slipped off the ladder.

After that, he'd hobbled to the parking lot and began trying car doors, finding none unlocked. Now he waited and watched. Thank God for the coat. He was rubbing his feet, trying to warm them up, and looking for anything he could wrap them in.

He watched as people exited the JCPenney. Through the open doors, Frank could see machinery and more people. There were guards at the door, and each person was checked as they left, probably to make sure they weren't leaving with contraband. Business as usual, he assumed, and that was a good sign—if they knew Frank was gone, the place would be in a panic.

Finally, Frank saw what he was looking for: an older woman, walking alone. She had been checked by a guard and now made her way in his direction. In his experience, women were just smarter than men. In this case, they were less likely to put up a fight. He felt bad about scaring the woman, but he needed to get away.

He moved between the cars, staying out of sight and tracking her until they intersected at her car, an old Ford. He waited until she unlocked the door and was putting her stuff in.

Frank stood up behind her, putting his index finger into her back.

"Don't panic," he said quietly. He felt her stiffen and start to lift her hands.

"No, keep your hands down," he said quietly, looking around. "I'm not going to hurt you. I just need to borrow your car."

"Oh Lord, oh Lord," she started saying quietly.

"Don't worry," he repeated. "I won't shoot—I just need to get out of here. Go ahead, climb in. I'll get in the back."

He pushed her in and climbed in the rear door. The back seat was filled with boxes and bags of clothes. He moved them around enough to lay on the back seat, then covered himself with a blanket.

She was just sitting there, praying quietly to herself.

"Like I said, ma'am, I'm not going to hurt you," Frank said. "Start the car and head for the guard gate. Make sure we get through with no questions, or I'll be forced to shoot you and the guard. I don't want to do that, okay?"

She nodded and started the car. It rumbled to life after a couple of tries.

"What's your name, by the way?"

"Tilda," she said.

"Okay, Tilda, just stay calm. I'm just trying to get back to my family."

She put the Ford in gear and drove slowly around the mall, approaching the gate. Frank recognized the guy from his last visit.

"You have a good night now," he said, waving at the woman. She nodded but didn't say anything.

Once they were off Northsiders property, she stopped at the light. "Where to?"

"I need your car, Tilda. Other than that, I don't care."

She thought about it. "I can stop at the bus stop—it's over a couple blocks."

"That's fine," he said quietly. "Not too close, though."

Frank felt around the boxes and bags, looking for a pair of shoes. It looked like she had a bunch of donation bags or stuff from Goodwill.

"Got any shoes back here?"

"No," she said. She stopped the car and put it in park. "Now what?"

He sat up and looked around. They were at the bus stop, a few empty spots between her car and the terminal.

"This is fine. Once the cops find your car, they'll get it back to you."

She glanced at him. "Okay."

"Take your stuff and go, and thanks."

"Thanks for what?"

"Not making me do something I don't want to do."

She shook her head and picked up her purse and another bag and got out, leaving the car running. Frank waited until she was well away from the car before he got out and into the driver's seat. He watched her go inside the bus station, then drove away. He had no idea where he was going, and no phone or map to get directions. But he'd been in this area of town before and drove in the direction that felt right. Minutes later, he ended up on the highway.

The drive seemed to last forever, but according to the little clock on the dashboard, it only lasted twenty-four minutes. Frank's head ached and he drove with bare feet on the hard pedals. His feet were freezing even with the heat blowing on them.

It was just past 10:30 p.m., and the rest of the world was settling in for the night. The world outside looked exactly the same. Had anyone even noticed he'd been gone?

A thin snow began falling on the car just as he got to the Cooper's Mill exit. He was heartened by the tall signs for the Tip Top Diner and his hotel near the off-ramp. When had the hotel noticed he was gone? He drove past the McDonald's and the liquor store and other places he recognized, but he had only one destination in mind. Finally, he turned onto Laura's street and parked in front of her place and stumbled up the driveway and banged on the door.

It never even crossed his mind how much he might scare her.

The door opened and she looked angry for about a half-second before she recognized him. He didn't hear what she said or any of the questions she asked. All he had the strength to do was walk into her apartment, cross to her couch, and collapse.

CHAPTER 96
Laura

Her apartment was soon abuzz with activity. Laura had called Chief King and left a message, and he called back to say he was on the way. He also said he'd arrange for an ambulance and Deputy Peters to meet at her apartment.

Laura waited on the couch with Frank. He looked horrible, skinny and ragged. His eyes were sunken holes, crazed, with dark bags under them. She'd taken off the weird, heavy coat—it smelled like smoke and beer—and wrapped him in a blanket. She'd put another blanket on his feet, which were red and swollen and cold to the touch.

The EMTs arrived first, lights flashing and sirens blaring. She waited at the door and let them in, pointing to Frank and telling them what she knew, which wasn't a lot. The two EMTs got to work on Frank, waking him up with smelling salts and assessing his condition while they took his temperature and blood pressure.

While they worked on him, Chief King appeared in her doorway. He watched over Frank and the EMTs, waiting for their assessment. King asked her again to repeat exactly what had happened and wrote it all down on one of his yellow pads. So far, Frank hadn't said anything.

Deputy Peters arrived around the time that Jackson woke up and stumbled out into the apartment to find his grandfather and a bunch of strangers talking. Laura got Jackson settled back into his room.

"Okay, the EMTs are wrapping up," Chief King said when she returned. "They say he's severely dehydrated and malnourished but otherwise okay. They want him to go in for treatment, but he's refusing."

"Sounds like Frank."

King nodded. "Can he stay here? He seemed reluctant to go back to the hotel."

"Of course. Has he said what happened?"

King shook his head. "I've only gotten snatches of it so far. He wants sleep, I think, more than anything, but we need a quick report. Let me get the EMTs out of here and we'll talk to him."

Laura nodded and King went back over and talked to the EMTs, who shook their heads and packed up their things. While trying to help them pack up, Deputy Peters knocked over one of their kits and spilled bandages everywhere.

One of the EMTs walked over to Laura. "He needs fluids, ma'am. We put two bags in him, but he'll need more. And rest. His feet were the worst—near frostbite, I'd say. If anything on his legs or feet turns black over the next twenty-four hours, admit him immediately."

She glanced over at Frank—he looked a little better and he wasn't shivering any more, both good signs.

"And he's undernourished," the EMT continued. "Wait until tomorrow for a big meal, but he can start eating in an hour or so if he's awake. Simple foods, like crackers or bread. And hot drinks, coffee or tea, though they can dehydrate, so be careful. Okay?"

"Got it."

The EMT handed Laura his card. "Call me or 911 if his condition worsens. He really should be admitted."

She nodded. "I know. I'll drive him to the hospital if he doesn't improve. And thanks."

The EMTs left and Laura made coffee and tea. King and Peters got settled around Frank, who was resting on the couch. He looked half asleep.

"You feeling better?" she asked, handing him a cup and setting the tray down on the coffee table for the others to serve themselves.

Frank nodded, sipping at the tea and the last of a bottle of Gatorade the EMTs had given him. "Yeah. Glad you were here. Don't know where I would have gone."

The chief leaned in. "So, what happened, Frank? Where've you been?"

"The Northsiders had me at the old mall in Trotwood. They grabbed me from my hotel room, tased me. Took me to their headquarters. I finally got away tonight." His voice was weak, thin and distant.

"The Salem Mall?" Deputy Peters asked, and Laura could see that both he and Chief King were jotting everything down.

"Yeah," Frank said. He sounded spent. "Took my car, too, they said, and all my stuff. Wallet, phone, everything."

"They emptied the room, Mr. Harper," Peters said. "Made it look like you checked out."

Frank nodded and looked at King. "They were convinced I was part of the task force. They…they tortured me."

"Jesus," Laura said quietly.

"I'm sorry, Mr. Harper," Peters said.

"Yeah," Frank said. "Waterboarding."

"What?" Chief King asked, shaking his head. "That's insane."

Frank nodded. "Yeah. There was nothing much I could tell them, but they kept asking about the task force. And the house fire—they wanted to know why I was investigating it." Frank sipped at the Gatorade and sighed. "They had me locked in this little room. I found a way through the ceiling. Had to carjack an old lady to get away. That's her car out front."

"I wondered about that," King said. "Stolen?"

"Yup. Don't arrest me. Or do, if you want to. I need the rest," Frank said, smiling for the first time.

As he recounted his story, Laura grew increasingly nervous and concerned for Frank's safety. It was too late now to be concerned, but it was crazy to think that all this stuff was happening to Frank a few miles away and King and Peters and Laura and everyone else were clueless, just going about their daily routines.

King and Peters questioned Frank, getting descriptions of the people involved and details about the mall. But when King wanted him to retell the whole story again so he could record it, Frank shook his head.

"I can't, guys. I'm exhausted."

King nodded. "Okay, you sleep, Frank. But you and I, we're going to have to go see Sergeant Roget at the task force tomorrow. I'll call him, send him my report tonight, obviously, but he'll have more questions for you, I'm sure. You up to it?"

"Yeah. Just make it after noon. I'm tired."

"I'll set it up. And I'll pick you up." King looked at Peters. "Have that car towed, searched, and impounded. I have a feeling the mall is about to be raided, so we'll hold that lady's car for her until after. But search it for drugs, just in case. And put a twenty-four-hour guard on this house."

Deputy Peters nodded, then looked at Frank. "Do you need anything else, Mr. Harper?"

"No, I'm good," Frank said, glancing at Laura. "I just need to sleep. And food."

King glanced at Peters, then back to Frank. "There's one other thing you should know," King said. "It might make you feel better, but you've got plenty on your plate already."

Frank sat up straighter. "I want to know what's happening."

King looked at him. "The Washington family, from the fire? They're alive."

Laura gasped. "What?"

She was shocked, but the look on Frank's face was something different, something bordering on anger. He opened his mouth to start to say something and then shook his head.

King quickly recounted the story of what had happened, and she saw

Frank become sadder as the story went on. All the rage inside of him was now useless, pointless. She could see him get more frustrated as he heard the details: the family had escaped, Jake Delancy had found out but kept the information to himself, he'd hidden them in a hotel in Columbus.

Laura wasn't sure how to feel about it. She was glad this family was okay, of course. But she wondered about all the wasted efforts from so many people, Frank included. And weren't the Dayton cops still investigating it as a homicide? Three homicides? How would they react when they found out it was all just a waste of time?

After a few more minutes, Frank ran out of questions and grew quiet. Laura looked at the chief. "I think we should call it a night, Chief. If he remembers anything else, I'll call you."

King nodded and tapped Peters on the shoulder, and they got up to leave. Frank stood, wobbly, a blanket wrapped around his shoulders, and shook their hands.

"Thanks, guys."

"Good to have you back, Frank," King said. "Glad you're not dead in a ditch somewhere," he said, making a joke. No one laughed.

"Yeah, me too."

Laura saw them out and closed the door, then sat back down on the couch. She wondered if Frank would want to talk some more, or if he would want something more to drink or something to eat. But she found him fast asleep. Laura pulled the blanket over him. She stood over him for a moment, relieved, and then headed to bed.

CHAPTER 97
French Toast

Frank woke to the smell of French toast, and his stomach rumbled. His head and feet hurt. He looked around, his back stiff, and saw Jackson sitting on the floor next to the couch, looking up at him.

"Hi Grandpa," he whispered. "Mom said not to wake you up, so I've just been looking at you."

Frank smiled.

"See anything interesting?"

"You look tired."

"Thanks," Frank said and sat up slowly, groaning. The couch was too soft—too many nights sleeping on the floor. He reached over and played with Jackson's hair.

"I missed you, kid," he said. His voice sounded like gravel.

"Me, too," he said. "Mom said you were on vacation but now you're back."

"That's right."

"Your car is gone. I looked outside but it's not there. Did you let someone borrow it?"

Frank smiled. "Something like that."

"The lights opened up."

Laura came in from the kitchen. "How you doing?"

Frank looked up at her. "Nothing some coffee and beignets wouldn't fix."

She smiled. "Nothing from Cafe du Monde in stock, but I'm making French toast."

"Special occasion?" Frank asked with a wink.

"No, not really," she replied. "Jackson, you have to be at school soon. Go finish getting dressed. And find your red bag." Every kid in his preschool carried a similar red bag with the student's name written along the top in Sharpie.

After he scooted away, Laura turned back to Frank. "Seriously, how are you?"

He groaned and changed position on the couch. "I'm probably not going to make it," he teased. "My feet are burning and my back is killing me. Can I just die on your couch?"

She nodded. "Sure, just don't make a mess," she smiled. "Advil?"

Frank shook his head. "No, I'm fine. I'll tough it out."

Laura nodded and then had a thought. "Hey, what about all your stuff? Your car and phone and wallet? Will they recover any of that?"

He shrugged. "Maybe. I'm sure they'll raid the mall at some point."

"Well, you need a phone," she said. "And you should cancel your credit cards."

"I just have the one," he said.

"All the same."

"I really liked that car," Frank said, shaking his head. "I'll ask about their plans—the chief and I are talking to the task force today."

"Well, you need a phone and some money, at least," she said.

Laura turned and walked back into the kitchen and returned with a tray with coffee and cream and sugar. It was the same tray she'd brought out on his very first visit to her apartment last fall when they were just starting to reconnect. He remembered being nervous that she might not want to see him.

He fixed up his cup of coffee while Laura left to get Jackson moving in the right direction. "Okay, everyone grab a seat at the table."

Still exhausted, Frank rose slowly and leaned over to pick up the tray. He heard a loud crack from his back, and it felt better immediately. It would probably be weeks before his body was back to normal.

Frank carried the tray over and set it on the table, then unloaded the contents and took a seat. There were three plates and a little cup for Jackson and suddenly he was overwhelmed with emotion. Sitting down at a breakfast table with his daughter and grandson—somehow, it had seemed out of the realm of possibility even twenty-four hours ago.

Frank excused himself and got the bathroom door closed before his entire body was wracked with shudders racing up and down his arms and legs. He leaned on the sink for support and looked at an unrecognizable face in the mirror. He looked like some weird hermit, rousted from a cabin in the woods.

"Christ. I look like the Unabomber," he said to the mirror.

He used the restroom and washed his face and hands and the visage in the mirror improved, but only slightly. But he was just happy to be free.

Frank went back out, and Laura and Jackson were both seated at the little table and eating.

"I made some eggs, too. Jackson loves eggs."

Jackson nodded, stabbing at the eggs with a fork too large for his little hand. "I used to hate them, but now I love them. My friend Katie at school didn't used to like them either, but she does now."

Frank smiled and waved his fork at Jackson's plate. "I love eggs. Should I just eat yours or get my own?"

"Get your own, grandpa!"

They ate together and chatted about the upcoming day and it was simple and warm and wonderful. Jackson had school from nine to noon. Laura wasn't due in to the salon until three. She would be dropping Jackson off at one of many sitters she used and wanted to take Frank shopping for some essentials.

"What happened to your phone?" Jackson asked.

"I lost it," Frank said carefully. "Your Mom's going to take me shopping."

Jackson nodded, smiling between bites. "I lose stuff, too."

"You should call your bank first," Laura said. "I can loan you my phone."

Frank nodded. "Thanks."

When they finished breakfast, Frank offered to clean up, and Laura bundled Jackson up against the cold outside and headed out, taking him to preschool. She kissed Frank on the cheek as she left. Her eyes were shiny but she didn't say anything.

He watched them leave and shut the door.

Laura was right. He needed to get his affairs in order, or at least get started. When tidying up from breakfast, he noticed Laura had forgotten to turn off the stove, something her mother used to do on occasion. After turning it off, he made himself another cup of coffee and sat down at the dining room table with her cell phone and started dialing.

He called Collier first. His boss was glad to hear from him, but Frank had to cut him off when he started asking too many questions. He made it clear he'd been held against his will and that he'd tell Collier and Murphy the whole story once he got back next week.

Frank's next call was to his bank in Birmingham. He only had two accounts, a checking and a savings account, along with a credit card. He explained that he'd been robbed, and once they verified his information, the bank teller checked his accounts for activity. Interestingly, there had been none over the last ten days.

"You got lucky," the woman said. "Usually they run up the card as fast as they can." She changed all his account numbers and issued new cards, offering to overnight them to Laura's house. He thanked her and hung up, relieved.

His next call was to Verizon. He reported his phone stolen and asked that it be wiped remotely, then ordered a new phone and had it charged to his account. The new iPhone 4S, an upgrade over his old phone, would also be overnighted as well. The customer service rep said Frank should be up and running again sometime tomorrow.

Frank was just hanging up when Laura returned.

"You left the stove on," he said, handing her back her phone.

"Really?" she said, looking over at the stove. "I'm usually more careful than that."

"Trudy used to do that," Frank said. "I got my accounts frozen and ordered a new phone and a new credit card. Should be here tomorrow."

Laura nodded, impressed, then handed her phone back to him. "Keep it in case you need it. For now, let's get you some toiletries and clothes. Sound good?"

"Yup," he said, grabbing the ratty used coat he'd stolen from the mall.

"And a haircut at the barbershop downtown. And a new coat," she added.

He held it up. "You sure?"

She looked at the ragged coat. "Definitely."

CHAPTER 98
Gone

Tavon's phone buzzed next to the bed. He reached over and grabbed it.

"Yeah?"

"Tavon," the voice said. It was Gig. "I need you to come in. Right now." Tavon grew more worried as Gig explained. People were freaking out—the old cop had escaped from the mall. Tavon had one job—get eyes on Harper.

"Where do you think he is?"

"Not sure," Gig said. "Last night, the chief of police in Cooper's Mill reported to the task force that Frank was alive and under guard. We've been going over the report. He describes the mall, getting tortured. Everything."

"Wow," Tavon said. He couldn't think of anything else to add.

"He's in Cooper's Mill, somewhere," Gig said. "Probably at the hotel, or his daughter's. Come here and switch out the Civic for another car and find him. And stay on him. And stay invisible."

"Got it."

Tavon threw on some clothes and headed out, switching cars at the mall again. As he drove, he wondered how the man had escaped. At Cooper's Mill, Tavon got off the highway and started to the hotel. He doubted Harper would return there, but it was worth a shot. Without the Camaro to follow, Tavon was at the mercy of luck. He watched the hotel for ten minutes, then drove to the street where Harper's daughter lived.

That's when he spotted the police car.

Tavon pulled over, parking about a hundred yards away from the duplex. Tavon could see two cops in the car. Were they watching the house? Or guarding it?

He settled in. Tavon had been smarter this time: for this stakeout, he'd brought snacks and two books to read.

CHAPTER 99
Tiny

The mall was swarming with activity. Gig was trying to keep a low profile—heads were going to roll over this, and he hoped his wasn't on the chopping block. Three members of the Council had been called in, and those already at the headquarters were being shouted at by the Dragon in the Foot Locker conference room. She was furious.

"How could he have escaped!" she asked for what had to be the fifth or sixth time. Sonny was in charge of the prison, and he was catching the bulk of her wrath.

"We're not sure, ma'am," Sonny said again. "We've got people looking into it. We know he climbed up and broke through the ceiling of his cell—"

"How long was he alone?"

"Overnight, ma'am," Tiny said. He was sitting next to Sonny. "He'd gotten his dinner and bathroom break, and I locked him in. This morning, we went to feed him…" he said and then tapered off. It was one of those situations where more speaking wasn't making things any better. Maybe Tiny was smart enough to figure that out.

Sonny took over. "He crawled through the ceiling and then—"

She held up a stack of papers—it was the report from the cop up in Cooper's Mill. "It says here he climbed up onto the roof," she screamed. "CLIMBED ON THE GODDAMNED ROOF! Then got down—what did he do, fly?"

No one answered.

She looked at the other report, put together by Sonny and Gig. "So, he climbs down from the roof—no shoes, mind you—and CARJACKS some old woman working in production. And just drives right out the gate?"

Sonny nodded. "Yes, ma'am, that's as much as we could figure out," he said. "She said he didn't hurt her—just dropped her off at the MTA."

Tiny leaned forward. "I'm very sorry, ma'am. I promise you we'll find out how—"

Gig was surprised at how quickly the Dragon drew her weapon. The small gun coughed and a hole appeared in Tiny's forehead. His mouth moved for a half-second longer, and then he flopped down onto the table. A puddle of blood spread slowly away from his head across the white conference room table, and a red mist hung in the air.

"They know who I am, you IDIOTS," she whispered. "Years I've been there. I had everything set up, even before I took over this gang. Have any of you morons ever worked on something that took years to set up? YEARS??"

She looked up from the table. "We have to move up the timetable. Part 2 today, Part 3 tonight."

Gig and the others looked at her, then at each other. It was too soon, wasn't it?

"Your package is ready, ma'am," Sonny said. "Part 2 can happen today. But for Part 3, we don't have all the information yet. We were planning—"

"I'll get the files today," she said. "They won't notice. And the bomb will cover it up."

No one said anything. No one seemed interested in disagreeing with her, not with Tiny's blood spreading slowly across the table in front of them.

"That...that should work," Sonny said.

Gig nodded. "We have the list already."

"Tonight?" she asked. "Can we go tonight?"

Sonny looked at the gun, still in her hand. A wisp of smoke flowed from the small barrel. "We just need the locations."

"Good," she said. "Get it started."

"One question," Sonny said gingerly. Next to him, Gig cringed and waited for the sound of gunfire.

"Yes?" she asked.

"The hospital. I have twenty men for that, but it might not be enough."

She looked at him and seethed. "Then...put...more...men...on...it."

Sonny nodded and stood, walking out quickly. The remaining men waited, the room falling silent. No one wanted to invoke her wrath by asking for directions or clarifications.

After a minute, the Dragon looked up and placed the gun on the table in front of her. She began reading from the report again. "He says he was tortured four other times after Gebhuza left. Who did that?"

No one answered, so Gig spoke up. "Um, that was Tiny and his men," he said, glancing at Tiny's blood on the table. "They may have been trying to get more information out of him."

"Or exercising their sadism," she said, spitting out the final word. "Not that I have a problem with harsh treatment, if it's done for a reason. For amusement of the bored? No. Gig, take charge of Tiny's men. You and your team did well snatching Harper. Find out how the man got out."

"Yes ma'am. I already have Tavon up in Cooper's Mill looking for Harper," Gig said. "We'll get eyes on him. Do you want us to take him out?"

She thought about it for a moment, then shook her head. "No, not yet. I need to go to work. Can't have anything mess with that."

Gig nodded and stood to leave, but she waved him back down into his chair.

"Hold on a second," she said. The Dragon turned to the others. "This location is compromised," she said loudly. "They will be coming. I want all the product on trucks and out of here by 6:00 p.m. Use the production staff. And all the chemicals and equipment—get started on moving those as well. At least get them on trucks and out of the area."

The others scrambled, taking notes. Gig expected someone to complain, but no one did. Everyone knew not to ask any questions. When the Dragon said do something, you did it.

"And I want all our records moved to Toledo," she continued. This was serious. "Gig, destroy our financial records and have the computers and backups destroyed, too. I want two copies—and only two—brought to me. Do it personally." She looked at them. "When the cops reconstitute, they'll raid this place. I want it empty. G0. Get to work."

Gig stood and left with the others, heading to his office. He got to work, concentrating on his task and trying to ignore the sounds around him. He could feel the rising sense of panic in the offices.

He created three full backup copies of the gang's financials, including all their account information, passwords, and other data, and saved them to three simple USB sticks, passwording and encrypting the single compressed file. He triple-checked the files to make sure they were all there, and then sighed and set his computer to begin formatting itself, deleting everything on the machine. While the formatting ran, he gathered all the paperwork he could find, including all the marked-up copies returned from Tavon.

That reminded him, and he called Tavon. The young man had checked the hotel and was now watching Mr. Harper's daughters' apartment, which was under a police guard.

Gig thanked him and walked back into the conference room, pocketing one of the USB sticks. Sonny was back and discussing the plans for tonight with the Dragon. Gig and Sonny had already talked at length about the teams and their assignments. Moving up the timetable to tonight shouldn't be a problem.

Gig handed the Dragon the two USB sticks.

"Two copies," he said. "The password is the name of your granddaughters' school." Her granddaughters were a fiction, as was the name of the school they attended. Very few people knew all the details of her cover story.

She nodded and took them from him. "Good."

"I also spoke to Tavon. He hasn't found Harper, he's parked outside Harper's daughter's apartment. The place is under police guard. I told him to stay there and keep me in the loop."

The Dragon nodded again and Gig turned and left, making his way to the old Banana Republic. Once there, he and T-Bone, Tiny's second in charge, inspected Harper's cell. Someone had put a tall ladder inside, and Gig climbed up to examine the hole Harper had apparently made in the ceiling. Gig popped his head through the hole—above the ceiling was a wide crawlspace that stretched in every direction.

Gig climbed down. "How did he get up here?"

T-Bone pointed at the walls and a set of thin strips of wood tacked there. "We think he climbed up these, then broke out the top."

T-Bone led Gig back to the loading area and pointed up.

"He came through to here, then tried the door, which was locked. Took my coat, then climbed this ladder to the roof. Do you want to go up?"

Gig looked up the ladder. It stretched away into the darkness. He shook his head. There was no point. He texted the Dragon his findings, then turned to the guards.

"We're clearing out. If you're on one of the teams, report to Sonny. If not, start cleaning everything up. By tomorrow, it should look like we were never here."

Chapter 100
Empty Desks

Tammy shook her head as she walked through the task force offices.

So many empty desks. This place was even more depressing then the hospital. She prayed for those who survived the attack, but many of the men and women she had worked with for months were now gone forever.

She walked through the main room and over to Roget's office, letting herself in. Being the senior admin staff member, she had keys to every room.

Tammy tidied Roget's desk, careful of her long nails. Roget was coming in for a meeting at noon. He'd been working from the hospital—in fact, yesterday she'd driven over two boxes of reports for him to read. His good arm was in a sling and his face was all bruised and Ms. Hawkins was in a coma.

The tears came on before she even realized it.

What would happen now? Half the task force was dead or in the hospital. Nothing could change that. Were the deaths of all these people worth cleaning up the streets?

Tammy walked back out into the main room, drying her eyes. Normally, this place would be busy. Now, only fifteen men and women were working, making calls and investigating the hundreds of leads that had come in since the raid on Riley's.

She stepped out into the hallway and was headed to the admin offices when the elevator dinged. The door slid open and Tammy saw Dottie, struggling with a metal cart loaded with three bags and a large box.

"You need some help, Dottie?"

"Oh, yes, thank you," she said, using a foot to block the elevator door from closing. "Did some shopping for the office and wouldn't you know I bought way too much."

The Sam's Club bags were crammed with Styrofoam coffee cups and a large pink box marked "Sweet'N Low."

"You been busy," Tammy said, holding the elevator door open as Dottie pushed the cart off. They turned, heading down the hallway into the break room.

"Yeah, they was having a sale," Dottie said, unloading the bags onto the counter. "And I got a new coffee maker, too," she said, pointing at the box on the cart.

"Sergeant Roget's on his way in."

"Yes, thanks for texting me. I wanted to be here for him. You takin' the meeting notes?"

Tammy nodded. "I'm going to get back to work," she said. "I tidied up his desk, but if you want to file some of his papers, he'd appreciate it. The place is a mess."

"Okay, I will. And I'm gonna put the coffee maker in the conference room. I need to make sure I'll get reimbursed for it," Dottie said, and began pushing the cart out of the room.

Tammy smiled and walked back to her desk, passing Jada, who looked up at Tammy.

"You okay? You been crying?"

"Yeah, I'm fine," Tammy sighed.

CHAPTER 101
Questions and Answers

Chief King drove, and Frank rode along with him, silent with his thoughts.

It reminded Frank of the ride he'd ever taken with King, driving to the Martin's house on Hyatt to conduct follow-up interviews in the kidnapping case. Frank had been cocky and thought he could just walk in and solve things.

"You gonna be okay?" King asked. They were heading south on the highway into Dayton.

"Yeah," he said.

"They tortured you," King said.

"Yeah," Frank said. "Tell you what—I'll save it for the interview, okay?"

King nodded. He was a good cop, Frank realized. Frank had thought the chief of the Cooper's Mill PD was good at his job, administering over the other cops on the payroll, allocating resources, etc. But now Frank saw him as something more: smart enough to know when to stop asking questions.

King filled the silence by telling Frank about

King drove south, filling the silence by recounting the task force's ill-fated raid on Riley's. King exited the highway at Main Street and drove through Dayton to the mayor's office, parking out front.

It was just before noon as King and Frank headed inside. After checking in at the lobby, they took the elevator up. For some reason, the elevator ride didn't bother Frank as much as it usually did. When the doors opened, they were greeted by a junior cop, who led them to the same conference room as before. One end of the table had piles of file folders and a large coffee maker, still in the box.

Sergeant Roget was already seated, waiting with a large, distinguished looking black man and another officer. A woman sat near the end of the table, ready to take notes. Roget's arm was in a sling, his face cut and bruised. He looked exactly like how Frank felt.

"This is Mayor Denton," Sergeant Roget said. The mayor nodded, shaking hands. "And Officer Stevens, and Tammy, one of our clerks."

After King and Frank sat, Roget got right to it. He asked Frank to recount his days at the mall again, even though they all had copies of King's preliminary report from last night. Frank went through it all again, talking quietly for the better part of a ten minutes. Tammy wrote everything down, stopping him at several points for clarification. Frank noticed that she had ridiculously long fingernails. Roget also jotted down notes at various points during the narrative.

The mayor interrupted Frank when he got to the Dragon.

"You're saying the Dragon's a woman?"

"Yes, sir," Frank said. "A black woman, fifty to sixty, based on her voice. And she was clearly in charge. She directed the people in the room. And based on their knowledge of your operations, I'd say another thing is obvious: you have a mole."

"That's unlikely," the mayor said. "Roget mentioned it, but I've just been through all the personnel files." He looked at Roget. "They're still on your desk, in fact. I went through the background checks on everyone here—I personally recruited every person. If we do have a mole, I can't figure it out."

"I've been noticing things for a few weeks now," Roget said. "But the raid confirmed it for me." He leaned forward. "There's also this… and this information is not to leave this room, okay? Tammy, don't write this down."

Everyone nodded.

"Agent Shales was killed yesterday," Roget said.

"What?" Frank said sharply.

Roget nodded. "He and three other agents from the Cincinnati office were ambushed and killed on the highway south of Dayton. Witnesses said a van pulled alongside their car and opened fire with automatic weapons."

"That's horrible," Chief King said. "He helped us with that kidnapping case last year."

The mayor nodded. "I'm the one that brought the FBI in. Now they're screaming at me for answers."

"You have a mole," Frank said. "That's the only answer."

"The Northsiders knew our attack plan for Riley's," Roget said. "Right down to our arrival time."

"That's true," the mayor agreed. "That doesn't mean they have someone on the inside." They discussed the possibility of a mole, then turned to planning an assault on the Salem Mall with the help of the Dayton PD. Frank let them talk for a minute or two before he interrupted.

"Look, are you done with me?" Frank knew he sounded rude, but he was too tired to care.

Roget nodded. "Yeah, but we need Chief King for a few more minutes. Why don't you get yourself some coffee or something? We'll make it quick."

He walked out of the conference room and found an empty desk near the windows. Out of habit, he pulled Laura's phone out of his pocket. No messages. He signed, realizing he had nothing else to do but wait for King.

Frank looked around—the room looked like every other police department he'd been in, even with the wide, tall windows that looked out over downtown Dayton. Rows of desks and chairs and white boards on the walls. The men and women in the room were mostly on the phone, probably tracking down leads. More than half the desks were empty. Had those men and women been killed in the raid?

Outside, the snow had started to fall again—it seemed like every time he looked out the window here, it was snowing. Laura had said a storm was coming in. Maybe this was it.

Frank needed some coffee. He'd gone a week without it and found himself craving the stuff, even the watery crap. He stood and walked through the room, searching for a galley or break room. Every police station had one.

He didn't need to be grilled. He'd had enough of coercive questioning in the last week to last a lifetime. If Roget and the mayor and King wanted to sit there and plan the raid on the mall, goody for them. But he wasn't interested. All he wanted was his car back.

Passing through a set of doors, he found a wide galley with coffee-makers, a fridge, and a small seating area with tables and chairs. He went to the coffee maker and found a pot of "regular" on the warmer. He'd never been in a police station that stocked decaf. Decaf was for civilians.

Frank fixed himself a cup and sat down. It wasn't bad—maybe his week off made all coffee taste better. He might never find any coffee as good as the brew from Café Du Monde, but this coffee was pretty good. Pretty damn good.

From somewhere else in the office, he heard her voice.

Frank froze, listening.

He had to be imagining it. No one would blame him, after what he'd been through.

No, there it was again. That voice. He heard her, talking to another woman, saying goodbye.

The Dragon.

She was here. Right now. In this office.

Frank turned and hesitated, setting down his coffee. He would know her if she opened her mouth in his presence. But SHE would know him on sight—she knew everything there was to know about Frank Harper.

He edged around the corner and looked in both directions, but saw no one. Frank rolled the dice and headed back to the bullpen, keeping his head down. He wasn't armed and needed to find backup. Fast.

Frank crossed to the conference room and walked in without even knocking, closing the door behind him. The official discussion must have ended as the secretary had already left. Sergeant Roget looked up at him, and the mayor and King turned to look at Frank.

"She's here," Frank said.

"Who?"

"The Dragon. I was getting coffee and heard her voice."

"Frank, what are you talking about?" Chief King said.

"I know what I heard," Frank said quietly. "Twice. She's your mole. She must work here."

The mayor looked at Roget, then back to King. "Mr. Harper, you've been through a lot over the last ten days."

"I know that, Mayor," Frank said. "I was there. You have no idea what I've been through." Frank looked at King. "Chief, you know I'm a lot of things," he said quietly to his only friend in the room. "I'm a drunk, and I'm impulsive, and I'm frequently in over my head," Frank said, realizing that his little speech was turning into a confession. "But have I ever lied to you?"

The chief looked at him and slowly shook his head.

"It explains a few things," Frank said quickly. "You said yourself the Northsiders seemed to benefit from the actions of the task force. And when I was being questioned, they already knew a lot about your people. You have a mole, I'm telling you. This woman works here."

"Bullshit," the mayor said. "I handpicked everyone on this task force."

King stood. "Where?"

"Break room," Frank said. "Come with me. If she spots me, she'll run. Or fight." King nodded and followed him out. At this point, Frank didn't really care if the Dayton folks believed him or not. He needed to track this woman before she got away.

He turned and left the conference room, King and the others trailing him to the break room. King had his hand on his gun and was looking around warily.

"Here?"

Frank nodded at the doors leading to the admin area. "Or back there."

"This is crazy," the mayor said and turned, walking through the doors labeled "Task Force Administration." The others followed. Frank saw it was a room with six desks, each piled high with paperwork and folders. Boxes lined the walls and more paperwork crowded a central table. Several of the desks held personal items, photos, and plants and the occasional stuffed animal.

One woman, the one from Frank's interview, looked up from her desk. The name on her desk read "Tammy."

"Can I help you?"

"Who else is here, Tammy?" Roget asked, his face a blank. Frank couldn't tell if he believed Frank or not.

"Just me, sir," she said, looking at King and his hand on his gun. "Why? What's happening?"

Frank stepped around Roget. "Hi. Can I ask, how many women work back here? We're looking for an older women, sixties, African-American?"

Tammy seemed a little taken aback by the question. "Well, there's me, and Dottie, and Shayla, and Joanna," she said, pointing to a desk for each name. "Dottie and Joanna are the oldest. And Jada and Barb, but they're both younger. Under 30. Why?"

Frank looked at King. "It's not her."

The mayor glanced at Tammy. "Anyone else in today?"

Tammy shook her head. "No, just me. Jada left at noon, and Dottie left a bit ago."

Frank and King spread out, looking around the tall filing cabinets and checking the rest of the room. There was no one else there.

"Clear," King said.

Tammy grunted. "What do you mean 'clear?' Is something going on?"

"I'm not sure," Frank said, the first bit of doubt creeping into his mind. He pointed at another set of doors. "Those lead out to the elevator?"

Tammy nodded.

King started through them, and Frank followed. They ended up back at the elevators, finding no one. Roget and the mayor stayed, talking to Tammy. King then started a circle of the floor, peeking into offices and the break room again. Frank stopped at the women's bathroom, located in the hallway near the elevators, and knocked.

"Cleaning service. This room occupied?"

There was no answer, so he walked in, checking each stall.

No one. He walked back out and followed King back to the admin offices. Roget looked up when they came in.

"Anything?"

King shook his head. Frank just felt confused. He'd heard the woman's voice—there was no imagining it.

"The only secretary back here was Tammy," the mayor said. "The staff has been with the mayor's office for years. Dottie has two granddaughters she's raising—her daughter is in jail. Joanna is obsessed with cooking, and her husband does professional BBQ. They travel around all summer going to competitions and festivals."

Frank shook his head. "I swear I heard it."

The other three men looked at each other. "Frank, why don't we take off?" King said. "You've had a rough—"

"I know what I heard," he said. He walked back out to the break room and the other men followed. Frank picked up his cup of coffee and sat. "She was here. I know it."

The mayor looked at his watch. "Gentlemen, can we wrap this soon? I have a 1:00 I need to make."

Roget gestured toward the conference room. King and the mayor followed the sergeant out. Frank stayed, sipping his coffee and listening for the Dragon. After a minute, he stood and wandered back into the admin offices.

"Hi," he said to Tammy. "Sorry about all that."

"Hey, it's not a thing, sugar," Tammy said, nodding at the computer screen in front of her. "I just finished typing up your interview and sent it to Dottie to proofread. With what you went through, I'd be hearing voices, too."

He sat at the desk across from her, curious.

"Tell me about the other women who work here."

Tammy sat back and smiled, crossing her arms. Frank knew immediately that she was a talker.

"Rosanna's—that's her desk you're sitting at—she and I started the same year, 2002. Coming up on 10 years. Likes to knit," Tammy said, holding up a scarf she was wearing. "Made us all scarves last Christmas. Her husband makes the best ribs you ever ate."

Frank looked around Rosanna's desk. There were family pictures next to the dark computer screen, along with a plant in a pot shaped like a pig. A framed certificate next to the plant read "Best Pulled Pork, Memphis BBQ Fest, September 2010."

"She in today?"

Tammy shook her head. "Yesterday. Jada was in, left before your interview. And Dottie was here—she just left. She was supposed to take notes for your interview but had to go."

"Dottie's the one raising her grandkids?"

"Two cute girls," Tammy said, nodding at her desk to Frank's right. "Poor things. Dottie's daughter got arrested, and Dottie had to step in and help. She's always gotta go to pick one of them up from school or to get them to some activity."

"And who else?"

"Well, Shayla," Tammy said, pointing at another empty desk with her crazy fingernails. "Started in '97. We've all been here since the last mayor," Tammy said. "She's a big girl, doesn't talk to a lot of people."

Frank stood and walked over to Shayla's desk and looked at her personal items—a plant and a signed photo of Billy Dee Williams attached to the wall. He pulled her desk drawer open and found it was full of bags of Cheetos and a half dozen Twinkie wrappers.

He wandered over and looked at Dottie's desk as well—she had a plant, too, and a framed picture of two young African-American girls. They looked happy, smiling and hugging on a playground.

"This them?"

"Yeah," Tammy said. "Kylie and Kritney. Ain't they cute?"

Frank nodded and started to set the frame down when he hesitated. He looked closer. There was something off with the photo. It looked TOO perfect. The lighting, the clothes the girls were wearing. It looked staged somehow.

On a whim, he flipped the frame over and swung open the little brads that held it together.

"What you doing?"

"Just checking something."

He popped the back of the frame off and took out the photo, flipping it over. The paper was too flimsy for photographic paper. The back of the page was an advertisement that read "PEOPLE MAGAZINE – SUBSCRIBE TODAY."

Frank held it up for Tammy to see.

"You're sure these are her granddaughters?"

Tammy nodded, and he turned the sheet around, walking over and handing it to her.

"They ever been in *People* magazine?"

She seemed confused, taking the magazine page in her hand. She flipped it back and forth several times.

"It's a fake," she said. "Someone cut it out of a magazine."

"They're fake," Frank corrected her. "There are no granddaughters. Those are two random girls that appeared at some point in *People*. Come on."

Frank walked back into the bull pen with Tammy following. Sergeant Roget and the mayor and Chief King were just coming out of the conference room. Tammy handed the photo to the mayor.

"Recognize these girls?" Frank asked.

The mayor nodded. "Yeah, Dottie's granddaughters."

"Flip it over, Sarge," Tammy said, her eyes wide.

He did, then looked up at them. "I don't understand."

Tammy spoke over everyone. "There ain't no granddaughters. Either that or they was famous enough to appear in *People* magazine."

The mayor looked at Roget. "Dottie?"

Roget's eyes went wide.

"She was supposed to sit in my interview today," Frank said. "Why did she back out?"

Roget looked at the rest of them. "She asked to leave early," he said. "Tammy volunteered to take notes instead."

Chief King leaned forward and took the magazine page. "Maybe she had other places to be when she found out who you were interviewing."

"I just sent it to her," Tammy said, still looking at the photo.

Roget looked at her strangely. "What?"

"The interview transcript. We always send each other our stuff to proofread. For typing errors, etc. She asked me to send the transcript along when I was done."

Frank was quiet for a minute, letting them debate. He was remembering something—

"I knew something was wrong," he said to himself.

Roget looked at him. "What?"

"While I was being tortured, they asked me what we talked about. You and me. During the interview. They wanted to know what we talked about when we were alone."

Roget nodded, explaining to the others. "After I excused the others. Dottie and Hawkins were sitting in, but I wanted to talk to you privately," he said, making a face.

"I don't care if they know," Frank said, then looked at the others. "Roget asked them to step out, then he asked me if I was high. And I was, I'll admit it. But Dottie, who was in the original interview, didn't hear that part."

The five of them grew quiet for a moment, each considering the situation. To Frank, it looked like Roget and the mayor and Tammy were all searching for an explanation. Or trying to figure out how badly they had been fooled.

Chief King cleared his throat and walked back into the conference room, and the others followed him inside, including Tammy.

"I think you have a situation here, Sergeant," King said to Roget and the mayor. "Last year I had a rogue cop on my payroll. I learned the hard way that things can go south in an instant. You have to assume the worst."

Roget looked at Tammy. "Was there anything out of the ordinary with

Dottie today? Anything strange?"

Tammy shook her head and tapped her fingernails on the conference room table. "Nah, other than she needed to leave early."

"That's it?" the mayor asked. "Nothing else?"

She shook her head. "I just can't believe it," she said, almost to herself. "I can't believe she's part of a gang." Tammy stood and left the conference room.

"Me neither," the mayor said, sitting back down. "If someone like Dottie or Tammy was a plant, they'd have everything. All our procedures, plans for our raids. Intelligence on every other gang in the region, names of their heavy hitters, last known locations. Everything."

Roget looked at Frank. "You said they asked about what you and I talked about."

"Yes. And they wanted to know other details about your men. Names, spouses."

"Why?"

"I have no idea," Frank said.

Tammy knocked and entered the conference room again. "Sorry, I forgot something. You asked about anything out of the ordinary with Dottie."

"Yes?" Roget asked.

"She brought in a bunch of coffee supplies this morning," Tammy said. "We put them in the break room. And a new coffee maker—she was worried about getting reimbursed."

"Where is it?" Frank asked.

"There," Tammy pointed.

They all turned and looked at the same time. Sitting at the end of the conference room table was the large coffee maker Frank had seen earlier, still in the sealed box and marked with a "Sam's Club" sticker, the kind they put on large purchases.

The mayor stood and walked over, looking at the box. He started to open it.

"Wait," Frank said. "What if it's not a coffee maker?"

The mayor stopped, his hands on the box.

"They blew up the strip club," Chief King added. "And you said they hit a warehouse in Cincinnati last week."

Roget nodded. "With a series of explosive devices."

The mayor put his hands down. "What do we do?"

Frank spoke up. "Anyone with bomb experience?"

The mayor nodded. "Hawkins and Brown."

Roget shook his head. "Both at Dayton General."

"Bellows?"

"Maybe." Roget turned and they all backed out of the conference room. "I want this floor cleared in two minutes," he yelled, getting everyone's attention. "Anyone know where Bellows is?"

"Here, Sergeant." A young man stood up from his desk.

Roget waved him over, then yelled at another member of the task force. "Get this floor clear. I'm not kidding. Mayor's office, too. In fact, just pull the fire alarm. Clear the whole building."

Bellows followed Roget back into the conference room.

"We have a reason to believe that box might hold an IED," Roget said, pointing. "How should we proceed?"

"Really, Sergeant?"

The fire alarm sounded, sending a shriek through the whole floor.

"How do we proceed?" the mayor asked again, his voice urgent.

"Standard procedure would be to clear the building and call in the Dayton PD. Bomb squad."

"Do you check it somehow to see if there's a device?" Chief King asked.

"No," Bellows said, shaking his head. "Most IEDs are set to trigger if investigated. Or they're controlled by a timer or radio detonator."

"Okay, let's clear out," Roget said, waving his left arm. "Bellows, call the bomb squad and coordinate with them."

King and Frank jogged out together. The mayor walked off in the direction of his offices to make sure everyone was out, and Roget did the same for his people. Frank hit the "Down" button and they proceeded to the lobby and out onto the street.

Those evacuated from the building crossed the street and waited, and Frank and King got into King's squad car to wait. King started the car and moved it, parking across the street.

King and Frank talked about the ramifications of a mole in the task force, a conversation similar to one they'd had last October about an employee of Chief King's.

In the minutes that passed, a firetruck and a van labeled "DAYTON POLICE DEPARTMENT BOMB TECH" arrived and Frank saw men rush inside. Men and women from the building, including Sergeant Roget and the mayor, continued to file out, gathering across the street.

Ten minutes passed. Finally, the bomb techs exited the building, two of them walking together and slowly carrying what looked like a heavy metal cooler. They climbed into the back of the bomb tech van and drove away.

Sergeant Roget and the rest of the building occupants began crossing the street and filing back into the building. Roget stopped at King's car and King rolled down the window.

"They opened the box. It was a device on a timer. They're not sure what it is, but they're taking it out to a parking lot by the river and will investigate it further. I'll call you when I know more," he said, then leaned around to look at Frank. "Thank you, Mr. Harper."

Frank just nodded and Roget turned to head back inside. The mayor waved at King and Frank as the chief King backed out of the parking spot and headed north, back to Cooper's Mill.

"I can't imagine keeping a cover for years like that," Frank said. "Think she got herself assigned to the task force?"

King shrugged. "Who knows. Maybe the whole task force was her idea."

Twenty minutes later, King dropped Frank off at Laura's apartment and waved as he drove away. Frank nodded at the cops guarding her duplex, then used the key Laura had given him to get in. Laura was at work and Jackson at the babysitter's house.

Inside, he hung up his new coat and went to make himself some coffee and eggs. He was famished. When he was done cooking, he put them on a plate and sat at Laura's couch and flicked on the TV, looking for something to watch. There was no local news on yet—it was only 3:00 p.m., and the earliest was NewsCenter 4 at 5:30.

He settled in to watch the national news. Everyone was talking about the 100-year anniversary of the sinking of the Titanic, coming up in three days. Every news channel was showing clips from the Leonardo DiCaprio movie, which had just been re-released in theaters, in 3-D this time. The anchors compared the movie version with the actual, real-life historical sinking.

What was "real life," anyway?

Was what happened to him in that mall 'real life?' If he'd described the waterboarding to ten people, nine of them wouldn't have believed him. If he'd told them what happened to him at St. Bartholomew's hospital—the shooting, the drowning, the anguish of leaving those people behind to die—no one would have believed him.

He ate his eggs and the leftover French toast. Why blow up the task force? Were the Northsiders so hell-bent on destroying them, they'd blow up their offices? What about the people who weren't at work, or those at the hospital? You couldn't kill them all.

You couldn't kill them all, right?

Frank had a thought. The Northsiders had been convinced that Frank was part of the task force, brought in to help. He was an unknown quantity to them. They were familiar with everyone else on the task force.

Dottie knew all of them, where they worked, what they reported. But

Frank was a fly in the ointment, and the Northsiders had been curious about what Roget and Frank talked about privately at the end of his interview. They probably thought he and Roget were discussing the case. Either that, or they though Frank was more involved than he was letting on.

It didn't explain all the questions, though. The waterboarding, the beatings. They wanted to know his involvement. And where the other task force members lived. They had asked for home addresses. And names of spouses and places the cops frequented. Why? If Dottie worked there, surely she could have gotten that information, unless it was locked up.

Home addresses. Did they know about Laura?

Frank stood and went to the window, looking out without moving the shades. He counted nine cars on the streets, and only one had a figure sitting in the driver's seat.

It was hard to tell from this distance, but it sure looked a lot like Tavon.

Frank went to find Laura's phone.

CHAPTER 102
Denied

Gig was in the counting room, helping them clear out the backup paperwork and box up the substantial amounts of cash. The Dragon came in and looked around, then walked over to Sonny, who had been helping with the money but had stopped to take a call.

"Hang up, now," she said to Sonny, who glanced up and swallowed.

"Yes, ma'am," he said and abruptly hung up his phone. "Can I help you?"

"Can YOU help ME?"

Sonny nodded.

"Yes, you can help me," she said. "The bomb should have gone off by now. But my spotters at the police station haven't seen anything. The bomb squad took it out."

Sonny looked at Gig, then back at the Dragon.

"I don't know what to say."

She looked at him and Gig, then seemed to lose the edge of her anger. She reached over and grabbed one of the stools and sat, putting her phone and the McDonald's cup she'd been carrying down on one of the rough-hewn counting tables. She sighed and looked at them.

"It's okay," she said. "I'm just angry. First that old cop escaped, and then Part 2 was a bust. At least I got the files."

Gig wasn't sure what to say. "They discovered the device?"

She nodded. "I was in the office and heard Harper was coming in for an interview. I barely missed running into him at the elevators on my way out. They found the device, evacuated, and called in the bomb squad to dispose of it."

Sonny shook his head. "That is disappointing."

"Yeah, that's an understatement," she said, picking up her Diet Coke and taking a sip. "All the more reason why tonight has to go off perfectly." Her eyes were on him. "You sent out the information?"

"Yes. And it will go perfectly, I promise," he said. "I'm personally leading the hospital group. And Gig will provide transport in and out as needed."

The Dragon looked up at them. "Good," she said, glancing around.

"Any word from Tavon?"

"He followed Harper down to the interview at City Hall, then back to Cooper's Mill. He's outside his daughter's place, watching him now."

She nodded. "Okay, work with the others and get this place cleared out. I will go talk to Mr. Kingmaker, see where we're at with the product." She stood and left without saying another word, and Gig noticed how Sonny visibly relaxed once she was gone.

CHAPTER 103
Stakeout

Tavon's phone buzzed next to him on the passenger seat. He reached over and turned down the classical music, then answered it.

"Yeah?"

"Tavon, it's Gig. I need an update."

Tavon looked up at the apartment. "Harper got a ride home from the police chief, and he's been inside her place now for a while."

Gig grunted, loud enough to be heard. "Good job today. Keep on him."

"Will do."

"You know what's happening tonight, right?"

"Yes," Tavon said. Everyone knew.

"Keep your phone on you. We might need help."

Tavon said he would and the call ended. Thank God Gig hadn't asked him to help one of the teams tonight. He'd much rather be on "old man" duty. Tavon knew what was coming and didn't want any part of it.

Someone tapped on the glass by his head.

Tavon turned and looked. It was a Cooper's Mill cop.

SHIT.

He smiled and rolled down the window. The old car had a hand-crank.

"Yes, officer?" The man's badge read "Peters."

"I'm wondering why you're parked here," the cop said. Tavon noticed his hand was resting on the butt of his gun. "Are you waiting for someone?"

At the same time, another cop stepped up on the other side of Tavon's car, his gun out and pointed at the window.

Tavon slowly lifted his hands and put them on the steering wheel. Looking straight ahead at Harper's daughter's apartment, he saw the front door open and Frank Harper stepped out onto her snowy lawn and waved down the street at him.

Ten minutes later, Tavon was handcuffed and sitting on the couch in the daughter's apartment. Harper and the Chief of Cooper's Mill PD were talking quietly, while the other cops were still searching Tavon's vehicle. King and Harper came over and sat across from Tavon.

"Tavon, right?" King said, looking at his notes. "Northsiders, one of the gang members wanted for questioning in the house fire that killed a family of three, right?"

Tavon looked at the carpet between his shoes and said nothing.

Harper leaned forward. "Look, kid. Do you know what they did to me at the mall?"

Tavon looked up. "I didn't have nothing to do with that."

"I know, I know," Harper looked at him. Tavon could see the man had been beaten and abused. "They waterboarded me. For investigating the fire."

"You know how they do that, right?" King asked. "They hold you down and pour water in your mouth until you feel like you're drowning. Over and over. Is that right, Frank?"

"Yeah, it is. And they beat me, nearly every day."

Tavon stayed silent.

"So why are you tailing me?" Frank asked. "The Dragon mad I got away?"

Tavon looked back down at the floor. "She ain't happy."

"I'll bet. If you followed me downtown today, I'm sure you know I had a long talk with the task force. You know she tried to blow up the building? Didn't work. We figured it out."

Tavon shook his head. "Won't matter, man. Won't matter."

King looked up. "What do you mean?"

Tavon looked at Harper. "Look, I was never...I didn't want that family dead. Whatever happened after...I didn't want that."

Frank leaned closer. "Guess what. I got a secret. I know something about the family that you don't."

"Tell me, man," Tavon said. He couldn't help himself.

"Nah," Harper said. "You waiting to kill me? Is that why you're at my DAUGHTER'S place?"

The Dragon would kill him if he talked. Or get Rubio or Slug to do it. Or go after his mom and sisters...

"I can't, man. I can't. They'll kill me."

The other two cops came in, and Tavon looked up. One held up the piece Tavon had in the car. King looked back at Tavon.

"I'm guessing that's not registered. That's a felony in Ohio," Chief King said. "Or you can help my friend out. Why are you tailing him?"

Tavon looked at the gun. "Just keeping an eye on him."

"Why?"

Tavon shook his head.

"Tell me," Harper said, leaning in closer. "Or whatever happens will be on you too. Just like the house fire."

"Stuff's happening. Tonight."

Harper leaned back. "Stuff. That helps. Okay, let's think about this," he said, brainstorming out loud. "Your boss tried to take out the rest of the task force today and failed. Getting me at the same time would've just been a lucky break."

"And me," King added.

"Yeah, Chief, but I don't think you're at the top of their hit list..." Harper said, trailing off.

Frank stopped him. "Tavon, your boss wanted to know the home addresses of every member of the task force. If she was employed there, why didn't she already have them? Why ask me?"

Tavon shook his head. "No clue."

"Is she hitting the cops? Is that what's happening tonight?"

Tavon looked up at Harper. "I told them I wouldn't help. Or drive any of them. That's why I'm watching you."

"Shit," Frank said quietly.

"What is it?" Peters asked.

"Chief, call Sergeant Roget," Frank said. "Right now. Put it on speaker."

King obliged, dialing.

"Yeah?"

"Sergeant Roget? It's Frank Harper and Chief King. Quick question—where do you keep your personnel files? With home addresses and such?"

"I have a file cabinet in my office, which I keep locked. Only a couple people have access. Tammy, the mayor, me, Hawkins," Roget said. "Why?"

"Can you go get the files?" Frank said. "We'll wait."

"Um, okay," Roget said. He set the phone down, and Frank and the others could hear sounds of papers being moved around for a minute.

Harper looked up at Tavon, who was busy keeping his mouth shut. "The Dragon's taking out all the cops. Tonight. In their homes. Right?"

Tavon looked at the ground and nodded slowly.

"Christ," Roget came back on the phone. "They're not here. The mayor borrowed and returned them. Said they were on my desk. They're gone."

"Okay, listen to me, Sergeant," Harper said slowly. "We caught one of the Northsiders outside my daughter's apartment up here. He's been tailing me all day. Between what he said and what Dottie asked me during my interrogation, we think the gang is going after your cops."

Roget laughed. "Of course they are, Harper. Didn't you hear about the explosion at the strip club? They've been gunning for us for weeks now—"

"No, that's not what he means," King interrupted. "Your cops. In their homes, probably tonight. That's why the files are gone—Dottie took them with her. Probably thought the bombing would cover it up."

"Tonight?"

Harper nodded. "Is that right?" he asked, looking at Tavon.

Tavon didn't know what to do. All eyes were on him, all these people trying to do the right thing. All trying to prevent even more death. Not like the Northsiders—they were always dealing it out, like to that burned family.

Finally, Tavon just nodded.

"Yeah," he said. "The crews are already on their way with addresses. The Dragon said tonight we end this."

"Shit," Roget said quietly. "I need to go, call it in to the switchboard. Get the word out."

"We can help, too," Chief King said. "I'll call Miami County and you call Dayton PD and Montgomery County."

"Don't forget the hospital," Tavon said quietly.

"What?" It was Roget, on the phone. "What did you say?"

"They're hitting the hospital, too," Tavon said. "Your wounded."

Roget cursed a string of words. "Okay. Got it."

The call ended and King went over to talk to Peters and the other cop. Tavon looked at Harper, who was just smiling at him.

"What?"

"I thought I might like you," the old cop said. "Even that first time, you were sassy as hell, but I could tell you were smart."

Tavon didn't know what to say. "Still on the Oxy?"

Frank shook his head and smiled again. "No, I'm not. Got your gang to thank for that. Put me through rehab, sorta. Maybe some good will come out of it," he said. "Oh, and the Washington family?"

Tavon felt his eyes narrow. "Yeah? What about them? You gonna tell me how they suffered, how it was all my fault? I know, man. I know. I can't stop thinking about them, okay?"

Frank leaned in and whispered.

"They're still alive."

CHAPTER 104
Couch Update

Twenty minutes later, Frank was still talking to Chief King and Deputy Peters when Laura came home. She walked in and looked around at them, seeing Tavon handcuffed on the couch. Jackson hugged her leg, unsure of who all these people were in his house.

"What happened?"

King and Peters smiled as Frank took her and Jackson in the kitchen and explained what had happened since this morning. After she sent Jackson off to his room, Frank filled her in on the interview downtown, the bomb scare, then coming home and figuring out he was being followed. He told her about confronting the young black man, now sitting on her sofa, and what was in the works for tonight.

"Things were so quiet when you were gone," she joked. She seemed unsure of what else to say and simply hugged him.

King walked over and greeted Laura, then turned to Frank. "We're heading out. You coming?"

Frank looked at the chief. "You want me along? I don't even have a weapon. Northsiders took it."

Peters nodded. "I got you covered."

"Yeah," Frank said. "Just give me a second."

The cops left, leading Tavon in cuffs out to their police car.

"I'm going to help," Frank said to her. "Is that okay?"

"We've already had this conversation," she said. "Don't you remember? In this room, too."

He was confused. "When?"

She pointed at the couch. "You said you were going to pass on helping with the kidnapping investigation. Right there on that couch. And I told you if you could help, you should. People were scared, and you could make a difference. Well, it's the same now."

Frank nodded. "Okay, you're right. I forgot."

Jackson wandered out of his room.

"Just be safe. Promise me."

"I will," he said.

"BE SAFE!!" Jackson yelled.

Frank smiled. Before he could answer, Jackson ran over and handed Frank one of his plastic dinosaurs. "That's Ben. He'll keep you safe."

Frank kneeled and hugged Jackson. "Thanks. I'll make sure to get him back to you." He stood and hugged Laura. "I promise."

"Okay," she said. "Go."

CHAPTER 105
Bloodbath

As it grew dark and snow began to fall, teams of young men fanned out across the city of Dayton and the surrounding suburbs. Each team knew where they were going—and were prepared for any resistance they might find when they arrived. Each team consisted of at least three young men and a driver. In some cases, larger teams were sent.

Tonight, these young men—and the growing organization they represented—would ascend to take their rightful place atop the power structure of this sprawling Midwestern city. Anyone who got in their way would be cut down.

In nearby Westwood, Officer Peter Patrelli was out for a walk with his dog, getting a little exercise in the steadily falling snow. It had been a tough week, and on this quiet Thursday night he was getting a little time to himself. He'd been injured in the blast at Riley's and was treated and released.

Although Officer Patrelli was armed, he wasn't on the lookout for trouble. Westwood was a quiet, upscale neighborhood with little or no violent crime. Patrelli walked, thinking about the explosion at the strip club and the planned assault on the Northsiders' headquarters.

His dog whined at something and Patrelli turned to see what it was and a young man was there, pointing a gun at Patrelli. The gun went off and Patrelli felt something like a punch to his chest. He looked down and saw a small hole in his coat. He never even had time to reach for his holstered weapon.

His dog barked and growled and lunged at the young man. There was another shot, this from another angle. The dog whimpered and fell. The shooters ran into the night, laughing, as Patrelli slumped to the snowy pavement. His final breath rattled out of his lungs, a thin wisp of vapor in the gathering night.

Chief of Police Dan Craig was sitting in his living room watching the local news. They were talking about the attempted bombing of the task force headquarters. He thought the whole thing was spinning out of control. It was the mayor's call, of course, but Craig had always hated the idea of a separate police force. Craig had tried to not take it personally, but it was difficult when the mayor went out and publicly recruited a separate "task force" to operate within the city.

He looked down at his service weapon, resting in his lap. He'd just finished cleaning and reassembling it. It was a ritual that calmed him. He thought about getting up and getting his backup weapon to clean as well, but his show came back on, a police drama. He loved seeing everything they got wrong.

Chief Craig was too engrossed in the show to notice movement outside his windows or to hear the low sounds coming from the second story, where his wife was sleeping. He mistook a low grunting sound upstairs for a chair moving. He had no way of knowing that his wife of twenty-three years had just been shot in her sleep by a man with a silenced weapon.

The cop show went to commercial and he stood, setting his gun aside on the table. Craig went into the kitchen to make a snack when a masked man stepped out from behind the counter, his gun aimed at Craig.

"Hey, what are you doing in my—"

The shot came from a different direction. Another masked man had followed Craig into the kitchen.

Craig felt a blast of fire in his back, and then the man in front of him fired as well, hitting Craig high in the chest. The chief of the Dayton Police Department collapsed to the floor. The last thing that went through his mind was that the shooters were amateurs—no one lined up on opposite sides of a target and shot at each other. There was too much of a chance of friendly fire.

Even at the end, Craig was working to solve a homicide—only, this time, it was his own.

Shayla was crossing the snowy parking lot of Del Meson, a popular restaurant in southern Dayton. She carried two boxes of takeout and watched her step on the treacherous pavement. The snow was really coming down and she didn't want to slip and fall.

From behind her, a car pulled into the parking lot and slowly pulled up behind her. The passenger window rolled down and the thin barrel of a handgun emerged. The muzzle flashed once, twice in quick succession. The portly woman was struck in the back and in the hand, and she cried out. The food containers dropped to the snowy pavement and Shayla collapsed on top of them, moaning as the car raced out of the parking lot.

The mayor's mansion in Dayton, Ohio, was located on a snowy hill overlooking the Great Miami River and the glittering downtown buildings. The mansion shared the hill with two other imposing structures, the Dayton Art Institute and the Dayton Masonic Temple, all recognizable landmarks to any native Daytonian.

The mansion was smaller than the other buildings, but still an impressive site with its distinctive, Spanish-style, ceramic roof and central courtyard. The building's stout concrete wall proved exceptionally easy to climb. The six shooters were over the snow-topped wall first, two teams of three. Each team had a driver that stayed outside the walls, providing backup and acting as spotters in case there was trouble.

The six masked men made their way quietly across the mansion's grounds. Carefully, they approached the front doors and found them standing open.

The place was empty.

In Centerville, eight miles south of Dayton, two groups of young black men exited two large homes across the street from each other. It had been a toss-up as to where the cop and his wife would be. Apparently, they often had dinner at a neighbor's house on Thursday nights. The teams met in the street.

"Anything? There was no one at their house."

A shooter on the other team nodded, pulling his mask down. "We got 'em. It was like a party or something. The cop and his wife. The other family—a couple and three kids."

"Dead?"

He shrugged. "Had to be done, right?"

Across the city, Northsiders teams struck. Surviving members of the Dayton Area Heroin Task Force were gunned down while sitting in their cars in traffic or at home, watching TV. A team broke in to Roget's apartment to make sure he hadn't returned, then trashed the place. Another team went to Hawkins' apartment and broke in but found it empty. Roget had called Hawkins' sister, who was staying at the apartment, and warned her to get out. Officer Bellows, responsible for calling in the bomb squad, was shot at through the window of his apartment while on the phone with dispatchers. He managed to chase down and kill two of his assailants.

Roget's warning calls ended up saving some of his team members. Dispatch sent a warning call, but some received the message too late.

Or never at all.

CHAPTER 106
SWAT Team

Three cars of men arrived in the parking lot of Dayton General. The men got out of their cars and gathered behind a row of snow-covered bushes by the parking lot. The sky was dark and snow around them fell at an alarming rate.

"I just heard—the other hits are going well," Sonny said. "Everyone ready?" The faces around him nodded. He looked at one of them. "Count?"

"Five in the lobby, three more in the ER entrance," the spotter said. He'd been onsite for hours, observing to get a count. "They rotate every hour. I don't know how many are up on six."

Sonny nodded. "Okay, we got twelve, plus twelve more coming. The cops got eight, plus six or so on the top floor. We can take them. Try not to shoot until we're all in." Sonny pointed as four more cars pulled in and waved at them as they passed. "That's the other team—they're going in through the emergency doors. We'll all meet at the elevators."

At that, several of them glanced up at the tall building.

"Remember, the injured cops are all on the sixth floor. We're taking the elevator, that other group the stairs, so we're gonna give them a head start. Meet on the top floor."

The men nodded. They'd been practicing this, doing mock raids at the mall and pretending one of the entrances was the hospital lobby. Running up and down stairs in full gear. Each member wore helmets, masks, stolen tactical gear, and vests that read "SWAT" across the front and back in large white letters. The other team, going in through the ER entrance, wore flak jackets that read "FBI" in large yellow letters.

Sonny got his men into position and waited. Moments later, he got a text: "Now."

He put the phone away and pulled on his mask, and the others followed suit. He had two guns, one in each hand, along with a black satchel with more weapons and ammo.

Sonny stood and made his way around the bushes, approaching the glass lobby doors. The spotter was right—there were no cops outside. To his right, he could see more of his men running toward the sliding doors of the emergency entrance. With a last look back, Sonny pushed open the doors and walked into the hospital lobby.

CHAPTER 107
Operation Confirmed

"It's happening," Roget shouted. "Right now."

Chief King was driving with Peters and Frank in the car. Sergeant Roget was on speaker, calling from Dayton General.

"Already?" King asked. "I figured we'd have more time."

"I'm getting reports from all over," Roget said. "Some of my men are down. Dayton PD is on alert, but I can't reach the chief. The mayor left his home and is headed to a safe location. I gotta go. Call me when you know more."

"Will do," King said, watching the road. Driving at fast speeds was always dangerous, even for experienced police officers like himself. But the snow, coming down hard, made it worse. His eyes played over the road and every car and object that loomed up out of the cold night.

When he had a break, he had Peters call the Miami County Sheriff's Office on speaker. King talked to the dispatcher, asking for all available units to head south to Dayton and coordinate with him or Roget.

While King shouted at his phone, Frank checked Laura's phone, pulling up the *Dayton Daily News* website. A video report came up but it was hard to hear in the car—the woman's voice was fast and hard to follow. From what Frank could tell, a group of armed men had attacked the chief's home.

"The chief of Dayton PD is dead," Frank said. "Newspaper's reporting him and his wife killed. In their home."

Chief King cursed under his breath. For the first time that Frank could remember, Peters didn't chastise him.

"I thought we got the word out early enough," King said.

"It's my fault," Frank said. "I should have broken out earlier. Or figured out why they were so interested in the cops' home addresses."

"No, it's likely they're hitting tonight because the bomb failed this morning," King said.

The chief roared down the highway, his lights blazing. His phone rang, and Peters answered, putting it on speaker. "It's Roget."

"Any news?" King asked.

"Nine down that I knew of. Seven others unaccounted for. Some families, too. Chief Craig and wife are dead. Dayton PD is circling the wagons, bringing in everyone. They're hitting the streets, checking on my other men and women and their own, just in case. They're sending me men here at the hospital."

King nodded. "Should we go to Dayton PD headquarters or come to you?"

It was quiet for a minute. "I hate to say it, but come here. I have a feeling this place is on the list."

"We're on our way," King shouted. "Hold tight."

"Okay," Roget said. "Be safe." The call ended.

"A police officer and his wife and five other people were killed at some kind of dinner party," Peters read from the police laptop mounted between the seats. "All executed around a dining room table."

"Christ," Frank said. "It's the Dragon," he said.

The radio came to life—it was Lola, working dispatch. "CM Dispatch to all Cooper's Mill units, all CM units. Please be advised: multiple officers down in Dayton. All backup requested except for CM2 and CM6, which are to remain on local patrol. Repeat: all units, minus CM2 and CM6, please proceed south, call in and await further instructions."

"Peters, call her back," King said. "Have her direct our people to the hospital and form a perimeter." Peters nodded as King changed lanes to go around a slow car in the fast lane that refused to get over even though King's lights were painting the entire interstate.

"At least they haven't hit the hospital," Peters said.

"Not yet." Frank glanced at him. "But the only way this plan of hers works is to get them all at the same time."

CHAPTER 108
Lobby

The lobby of Dayton General looked like a bloodbath.

When Sonny and his men had entered, the cops had seen the SWAT vests and hesitated. It was the only advantage Sonny had needed. The Northsiders opened fire, mowing down cops and hospital staff alike.

Now, a few minutes later, two of his team were out of the fight: Slug had been struck in the leg, and Sonny had sent him outside. The other gang member had taken a shot to the head and was sprawled in the middle of the waiting area, a puddle of red still spreading around his head.

"Form up on me!"

They gathered around Sonny behind the abandoned information desk. The rest of the room was nearly empty—the hospital staff had either fled or been cut down.

"What happened to Slug?" one of them asked.

"Ran outside," Sonny said. "Took one in the leg. He'll be back."

The last cop was taking potshots at them as they talked, and then suddenly, the sound of automatic gunfire filled the lobby and the last cop fell, silenced. Sonny peeked over the counter and saw other black men in FBI gear approaching from the ER, his other team. Sonny stood and walked to them, high-fiving Rubio, the leader.

"Any trouble?"

"Nah," his friend said, holding up the guns. "It's been a while since I shot an automatic. Lose anyone?"

Sonny nodded at the body. "One, plus Slug got winged. I sent him to the parking lot to watch for backup. You?"

Rubio shook his head. "Cakewalk. Jackets worked great."

"Good. Okay, you guys take the stairs. We'll wait four, then head up on the elevators. Text me if you are delayed."

"Will do." Rubio pointed his men to the wide stairwell and started up.

CHAPTER 109
Gear Up

Roget walked out of Hawkins' room. He'd been fielding calls from the mayor, now in hiding, and Chief King. "What's happening?"

The on-duty officer looked over at Roget, one hand on his radio. "Gunfire in the lobby. Reports of at least ten men, dressed like SWAT. Our men and the security guards are not responding."

The nurses and doctors were in a state of panic—Roget could see them yelling into telephones, trying to reach other parts of the hospital. Hawkins' nurse looked directly at him and he could see the look of terror on her face.

The Northsiders were here to finish the job. He'd hoped he was wrong, but it had to be them. Roget felt a shiver run up his back. Roget looked up at the cop.

"Get your men to the elevators and stairs. Do you have extra sidearms?"

"I'll see," he said and ran off to gather the others.

Roget had his service weapon—he never went anywhere without it—but his injured were sitting ducks. Who armed themselves in their hospital beds? This was a hospital, for Christ's sake. His men and women were concentrating on healing, not defending themselves.

Roget had a gun, at least. Even shooting with his left hand was better than being a sitting duck.

Chapter 110
Dayton General

The police band was chaotic. Calls kept coming in over the air announcing an officer down or under fire. King had switched the radio over to the Montgomery County channel. Frank heard the panic in the dispatchers' voices.

"You recognize any of those addresses?" Frank asked.

"Nope," King said, changing lanes to avoid rear-ending a slow-moving semi. "Not downtown. Sounds like the suburbs."

More reports of shots fired came over the radio, this time from the hospital.

"Clearing out the lobby," Frank said quietly. "Before they head up."

King nodded. Frank felt the car sped up as King swerved around a driver that was doing two things wrong at the same time: changing lanes and ignoring King's flashing lights and sirens. To avoid a collision, King traveled a short distance on the shoulder, then moved back over into the fast lane.

Frank and Peters kept quiet.

They finally exited I-75 and merged onto a smaller highway Frank didn't recognize. King got off at the first exit, barely slowing at the bottom of the ramp. He took the corner roughly, skidding on the snow, and Peters and Frank grabbed for something to hold on to. King slowed at the lights, at least, before plowing through them.

"Is that it?" Frank asked, pointing at a large building on a hill to their left.

"Yep," Peters said.

King slowed and turned into the parking lot in front. The tall hospital towered over the lot, and King slowed as he passed the emergency entrance and approached the lobby.

"Okay," King said, mostly to himself, parking at the curb.

They were climbing out of the car when someone started shooting at them. Frank ducked and stayed down while Peters and King returned fire. Frank peeked up just enough to see what was going on. They were trading shots with a guy in a familiar tricked-out Honda Civic—it had to be one of Tavon's mates.

After a second, the assailant slumped down and stopped firing. King ran in the direction of the Civic, his gun up. Frank stood up and looked around for more gunmen.

"Come on," Peters said, going to the trunk and opening it. Inside were bulletproof vests, shotguns, handguns, and a box of ammunition in several different sizes.

"Nice," Frank said. Peters pulled out a vest and handed it to Frank, then started putting one on himself. It was just like the night Peters and Frank had raided that kidnapper's house and saved those girls. King walked back over to the trunk as Frank was picking out weapons.

"You guys get him?"

King nodded, reaching for a vest. "Spotter. They know we're here."

Frank ended up picking out three handguns and a shotgun. He loaded them fully, then tucked two of the guns in his waist and one in his new boots, the ones Laura had bought for him this morning at Target. When he was ready, he walked over to the Civic.

The guy inside was one of the men with Tavon, the big aggressive one. He was slumped over the wheel and missing half his head. Frank felt for a pulse, just in case, and took his weapon, sticking it in his belt in the small of his back.

Frank jogged back over as King finished with his vest. "Ready?"

Peters and Frank nodded and followed King to the doors of the lobby.

Inside, it was a massacre: at least five dead cops; two dead gangbangers, each wearing black masks and "SWAT" jackets; dead civilians. Some of the hospital staff was checking them, searching for wounded among the dead. Peters went to check on the other dead gangbanger by the door, kicking his weapon away before taking his pulse. "He's gone."

King and Frank were checking the cops—there were five, all Dayton PD. "Nope," Frank said, shaking his head. Peters made a point of gathering up the weapons and putting them in a drawer behind the information desk. "No need to leave loaded weapons lying around."

"Good," King said, pointing at the stairs. "Ready?"

Frank followed King to the base of the open staircase, looking up through the middle. He heard gunfire from above, and they started the climb. Thirty seconds later, King and Peters were trading shots with "SWAT" members on the stairs two flights up. Frank was following, covering their back.

"What do we do now?" Peters yelled, crouched down behind a concrete wall.

They exited the stairwell to avoid getting shot, and King looked around the fourth floor for options. Frank could see he was desperate to get up to six, but they were pinned down.

"Elevator?" Frank yelled.

King shook his head. "No, no cover," he said, pointing at the elevator doors. "We'd be sitting ducks once the doors opened."

Peters looked around and ducked when another volley of shots started, shattering the wall next to him. "Other stairs?"

"Maybe," King said, stepping away. Frank saw him jog down the hall to the elevator and inspect the wall next to it, but Frank couldn't see what he was studying. King walked back over. "There are stairs on either end of the floor, plus the main stairs here in the middle. Only one elevator. Have to assume it's covered."

"We're gonna get killed out here, cousin," Peters said and King nodded.

"Okay, Frank, come on."

King and Peters took off running and Frank followed, running backwards as fast as he could, covering their retreat. King told Peters to call it in, and Frank heard Peters talking on his radio, giving his location. Hopefully someone was coordinating the efforts of several police departments.

Once it was clear no one was following them, Frank turned and ran after them.

Peters and King stopped at the far doors, pushing through and starting up the stairs, when Frank yelled for them to stop.

"What?" King asked.

"Come back and try the door," Frank said, pulling the door closed between them. Peters pushed on the handle, but it didn't open.

"Internal security," Frank said, letting them back in. "We'll get locked in the stairwell. Is there a badge reader or something on the wall out there in the hallway?"

King looked and nodded. "We'll need a badge."

"I'll watch the hallway," Frank said, and King and Peters walked away, searching the nearby rooms and offices for a passkey—or an employee of the hospital.

Up on six, Roget was trying to hold off the assault. At least eight masked men wearing SWAT jackets had come up the main staircase. Their first move was to scatter the cops and guards on this floor and surround the elevator. Moments later, the elevator bell dinged and the door slid open and more masked men ran out. They had quickly seized the primary nurse's station, located next to the elevator, and started shooting.

Now, the assailants held the middle of the floor and the elevators. The cops were using coordinated firing but were outnumbered. The attackers seemed to have unlimited rounds, automatic weapons, and grenades—the hallway between here and the nurse's station already looked blackened and ruined.

Roget was firing as best he could with his left hand. The rest of the police officers, along with the three security guards, had backed down the east wing. One officer spun and fell, his arm ragged and bloody. He was with the Montgomery County Sheriff's Office.

"Help him!" Roget yelled at one of the other officers. "Pull him in behind cover!"

Once he'd heard about the attack in the lobby, Roget had worked with the panicked nurses to move most of his injured into the last three rooms at the far end of the hallway. He figured the smart thing to do was to defend as small an area as possible.

He hadn't counted on the grenades.

Now, Roget and the cops were defending the rooms behind them. All his men were here, halfway down the east wing, except for two that were stationed at the end to defend the east stairs.

Another cop fell, one standing right next to Roget. The top half of his head was gone. A nurse, cowering in the hallway, looked at the injured man and then looked away.

"You need to get out of here," Roget told her. "Get your staff and get back to the last three rooms."

She nodded and grabbed another nurse, pulling him after her.

Suddenly, Roget saw the situation through her eyes. They were trapped, with a group of armed gunmen slowly progressing down the hallway. She had probably already seen some of her co-workers fall. Roget had passed more than one dead person in scrubs. Roget looked around at the officers around him.

"Okay, we're pulling back," he said. "Get to the end of the hall and fortify that position. Cover the last three rooms. I just heard reinforcements are coming—should be here in five minutes," he lied.

As a group, the cops and hospital guards began backing down the hall away from the nurse's station, ducking into open rooms for cover. As some retreated, others fired, covering them. Roget didn't like retreating, but it was better than being overrun.

"Just keep firing!"

Sonny pulled out some gauze he found in an abandoned medical cart. He balled it up and pushed the wad of gauze into the hole in his shoulder. It was bleeding freely. He yelled at his men—they still didn't understand the concept of sustained firing.

"I'm running low," Rubio said, and Sonny pointed at the bag on the ground between them.

"I brought 3,000 rounds," he said, wrapping tape over the gauze. The bullet had gone in and out of his shoulder and hurt like hell.

Some of his men were solid, but others weren't. Sonny could see that now. They'd all been full of swagger before. He'd hand-picked them for their bravado. But put them in a firefight, and you quickly learned which ones were truly brave—and which ones were good at pretending. Or which ones were only good at video games.

They were going up against professionals. If this didn't end soon, backup would wipe out the Northsiders.

"Keep moving up," he yelled. "Keep firing!" Bones, one of the men on loan from the recruitment side, nodded and started shooting back.

"You gotta keep firing," Sonny said to the others, nodding down the hall. His men looked over at him. Some of them were scared. Sonny leaned over and dug through the bag—the handle was slick with someone's blood. He found what he was looking for, pulled the pin, and threw it. The grenade rolled down the hallway toward the cops and detonated, showering the cops and the hallway around them in fire.

It took nearly seven minutes of searching to find a badge.

Frank stood, nervous the whole time, watching the corridor in front of him and the doors to the emergency stairs behind him. He jumped every time he heard another round of gunfire. There was clearly a firefight going on upstairs, punctuated every so often with a loud "BOOM!" He hadn't heard a grenade in real life in decades, not since the military.

Peters and King returned, King holding up a badge with a magnetic stripe. "Sorry, took a few rooms. Found it in a desk."

"What was that sound?" Peter asked.

"Grenades."

Peters' eyes widened.

King went back out into the stairwell and tried the key card—it worked. Peters and Frank followed him up to the stairs to the top floor. King tried the key card and it worked here as well.

"Okay, here we go," King said, pulling the door open.

Frank looked down the long, sixth-floor corridor in front of him. Half-way down, it looked like carnage—bodies, blackened and falling ceiling tiles, and bodies. Past that, he could see the backs of a bunch of men in SWAT vests.

"There they are. Get down," Frank whispered. They hugged the walls and found an open room to duck into. "What's the play?"

King looked down at his gun. "I'm running low on ammo and not in the mood to take them on directly."

"Is there any other option?" Peters asked.

"Not that I see," Frank said. "But even with the guns we took off those guys in the lobby, we won't have enough."

Peters and King nodded. Finally, King looked up at him. "Well, we can't just sit here and do nothing," he said. "Peters, come on."

They got up to leave, and Frank stood, following.

Back out in the hallway, they held their fire and moved down, making it halfway to the center of the floor before they were spotted and one of the gangbangers fired at them. King and Peters ducked into one room, while Frank found one across the hall, returning fire around the doorjamb.

"Now what?" Frank yelled to King.

They were coming.

It was nearly over, Roget thought. The nurses were hurrying to get patients off their gurneys, placing them underneath for protection. Automatic gunfire spattered the walls around Roget and the others. Bullets ricocheted off the metal doors that led to the stairwell. Roget and the others were running low on ammunition, saving their shots for when one of the gangbangers showed themselves. Roget knew it was going to be close. He called in for backup again, hearing the desperation in his own voice. They were pinned down, defending the wounded. And running out of time.

Rubio had fallen, shot through the head. The hallway was thick with smoke, making it hard for Sonny and his remaining men to aim. And they were firing in two directions now. Some other cops had come up the western stairs and were firing at them from behind.

"Keep at it!" he shouted.

Two of Sonny's men ran up the hallway. One of them was T-Bone. "There are only three of them on the west side."

Sonny nodded. "Take two men and head west. Take out those new cops. We can't fight people on both sides," he said.

T-Bone nodded and moved away, taking two of the guys with him. They hugged the walls and moved back toward the nurse's station and main stairwell, where they'd come up.

"Good job, guys," Sonny shouted. "We got cops behind us. Move up, shoot anything that moves!"

Sonny threw another grenade.

Roget saw the grenade rolling in and knew what he had to do. He stood and ran for it, grabbing the device and throwing it back toward the attackers with his right hand, grimacing. He landed hard against the wall and felt something crack in his shoulder. The grenade rolled away and detonated, blowing out a door and knocking back some of the attackers.

But after only moments, they returned fire. Somehow, the incoming fire became even worse. Roget backed into another room and used his one good arm to signal his men. At least they had police training and knew how to work together as a team.

He pointed, signaling them fall back into the three remaining rooms: Hawkins' room at the end of the corridor next to the stairwell, and one on either side. Roget glanced at the stairwell door but shook his head. There was no way to get everyone down the stairs.

No, this was it. The last stand.

Roget backed into Hawkins' room and returned fire. He emptied his clip, something he'd never done before. You always replaced the clip before you ran out. Dry firing a weapon could damage it. Of course, running out of bullets was a last-ditch scenario.

He was reloading when he saw the other grenade go through the door and into the room on the left and there was nothing he could do except wait for the sound. The grenade went off, blowing out windows and throwing patients and nurses and equipment into the air. Another hospital security guard, this one on fire, staggered out into the hallway and was gunned down by the attackers.

Roget was running out of men. And bullets.

T-Bone moved down the hallway, looking for the cops. One of them ducked his head around the corner.

It was Harper. The old man, back again. T-Bone laughed and fired, shattering the window above the old man's head. "Harper, is that you? Couldn't stay away, could you?"

T-Bone and his three men sprayed the hallway walls on either side with bullets, tracing lazy circles in the drywall. "That was smart how you got away. You know the Dragon killed Tiny over it?" he shouted over the gunfire. "She was pissed!"

"Good," he heard the familiar voice come back.

T-Bone suddenly wished he'd grabbed one of the grenades. He kept firing, walking toward the doorway where Harper had disappeared. The other gangbangers stepped around the corner of the door opposite Harper's and fired indiscriminately into that room. T-Bone motioned for them to look into Harper's room, but they weren't paying attention.

T-Bone shook his head and rounded the corner, spraying the room with bullets and putting holes in the bed and chairs and equipment and the curtains on either side of the windows. The glass shattered and a cold gust of wind blew in.

He emptied his clip and started to reload when a figure stepped from the bathroom.

"Hey, dumb ass," Harper said, his gun up. "You never empty your clip."

T-Bone saw him pull the trigger and felt something weird happen to his vision. He shook his head and tried to say something and fell over onto his face.

Frank stepped over to the doorway, kicking the gun away from T-Bone. Thanks for beating the crap out of me for a week, he thought. Frank leaned around the corner and shot another gangbanger in the back. He was firing wildly into the room where Peters and King were hiding. He heard more shots coming from the room, and the third shooter fell.

From the doorway, Frank asked, "You guys okay?"

"Yup, clear," he heard. He looked around the corner. Peters and King were peeked up from behind a desk, which they'd flipped over to use as a shield. "Yeah, we're good."

Frank bent over and checked the other two shooters. They were hurt, but not dead. Frank noticed they were all wearing Kevlar vests. Suspecting as much, Frank had shot T-Bone in the face.

"Well, at least now we have automatic weapons," Frank said.

They ziptied the injured gangbangers and took their weapons and extra ammunition. When they were ready, King and Frank leaned back out into the hallway and ran, proceeded past the elevators and the nurse's station.

It looked like a war zone. The walls were blackened and ceiling tiles had been blown out. Every surface seemed riddled with bullets. And there were bodies everywhere, cops and "SWAT" members alike.

Peters stepped over the body of a fallen patient, bending over to check for a pulse before moving on.

King grunted as they made their way down the hall. There was a firefight going on at the end of the hall, eighty feet away. They stayed low, moving as a team from doorway to doorway and hiding behind fallen equipment.

"Hold your fire until we get close enough to make a difference," King said to them. "Especially you, Floyd. Use the automatics until you run out, then switch to the other weapons."

Peters looked at his cousin and nodded.

Roget and his men had been pushed back into the last room at the end of the hallway. Grenades had been thrown into the rooms on either side, sending patients and cops flying. Everyone in those rooms was probably dead.

Two grenades had been thrown into Roget's room as well, but he'd managed to spot them and throw them back. The returned grenades had to be hurting the attackers, right? These were kids with no training—all they had was an overwhelming number of weapons.

Roget glanced around. He had four men left, plus two nurses and three patients cowering in the large bathroom. The window had been shattered, and snow was blowing inside, coating the hospital bed and equipment in a layer of snow.

"Sergeant, I'm running low," one of the cops told him. He was with the Miami County Sheriff's Office, north of Dayton. Roget was glad he was here, but could only shake his head.

"I'm nearly out," Roget said. "And I've scavenged all the weapons I could," he said, referring to the cops who had given their lives to protect him and the injured members of the task force.

The officer nodded and crawled away. Roget could tell he was looking for a low place to return fire. In his mind, Roget wished him luck.

They would need it.

Roget slid on the floor, backing up against the closed bathroom door. He would defend those inside, giving his life if he had to. Hawkins was in there, along with two patients and two nurses, including Hawkins'. She was probably going to die, too.

Roget sat back against the door, his gun out. He was nearly out of ammunition, so he watched for incoming grenades. Hopefully, if one came, it would land near enough to him for him to grasp and throw back.

Sonny rummaged through the black satchel, looking for another gun or more ammunition. He was running low—the cops had to be out by now, right? Of course, Sonny and his men had been firing randomly, wasting their own ammunition.

He felt to the bottom of the bag and scowled. Nothing.

"Save your ammo," he growled to the others. "Three-shot bursts." He had six men left, including him, and they were positioned about three quarters of the way down the hallway. Ahead, more of his men had attacked the rooms on either side of the hall before falling. They were making progress—all that was left was the final room, but they were putting up one hell of a fight.

"You got any more grenades? I'm good with grenades."

Sonny looked up—it was Sharps, eyeing the bag.

"Yeah, two left. Take one, I'll keep the other."

"Okay," he said, digging one out.

"But they keep throwing them back," Sonny said.

"You just have to cook 'em," he said.

Sonny made a face. "What?"

"You gotta cook 'em," Sharps said. "Don't you play *Call of Duty*? You pull the pin and hold the grenade. Count to three before throwing it. It's called 'cooking' them."

Sonny nodded. "Okay," he said. "Just do it! Hurry!"

Sharps took the grenade and crawled down the hallway ten feet. Then he held up a grenade and smiled at Sonny.

"Check it out. It's easy," Sharps yelled and pulled the pin and pointed at the grenade and counted loudly.

"One!"

"Two!"

The grenade went off in his hand like a small bomb.

Sonny looked away as fast as he could but the initial flash seared his eyes, blinding him. The explosion washed over them, heat and light followed by parts of the fragmentation grenade—and parts of Sharps. The blast also took out two more of Sonny's men and threw others to the ground.

Sonny shook his head, his vision swimming into focus. It looked like someone was coming down the hallway at him—it was those other cops, the ones T-Bone was supposed to take care of. They were hiding behind equipment. If they were going to attack from the west, Sonny needed to take them out. He shook his head and yelled at the others to regroup.

"What was that?" King asked.

Frank stepped back into the room. "Grenade. Went off right in the middle of them," he said. "This is our shot."

King nodded and made his way into the hall. Peters ducked out from behind the doorway and started after King, with Frank right behind him. All three had their automatic weapons out, level, moving as a group. When one passed in front of the other, they pointed their guns at the ground to avoid accidentally shooting their compatriot in the back.

They moved quickly up the hallway, taking advantage of the lull in the action. King was at a dead run and Peters and Frank raced to catch up with him. King got as close as he could and waited until there was cover on either side before firing.

It looked like most of the attackers were down, flattened by their own grenade. King opened fire, and Peters and Frank joined in, shooting at the men they could see.

A head popped up and the shots came immediately. The guy was shooting blind. Frank ducked into a room.

King saw it, too. Instead of firing, he shoved Peters out of the way. The bullets missed them both, passing where Peters had been standing. Instead of stopping, King ran forward, cutting the distance between him and the man firing. King was less than ten feet away from the shooter, and Frank ran after him. King shot the man on the ground, two bullets to the chest.

King stopped running and another man on the ground behind King lifted his weapon to return fire.

Frank pulled the trigger.

The prone shooter didn't have a chance. The short distance meant Frank was accurate enough to strike the man in the head.

Frank ran up next to King, who was pulling the gun out of the man's hand. King pointed it at the other men, all of whom were on the floor and not moving. None of them lifted their heads to offer resistance.

"Stop shooting!" King shouted. "This is over!"

Two of the men, the only two still moving, dropped their weapons and rolled over onto their stomachs, putting their hands behind their backs.

"Frank, cover them. Peters, get them ziptied and into a room we can secure."

Frank nodded as Peters came up behind him, pointing his gun at the men on the ground. King moved past the prone men, his rifle pointed at each as he approached and kicked their guns away. He continued past them and down the hallway to the door.

"Cooper's Mill PD!" he shouted. "Do not fire!"

Frank saw him go into the last patient room and glanced at Peters.

"Exciting enough for ya?"

Peters nodded. "Maybe a little too much."

Roget was leaned against the bathroom door and heard the explosions go off, followed by more gunfire. None of which appeared to be coming in this direction. He heard voices shouting and more shots, and then nothing.

"Cooper's Mill PD!" came from outside the door "Do not fire!"

"In here, officer," Roget said. He tried to yell it, but it came out like a whisper. He tried again. "In here."

A man came around the doorway, his gun out. It was Chief King.

"Thank God," Roget said. "Good to see you."

King came over and kneeled next to him. "Are you hit?"

"Yeah, but not bad." Roget slid sideways and pushed the door open behind him. "It's okay, you can come out now," he said to the nurses and patients inside. "It's all over."

King nodded and left Roget on the ground. Two nurses and three patients emerged from the small bathroom.

"Can you help him and the others?" King asked. "And alert the rest of the hospital that it's over? We have lots of injured."

The nurse nodded. "We have protocols for this. Is the nurses' station clear?"

King nodded at the nurse as Frank came into the room. "The shooters are all incapacitated. We're moving them into one room to secure them."

The nurse walked away, leaving to call for help. More cops began arriving, shouting to make everyone aware of their presence and to help secure the scene.

"You okay, Chief?" Frank asked.

King nodded and tabbed the radio on his shoulder.

"This is Chief King to all units. Dayton General is secure, but multiple officers down. Assistance needed at Dayton General, lobby and sixth floor. Be on the lookout for additional assailants."

While he talked on the radio, Frank looked around the room and moved to check the fallen officers and patients. He found a nurse with a leg wound behind a bed, and helped two other nurses get a woman patient onto the bed. She was passed out, her head wrapped in thick bandages. Behind him, Frank could hear King on the radio.

"Be aware Dayton General's facilities are largely compromised— EMTs should find alternate treatment locations until they're back up and running."

Sergeant Roget came over and stood by the bed, putting a hand on the patient. He looked at her for a second, then glanced at the nurse.

"Is she okay?"

The nurse nodded. "She'll be fine."

Frank smiled and backed away, leaving them alone. Roget looked like he'd been to war and back. If he had to guess, Frank figured they all felt that way.

CHAPTER 111
Talk it Out

"You okay?"

Frank looked up at Laura. It was Saturday morning, two days after all the craziness at the hospital. They were sitting in booth number three at the Tip Top Diner, enjoying a nice breakfast before he headed south to Birmingham. In spite of his adventures, he needed to be back at work on Monday morning or he'd be out of a job. Jackson was playing at a friend's house—Frank had already said his goodbyes this morning. He'd wanted a quiet breakfast with his daughter—he had something to tell her.

"Yeah," he said. "Am I quieter than normal?"

Laura nodded, pointing with her toast.

"Yes, you are. Did you get everything back? You look like you're missing your favorite teddy bear," she said with a smile.

"No, it's not that," Frank said. "The Camaro wasn't even scratched. All my stuff was inside except for my money. And my phone, which they never found."

The Dayton PD and other agencies had raided the old Salem Mall on Friday afternoon. Based partly on information provided by Frank, the Dayton PD sent in nine squads of police officers to seize the Northsiders' operation. There had been no casualties on either side— only a few Northsiders had been inside the mall. A few of the higher-ups had been captured, but there was no sign of the Dragon or most of the gang members. And all the drugs and production equipment—along with any money on site—were long gone.

The Dayton Area Heroin Task Force was no more, officially folded into the Dayton PD and falling under the auspices of Chief Craig's replacement. They had done good work, of course, but no one wanted to be part of such a cursed organization. Police departments all over the nation would study what happened with the task force and, hopefully, learn from its mistakes.

"You're quiet again," Laura said. The waitress had come twice in the last five minutes, refilling their cups. "Thinking about the Washingtons?"

"No, they're gonna be fine," he said. The family had not been on his mind for hours, a nice change. He'd visited with them yesterday and they were happy, no longer under threat of retaliation from the Northsiders. Markeys was thinking about settling back in Dayton, now that the Northsiders were gone.

"You sure you're okay?"

He looked up at her. "Yeah. I just...I had a lot to think about, in the time when I was..."

"Kidnapped?"

"Yeah," he said. "It sounds silly when you say it like that."

"It wasn't silly. I was freaking out, yelling at Chief King and the others to look for you," Laura said. "They got sick of me, but I was worried."

"Everyone probably thought I was drunk in a ditch somewhere."

She nodded, her mouth full. "As time went on," she said, and finished chewing, "we got more and more worried."

He nodded, not sure what to say about that. "I'm sorry to put you through all that, Laura."

"It's okay."

He took another bite and chewed and then set his fork down and sipped from the coffee. "Actually, I meant that I had a lot of time to think. And there is something I need to tell you, something that I think might help you understand me better. Something I should have told you, or someone, a long time ago."

She stopped eating and looked at him strangely. He hadn't meant to sound ominous, but that was the way it came out.

"I need to tell you about what happened after Hurricane Katrina," he said quietly.

The story started quietly, in fits and starts, while the two of them continued eating. He began with the events that happened to him in the days after Katrina broke the levees and flooded his beloved city of New Orleans. He spoke quietly, sharing his story. She asked a question or two, here or there, but for the most part remained quiet as he explained what happened, ending with swimming out of the flooded hospital and being rescued. In the time it took to tell his story, the waitress came with coffee twice and offered to heat up his food.

When he finished, he went back to eating. Frank wondered what was going through Laura's mind as she processed the story. He knew what it had meant for him. Talking about Katrina seemed to make the story less powerful, somehow. And his claustrophobia seemed better.

"That's...that's terrible, Frank," she said after a minute. "I can understand how that would mess you up. Did you ever tell Mom?"

He looked up at her and shook his head.

"Not something I've ever told anyone," he said. "But...when they waterboarded me? It brought back all those memories. I was there again, getting shot, bleeding in the water. I remembered every detail, stuff I'd forgotten."

She smiled at him, not something he was expecting.

"Something funny?"

"Yeah," she said. "You get shot a lot."

He smiled. "I do, don't I?"

Laura nodded.

"I almost got shot again on Thursday," he said. "Managed to avoid it this time."

"Good," she said, glancing over her shoulder at the dessert case. "Maybe I'll buy you a piece of cake to celebrate." Her smile was real this time, stretching from ear to ear.

"Oh, now you're just making fun of me."

"I am. But seriously, you should work on that whole 'getting shot' thing. It's becoming a bad habit," she said.

Frank smiled. It was nice to be open with Laura like this. To have a real conversation and even joke around a bit. They settled back into their breakfast and soon finished it off. Laura asked a few more questions about St. Bart's, clearly empathizing with him.

"So, looking forward to getting back to work?" she asked, pushing her empty plate away.

"I am, actually," he said. "Clean and sober feels weird. Collier might not be my biggest fan, but I really want to make a go of it."

"He seemed to like you."

Frank looked up, confused for a second. "Oh, that's right. I forgot you spoke to him. He's one of those people...well, I guess I'd have to say he's disappointed in me. Not living up to my full potential, he said once."

"I would agree, in some ways," she said quietly. "The drink, Frank. You gotta get a handle on that."

He looked at her. "I know. It's like it gets hold of me..."

"It's a disease," she said quietly. "It's called alcoholism, and lots of people have it. They deal with it. Every day. You need to be one of those people—start a program, get some help. Okay?"

He nodded.

"Seriously," she said. "Do it for Jackson and me, but mostly, do it for yourself. And the Oxy—is that over with?"

He nodded. "Yup, can't afford it."

"That's not funny."

He looked at his cup of coffee. "I know I should be angry at the

Northsiders, but I feel like they've somehow given me a second chance," he said. Frank swirled the cup in his hand and watched the coffee rise along the walls of the cup. "They had no idea what they were doing, but going cold turkey wasn't something I could have done on my own."

"They were like your own private treatment center," she said, teasing him. "Like the ones the Hollywood stars use. Except this one was free."

"And dangerous," he added. "What would their motto be? 'You'll get sober, or die trying?'"

She shook her head. "Maybe it's not the best business model."

He nodded. "But I am looking forward to being back at work." He looked back at her and smiled. "Maybe this time, I'll actually be good at it."

CHAPTER 112
SSDD Again

Monday morning. Back to normal. Or at least the new normal.

Frank Harper locked the Camaro and started across the parking lot, heading for the ABI building. For once, he was excited about going to work.

He knew it would be hard to stay on the wagon. Maybe drinking was just in his DNA. But he'd told Laura the truth—he was going to get a handle on it. And he meant it. And he was excited about returning to work. He vowed to knuckle down and get serious about the cold cases. In fact, he even had some ideas about how to speed up the investigations.

Juggling his coffee, Frank dug out his badge and entered the building. Inside the lobby, there was a reception area and several wide, outdated couches spread around for the occasional civilian visitor. Across from the elevators, an officer stood next to the metal detector. He recognized Frank and smiled.

"Welcome back, Mr. Harper," the officer said. "Heard you took a couple weeks off. How'd that go?"

Frank took the stuff out of his pockets—keys, coins, new phone—and put it in the plastic tray, handing it to the officer along with his bag.

"Yeah, it was good," Frank said. No need to confuse the guy with facts. "Saw my daughter up in Ohio."

"That's nice," the officer said and then looked at him. "Weapon?"

"Nope," He didn't feel like explaining to the man that his weapon had been taken by the Northsiders and was currently missing. The gun had been entered into the ATF's national database, in case it ever showed up in connection with a case. And now Frank would need authorization from Collier before he could get a new one as his daily carry.

The officer ran the plastic tray through the x-ray machine next to the metal detector, then nodded Frank through the metal gateway. The officer stepped around and started handing Frank's stuff back.

"All right, there you go," the officer said. "Same shit, different day, am I right?"

Frank smiled and waved his cup of coffee at the man.

"Not today, my friend. Not today."

Epilogue

The black limousine moved through south Chicago, weaving around the city traffic. The vehicle passed through an industrial area, with both sides of the road lined with factories and warehouses. Most seemed empty, or had seen better years. The dark windows of the vehicle reflected the bright blue sky and a succession of dormant smokestacks.

Inside the vehicle, a distinguished-looking black man pointed and gesticulated at the windows. The man was dressed to the nines, the sleeves of his suit were adorned with diamond cuff links bearing his initials. On more than one occasion he'd mentioned how he'd met President Obama, Chicago's favorite son. Of course, that had been "before," which seemed to indicate the undefined decades before the man became the President.

In the rear of the limousine rode an immaculately-dressed older black woman and a young black man in a tidy suit. They listened to the man speak and followed as he pointed out buildings on their route.

"That property was abandoned in 2009 when the factory went into foreclosure," the commercial real estate agent said, pointing at a block-long brick factory. "280,000 square feet on five floors. Lots of room." The building was surrounded by a parking lot that had not been resurfaced in decades. Grass grew from the cracks, and a good-sized pine tree sprouted from the center of a dilapidated guard shack.

"They were like all the others. When the housing market crashed, the need for building materials plummeted," the agent continued. His words sounded practiced, honed over time. Apparently, he'd been showing these properties for similar buyers. "They couldn't keep up with the cheaper Chinese imports and ran out of cash."

The young man leaned forward.

"Thank you, sir, but we're looking for something a little more manageable. Something around 40,000 square feet," Gig said. "And, like she said, we also will provide security, if possible. Our expertise is in production and security. And efficient operations."

The older woman leaned forward and smiled, patting the real estate agent on the hand. "It's what we do best," she said. "We need a large production facility, first and foremost. But we can also help people reach their full potential, based on organizational tenets from decades ago. We use them to help our organizations run more efficiently."

The real estate agent nodded, understanding.

"That makes sense, ma'am. And there are many organizations around here that could be improved, if you are a consultant."

"I am," she said, smiling.

"I know several properties south of here, near the airport, that are large enough and in good enough condition to warrant security details," the agent said. "In addition, I can look into which local municipalities need that sort of service, if any."

"We own a new security company," the young man said, handing the agent a card. "We'll also be needing a substantial amount of warehouse space. At least another 20,000 square feet, on-site if possible. We have a lot of product to store."

The agent looked at the card. It looked clean and fresh, newly printed. The paper was thick. The card included a temporary address in the downtown and a symbol, which to him looked like two stark jagged white lines on a field of black. The lines spelled out "S.S." The card read "Southsiders Security, LLC."

"Thank you," he said. "I thought I knew all the private security firms on the southern side of Chicago. You new in town?"

The Dragon nodded, leaning forward.

"Yes, we're new. But we've got big plans."

About The Author

Greg Enslen has written and published six mysteries and thrillers, including the Amazon bestsellers "*A Field of Red*" and "*The Ghost of Blackwood Lane*." He also writes about technology and pop culture, including his popular "Binge Guide" series for "Game of Thrones" and "Mr. Robot." Greg lives in southwestern Ohio with his wife, three children, four dogs and an indeterminate number of cats. Greg enjoys writing late at night, after the house is finally quiet. Read more about Greg at **www.gregenslen.com**. For more information, please see his **Amazon Author Page** or visit his **Facebook fan page**.

Books By Greg Enslen

All titles are available on Kindle:

Frank Harper Mysteries
A Field of Red
Black Ice
White Lines

Fiction
Black Bird
The Ghost of Blackwood Lane
The 9/11 Machine

Guide Series
A Field Guide to Facebook
"A Viewer's Guide to Suits," Season One
"A Viewer's Guide to Suits," Season Two
"A Viewer's Guide to Suits," Season Three

Binge Guides
"Game of Thrones: A Binge Guide" for Season 1
"Game of Thrones: A Binge Guide" for Season 2
"Game of Thrones: A Binge Guide" for Season 3
"Game of Thrones: A Binge Guide" for Season 4
"Game of Thrones: A Binge Guide" for Season 5
"Game of Thrones: A Binge Guide" for Season 6
"Mr. Robot: A Binge Guide" for Season 1
"Mr. Robot: A Binge Guide" for Season 2

Newspaper Column Collections
"Tipp Talk" 2010 Newspaper Column Collection
"Tipp Talk" 2011 Newspaper Column Collection
"Tipp Talk" 2012 Newspaper Column Collection
"Tipp Talk" 2013 Newspaper Column Collection

CAN I ASK A FAVOR?

Thank you for reading this book - I hope you enjoyed it. If you enjoyed this book, found it useful or otherwise then I'd really appreciate it if you would post a short review on Amazon. If you could, take a few minutes out to write a review of this book on Amazon, Goodreads, Facebook or any other place you feel like sharing. If you'd like to leave a review for one of my books, please visit the link below:

http://bit.ly/geauthor

Reviews are the best way readers discover new books. And, believe it or not, the sheer number of Amazon reviews affects how Amazon lists book titles. So swing over there and jot down a couple of sentences. Good or bad, every review helps increase the "social buzz" of the book. I would truly appreciate it.

And thank you for your support!

— Greg Enslen

CPSIA information can be obtained
at www.ICGtesting.com
Printed in the USA
FFOW03n0808220717
37963FF

9 781938 768767